PRAISE FOR PHOEBE CONN
AND *WILD DESIRE*!

"A great Western romance…[that] will capture your heart. For a Western with action, romance, and a little sensuality mixed in, this is a book fans and all readers will have to try."

—*Romance Reviews Today*

"Phoebe Conn has done it again with her novel, *Wild Desire*. This historical romance is a pure delight to read from cover to cover."

—Roundtable Reviews

"Ms. Conn packs quite a wallop with [*Wild Desire*]."
—*The Midwest Book Review*

"A pleasant, realistic Western romance for fans of the subgenre."

—*RT BOOKclub*

A PIRATE'S PLUNDER

"Oh, yes, I am," Chris concurred. "I'm very, very good."

He tilted Sarah's chin and leaned down to kiss her. Rather than remaining frozen in place as she had in the past, she leaned against him and parted her lips. Readily accepting her encouragement, Chris cupped her face between his palms and nipped at her lower lip before slipping the tip of his tongue into her mouth. She tasted vaguely of oranges and the promise of something even more delicious.

Chris opened his eyes, and he found Sarah regarding him with a bewildered gaze. Pleased to have gotten the best of her, he laughed. "Surely you've been kissed before, Mrs. Hadley," he chided softly.

PHOEBE CONN

Midnight Blue

LEISURE BOOKS NEW YORK CITY

To Jeff and Drew
Thank you for the love, music and laughter.
You are the best of sons.

A LEISURE BOOK®

May 2006

Published by

Dorchester Publishing Co., Inc.
200 Madison Avenue
New York, NY 10016

ISBN 0-8439-5709-3

The name "Leisure Books" and the stylized "L" with design are trademarks of Dorchester Publishing Co., Inc.

Printed in the United States of America.

Visit us on the web at www.dorchesterpub.com.

Midnight Blue

Chapter One

Summer, 1781

Captain Christopher MacLeod braced himself against the *Island Belle*'s starboard rail and trained his spyglass on the merchantman gliding across the horizon. His remarkable skill as a privateer had brought him a fortune during America's lengthy battle for independence, but he remained eager to share the profits on the sale of this enticing prize with his crew.

He snapped the spyglass shut and turned to his mate. "This looks too easy, Mr. Corliss. We've half a day's light remaining. Maintain our present distance and, if the mood strikes me, we'll take her just before sunset."

Rob Corliss was a wiry, red-haired man of twenty-eight. His face was liberally dusted with freckles, but he was so good-natured that women always described him as handsome without ever being able to explain exactly why. He stood nearly six feet tall but still had to look up at the captain. After sailing with Chris MacLeod for three years, he had quickly come to understand that the captain was a deliberate man who could not be rushed. He had

1

complete faith in MacLeod's judgment, however, and nodded in agreement.

"Aye, Captain, the *Island Belle* will serve as an attentive escort."

Chris handed the mate the spyglass and continued his stroll along the schooner's well-scrubbed deck. Sleek and fast, the *Island Belle* was armed with a long gun mounted on a swivel amidships. Along each side, she carried four snub-nosed cannons, known as carronades after the foundry on the Carron River, Sterlingshire, Scotland, where they were cast. They lacked the range of the long gun but were deadly accurate in a close, broadside attack. The cannons could be made ready to fire in an instant.

As Chris moved past, he nodded to acknowledge his gunners' predatory grins. He had left Port Royal, Martinique, with more than a hundred hands, but after sending prize crews to guard prisoners and sail captured vessels into American ports, his crew now stood closer to seventy-five. All were fiercely loyal to their tall, raven-haired captain. Scion of one of Virginia's wealthiest families, Christopher MacLeod had chosen to fight the British at sea and had taken command of his own ship soon after turning twenty-one. Now twenty-five, he had the keen eye and tough, lean build of a seasoned Revolutionary War veteran. He was among the most successful privateers and took great pride in the fact that his kind had accounted for more captures and sinkings than the United States Navy.

When he reached the stern, Chris gripped the rail and inhaled the exhilarating sweetness of the salt-scented breeze. As restless as his crew, he longed for a real fight, but he doubted this merchantman would provide one when there was such a great risk of their taking high casualties. While it always required a large measure of will to wait, he enjoyed taunting the crews of Loyalist merchant vessels almost as much as demanding their surrender. He could easily imagine the men scurrying around this ship's deck searching for places to hide rather than for secure positions for defense, but merchant seamen would have had little practice with their weapons and be unlikely to fire them with the deadly accuracy of the *Island Belle*'s highly experienced gunners.

He doubted the war would continue much longer, what with the French such willing allies. When peace came, after what he was confident would be an American victory, he would take up the merchant trade himself. He was not looking forward to that bittersweet day, and for now he was an ambitious, coldly calculating privateer.

Relying upon instincts that had served him well, he stalked his prey until the sun dipped low and lent the waters off the southern coast of America a blood-red glow. He knew the hapless souls on board the merchantman would be praying for darkness to bring hope for escape, but he had no intention of allowing this ship to slip away. He laughed to himself as he gave the order to attack, and the *Island Belle* swiftly closed the distance between the ships. When he could read the name of the targeted vessel as the *Beatrice,* he signaled his gunners to fire. A single shot over her bow forced a prompt surrender. Just as he had anticipated, taking the ship was no challenge at all. He hid his disappointment and was among the first to board his prize.

In an expansive mood, he greeted the captain of the *Beatrice* in a civil, if not particularly respectful, fashion. "I've no lust for blood," he swore. "We've yet to lose a prisoner who behaved himself. Now, I want every man on deck, and your weapons stacked in a neat pile in the bow. That includes whatever personal arms your men might carry, right down to their razors."

A stocky man in his thirties, Captain Gregory Newton foolishly replied with a curse meant to freeze Chris's blood. Chris chuckled, as though he found the insult amusing, and then, with a single savage blow, dropped the belligerent fool to his knees. Dazed, Captain Newton cupped his hands to shield his broken nose from further injury. As the blood oozed through his fingers and dripped down his throat, he uttered a low, keening moan. His crew, which had been huddled around him, backed away in an awkward shuffle.

Disgusted the fellow was so lacking in courage, Chris stepped around the *Beatrice*'s captain to address the rest of the captured crew. In a threatening baritone he said, "Is there anyone else who fails to understand who now commands the *Beatrice*? If so, come forward and I'll deal with you one at a time."

A privateer's crew always ached for a fight, but there were no similar cravings for violence among the seamen serving on board a merchantman. Surrounded by men from the *Island Belle* who appeared anxious to use their cutlasses to slice up any obstreperous souls, none of the defeated crew responded to Chris's challenge.

Chris waited, however, his stance and expression darkly menacing until, thoroughly cowed, there wasn't a man among the *Beatrice*'s disheartened crew who dared meet his gaze. He waited a moment longer, as though enjoying their discomfort, then turned away to address his mate.

"Take a search party below to root out stragglers, Mr. Corliss." He caught a sudden startled glance passing among the crew of the *Beatrice* and called to Captain

Newton, who sat slumped back on his heels. "Are there passengers on board?" he asked.

The injured man shook his head emphatically, then winced at the pain he caused himself—but in less than five minutes, Rob Corliss returned leading a woman dressed in a flowing black cloak. Her hood was pulled low to conceal her face, and with every step, she struggled against the mate's confining grasp.

Thoroughly annoyed, Chris clasped his hands behind his back and widened his stance as he waited for Rob and his reluctant companion to reach him. "You claimed there were no passengers, Captain. Should I assume this woman is your wife?"

Gregory Newton peered up at Chris. Then, clearly befuddled as to how to respond, he quickly glanced away. Despite his initial show of bravado, he now appeared utterly wretched and seemed almost to shrink in on himself and grow smaller.

Chris shook his head with real regret. "While I always advocate the truth, I gave you sufficient time to fabricate a convincing lie. If she isn't your wife, is she perhaps the darling *Beatrice* for whom this splendid vessel was named?"

He fully expected to find a common whore, but when he reached out to yank back her hood, Chris discovered a young woman of exceptional beauty. Her eyes were an unusual deep blue and while shadowed by a long sweep of dark lashes, defiance blazed clear to their indigo depths. A wild mass of tightly coiled blond ringlets framed her classic oval face, and a bright blush heightened the peach tones of her flawless skin. Entranced, Chris was convinced such a lovely creature would surely exude an aura of innocent sweetness were she not wearing such a fierce scowl. Still, her expression failed to mar the delicate perfection of her small, straight nose, nor the exotic slant of her high cheekbones.

Before he could gather his wits to speak, she broke away from him with a hostile shove. "Unhand me, you filthy pirate!" she demanded in a cultured tone with a soft Southern accent. She was wearing black kid gloves and, having successfully rejected Chris's touch, used both hands to clutch her cloak more tightly around her shoulders. The soft woolen garment flared open at the hem to reveal a black satin skirt and the tips of black kid slippers.

Astonished as much to find such a remarkable woman as by her insulting demand, Chris responded with a deep chuckle that echoed through his crew and deteriorated into rude snorts. Clearly this was a fine lady who was used to being obeyed, but she was in no position to order anyone about today.

Chris's navy blue frock coat, waistcoat and breeches were well tailored of fine woolen fabrics, but other than the gleaming silver buttons, held no ornament. He preferred boots to shoes, and when he doffed his cocked hat and bowed low, he looked like the proper gentleman he considered himself.

"I'm no pirate, my lady, but a privateer with a commission issued by the Continental Congress. I'm not filthy, either, but if you'd prefer to judge for yourself, I'll provide you with an ample opportunity later this evening."

At that suggestive invitation, a flicker of fear widened his captive's eyes, but she quickly suppressed it and continued to regard him with open contempt. He admired a woman with spirit, and clearly this pretty lass had the attribute in abundance. Greatly intrigued, he glanced over his shoulder at Captain Newton.

The injured officer had drawn his handkerchief, but

blood still seeped through the linen to spatter his shirt. "The captain appears to be unable to explain your presence on board," Chris remarked as he turned back toward the belligerent young woman. He then swept her from head to toe with a lazy glance.

Designed for protection from the elements, her cloak served its purpose well, but he imagined that her figure must be every bit as splendid as her face, and he longed for a better view. Anticipating such a delight, he swallowed a wolfish growl and forced himself to be patient.

"Are you perhaps a stowaway?" he teased with a wicked grin.

"Certainly not," she swore, but a quick flick of her tongue over the enticing fullness of her lower lip revealed a wavering resolve.

It was far too suggestive a gesture to escape Chris's notice, and he wondered how she would taste. His mother's delicate pastries came to mind, and he longed to lick sparkling sugar crystals from this defiant beauty's lips. He had always appreciated a striking woman, but this wild-eyed vixen had presented herself at a most inopportune time. He turned mocking, to control his own emotions as much as to subdue hers.

"Did you actually pay for passage on the *Beatrice*?" He rolled his eyes toward the rapidly darkening heavens. "Where could you have been that you were unaware that the United States and Great Britain are at war?"

"This cursed conflict has cost me a great deal," the woman hissed angrily. "I meant to escape it."

Chris dipped his head slightly and leaned closer, as though intent upon confiding an intriguing secret. "I'm so sorry to disappoint you, my lady, but you'll not see England any time soon. Are you traveling with a maid?"

The young woman raised her chin proudly. "I'm fully capable of looking after myself, and have no need of servants."

The sun was sinking into the sea, and as the breeze strengthened, Chris caught a hint of perfume. It was a floral scent—carnations, he suspected—and as provocative as she. He had occasionally encountered passengers in the past, and had sent them off to port as prisoners under the watchful eye of a prize crew. None had been female, however, and he was not even tempted to leave this luscious morsel on board the *Beatrice*. With the merchantman now lashed to the side of the *Island Belle*, he would have to carry the young woman only a few steps to make her his guest.

A sly grin that his crew seldom glimpsed spread across his well-shaped lips. "Is your luggage packed?" he asked.

The blonde stared at him coldly. "Of course it's packed. I have only a single trunk. Will you stoop to calling it booty?"

Chris nodded to his mate, who had been following their exchange with a befuddled frown. "Send a man to fetch her belongings, Mr. Corliss. Then make the rest of our prisoners comfortable for the night. Our men already know which among them is to remain as the prize crew, and where they're bound. As soon as you're satisfied the *Beatrice* is secure, we'll separate and be underway."

"Aye, Captain. We know what must be done," Rob assured him. But he regarded the pretty young woman with a troubled glance before turning away.

Chris saw a questioning light fill his captive's dark eyes, but he plucked her off her feet before she could ask his intentions. She had delicate features and dainty hands but weighed more than he had anticipated. Not wanting to appear clumsy, he quickly adjusted his hold on her.

"You're surprisingly heavy, my dear. I hope the extra weight is due to expensive jewelry tucked into your pockets rather than an excessive love of sweets."

Infuriated by the crass comment, the woman made to slap him, but Chris dodged the blow and swung her over the side of the *Beatrice* and up onto the deck of the *Island Belle*.

"Put me down!" she shrieked, and dislodged his hat with a flying elbow. She then grabbed for his hair. Straight rather than curly like her own, it was a thick sable that came loose from the bow at his nape and slipped through her fingers until she caught hold with a fierce grasp.

"Duck your head," Chris directed as he carried her down the companionway to his cabin, but she continued to twist and turn in his arms. "I swear, there's more fight in you than the entire crew of the *Beatrice*, but you needn't be so obnoxious." He lowered his voice to make a sincere promise he hoped she would believe. "I mean you no harm."

When they reached his cabin, he cautiously waited for her to turn loose his hair before he placed her on her feet and stepped away. "Allow me to introduce myself. I'm Captain Christopher MacLeod, but I'd be pleased if you would call me Chris."

His captive surveyed the oak-paneled cabin with an anxious glance, but, feeling trapped, reacted with another clear challenge. "I'll not call you anything but a black-hearted scoundrel."

"Refer to me by a pet name if you wish," Chris offered with unabashed good humor.

A pet name? Only the vilest of insults came to his captive's mind, but she bit them back. Having felt the strength of his well-muscled shoulders and arms, she knew that, despite his rude complaint, carrying her had scarcely taxed what had to be considerable endurance.

Her gaze narrowed as she watched him rake his hair out of eyes that were a bright, clear blue. His features were unmarred by the brutality of his profession, but that he was such a handsome bastard made little impression on her. He was a seafaring bandit in her view, and as welcome a companion as a cottonmouth moccasin.

Appalled by that fearsome image, she again raised her hands to hold her cloak securely at her throat. "Do you make a habit of amusing yourself at the expense of defenseless women?" she asked.

"Every chance I get," he assured her in a husky whisper. He then gestured toward the table.

"Please sit down. I don't keep any weapons in here, so you needn't bother to search my effects unless you'd gain some perverse pleasure from doing so. I have business which requires my attention, but I'll send you a pot of tea and join you later for supper. One of the benefits of being a privateer is the ready access to luxuries not easily found ashore, and I can promise you a delicious meal."

"I'd rather starve," she vowed, and while relieved that he was leaving her for the moment, he had failed to provide a vital piece of information. "Wait," she called as he moved toward the door. "Where are you taking me?"

Chris's dark brows dipped in apparent puzzlement. "I'm not taking you anywhere, my dear. We replenish our stores each time we take a ship like the *Beatrice,* and we don't return to port until I'm bored. With a woman as charming as you on board, that might not be for a very long time."

His teeth were even and very white against his deeply

tanned skin, but she found his grin as utterly revolting as his taunting compliment. "You are a presumptuous swine," she countered.

Rather than respond with an equally brutal assessment of her character, Chris blew her a hasty kiss and went on out the door, but he took what he saw as a necessary precaution and locked it behind him.

Amused, he whistled as he returned to the deck. He plucked his black ribbon from where it had fallen, retied his hair, and then replaced his hat. He had longed for a fight, and even if he had not gotten the kind he would have liked from the crew of the *Beatrice,* he looked forward to a most entertaining argument later that night.

Chris's most unwilling guest heard the key turn in the lock, removed her gloves with a vicious yank, and flung her cloak over one of the chairs near the table. The neatly kept cabin was no larger than the pantry at home, and so thoroughly masculine that she felt doubly out of place.

That her voyage had begun with such high hopes only to be sabotaged in such a dreadful manner made her feel sick clear through, but unable to merely sit and brood, she was drawn toward the cabin's two small-paned, rectangular windows. Located in the stern of the ship, the captain's quarters provided her with a final glimpse of the *Beatrice* as the ships parted.

When she had booked passage aboard Captain Newton's ship, he had not impressed her as a coward, but clearly he had put up little in the way of a fight before they were boarded, and she blamed him as much as the despicable MacLeod for her present disastrous situation. Pressing close to the cool glass, she watched until the merchantman's sails had vanished into the moonless night.

Fighting a painful sense of abandonment, she pushed away from the window and prowled the cabin with a seething grace. The captain's belongings were stowed in lockers built into every available space, but she was unimpressed by the cleverness of the design. She noted the lemony scent of the polish rubbed into the oak and the gleam of the brass fittings, but the cabin was still a prison cell.

A knock at the door startled her, and she quickly grabbed the nearest chair for support. "You needn't wait for me to invite you in," she called. "I'll not do it."

The cook's helper unlocked the door and peered in. A chubby lad with unruly straw-colored hair, he forced a timid smile. "Excuse me, miss, but the captain said he promised you tea. If you'd care for something more, I'll run to fetch it."

While she was relieved it wasn't the captain back to torment her, she nevertheless turned her back on the boy. "Just leave it," she ordered crossly.

She heard him place the tray on the table but did not glance over her shoulder until he closed the door on his way out. She held her breath then, hoping he would leave it unlocked, but after a brief hesitation, he turned the key in the lock with a disheartening rattle.

He had brought her tea in an elegant china pot decorated with tiny violets, complete with matching cup and saucer. There were lemon wedges and several cookies that were as thin as crackers. A small silver teaspoon rested on a freshly laundered linen napkin.

"The whole lot is probably stolen," she murmured softly, but too thirsty to shove the tray off onto the floor as she would have liked, she sat down and poured herself a cup of tea. She was sipping a second cup when the captain hastily unlocked the door and burst back into the cabin.

"Have you no manners at all?" she greeted him. "At least the boy who brought this knew enough to knock before he entered."

Chris removed his hat and tossed it on his desk. "As well he should, but this is my cabin after all, and no one knocks at his own door."

He watched her raise the teacup with as serene a gesture as any he had ever witnessed in his family's parlor, but the stubborn tilt of her chin kept him wary. No longer covered by gloves, her hands were lovely, her fingers long and slim with gently rounded nails. As she raised her left hand to brush away a stray curl, he caught sight of a gold wedding band.

When the captain of the *Beatrice* had not claimed her, it had not even occurred to him that she might be another man's wife. That was more than enough of a shock, but before Chris could gather his wits to speak, she set her cup aside and rose to face him. He would have thought her black gown enormously flattering with her fair coloring, had the thickness at her waist not made it obvious that she was more than a few months pregnant.

"My God," he gasped. "Why didn't you tell me you were expecting a child?"

She merely shrugged, as though surprised by his dismay. "Why would I confide something so personal in a corsair who's not shown the slightest regard for my welfare?"

On deck, her eyes had been a rich, midnight blue. Now, in the dimly lit cabin, they appeared almost as black as her gown, which made her steady gaze all the more venomous. She was tall for a woman, but even if she had been petite in stature, her bearing would have been regal.

13

Chris was accustomed to being in command of any situation, but with shock sucking the wind out of him, he suddenly felt as though he had fallen overboard. He gulped for air to stave off the panic of drowning, but the quick breath failed to restore his sense of control.

"I'm sorry," he began haltingly. "Perhaps we might begin again. When I introduced myself, you failed to provide your name."

"Call me whatever you wish. I'll not respond."

The only trace of fear Chris had seen from this razor-tongued vixen had come when he had offered to prove he wasn't as filthy as she had assumed. He glanced toward his bunk, then circled the table with two easy strides.

"I'll continue to treat you as a lady only as long as you behave as one. Now, it's been a long while since I spent any time with a beautiful woman, even a most unwilling one. I don't care whose wife you are or when that brat is due. If I wish to be entertained, you'll do your best to please me."

She raised her hand to erase his smirk, but he caught her wrist in midair. He yanked her close, and to underscore his threat, gave her a long, punishing kiss.

He had meant to subdue her passions rather than inflame his own, but when his heart began to race, he realized just how stupid he had been. Her lips were whisper-soft, her taste every bit as delicious as sugar-coated pastries, and he pushed her away before he lost all trace of reason.

Unwilling to wait for his breathing to slow, he hoped she would mistake his reaction for furious anger rather than the betrayal of fierce desire it had truly been. "Sit down," he directed harshly, "and tell me your name, where you're from, and why you chose now of all times to visit England."

His captive raised trembling fingers to her bruised lips. She despised everything about this brutish captain, but to her everlasting shame, in the instant before he had become so rough, his kiss had actually been quite pleasant. Then he had ruined it, as she was certain he must ruin everything he touched. Had there been a knife on the table rather than a teaspoon, she would have plunged it into his heart. Her hand shook as she lowered it to her side.

She slipped into the chair farthest from his bunk. It was bolted in place, as the chairs had been on the *Beatrice,* but she would have liked to have shoved it back in a clear show of her mood as much as to allow more room for her swollen abdomen. She hated feeling so horribly confined, and for a moment forgot what she had been asked.

"I'm Sarah Godwin Hadley," she finally announced. "I lost my husband in March, and I wanted our child to be born in England as he had been." Her words were proud.

Chris was elated to find her a widow, but the resulting shame quickly dampened that inappropriate burst of joy. "Your husband was a British officer?" he asked, forcing his voice into a more reasonable range.

Sarah nodded. "Yes, and a fine one. He was among the men Cornwallis lost at Guilford Courthouse."

She was speaking in a soft if spiteful tone, but Chris was still completely unnerved. He began to pace with a restless stride timed to his ship's slow roll. "I am sorry for your loss, Mrs. Hadley, but sailing for England was a foolish if noble choice. From the looks of you, you'd have had the babe long before you reached Great Britain, even if we had not intervened."

Sarah straightened her shoulders. "I still have two months before the birth. That's sufficient time to reach England."

"Obviously not, sailing these treacherous waters," Chris pointed out.

He had known her sympathy to be with the British cause, but he had not imagined she would be a British officer's widow. That made her not merely an adversary but an extremely dangerous one. He could not recall ever speaking to another woman—or man, for that matter—who had thrown his every word right back in his face. Being high-spirited was one thing, being an ill-tempered shrew quite another.

It was too late to send her along with the prisoners on board the *Beatrice,* and now, knowing her condition, Chris could not have done so in good conscience anyway. He felt as though he had trapped a wild panther that was much too beautiful to kill and skin, although he sure as hell didn't want to keep it around alive. The problem was, he had absolutely no choice.

He swept his cabin with an expansive gesture. "We'll simply have to make the best of this regrettable situation, Mrs. Hadley. But I meant to offer you my cabin, not share it with you against your will."

This time, Sarah was the one to issue a bitter laugh. "Liar."

Chris opened his mouth to remark on the fact that he doubted her husband had regretted dying with such a quarrelsome bitch awaiting him at home, but he had been raised to be more respectful of women and bit his tongue.

"Don't tease me, Mrs. Hadley, or I'll think you crave more than a single kiss."

Sarah glared at him, but when she remained quiet, he took it for a victory. That she did not care for him was obvious, but he wondered if affection terrified her because she feared for her child, or merely because her late husband had been an inept lover. He would save that impertinent question for the next time she defied him.

"Where is your home?" he asked. Relaxing slightly, he propped his hands on the back of the chair opposite hers.

"That's really no concern of yours," she responded coolly.

"Oh, but it is. I'll make no promise to arrange for your safe return, but if I've no idea where you're from, I can't even consider it."

Sarah clasped her hands more tightly in her lap. This bastard was undoubtedly toying with her. Still, she saw no possible risk in revealing the truth. "I'm from Charleston, South Carolina—but I doubt you've the courage to take me there."

Chris straightened. "It's not a matter of courage, but of common sense."

Sarah Hadley had the most expressive eyes he had ever seen, and with a tilt of her head and narrowing of her gaze she could convey a truly stunning array of moods, all of them tinged with dark loathing. Chris thought perhaps he had never met a woman who was as furiously angry as this rare beauty. Perhaps she hoped to goad him into killing her so she might join her husband in paradise. If that were the case, he would not oblige.

The cook's helper knocked at the door Chris had left slightly ajar. "Will you be wanting supper now, sir?" he inquired.

Chris had seldom felt less like eating. "I'll call you when we're ready," he replied, and this time he made certain the door was closed.

"Now, where were we? Oh, yes, you'd mentioned

Charleston. I've visited your beautiful city on numerous occasions. I know all of South Carolina has suffered terribly during the British occupation, but once the war is won—"

"Your side will surely lose, Captain, and then you'll be hanged for piracy, which is precisely what you deserve."

She was obviously relishing that dark prediction; Sarah's eyes smoldered with an intensity Chris would never have thought possible from a woman with such delicate coloring. There was nothing truly fragile about her, however—except for her condition, which he resolved right then to make every allowance for.

"The United States has fought too hard for our independence to ever surrender, Mrs. Hadley. Now, I suggest we confine our discussions to less inflammatory interests for the remainder of the voyage."

"There's no need to prolong things," Sarah was quick to disagree. "While I would naturally prefer Charleston, you could put me ashore anywhere along the South Carolina coast."

Chris weighed his words thoughtfully before he replied. "I told you I'd make no promises, and I've no intention of going ashore in South Carolina or anywhere else, Mrs. Hadley. When I decide we've captured a sufficient number of ships, we'll return to the West Indies."

Stunned, Sarah sagged back in her chair. He had just confirmed her worst suspicions: he was a cunning liar. From that moment on, no matter what he offered to win her cooperation, she would not be fooled. She swallowed the bile-flavored taste of virulent anger and hated him all the more.

"The West Indies?" she repeated numbly. "Where the French undoubtedly regard you as a great hero."

Her voice dripped with sarcasm, but Chris was well

past the point of being annoyed. "Yes, as a matter of fact, they do."

"I despise the French. They seize upon any excuse to make war on Great Britain."

Chris's expression hardened into a mask every bit as forceful as his words. "My mother is French, so even if they had not become our allies, I would still have a great affection for them."

Clearly he was daring her to keep her opinions to herself, but Sarah stubbornly refused. "The MacLeods must have come from Scotland, though—or did you merely adopt the name to avoid disgracing your whole family with the taint of your piracy? Assuming, of course, your kin possessed any honor to lose."

He would have struck a man for such a grave insult, but he channeled his rage in the direction that would upset her most. "My parents met during the French and Indian War, when my father went to Acadia to aid in the expulsion. An Acadian, my mother had no wish to even know him, let alone accept his affection, but he is an extremely charming man.

"I doubt she was as arrogant in her rejection as you, Mrs. Hadley, but my parents provide ample evidence that love has no respect for the political disputes that drive countries to war. I'll warn you now, however, that if you should fall in love with me, I'll insist you observe a full year of mourning before we wed."

He was already out the door before Sarah could respond, but it amused him to imagine her choking on the vile stream of insults his comment must surely have inspired. He was not seriously interested in a British officer's widow, but taming such a volatile creature was exactly the type of challenge he relished.

Not wishing to expose the cook's helper to her abuse, he decided to fetch their supper himself, but believing the longer he waited, the hungrier, and therefore more agreeable, Sarah Hadley would become, he took his own sweet time going about it.

Chapter Two

Sarah emptied a recessed bookshelf and hurled half a dozen leather-bound volumes across the cabin before she realized how futile the gesture truly was. The captain would no doubt retaliate by removing his books. Then she would have only the single novel she had packed for amusement.

It wasn't until she kicked a book aside that she noticed it was written in French. A quick perusal revealed that they all were. Now with no hope of a diversion, she sank down on the bunk in a dejected heap.

Tears welled in her eyes, but she refused to cry, and, still furious with the captain for his ludicrous taunt about love, she succeeded in blinking away any hint of moisture. Rogues held absolutely no appeal for her, and she had no doubt that had her incipient motherhood not been apparent, Christopher MacLeod would have raped her repeatedly. That he held sufficient respect for her condition to protect her from what were surely his lustful tastes provided scant reason to rejoice, however.

What did she have, eight weeks at the most before she

would be slender again? she worried. She had heard some women had killed themselves rather than live with the horror of rape, but she would have a child to raise and would never abandon a tiny babe. Even if she did not have an infant to tend, she would never resort to suicide when in her opinion a rapist disgraced only himself, rather than his innocent victim.

She wrapped her arms around the bowl of her belly and fought to make sense of the hideous turns that plagued her life with such wretched frequency. She had had such blissful expectations for her marriage to Michael Hadley, but all too swiftly his death had brought an end to those beautiful dreams. As alone as she had ever been, she felt cursed, but she had done nothing to deserve punishment this severe.

Except to be born female, of course. Her father, a demanding Anglican priest, had never let her forget that grievous error. Her mother, a woman of such angelic sweetness she never raised her voice above a hushed whisper, had not once come to her defense. An only child, for as long as Sarah could remember she had felt out of place in her parents' home. She had not once been complimented for being a bright little girl, but instead constantly criticized for being willful and disobedient. She had even had the audacity to be born on a Sunday morning, which had forced her father to be late for the ritual he conducted with such desperate precision. His incense-scented church had never been a peaceful refuge for her, but instead an extension of the earthly purgatory she had been forced to endure.

Her father had threatened her with the fires of Hell for the smallest infraction of his household's innumerable and often contradictory rules. Her mother had merely complained of a debilitating headache and taken to her bed whenever Sarah turned rebellious. Alienated by them both, she had never paid the slightest attention to either of her parents.

She had much preferred the attentions of the British officers her father befriended. They were such charming men, who wore splendid uniforms and brought her amusing presents and delicious treats. They had cuddled her close, called her an adorable child, and loved her as her parents never had. As soon as she had reached marriageable age, she had wed the first officer to propose. Michael Hadley had treated her with a reverence bordering on awe, and she had vowed to repay him by being an exemplary wife. She had been, in fact—although her love had never even approached the worshipful depths of his. He had been the ideal husband, and would surely have been a wonderfully loving father, had he lived to see his child born.

A painful lump filled her throat, for she truly believed Michael ought not to have been killed and the *Beatrice* ought not to have been captured by some half-French devil. Weary after an emotionally exhausting day, she curled up on the bunk and closed her eyes. The linens were freshly laundered and smelled faintly of sunshine, but sleep would not come, only the echoes of her father's angry tirades, which swiftly blurred into Christopher MacLeod's foul taunts.

When the captain finally returned to his cabin, Sarah's temper had not even begun to cool. She immediately sat up to reply to his last insulting boast. "I'd sooner wed one of the rats swimming in this cursed ship's bilge water than you, sir."

"You'd make a charming couple, too," Chris responded with a teasing wink. He was badly disappointed that he had obviously not stayed away nearly long enough to induce civility in the wench, but he did not want to deprive her poor child of nutrition, and so refrained from making a further comment on her colorful outburst.

"I keep live chickens on board for eggs and meat, and while it's unimaginative fare, it's a damn sight better than salt-beef and hardtack," he told her. "I had hoped the *Beatrice* might carry some tasty provisions, but alas, the cook apparently relied on bacon and ham to fill the captain's table. I'm not fond of either."

Sarah watched him arrange the covered dishes on his table. "Do you usually wait on yourself?"

"No, but I'd rather not subject the cook's helper to your temper. He's a shy lad, you see, and I'll not have him abused."

Sarah started to rise, but the ship took a sudden rolling lurch in the opposite direction, and she was forced back down on the bunk. "And just what do you call taking me captive, Captain? An act of charity?"

"In your case, that's precisely how I'd describe it. I don't recall ever meeting anyone in greater need of rescue. Now come sit with me here at the table, and let's eat this delicious meal before it grows cold."

Under better circumstances, the savory aroma of roast chicken mixed with rice and carrots would have been enticing, but Sarah stubbornly remained where she sat. "I don't see any reason for us to share our meals. After all, no prison warden dines with the inmates."

Chris had brought a jug of wine and two pewter tankards. He filled them both, arranged the pewter plates and sterling utensils; then, satisfied the meal had been properly presented, he opened his napkin and sat down to eat.

"This is awfully good," he emphasized with an appreciative hum. "Frankly, I don't care with whom prison wardens care to dine," he confided between bites. "I find you to be such an exciting companion that I'll not miss a minute we can share. In fact, I've decided to stay with you tonight."

While horrified, Sarah muted her revulsion and merely regarded his sly smirk with a malevolent stare. "Then you lied when you said you'd not meant to force me to share your cabin, for I am most unwilling."

"That was no lie," Chris argued, "for I hadn't meant to share the cabin then. Now that I've had the opportunity to sample your charms, you've inspired me to change my mind. Come and have supper with me," he invited more firmly.

Sarah felt sick with fright. She knew it would be useless to plead for her honor, and she was far too proud to resort to such a pathetic ploy anyway. "If I'll have to contend with you later," she murmured darkly, "I'd rather do it on an empty stomach. But truly, I've lost my appetite."

Chris took a sip of wine and let it trickle slowly down his throat. "I'm sorry to disappoint you, my dear, but I plan to hang up a hammock rather than wedge myself into the bunk. In your present condition, you'll take up too much room for either of us to be comfortable."

Sarah doubted he would stay in his hammock more than five minutes, but the insulting comment on her size still hurt. "You bastard," she snarled.

"Would you prefer the hammock?" Chris replied. "I doubt you're used to sleeping in one, and I'd not want you to fall out and risk harming your child. I'm already growing fond of the little tyke. What do you plan to name him?"

Astounded by the smoothness with which he wove insults into innocuous conversation, Sarah simply stared. She could not fault his table manners or his appearance, but he was easily the most objectionable individual she had ever met. Rather than respond, she turned her back on him.

"Sarah," he called with a deceptively musical lilt, "I won't remind you again to behave like a lady. Now, face me this instant and tell me what names you've selected."

The strained tone that flavored his command was a clear warning to take care, and while Sarah knew she would be wise to obey, she hated to give in. After a long hesitation, she swung back toward him but kept her eyes focused on her tightly clasped hands.

"I have a whole string of names from which to choose if the baby's a girl, but if it's a boy, I'll name him Michael for his father."

Chris wiped his mouth on his napkin and broke into a wide grin. "What a remarkable coincidence. That's my name too."

"You introduced yourself as Christopher. Can't you keep your lies straight?"

Chris took another bite of chicken before he replied. "I've told you no lies, Sarah. My father wanted to name me Michael, but my mother preferred Christopher. They reached a compromise with Christopher Michael. Michael is a fine name, and I'm sure your son will be happy with it."

That he had called her by her first name as though he had that right galled her all the more. She felt nauseous, and feared it wasn't only because Chris intended to share the cabin. He raised his tankard in a silent toast, and for the first time she noticed the knuckles of his right hand were scraped raw and swollen.

"I thought one of your crew must have beaten Captain Newton, but you did it yourself, didn't you?" she asked.

Chris noted the direction of her glance and, after taking a drink, replaced the tankard on the table and flexed his hand. "It's a shame you missed hearing his comment, for I'll not repeat it, but you can be assured that he deserved a lot worse than I gave him."

"I'm amazed to learn anything he could have said would have upset you. I assumed pirates heard so many vile insults they swiftly became inured to them."

Chris leaned back in his chair but remained far from relaxed. "Most people know better than to insult me, and you ought to consider your words more thoughtfully before you speak."

Sarah paused a moment to ponder his unwanted advice but twisted it as artfully as he did his promises. "I'll endeavor to be more creative then, Captain."

That had not been what Chris wanted to hear, but he let the comment pass for the moment. Hoping they would have an easier time discussing the ship's routine, he searched his mind for something that would concern her and quickly found it.

"Keeping water fresh on board ship can be a problem, but we took several barrels the *Beatrice* will no longer require, and I've arranged for you to be given an ample daily ration for hygiene and laundry."

"You are too thoughtful," Sarah replied.

Chris nodded. "Yes, I know. It's one of my few faults."

Sarah watched him bring a bite of chicken to his mouth. While the gesture did not appear awkward, she was glad he had hurt his hand and hoped it was causing him excruciating pain. She wondered why he had not bandaged his knuckles.

"Have you a physician on board?" she asked.

Alarmed, Chris paused in mid-bite. "Why? Are you feeling ill?"

"How could I feel otherwise? Do you honestly believe I could enjoy being held prisoner by a pirate who speaks nothing but lies?"

Chris laid his fork on the edge of his plate. "I'm not going to repeat this again, Sarah, so please remember it this time: I'm a privateer with a commission. My part in this war with England and the Loyalists supporting her is to disrupt shipping and make commerce not merely difficult but unprofitable as well. I'm an honorable man and will never lie to you.

"As for your health, my mother is what the Acadians referred to as a *sage femme*. She is an accomplished healer, and her herbal cures are more efficacious than the remedies most medical doctors prescribe. She provided me with sufficient stores of herbs and elixirs to treat most illnesses. So you see, you're sure to be in excellent health as long as you're in my care."

As usual, he looked far too pleased with himself, and Sarah sincerely doubted he knew anything at all about herbal cures. Bravely, she put her worst fears into words. "Do your skills include midwifery?"

Appalled that her condition might require it, Chris took care to hide his dismay. "Childbirth is a natural process, not an illness, but the answer is yes. Should you go into labor while on board the *Island Belle,* I'll deliver your babe. In fact, I shall look forward to it."

"Yes, I just bet you will," Sarah responded through clenched teeth.

Chris wondered if he shouldn't have searched her for weapons, then decided, had she been armed, she would have attacked him long before this. "My first obligation is to keep you healthy. Now I'll not ask you to join me again, Mrs. Hadley. Either you bring yourself to my table immediately or I'll be forced to carry your plate over to my bunk and stuff this fine meal down your throat."

"That would be a complete waste of your time, Captain, as I'd surely vomit it right back into your lap."

Chris produced an excellent imitation of her voice. "Yes, I just bet you will."

He looked down at his plate and tried to decide what to do with her without allowing her to see just how deeply perplexed he truly was. He had seen only a beautiful woman, albeit a furious one, and had grabbed her without thinking past the initial delight her presence would surely bring. That wasn't like him, and he now regretted his failure to consider other options, but a quick review reminded him that once he had taken the *Beatrice,* he had had none where she was concerned.

"Newton was a fool to have you on board," Chris announced suddenly. "The hold of the *Beatrice* was full of rice, and while I appreciate the addition to our diet, a thousand loads of rice aren't worth the risk of a single human life, most especially not a life as precious as yours."

He rose and threw his napkin down on the table. "Perhaps you'll have more appetite without my company. Don't wait up for me as I'll be quite late, but you really must pick up the books you've dropped before you trip over one and hurt yourself."

Sarah listened attentively, waiting for him to turn the key in the lock as he left her, and she was not disappointed. She had no idea what had inspired him to refer to her life as precious, but she was certain it had to be another of his vile tricks. As for his remark about returning late, she did not believe that any more than he must believe she had merely dropped a few of his books.

Her food would still be warm, but she did not move to the table. She knew Chris was right, that she should eat for her baby's sake if not her own, but the mere thought of food made her gag. She sat for a long while before rising to take a single bite of chicken, but that was all she could tolerate.

As she gathered up the books and returned them to the shelf, she wondered what had happened to her trunk. How was she to prepare for bed without a brush for her hair or a nightgown in which to sleep? Afraid Chris would be unlikely to allow her any time to sleep, she returned to the bunk and fidgeted nervously before finding a comfortable pose. More than two hours passed before she became too sleepy to remain awake, and then, still fully clothed, she finally lay down to rest.

It was after midnight when Chris returned to his cabin, and he was surprised Sarah had failed to dim the lamps. He was grateful she was asleep, if still in her dress, then realized the fault was his for failing to produce her trunk. He was ashamed to have overlooked such an obvious detail. The poor dear had had no choice about sleeping in her clothes; but unwilling to risk another spiteful encounter, he chose to wait until morning to rectify his error.

He feared he had frightened her needlessly by announcing his intention to share the cabin, but she defied him so readily he did not dare leave her alone for extended periods. He hung up the hammock he had tucked under his arm and peeled off his jacket, waistcoat, and boots. He turned the lamps down low, then climbed into the hammock and stretched out to get comfortable. It had been several years since he had used one of the sagging nets as a bed, and it took him a while to feel secure enough to relax.

His mind refused to follow his body's example, however, and kept churning over provocative images of Sarah Hadley. She was a haughty creature who taxed his patience severely, but while it made absolutely no sense, he actually found her appealing. She was bright and a delight to behold. The war could not last forever, and once America and Great Britain made peace, she would no longer have a reason to hate him. Not that a woman with her fiery temperament required an excuse, but he sincerely hoped they would not remain enemies forever. Finally, he was lulled to sleep with his thoughts still full of her.

Chris was startled awake before dawn. For an instant, the subtle drape of the hammock left him disoriented, but he quickly recalled where he was and why. He was by nature a light sleeper, and while Sarah appeared to be doing her best to muffle her sobs, he heard her distress. With good reason to believe he was the cause of her sorrow, he grabbed hold of the side of the hammock and rolled out. As soon as his feet touched down, he heard Sarah gasp in surprise.

He knelt beside the bunk and took her hand. "Yesterday wasn't a particularly good day for either of us," he whispered. "I'll help you remove your gown and petticoats, and you can sleep in your chemise. I'll have your trunk brought down first thing in the morning."

Recoiling from his touch, Sarah yanked her hand from his. Although he sounded remarkably sincere, she knew better than to trust him to help her disrobe. Surely he would simply strip her nude and then laugh at the thickness of her waist. She was not about to provide him with such an appalling opportunity.

"Leave me be," she ordered through a choked sob.

"I'd like nothing better, but your weeping woke me, and I'll not be able to get back to sleep knowing you're miserable. That's such a beautiful gown. Surely you don't wish to sleep in it and wrinkle it badly."

His expression was surprisingly tender in the dim light, and he was coaxing her in a soft, low voice—but Sarah would never trust his kind. It had been a Patriot who had killed Michael, and that was the cause of her tears.

"My clothes are scarcely a major concern," she snapped.

"I realize that, but I do want you to be more comfortable."

Sarah sat up, then pulled away to huddle in the far corner of the bunk. "I'll never believe your honeyed lies, Captain. You'll have to beat me senseless to have me, which I imagine you'd rather enjoy."

She had inadvertently left him plenty of room, and

Chris moved to sit down on the edge of the bunk. He reached out and laid his hand on her knee. "I'd enjoy having you certainly, but I'd never beat you, Sarah, nor do I think I'd have to."

He waited for her to hiss some vicious retort, but she kept still, and that confused him. He strove to confuse her as well. "We're both wide awake so we might as well talk. Tell me about Michael Hadley," he said.

"You're not fit to speak his name," she replied in a harsh whisper.

"Perhaps not, but I'd still like to know more about him. Tell me something interesting, anything at all."

Sarah feared he would take great delight in twisting whatever she said into an insult, but at the same time, she felt obligated to defend her late husband. She sighed softly and wiped away the last of her tears on her fingertips.

"He was very kind," she finally revealed.

"Kind?" Chris thought it an extremely unlikely attribute for such a recent widow to praise. She was a vibrant young woman, and he could not even imagine her marrying a man who did not match her stirring intensity. He had expected her to remark upon Michael's intelligence or passionate commitment to the British cause. Compliments for the man's fine appearance or charm would not have surprised him. But kindness? That made no sense whatsoever.

Sarah had not expected Chris to understand, and so she was not disappointed by his failure to appreciate Michael as she had. Michael Hadley had been many things: tall, strong, handsome, and greatly admired by his troops, but he had treated her with a gentle sweetness she would always treasure. That she had lost the only love she had ever known brought a fresh torrent of sorrow, and she covered her face with her hands and again wept bitter tears.

Chris had no idea what he had done to reduce his captive to such a pitiful state, but knowing her to be strong-willed, he feared she had regarded his question as a criticism of the late husband she had clearly adored. He reminded himself that she was a very pregnant widow, and he blamed himself for being stupidly insensitive. He reached out to pull her into his arms, and while she struggled against him briefly, she was much too distraught to wage more than a token resistance to his sympathetic embrace.

Her curls were soft against his cheek, and pulling her closer still, he again inhaled the delightful scent of carnations. He longed to repeat the reassurance that he was an honorable man, but overwhelmed by desire and fully aroused, his thoughts refused to tread a righteous path.

He refused to act on those tormenting thoughts, however, and instead patted Sarah's back gently. He was grateful the voluminous folds of her gown provided a much needed cushion between them, but he could now easily detect how slender she truly was. Motherhood might have swollen her breasts and rounded her stomach, but she was as delicate as an exquisite porcelain figurine.

Perhaps that was why she argued so fiercely, for clearly she lacked the physical strength to defend herself. He did not want her to fear that she would have to. Aching for so much more, he kissed her temple and, keeping his hold on her light, rocked her gently in his arms. No one at home thought of him as unkind, but with Sarah so eager to hate him, he doubted she would ever notice that he was also a thoughtful man.

She moved her hand to his shoulder, holding on to him now rather than shoving him away, and he nearly moaned with joy. He had known a great many beautiful women, but the war had been his chief concern for so long that he had failed to form a lasting bond with any of them. Now, as he held this lovely young widow, he had no doubt that she would betray him in an instant, but she felt so incredibly good in his arms that, for the moment at least, he gladly accepted the risk.

He fought the increasingly painful yearning to possess her, and continued to cradle her tenderly until she had exhausted her tears. He dared not repeat his offer to help her out of her gown, and instead allowed her to slip out of his arms. Returning to his hammock, he eased down into the netting's folds and wondered where he would find the strength to walk away from her again tomorrow.

The next time Sarah opened her eyes, sunlight filled the cabin and Chris was standing at his desk shaving. Fully clothed he presented an imposing sight, but stripped to the waist, his stance wide for balance, he was an all too virile pirate. The muscles rippled across his broad shoulders as he slid his razor up his throat, and Sarah held her breath hoping that he would slip—then just as quickly prayed he would not.

She watched him through a thick veil of lashes and struggled to recall their late-night conversation. She had only a vague memory of the details, but she was certain it had gone as poorly as all the others. She might have survived the first night in his cabin unharmed, but she did not regard it as a positive sign when he could so easily turn his gleaming razor on her.

The fear of that gruesome possibility tightened her

chest with a painful ache. Struggling for breath, she slowly raised her glance and met Chris's in his small oval mirror. She wondered how long he had been watching her, and was angered he had not even allowed her the privacy to sleep unobserved. Caught spying on him in return, she sat up slowly.

"Good morning, Mrs. Hadley." His grooming complete, Chris toweled away the last residue of the bayberry soap he had brought from home and turned to face her.

"It can't possibly be good for me, Captain," she replied.

Sunlight streamed through the portholes in the stern, and the soft, golden glow lent Chris's bronze skin the high polish of marble. Sarah's gaze followed the crisp curls that fanned across his broad chest then narrowed to a thin trail over the flatness of his belly. His britches were slung low on his narrow hips, accenting the length of his well-muscled legs, and the fine leather of his black boots gleamed darkly.

A slight smile curved across his lips, and a curious light brightened his gaze, but Sarah refused to be taken in by his apparent good humor. Clearly he was in no hurry to don a shirt, and with his hips thrust forward slightly, his stance was a clear challenge. She assumed he wanted her to complain about his lack of attire so that he could remind her that this was his cabin, after all. To avoid that trap, she made no mention of his state of undress and instead glanced toward the table.

"There's tea and biscuits for breakfast," Chris noted, "and I want you to eat several oranges."

"I doubt that I'm in any imminent danger of succumbing to scurvy."

"Perhaps not, but they'll be good for you nonetheless," he insisted.

Sarah was relieved that the dinner dishes had been cleared away, but somewhat surprised that he had not left her meal on the table as all he would provide until she had finally eaten it. She thought she would make do with a cup of tea, but as she rose and started for the table, she grew faint and had to sit right back down. The whole cabin seemed to be spinning wildly around her, and she quickly tucked her feet up under her skirt and lay back down.

"Maybe later," she promised weakly.

"Sarah?" Chris hurried to her side. She looked pale, and it frightened him. "Are you always troubled by morning sickness? Is that the problem?"

Sarah raised her hand to plead for silence. "Just leave me be."

"You didn't eat anything last night. Had you eaten before coming on board the *Belle*?"

Sarah looked up at him, but when her vision blurred again, she wished she had kept her eyes closed. "I didn't simply come on board; I was kidnapped."

Chris pushed her legs aside and sat down on his bunk. "That's not really the issue here, Sarah. I asked if you'd eaten anything yesterday. Now answer me."

Sarah never felt well enough to eat in the morning anymore, and with pirates pursuing them all afternoon, she had not felt up to eating later in the day either. She licked her lips. "Perhaps I'm just a poor sailor," she murmured.

Chris reached out to stroke her curls, and for once she did not flinch at his touch. He feared it was simply because she did not feel up to objecting, rather than any sudden aching need for his comfort. He wrapped a glossy curl around his finger, then unraveled it with a slow tug.

"I think you're sick because you haven't eaten," he argued. He left her for a moment, then came back with a cup of tea. He raised her head and brought the pretty china cup to her lips. She took a sip without his having to urge her to drink, and he considered it real progress. He was about to compliment her, then caught himself—surely she would only object and cease even this small show of cooperation.

He waited until she had finished the tea and then brought her a biscuit. "Our cook is better than most, and he bakes these every morning. A sailor's lot is miserable on most ships, but I say there's no excuse for rotten food and mistreatment."

Sarah rested her hand lightly on his. "Why, Captain, do you wish to inspire me to join your crew?"

The color had returned to her cheeks, and, greatly relieved that she felt well enough to tease him, Chris laughed easily. "Lord, no. You'd provide a terrible distraction. No one would get any work done."

He broke off a bit of biscuit and guided it to her mouth. Her teeth were as pretty as pearls, and he was reminded of the last time he had fed a woman a bite of bread. They had been on a picnic along the banks of the James River. It had been such a pleasant interlude, but it bothered him not to be able to recall the young lady's name.

When Sarah finished the biscuit, Chris peeled an orange and gave her a section. She took a bite, the juice spilling down her chin, and she caught it with her fingers. "Am I moving too quickly?" he asked.

"No, this is fine." Despite her best intentions, Sarah was sharing a bunk with a half-clothed pirate, and for the moment, it did not feel wrong. The spicy scent of his soap brought the unwanted memory of his late-night embrace, and she wished he reeked of something vile rather than smelling so pleasant. With sudden inspiration, she wondered if she might not be wise to encourage Chris's company to the point that his crew became jealous and mutinied, but then where would she be? She agonized, then discarded the scheme as absurd.

She was so obviously preoccupied, Chris did not press her for conversation. When she finished the first orange and refused another, he had no excuse to remain with her and reluctantly rose and rinsed his hands in the last of the water he had brought to shave. Filled with an uneasy sense he had just missed an opportunity to forge an accord, he dressed in a clean shirt and pulled on the waistcoat and coat he had worn the previous day.

"I'll send the water I promised," he remarked as he reached the door, "and your trunk. Rest until you feel better, though. I won't have you risk a fall while you dress, and you needn't repeat how disagreeable you'd find my assistance. I'll stop in later, and if you feel up to taking a stroll on deck, I'll escort you. I can't allow you to move about the ship on your own. I'm sure you understand why."

Sarah wondered if it was because he feared she might scuttle the vessel, or if he was more worried his men might abuse her. She did not care to seek clarification when whatever his concern, he would be unlikely to tell the truth. She let him depart without comment and remained snuggled on the bunk until the young man she recognized as the cook's helper brought her a bucket of hot water.

Sarah held her breath as she sat up to greet him, but her earlier dizziness did not return. "Won't you please tell me your name so that I might thank you properly?"

"It's Charley Black, ma'am," he replied.

"Well then, thank you, Charley."

Embarrassed by her pretty smile, Charley averted his eyes and cast a nervous glance around the cabin. He knew how the captain liked to have things done, but he had no experience serving fine ladies. Uncertain just what to do with the water, he set the wooden bucket down on the table and backed away. "I'll fetch your trunk," he offered, then bolted out the door. He left it unlocked.

Unfortunately, Sarah did not feel up to following. Nor could she take any comfort in remaining where she sat, for while the captain's quarters were now familiar, she knew better than to make the mistake of becoming complacent, and therefore careless. Desperately needing the strength that had deserted her that morning, she rose and took a tentative step toward the table. She still felt a bit shaky but held fast to the back of a chair until she was confident she would not fall.

She had never enjoyed being cooped up indoors but would not look forward to going up on deck when Chris could so easily notice her pleasure and keep her imprisoned below for the remainder of the voyage simply to punish her. He could surely be counted upon to try to break her spirit in countless ways, but her father had never succeeded in that feat and she swore no pirate would either.

When Charley returned with her trunk, they debated a moment about where to place it, then he again fled as swiftly as before, and Sarah was amused by how badly she appeared to frighten him. There he was, at sea among pirates, and he found a lone female terrifying. She had no hope the rest of the crew would share Charley's trepidation where she was concerned, and that she would have to rely upon Christopher MacLeod to protect her was not at all reassuring.

The mere thought of the captain made her hurry to bathe and dress, but with a single bucket of water, she had to bathe first and then rinse out her lingerie. She had just donned a clean chemise when the *Island Belle* suddenly changed course, and soapy water slopped all over the table. She again grabbed for a chair to steady herself, and in the next instant she heard the thunderous roar of cannon fire. She sent a frantic glance toward the windows in the stern and glimpsed a British brig in full sail bearing down on them with amazing speed.

She extended her arms for balance as she stepped toward her trunk; then, unwilling to waste any time unpacking another gown, she slipped into the black satin dress she had slept in. She had just sat down on the unmade bunk to pull on clean stockings when Chris burst through the door.

"Good. You're dressed." He reached out his hand. "Don't bother with shoes. Come up on deck; I want you to see this."

Sarah started to rise but was thrown into Chris's arms as cannon fire again rocked the ship. "How can you possibly be smiling?" she asked. "Aren't you terrified of being sunk?"

Chris laughed at the absurdity of that notion. "I'm just playing with them. The *Island Belle*'s out of their range and we'll stay that way. Did you hope that I'd surrender and use you as a hostage to bargain for my life?"

Sarah pulled free of his grasp. "It's not a bad plan."

A teasing glint filled Chris's eyes, and when he inclined his head as he reached for her again, she knew he was going to kiss her. Anxious that the tender touch of his lips would swiftly turn bruising, she braced herself, but his hasty kiss was over in an instant. She then had to sweep her hair out of her eyes as the exuberant captain led her up the companionway screaming a wild war whoop she feared only another bloodthirsty pirate could appreciate.

Chapter Three

Chris led Sarah to the stern, then placed one arm around her waist and the other on the rail. He pulled her so close that the whole length of her body was pressed against his with the graceful ease of a gentle smile.

"I can play tag with them all day if I choose," he laughed, "but for some reason, enraging the Royal Navy has lost its appeal."

Sarah wondered if she might be to blame for his lack of interest in the enemy, but the alarming possibility was far from flattering. Buffeted by the wind, she clung to the rail. "You overtake the slower merchant craft that can't give you a battle and elude the heavily armed warship that could. Is that how you wage war on Great Britain?"

"Precisely." Chris had met Sarah at sunset and had studied her delicate features at length under the soft lamplight in his cabin. Now, in the bright morning sun, she fascinated him anew. Her profile was as superb as the finest cameo, and he longed to reach out and trace the gentle sweetness of her nose and the lush fullness of her lips, but wisely he kept his free hand locked on the rail. It had been her beauty that had first bewitched him and then the fire of her temper, but with her full attention focused on the British ship, he made a startling discovery.

"You're much younger than I thought," he confessed when she glanced his way. "Are you even sixteen?"

Sarah gestured toward the vessel giving them a valiant, if futile, pursuit. "This is scarcely the time to exchange personal information, Captain. What if you've misjudged the range of their cannon?"

For an instant, Chris lost himself in the liquid depths of her indigo eyes, but then another cannonball sent up a huge wave. As it splashed off the stern, he turned to shield Sarah from the spray.

"I'd never make such a careless error," he vowed. "War is a deadly sport, and it deserves to be played well."

"This is no mere game!" Sarah denied, but her voice was lost in the howl of the wind filling the sails, and she was forced to lean close to be understood. "No rational man dismisses war so flippantly, Captain—at least not after he's seen his friends die."

"We'll all die eventually," Chris reminded her. "No one escapes Earth alive. Now stop evading my question and tell me how old you are."

Sarah thought him completely crazed. The British warship might at any second catch a strong gust of wind and surge forward with enough momentum to hurl cannonballs right into the *Island Belle* and dissolve the graceful ship in a hail of jagged splinters. She was tempted to throw herself over the side and swim for the brig, but weighed down by a heavy gown, such a frantic gesture would surely cost her not only her own life but her dear babe's as well. When Chris tightened his hold on her, she felt trapped and feared he had read her mind.

"I'm eighteen," she finally admitted grudgingly, but

she could not look his way again when the danger to them all was so great.

"I have a brother who will be eighteen in a few months," he replied.

Sarah responded sarcastically. "Fascinating." She could see the brig's crew dashing around the deck, and glanced over her shoulder to see what Chris's men were doing. When she discovered several were merely observing her, she quickly refocused her attention on the British warship.

"There has to be a price on your head," she warned.

"Perhaps." He continued to regard her with a knowing smile. "What would I be worth to you?"

Sarah caught a glimpse of a British officer in the bow of the brig, and her heart lurched. Desperately eager for the ship giving chase to overtake them, she ignored Chris's provocative question and wished she had had sense enough to devise a plan to hide should there be an attack. Then, when the first British officer came on board the *Island Belle,* she could have come out to provide an enthusiastic welcome.

Hoping it was not too late for such a ruse, she sagged against Chris's arm. "I'm afraid I'm still not feeling well," she murmured sadly. "I'd like to go below, please."

Chris appeared to be sincerely pained. "I'm sorry you're not enjoying this as much as we are."

Her effort to feign illness forgotten, Sarah spit out her reply. "How could you even imagine I'd take pleasure in this ghastly spectacle?"

Despite his confident boasts, the gunners aboard the brig succeeded in improving their aim, and with the next cannon volley Chris and Sarah were drenched with high-flying spray. Chris kept a firm hold on Sarah's arm as he shouted an order, and the helmsman corrected the *Island Belle*'s course to catch the full force of the wind. Then, with a soaring ease, the schooner's speed increased to near flight and, barely skimming the surface of the sea, she drew easily away from her pursuer.

Sarah felt the angle of the deck shift beneath her feet and quickly broadened her stance for balance, but there was no saving her plummeting spirits. Tears filled her eyes, and she watched in tormented silence as her chance at rescue faded in the *Island Belle*'s foamy wake. She waited until the British naval vessel was no larger than a thimble in the distance and then, truly sick with disappointment, repeated her request to go below.

Splattered with saltwater, she was positive she looked sufficiently pitiful for Chris to grant her plea, but his long hesitation worried her. "You invited me to take a stroll," she reminded him, "but I'd rather not tour the deck barefoot and in a sopping wet dress."

Chris sent a last glance toward the brig and then, confident he could spare a moment to escort Sarah below, he took her hand to steady her step. As they started across the deck, the wind sculpted her damp gown against her rounded abdomen, and the crew's admiring glances immediately turned to astonished stares.

Chris heard the shocked whispers before Sarah did and hurried her below, but he knew as soon as he returned to the deck, he would be bombarded with questions more dangerous than the British cannon fire.

When they reached his cabin, Chris pushed open the door but did not follow Sarah inside. "You'll need more hot water," he offered. "I'll send Charley down with another bucket."

"I dare not exceed my daily ration, Captain. I'll just have to make do with what's left in the one he brought me this morning."

Chris shook his head. "Oh, no, for then you'll surely complain later of how I've mistreated you." He pulled the door shut but this time failed to lock it.

Just as he expected, Rob Corliss was waiting for him at the top of the companionway. "Yes, I know," he said to the mate. "She's very young and very pregnant. What did you expect me to do? Put her in one of the lifeboats and hope the British would find her adrift?"

Rob responded with a confused shrug. "I've no idea what to suggest, but everyone knows having a woman on board is bad luck, and a woman in her condition can't possibly give you any joy."

"That's where you're wrong," Chris assured him. "Mrs. Hadley provides a veritable garden of delights." He watched Rob's expression fill with disgust, but his mate's disapproval was of slight concern.

"She's a widow from Charleston, and because I won't risk entering a British-held port, she can't return home. Nor will I abandon her, alone and friendless, anywhere else.

"You needn't concern yourself, however. I'm not abusing her in any way," Chris stressed convincingly. "In fact, I'm the one who's suffered the abuse. Now, let's see if we can't find another merchantman ripe for the picking before we set a course for the Caribbean."

Rob nodded, but his expression was no less bewildered. "Aye, Captain, but I fear our luck won't hold. It sure didn't for that young woman's poor husband."

"One British officer won't be missed. Get back to work, Mr. Corliss, and leave me to plot our strategy."

Rob hated to jeopardize what had been a cordial relationship, but he felt compelled to speak. "Mrs. Hadley could have my cabin, sir, and I'll hang a hammock with the crew."

Chris frowned slightly as he considered Rob's offer, but he quickly discounted it as unworkable. "She'd not even have the room to turn around in your quarters. It would be like imprisoning her in a cell, and I'll not do it. She's a fragile creature and not only requires, but deserves, far better care."

"And you're providing it?" Rob asked incredulously.

Chris would never have tolerated a challenge to his authority under any other circumstance, but Sarah Hadley's exotic presence did not fit any of the usual dilemmas they encountered at sea.

"What's your real question, Mr. Corliss? Are the men wondering if I'll share her as I do privateering's other rewards?"

Aghast at the question, Rob's freckles disappeared beneath a deep scarlet blush. "Some might have wondered about it before they saw she was with child, but no, sir, not anymore they don't."

"Good. Now, I suggest everyone keep a sharp eye out for trouble on the horizon rather than create problems here on the *Island Belle.*"

Chris walked away before Rob could respond, but there was nothing the mate could possibly say about Sarah Hadley that he had not already told himself. No privateer took his mistress to sea, and with good reason—but Sarah was most definitely not his mistress.

"Eighteen!" Chris muttered under his breath. When he had last seen his brother, the gangling youth had been a long way from a man, but Sarah was all woman at eighteen. She was so fiercely determined that he could scarcely imagine her ever having been a child. She would have been an adorable moppet with her crown of golden curls, but she was so full of life that he doubted she had ever enjoyed playing quietly with dolls.

He paused at the rail and reluctantly admitted he was as thoroughly distracted as his crew must assume, and promptly forced himself to begin a detailed inspection of every inch of the ship's rigging and sails. They carried plenty of spare canvas, but he did not want to have to call for it should a sail rip while they made the kind of hasty escape they had made that day. Perhaps Sarah would have had more respect for him had he attacked the brig. He laughed to himself as he thought how greatly such an unexpected maneuver would have shocked the men of the king's Navy. It was always wise to do the unexpected, he mused, and feeling decidedly optimistic, he looked forward to sharing his next meal with the alluring Widow Hadley.

Sarah's hands shook so badly she had great difficulty removing her gown. The black satin was trimmed with black velvet ribbon at the neckline and the sleeves were edged with a deep ruffle of black lace. It was her favorite gown despite its somber hue, and she prayed it had not been ruined.

She shook out the saltwater, lay it over a chair, and cursed the captain for not allowing her the time to don her cloak; her dress would be dry had she worn it, and she resolved right then not to appear on deck without it ever again.

Before removing another gown from her trunk, she sent an anxious glance toward the windows. Although she dared not hope the British warship would have reappeared, that there were no white sails dotting the horizon deepened her already wretched sense of abandonment. Upon sailing from Charleston, the vastness of the gray-green ocean had been a comforting sight, but after being fired upon, the sea's restless rhythms mirrored her own anxiety far too closely to offer solace.

A soft knock at the door forced her to use her damp dress as a modest shield, but it was only Charley carrying another bucket of hot water and a clean towel. She thanked him, and briefly considered asking a few questions about the captain, then decided there was too great a risk the boy would run straight to him and repeat her every word. There might possibly be someone on board who could provide useful information, but not the cook's timid helper.

As he had earlier, Charley fled as soon as he completed his errand, and Sarah hurried to use the hot water before it cooled. The bucket was much too small to serve as a tub to launder her gown, so she again lay the beautiful black garment across a chair, where it rested beside the lingerie she had rinsed out earlier. She then washed the salt spray from her hair and wrapped the towel around her head.

Still dressed in her ribbon-trimmed chemise and petti-coats, she curled up on the bunk and endeavored to formulate a plan to survive this miserable captivity. First of all, she was in desperate need of an ally. Unfortunately, she had not been on deck long enough yesterday nor today to recognize any of the *Island Belle*'s crew, with the sole exception of Mr. Corliss; the red-haired mate's vivid coloring made him impossible to mistake. They had met under regrettable circumstances on board the *Beatrice,* when he had forced her up on deck. His hold on her arm had been firm rather than bruising, but was that sufficient proof to assume he might treat her well at other times?

"Probably not," she predicted darkly.

Preoccupied with the need to find a friend, she towel-dried her hair and vowed to spend every minute on deck that the crazed Captain MacLeod would allow. She would learn to identify the rest of his crew first by sight and then by name.

While she had no real reason to hope MacLeod's crew were any more rational than he, she believed the odds were good that at least a few among them would have a firmer grip on sanity. She prayed that from among those hardy souls she would be able to find a protector who would aid in her escape should another British vessel appear. Her only fear was that one man would not be nearly enough.

Then there was Christopher MacLeod himself, she agonized. She now believed it had been extremely foolish to antagonize him when he had just proven his grasp on reality was tenuous. What if she had provoked him to a murderous rage? Would his crew have stepped forward to shield her from harm, or drawn lots to sate themselves on her lifeless body?

Sickened by that gruesome mental image, she forced herself to think more calmly. She had learned to fight anger with anger as a child. The tactic had served her well thus far, but if the captain's moods were erratic, then she had been fortunate to meet him while he was elated over the capture of the *Beatrice*.

The cleverness he had shown that morning in eluding the brig might keep his mood buoyant throughout the day, but what of tonight, or tomorrow? Should he become depressed, would her mere presence annoy him to the point her life might truly be in grave danger?

"I am already in mortal peril," she reminded herself, but she had never been able to simply sit and sulk.

She left the bed and removed a dark blue gown from her trunk. As she pulled it on, she was sorry it wasn't prettier; but, newly widowed, she had packed none of the brightly colored clothes Michael had loved. She slipped on her stockings and shoes, then realized her cloak would be the only apparel the ship's crew would see. Still, with her fair coloring, the dramatic black garment was extremely flattering. Hadn't Michael always told her so?

Overcome with a poignant longing for the happiness she and her husband had shared all too briefly, she cried out, "Oh, Michael, I miss you so."

Hearing Sarah's voice, Chris assumed Charley was with her, and he did not pause to knock before coming through the door. He was quite naturally puzzled to find her alone.

"To whom were you speaking just now?" he inquired.

Seized with a sudden inspiration, Sarah's face lit with a triumphant smile. She was convinced he was unbalanced, a crazed demon who lived for the thrill of conquest or flight. She also believed that if she made her behavior as mercurial as his, it might speed his progress toward total disintegration. She might even be able to convince him to put her ashore before he lost the ability to command. That hope made her smile wider still.

"I was just singing to myself," she explained in a sultry whisper.

Chris had to grab for the door to steady himself. He had seen Sarah Hadley furiously angry, obnoxiously sarcastic, and completely despondent, but he had never seen her smile, and the effect was dazzling. Her dark blue gown was as demure as the black satin. The neckline was draped with a silk fichu and the cuffs bordered with deep lace, but against her creamy smooth skin, the result was

anything but retiring. For a long moment, he could not recall what question he had asked, then decided it made not
the slightest bit of difference.

He cleared his throat to make certain he could speak.
"If you feel up to it, we've time before dinner for the stroll
I promised. Of course, if you're still not well—"

Sarah reached for her cloak. "Your quarters are handsome, Captain, but I do believe a change in scene will do
me good, as will the exercise."

Chris came forward to help her on with her long black
cloak, and when she stood staring up at him, he had a difficult time tying the satin ribbon at her neckline. He
could feel her watching him and deliberately refused to
meet her gaze when he knew how easily he would become lost in it. Instead, with deep concentration he fashioned a crooked bow, gave it a final nervous tug, and took
her hand.

Sarah waited until just before they reached the deck to
pull her hood into place over her curls. She then wound
her arm around Chris's and moved as close to him as she
had always walked beside Michael. She had not realized
until that very instant that the two men were nearly iden-
tical in size, or would have been, had Michael still been
alive. Her hood hid her resolute smile, but she dipped her
head in a silent salute to her late husband.

Eager to put her plan into operation, she searched the
deck for the mate and found him easily. He was standing
at the wheel beside the helmsman. She nodded slightly to
acknowledge both men, then gave a mere hint of a smile
before modestly lowering her gaze in a gesture calculated
to provoke sympathy for her plight.

Whenever Chris paused to speak to a member of his
crew, she searched out another man standing nearby and

offered a similarly winsome smile. She had never had to resort to such flirtatious behavior in the past, and had decried it in other young women as maddeningly superficial, but at present, it was the only method available to win support from the crew. Chris had already remarked on her youth, and with just a little effort, she could appear even younger than her eighteen years. With that goal in mind, she licked her lips and adopted a pretty pout.

Each time Chris glanced in Sarah's direction, her softly draped hood obscured his view of her face, but the amazed glances she was drawing from his crew were a clear indication that she was playing some sort of trick. Finally, too curious to tolerate being the only one left out of the fun, he drew to a sudden halt and pulled her around to face him. She gazed up at him, her eyes wide with an expression of innocent surprise, but he had seen the explosive side of her nature too often to be fooled.

"Just what is it you're doing, Mrs. Hadley? My crew appears to be so thoroughly entertained that I must insist you amuse me as well."

Sarah's glance slid down the row of silver buttons on his waistcoat before returning to his face. It was an insolent gesture, one that appraised his masculine appeal and then promptly dismissed it as unworthy of her notice. "Why, Captain," she murmured in a throaty whisper, "I've absolutely no idea what you mean."

Chris watched her turn away, her smile seductively sweet as her gaze fell upon Rob Corliss. The flustered mate blushed but broke into a broad grin. He started to back away, and nearly tripped over a coiled rope before he began to pay more attention to where he was bound than to the lovely young widow.

"That's enough," Chris scolded harshly. He took Sarah

by the arm and propelled her right back to his cabin. He took the precaution of closing the door and even then lowered his voice before confronting her. "Just what was it you were doing up there, Mrs. Hadley? Do you intend to make pets of my crew?"

Sarah slowly loosened her cloak's lopsided bow, then slid the heavy garment off her shoulders and, with a graceful swirl, laid it across her trunk. "If I've offended you somehow, Captain, I'm sincerely sorry," she replied sweetly.

Rapidly losing patience, Chris propped his hands on his hips. "While you're in such an obliging mood, perhaps we can become better acquainted."

"Of course. I'll be happy to satisfy whatever curiosity about me you may have."

Chris had heard friends criticize women for being unpredictable, but he did not believe that was one of Sarah Hadley's undoubtedly many flaws. She was simply striving to manipulate him, and he was appalled. He wondered just how far she would take her game and stepped closer to find out. When she failed to back away, he moved closer still. He raised his hand to trace the delectable curve of her cheek.

"Have you simply come to your senses, Mrs. Hadley, and realized that you'll receive far better treatment from me if you're cooperative?"

Although his fingertips were warm, Sarah had to fight to suppress a shudder that would have belied her words. "Yes," she agreed after a convincing hesitation. "Upon reflection, I was impressed by the masterful way in which you eluded capture by the Royal Navy. Clearly you're a much finer captain than the man in command of that brig."

"Oh, yes, I am," Chris concurred. "I'm very, very good."

He tilted Sarah's chin and leaned down to kiss her. Rather than remaining frozen in place as she had in the past, she leaned against him and parted her lips. Readily accepting her encouragement, Chris cupped her face between his palms and nipped at her lower lip before slipping the tip of his tongue into her mouth. She tasted vaguely of oranges and the promise of something even more delicious.

Chris opened his eyes and found Sarah regarding him with a bewildered gaze. Amused to have gotten the best of her, he laughed. "Surely you've been kissed before, Mrs. Hadley," he chided softly.

Indeed she had, but she had not expected him to be so tender when he had treated her far more roughly in the past. Her heart fluttering in panic, she glanced down at the fullness of her figure and spoke the first thought to enter her mind.

"You have the advantage here, sir, for no matter what I claim, you'll not believe me a shy virgin."

With that saucy retort, Chris was convinced she was merely toying with him, but he no longer cared. If she wanted to play, then so did he. He brushed gentle kisses over her thick sweep of dark lashes, then her delicate ears, before searching out the pulse at the base of her throat. Her heart was racing as wildly as his own and, again tilting her chin slightly, he grazed her lips with a feather-light kiss, drew back slightly, and waited for her to come to him. In less than a heartbeat she pressed her lips to his, and he wrapped her in a fond embrace and gave her a long, slow, deep kiss that felt so good it was sheer torture to bring it to an end.

Sarah knew just how dangerous a game she was playing, but as she watched a teasing glint fill Chris's eyes, and a rakish grin spread across his lips, she feared she had tricked only herself. Christopher MacLeod might not have a sure grip on his sanity, but he certainly had a firm hold on her.

She could not abandon her ruse without arousing his suspicions, and so she continued to smile while searching her mind for a plausible excuse to pull away. At last, she recalled the splendid one he had supplied himself.

"You were right to admonish me to observe a year of mourning," she announced with what she hoped he would mistake for sincere regret rather than the desperation it truly was. "Now I suggest we have dinner and forget this unfortunate incident ever occurred."

As she tried to slip free of his grasp, Chris pulled her back into his arms. "You're forgetting something, Sarah."

His knee was pressed firmly against hers, and before she could suppress the impulse, she slid her hand beneath his jacket and ran her palm over his hip. "I sincerely doubt that, Captain," she replied.

The boldness of her touch shocked him, but it made Chris long to explore the depths of her knowledge. He began to think Michael Hadley might not have been such an unlucky man, after all. "You promised to satisfy my curiosity where you're concerned."

"Yes, I did, and it would be very wicked of me to break a promise," she assured him.

There was something about the way she stretched out the word *wicked*, turning it into a boast, that was as intriguing as her luscious kiss. It made all her actions suspect, and while at first Chris hated to accept where that wicked streak might have led her, he could not reject those dark possibilities either.

Charley interrupted them. He brought dinner, and they had to rearrange Sarah's damp clothing to empty two chairs. Not wanting to watch her starve herself again, Chris waited until they had finished their meal to challenge her.

First he refilled their tankards, but Sarah had swallowed only a few drops of wine. "Would you prefer ale?" he asked.

"No, thank you, Captain. I have very little tolerance for spirits."

Chris was amused by the thought of her becoming too tipsy to argue. "I wish that you'd told me. From now on I'll see you have tea with your meals."

They had been served a chicken pie with a rich, vegetable-laced sauce and flaky crust. Sarah had nearly finished before she realized it was essentially the same meal she had refused the day before, but merely baked in a crust. Surprisingly hungry, she feared she had eaten too much and would be sleepy all afternoon. She raised her hand to cover a wide yawn and then apologized.

"Forgive me, Captain. I didn't sleep well last night; but then, I'm sure you know what was troubling me."

Now that they were finished with their meal, Chris set their plates aside and folded his hands in his lap. "Your youth is what troubles me, Mrs. Hadley, as does the fact that you've been rather conveniently widowed."

"My God," Sarah cried, sorry she had lowered her guard for even a second. Encouraging his kiss had been the height of folly, but she had not dreamed he would turn mean so quickly. "What a ghastly thing to say."

Chris raised his hand to plead for silence. "Just hear me out. Both sides in this war have resorted to using spies, and a great many of them have been women.

Women have the advantage over men in that they're able to pry secrets from their lovers' lips that not even the most ambitious male agent could ever extract. I actually believed your story about being a widow who wished for her child to be born in England—until you abandoned your righteous anger in an attempt to manipulate me and my crew with your considerable charm."

Sarah's eyes widened slightly for, even knowing the captain was dangerously unbalanced, she had no idea how to counter such wild ravings. Too shocked to compose an immediate defense, she stared at him in numbed silence. His manner was deceptively calm, his mellow voice even, but his supposition was so outrageous she was more terrified of him than ever.

Chris mistook Sarah's stunned silence for an admission of guilt. "I think you left Charleston because it will be too dangerous for you to remain in America if the Patriots win the war, which indeed we will. I doubt you've ever had a husband, and your pregnancy might be no more than a feather pillow you've weighted to distort your slim figure.

"I'll grant you that it's a clever ruse," he continued. "But now that I've caught you, I just might return you to shore. Only I'll choose a port we control and make certain you stand trial for your crimes."

Sarah feared Christopher MacLeod's thoughts must careen around his brain with the same rolling motion as his ship rode the waves, and she had no way to counter his astonishing fabrication of her past. Spies were hanged when apprehended, but she was no spy. But how could she prove her innocence if the accusation were made by someone as convincing as Christopher MacLeod? Would she even be granted an opportunity to plead innocent to such a ridiculous charge?

With exaggerated care, she rose from her chair and went to Chris's side. She took his hand and pressed his palm to her belly. "The babe's kicked me all through dinner. Just wait a moment and you'll see this bulge in my shape is no pillow."

Chris waited, and waited, but all he felt was the smoothness of her gown and the enticing warmth of her hand. He was about to demand that she shed her dress to offer proof of her condition when Sarah moved his hand lower, and he at last felt the babe give a fluttering kick.

An ageless sense of wonder swept through him, and he knew regardless of whatever sinister crimes Sarah Hadley might have committed, she was most definitely with child. He pulled his hand away and rose to face her.

"Pregnant women are never hanged," he announced reluctantly. "So it looks as though your luck will hold."

"Luck!" Sarah placed her palms against Chris's chest and shoved him right back down into his chair. "It was not luck that made me a widow at eighteen, nor luck that brought me aboard your cursed *Island Belle*. The next time we sight a ship put me in a lifeboat and set me adrift. I don't care whose ship it is, either. I would rather be with anyone than you when you laugh at death and malign virtuous widows as spies!"

Chris hauled himself to his feet and stared down at her with a glance every bit as darkly menacing as her own. "You are a consummate actress, my dear, and if the British didn't have you spying for them, then they are even more incompetent than we all suppose." Certain she would slap him for that opinion, he reached out to grab her wrist.

"Careful, Mrs. Hadley," he warned. "A captain has as much power as King George aboard his ship, and I tolerate only obedient subjects. Now, I suggest you take a nap, or write poetry, or embroider, however you usually spend your afternoons, but you're not to make another bit of trouble for me."

Sarah held her breath as she waited for him to enhance his demand with another vile threat, but he simply stared at her, his expression one of such hardy disgust that she fully expected him to spit on her. He had a firm hold of her right hand, but she curled the fingers of her left, ready to claw his face if he resorted to something so crude. She refused to look away, channeling every bit of the fury he so consistently provoked into her gaze.

Chris felt the searing heat of Sarah's hatred and again marveled at how cleverly she had hidden it from his crew. From the reactions he had observed, she had flirted with his men in what had to be an attempt to win their sympathy and to sabotage his command. While he had to grudgingly admire her audacity, he would not allow her another such opportunity.

"From now on, Mrs. Hadley, you'll only be allowed on deck after dark, and that privilege will be extended only if you've behaved yourself and completed whatever task I've assigned you for the day. As long as you behave in a ladylike fashion, you'll have a pleasant voyage, but don't cross me again or you'll beg to be tossed over the side."

He released her so quickly, she stumbled toward his bunk and missed the chance to rake him with her nails. He locked the door, but it did not faze her. At home, she had spent almost as much time locked in her room as out, and because she so greatly preferred her own company to his, it was a relief to have him gone.

She moved onto the bunk and hugged herself tightly. She had absolutely no idea what sort of tasks the deranged Captain MacLeod might expect her to perform, but she would not even begin until she was good and ready.

She closed her eyes and took a deep breath, but despite her distress, she could still feel the gentle caress of his lips and the heat of his hand against her belly. She cuddled his pillow as exhaustion swept her into a taunting dream where there was no escaping a damned pirate, nor his possessive kiss.

Chapter Four

Too frustrated to pace the deck, Christopher MacLeod gripped the rail and wished it were the Widow Hadley's slender neck. His hands ached before his temper began to cool. Then, forced to relax his stance, he realized just how foolish it had been to threaten the perplexing young woman. Now he would have to actually produce some useful work for her to perform. He was still scowling with the effort when Rob Corliss approached.

"The day is a fair one, Captain. The wind's steady and there's been no further sign of the British."

Chris nodded absently, for he would relish an opportunity to fire their cannon. "The British are still in pursuit, hovering just over the horizon," he predicted darkly.

"Can you actually feel them?" Rob asked.

What Chris felt was barely suppressed rage, but the Royal Navy made a far better target than Sarah Hadley and he blamed them happily. "Aye, that I can. It's not as clear a sign as the shifting winds heralding a storm, but their rotten stench hangs in the breeze."

Rob drew in a deep breath, but all he smelled was the sea. He then followed the captain's gaze, but again sighted only the shifting ebbs and swells surrounding the *Island Belle*. "Perhaps I spoke too soon, and the day is not nearly as fine as I thought."

"Perhaps," Chris murmured, but it was not truly the British that plagued him. He hated to admit what a sorry mess he had created for himself and veiled the seriousness of his request behind a casual tone.

"Mr. Corliss, while we have little to do but watch for our enemies, perhaps you will assist me in keeping Mrs. Hadley occupied with some time-consuming chore. I seem to be at a loss to devise one."

Now equally flummoxed, the mate grabbed for the rail. "I doubt she could provide much help to the cook."

"Don't be absurd. It cannot involve physical labor."

"I meant no disrespect, sir. I was merely eliminating the unsuitable."

"Then you've made an excellent start."

"Well, yes, sir, that was my intention." Rob pursed his lips as he considered the many tasks required to keep the *Island Belle* afloat, none of which was usually performed by a beautiful young woman in an advanced state of pregnancy.

"There is your laundry," Rob offered after a lengthy pause. "But that would be most improper."

"Agreed."

Rob stared down at his boots and then up at the cloudless sky while he silently discounted increasingly unlikely options. "We do have several bolts of muslin," he finally recalled. "She could roll some into the appropriate lengths for bandages, should they prove necessary."

Relief washed through Chris's features, followed by a slow, satisfied grin. "Thank you for the fine idea—but the muslin might also be used to fashion her infant's clothing if she has none prepared. Making tiny garments might keep her involved for weeks."

"A true inspiration, Captain. Set her to work on what she'd want to accomplish on her own!"

Chris slapped the mate on the back and turned away, already beginning to refine his plan. He was confident that with but a little effort he would remain ahead of the willful widow, and with surprise working to his advantage he returned to his cabin in a far better mood than when he had departed.

He found his comely guest curled atop his bunk asleep, and he forced himself to turn away rather than tarry to contemplate her remarkable beauty. He was then chagrined by how vividly her enticing image remained fixed in his mind. Confining her to his cabin would provide no respite at all, he worried. Not if she continued to cloud his thoughts as tenaciously as she clung to his side.

Sarah had packed her favorite book at the bottom of her trunk and, awakening from her nap desperate for a diversion, she was rapidly shuffling through her belongings to retrieve it when Chris knocked at the door.

"If that's Charley, please come in. If it's the captain, just leave me be," she said.

Chris entered and closed the door quietly. "Charley rates a polite welcome, but I do not?"

Sarah sat back on the bunk and twisted a stray curl behind her ear to clear her vision. Christopher MacLeod was definitely a fine figure of a man, but like many a handsome appearance, his masked what had to be a wide nasty streak.

"How can you possibly imagine that I would welcome your tedious company?" she asked.

"Force of habit, I suppose, but then, you're unlike most of the young women I've met, Mrs. Hadley. Now, let's not quibble over the reason for my visit. I've devised your first task, and while you're apparently occupied spilling out the contents of your trunk, this won't require but a moment."

"Surely you possess more stamina than that, Captain," she challenged.

It took Chris several seconds to realize she was blatantly referring to his sexual prowess, but then he burst into hearty laughter. "You may rest assured that I have remarkable stamina, but we'll save that treat for another day."

He remained smiling as she dipped her head and stared at him coldly. Clearly her audacious comment had been a broad taunt rather than an invitation, and for the moment, at least, he had the necessary resolve to resist her many charms. She continued to confound him, however, for he had never met another elegant beauty who had dared offer such bold opinions.

Fortunately for him, he would continue to hold the upper hand. Rather amused, he cleared his throat. "Let me begin again. I have generously decided to provide a choice. We have plenty of muslin, from which you might fashion the necessary little garments for your infant if you've not packed them. Or, if you'd prefer, I have a French dictionary that translates words into English and an ample supply of books to assist you in mastering the language."

Dumbfounded, Sarah's expression filled with horror. "You expect me to learn French?"

"*Oui, madame,* it's a lovely language, soft and poetic. You will find it far easier to communicate on Martinique if you speak it well."

"I would sooner sprout a forked tongue and converse with serpents."

"Then I will send you the necessary muslin, needles, and thread. The light here in my cabin is better in the morning, but it's still bright enough to sew for a while today. Should you tire, however, you have my permission to indulge yourself with another nap."

He went out the door and locked it before she could draw breath to reply, but he knew exactly how she would greet him upon his return. That her mood was so predictable made him laugh again, but he was careful to adopt a more serious expression before crossing the deck. After all, the outspoken young woman was a horrible burden, and he did not want his crew to suspect otherwise.

Sarah managed to stave off a shrieking fit, but in truth, her handiwork had never in the past progressed beyond the level of a clumsy child's. Her stitches were perpetually uneven, and her needle pierced her fingertips so often that every bit of fabric she touched was quickly bloodstained beyond repair. Despite her mother's patient instruction, she had not perfected the art of embroidery, nor learned to crochet well either. But of course, her lack of skill with a needle was but a minor offense in her father's precisely run household.

"And I am truly to fashion garments for my precious babe?" she moaned. She could have more easily studied the ship's nautical charts and plotted a course for England.

Then she recalled the captain's mention of *another* nap, and realized he had inadvertently revealed a return to his cabin while she'd slept. The possibility of being spied upon made her flesh crawl, and she rubbed her arms to dispel the unwelcome sensation. Clearly the man possessed not a single admirable quality, other than his obvious ability to command.

He was a devious, unprincipled sort, and while she would never stoop to his level, she swiftly devised a plan. Even with little skill, if she concentrated diligently, she would surely be able to produce a single tiny smock. Whenever the captain appeared, she would pretend to pause in her sewing and, seeing the garment upon her lap, he would quite naturally assume that she had already fashioned several.

He might wear finely tailored garments, but he would use a needle the size of a nail and coarse thread to repair a torn sail, and be unlikely to be any judge of the quality of her handiwork.

"I must be sure to hide what's left of the muslin and ask for more," she mused softly, delighted to have anticipated such a need to make her ruse convincing.

Her mind at ease for the moment, she continued the search through her belongings. When she at last found her favorite book hidden among her petticoats, she hugged it to her bosom. She had read it more than a dozen times, but *Evelina* never failed to lift her spirits.

Like herself, the lovely heroine had also been raised in a parsonage, but she had had such wonderful adventures in London society and wed the dashing Lord Orville. While published anonymously, the popular book was rumored to have been written by a woman. Sarah was positive that it must have been and, in a flash of inspiration, recognized that the recent dire turn of events in her own life might easily inspire a novel.

Her father would surely die of shame, but her mother might actually read a book she had penned. Lost in the possibility of becoming an author, she was startled when

Charley knocked at the door. He entered carrying the promised lengths of muslin, and a small wooden box containing sharp sewing needles, pins, and thread. When he lay everything upon the table, Sarah left the bunk to run her fingertips along the muslin's crisply folded edge. It was finely woven but smelled faintly musty, as though it had long lain at the bottom of a chest. There was also the matter of shrinkage.

"This must be laundered before I begin," she stated sweetly. "Is that someone's job, or must I request hot water and see to it myself, as I did with my own things?"

Perplexed, Charley unfolded the fabric. "I don't see no dirt, ma'am. The captain's real particular about how things are kept."

"Yes, I'm sure he is, but this needs to be freshly laundered, maybe even a dozen times before it will smell sweet and be soft enough for a baby to wear."

Badly embarrassed by the reference to her expected child, as well as her laundry, still draped carelessly about, Charley's deep blush scalded his ears. Unable to acknowledge his error, he grabbed up the muslin. "I'll see to it myself, ma'am."

"I hate to cause you any additional work." Her words dripped with a honeyed sincerity, but he was so eager to flee that he sprinted through the door and did not pause to lock it.

Because an unlocked door offered nothing in the way of true freedom, Sarah returned to her trunk. Her mother had given her a diary when Michael proposed, and she had set down her fears as well as her joy at their coming marriage. Then they had wed, and everything about being a wife had been so wonderfully new, she had not known how to describe it. Her entries had been few and fleeting up until Michael's death and, crushed by grief, she had not written a word thereafter.

The journal lay at the very bottom of the trunk. She ran her hand over the leather binding and wished she had recorded each of the blissful days she had shared with her husband. They were a painful blur now, but in truth, she and Michael had shared many happy hours.

Now she would use the book to keep a log of her time aboard the *Island Belle*, and while she would never divulge the intimate details of her own life to entertain readers, this experience aboard a privateer, no matter how unwelcome, would provide an authentic taste of adventure that would surely be popular. Why, were she to publish it, her book might even sell more copies than *Evelina*, she dreamed.

Forcing away such hopes as unseemly pride, she opened the book to a blank page, borrowed pen and ink from the captain's desk, and quickly made a few notes on the surprising twists in her journey. Not wishing to share them with the odious captain, she returned the diary to her trunk, where it would lie unnoticed among her lingerie.

Chris entered his cabin trailing a banner of wet muslin. "You are not, under any circumstances, to order my crew to do your bidding. Is that clear?"

Sarah had vowed to remain calm in the face of his anger, and now she simply stared at him. Had he wished to do her some grievous harm, he would surely have done so by now. Still, she took care to appear puzzled rather than incensed as she truly was by his ridiculous rebuke.

"Is that the muslin Charley insisted upon laundering for me?" she asked sweetly.

"It is, and it could not have been his idea."

"You underestimate him, Captain, but I fear that is scarcely the issue."

Chris's dark brows dipped menacingly. "I believe I was quite clear as to the issue. You are not to order my men about as though they were your personal staff."

"I quite agree, although what a lady would do with cutthroats for servants is beyond me. As for Charley, he was merely following your orders, not mine."

Chris tossed the damp fabric on the table, where it nestled in a soggy puddle. "How, pray tell, did you reach such an absurd conclusion?"

Sarah squared her shoulders but continued to address him softly as she recounted Charley's generous offer of help. "Muslin tends to shrink a bit and must be washed before it's cut to fit a pattern. There would be absolutely no point in sewing garments that would have to be laundered before a babe wore them if they then shrank to an inappropriate size."

Chris opened his mouth to argue, but her explanation made so much sense, he knew he had already lost. Charley had mumbled something about softening the cloth for her babe, so clearly they had discussed the fabric's use, even if the lad had not fully understood.

"In the future, Mrs. Hadley, you will consult with me, and I will decide what needs to be done and by whom."

Sarah shrugged slightly. "As you wish, Captain. I am merely a prisoner here."

"You are my guest," Chris uttered through clenched teeth, but in the next instant, he caught sight of a white sail in the window behind her. He swore as he grabbed the still dripping muslin and tore out of his cabin.

Following his gaze, Sarah raised up to peer out the window and nearly shouted for joy. The brig was again in

71

pursuit, which meant she might escape yet, and with her copy of *Evelina* and her diary clutched tightly in her hands, she was more than ready.

The *Island Belle* changed course with a rapidity that forced her to grab hold of the side of the bunk to escape being hurled headlong into her open trunk. She could feel the ship gathering speed as wind filled the sails. The graceful ship cut through the water with razorlike ease, but at such a precarious angle, Sarah feared they might swiftly capsize. Trapped belowdeck, she would surely drown along with the pirate crew.

The captain, however, would probably bob right up to the surface and describe himself as an innocent hostage rather than admit to being the brigand he was. She imagined that he would be quite convincing too, and the unsuspecting British captain who took him on board would no doubt be murdered in his bunk. Even if they had been sailing calm seas, that was far too gruesome a thought to commit to her diary.

When the brig began to fire on them, she considered the British fools to waste their ammunition when they were out of range, but she continued to study their pursuit with rapt attention. To her delighted surprise, a second brig soon appeared, driving down on them at a sharp angle from the first.

If the Royal Navy forced Captain MacLeod to fight, the resulting danger would be as great as drowning. The cabin door was unlocked so she would not be trapped below, but being up on deck where a shattered mast and miles of rigging might come crashing down on her was not a happenstance she would risk.

The sun was low on the horizon, exactly as it had been when the *Beatrice* was boarded. Had she been a prisoner only a day? she wondered absently; it felt so much longer. Indeed, her whole body ached with the strain.

The babe kicked her, an insistent reminder of his presence—as though she could ever forget him—and she patted her abdomen soothingly.

"We have not come so far to die clinging to wreckage adrift on the waves," she assured him. She knew better than to hope that Chris would ever surrender, but that their survival depended upon a pirate's unholy skill was still terrifying.

The menacing appearance of the second brig sent a rumbling murmur of disbelief through the *Island Belle*'s crew. A few were eager to fight, but most did not like their odds when they were so badly outgunned.

Finally Jacob Shorter, a tall, gaunt seaman with hunched shoulders, spoke the others' fears aloud. "The skirt's changed our luck," he vowed. "No good ever come from havin' one on board. No skirts, I say."

The sly comment rippled around the deck until the gunners took it up as a hoarse chant. Rob Corliss caught the insidious whisper before the captain, but if the superstition was being voiced loud enough for him to overhear, he knew Chris soon would. Unwilling to allow the situation to deteriorate that far, he kept a close watch on the crew and soon noted the true hub of discontent.

" 'No skirts,' is it, Shorter?" Rob called to him. "The captain doesn't agree."

"If you don't mind my saying so, Mr. Corliss, the captain ain't thinking with his head." Shorter winked at a man standing nearby, and was rewarded with a hearty chuckle.

Rob was well aware that he lacked Chris's imposing

presence, but then, he was not a MacLeod, and had not been born expecting to be obeyed, either. Nevertheless, he intended to captain his own ship one day, and he projected his own steady strength. He gestured to bring Jacob Shorter a step closer and spoke in a clipped, threatening tone.

"I do mind, and unless you'd care to repeat your insulting opinions to the captain, keep them to yourself. Otherwise, I'll have you whipped. Or I could whip you right now and save us both the wait."

"No, sir." Jacob raised his hands and backed away. "We'll be cursing the British is all."

"See to your duties instead," Rob ordered.

"Aye, sir, that I will." Jacob ducked his head as he turned away, but a devilish grin tickled his lips.

Jacob Shorter was an experienced hand who looked after the younger men, or Rob would have given him more than a warning, but he was not entirely satisfied with their exchange. Then again, he was not pleased to have a woman on board, himself. Still searching for a way to broach that delicate subject, he approached the captain.

With spyglass in hand, Chris studied the looming threat posed by the larger ships. "I told you I could smell them," he began, "but something's not right."

"An understatement if ever I heard one," Rob countered. "Sir, the men are concerned—"

"As well they should be. The British know they can't catch us, so this joint pursuit can mean only one thing: a clumsy effort at a trap."

"A trap, sir?" Rob glanced over his shoulder to survey the men grouped nearby. Their scowls spoke volumes, and he could not decide which was worse: the fury of the British Navy or a crew bent on ridding the ship of a lovely young woman. That she had to be equally anxious to leave only complicated matters.

"Obviously the *Island Belle* has been an even greater scourge than we imagined," Chris continued. "They're attempting to drive us west. We'll change course, Mr. Corliss, southeast to flank them, then due south."

"Aye, sir." Rob now hesitated to mention the crew's surly mood. The sails had slackened from lack of wind, but that slowed the brigs' pursuit as well as their own progress. If they outsmarted the British yet again, the crew would wash down their complaints with rum. Hoping to avoid trouble in that way, he strode off to relay the change in course.

Chris remained braced at the rail. The *Island Belle* was alive to him, more bird than ship at times like these, when her speed nearly carried them aloft. He watched as the British vessels attempted to change course as well, with one coming perilously close to ramming the other.

"There's not a man between them worthy of command," he mused to himself, but he continued to study the brigs' reckless pursuit until both distance and darkness rendered the effort impossible.

Hunger finally drove Chris belowdeck, and he found Sarah holding a lacy christening gown. "Why didn't you mention that you'd packed clothing for your infant?"

She was surprised he was not gloating over his latest victory, but she had refused to give in to tears when the second opportunity at rescue had disappeared as swiftly as the first. She was by no means resigned to her fate, however.

"You needn't pretend that you care a whit about my babe's wardrobe," she exclaimed.

"You're right, it doesn't concern me, but I don't like being lied to either."

"You are scarcely my confidant, Captain, but to ease your mind, this beautiful gown is all I have. I expected to have other garments made in London."

"Providing that you arrived. I, on the other hand, refuse to leave anything to chance. Now let's just enjoy the evening meal."

Her stomach still tied in a painful knot, Sarah moved to her place at the table rather than dispute such an innocuous command. She had put away the clothing she had laundered that morning and suddenly wondered what had become of the muslin.

"I don't suppose you were able to give much attention to the muslin you insisted I use, but I shall be unable to sew a stitch without it."

Chris frowned slightly. He vaguely recalled flinging the damp cloth aside as he returned to the deck, but he had not seen it since. "You can't sew now anyway," he replied. "When you have such beautiful eyes, I'll not have you straining your sight here in the dim light."

Unaccustomed to such flattery, Sarah responded with a dismissive laugh. "Please, Captain, any effort to charm me is completely misguided."

"It was merely the truth, madame. I save whatever charm I might possess for far more agreeable company."

"Good, then we understand each other—about one thing at least."

She wore an all too satisfied smirk, but rather than discount her opinion, he remained silent. If she wished to gloat, then so be it; he would still have the only voice that mattered. Yet the day had left him with a lingering sense of foreboding, and he ate the chicken stew Charley served without comment.

Sarah merely picked at her food. She much preferred

a disagreeable companion to a silent one. Her father had so frequently lapsed into an appalled silence around her that she could not tolerate being ignored.

"You're frightened, aren't you?" she surmised aloud.

"Frightened of what?" Chris scoffed. "Captains who'll sooner collide and sink both their ships than cause us any damage?"

"Laugh if you must, but I can see that you're worried."

"You're all that concerns me for the moment, and you'd be wise not to provoke me."

He got up and left the cabin before Sarah could respond, but his mood had been so dark that she was certain she had guessed the truth. He had been more than merely preoccupied, and with two warships trailing them, he had every right to be. Suddenly rescue did not seem like such a distant prospect.

That glimmer of hope sparked her appetite, and she reached over to take a half-eaten biscuit from Chris's plate and savored every crumb.

While Sarah did not weep for Michael, her second night on board the *Island Belle* was no more restful than the first. The oil lamps were burning low when she awakened in the morning, and for a moment she thought it must still be night. She sat up, yawned and, eager to sight the British, was disappointed to find a thick gray mist clinging to the windows.

She left the bunk to fetch a handkerchief and rubbed at the small glass panes, but wiping away the interior condensation failed to improve the view. She felt as though she had tumbled to the bottom of a long, gray sock, and it was frustrating to be unable to crawl out.

Then she noticed how flat the ship rode the water, as

though they were not moving at all. There were the usual creaks and groans from the hull, and an occasional shout from a seaman, but the ship was as unnaturally quiet as the gray dawn.

The wind had proven to be as uncertain as her fate and, unwilling to face the day in her nightgown, she quickly shook out the black dress she feared had been ruined by seawater. When the fabric shone with its usual dark sheen, she hastened to dress, but she was still brushing her hair when the captain gave a hasty knock and entered.

He came to such an abrupt halt when their eyes met, it appeared as though he had forgotten she shared his cabin. Insulted anew, she took a step toward him.

"I can't see anything from here," she greeted him. "Can you sight the British from on deck?"

Chris shook his head and shrugged off his coat. "No, we left them far behind. Now, if you can possibly manage to be quiet for an hour or two, I'm taking the bunk."

If he had kept watch rather than sleep all night, then their situation had been as dire as she feared, which was scarcely good news. "The British are going to attack us, aren't they?" she murmured softly.

"Not when they can't find us," Chris explained wearily. "But no one can find anything in fog this dense. I've remained drier in a monsoon."

Unconvinced his lack of concern wasn't prompted by stubborn pride, Sarah moved aside. She had made up the bunk and gestured with a careless air. "You're welcome to the bed, but it's a shame it's not more comfortable."

Chris paused, so close that their toes were nearly touching. "Are you offering a soft shoulder, or perhaps—"

"You swine!" She raised her hand, but he caught her wrist in midair.

"You really must be more careful," he scolded softly. "I've been awake too long to maintain my usual gentlemanly reserve."

"Had you possessed any gentlemanly qualities to begin with, I'd not be here!" She wrenched herself free of his grasp and grabbed the back of a chair for support.

"A good point," he conceded. Then, dismissing her with a nod, he stretched out on the bunk without removing his boots and instantly fell asleep.

Sarah rubbed her wrist, but his hold had been so light she wasn't bruised. There was something infinitely worse about being in the captain's cabin while he slept than when he was awake. His breathing was slow and deep, without any trace of a rattling snore, but it wasn't reassuring.

She distracted herself momentarily by attempting to describe the unsettling sensation fluttering in her stomach to better commit the experience to paper, but she shook too badly to hold a pen and began to pace. The sea was so calm that she could traverse the cabin without expending much effort to maintain her balance, but her true equilibrium spun wildly out of control.

Chapter Five

Jacob Shorter scratched his bristly chin and muttered, "Cursed brigs, no wind, and a bone-aching fog. What's next, you suppose?"

Sean McBean, who was nearly as round as he was tall, pondered the question a moment and then offered, "The plague?"

Jacob cuffed him hard. "Don't even be thinkin' it. I heard tell of a plague ship come driftin' into port with naught but skeletons for a crew."

"Which harbor was this?" Rob Corliss asked pointedly. He had been circling the deck and could not abide such superstitious drivel. "A ghost ship story must have a specific port. Otherwise, it's merely a drunken fable."

Jacob squeezed his eyes shut, straining his memory, but finally shook his head. "Can't recall, sir, but it happened. Plague killed 'em all, right down to the towheaded cabin boy."

"A terrible tragedy indeed," Rob offered with scant sympathy. "Don't be inviting another, Shorter."

"No, sir, that I won't."

McBean waited until the mate had moved on, then

quickly looked over his shoulder. "What tragedy could that be?"

"The one that'll befall us if we don't finish scrubbing the deck. But being idle ain't the root of our troubles."

"The skirt?" McBean mouthed silently.

"Aye, the skirt came aboard wrapped in bad luck."

McBean nodded rather than admit he could not fault the captain for keeping such a fine-looking woman tucked away in his cabin. But if the eerie fog failed to lift soon, he would go along with tossing the skirt over the side. But if they didn't have a bit of fun with her first, even with a rounded belly, it sure would be a terrible waste.

When Chris awakened, the windows above him showed the same disheartening expanse of gray. Sarah was seated at his table, her cheek resting on an outstretched arm. She was sound asleep but could scarcely be comfortable. He cursed his own lack of manners in not hanging a hammock elsewhere to leave her the bunk.

Thinking that, in such miserable weather, she might as well sleep the day away, he rose to transfer her to the bed. But the instant he scooped her into his arms, she attacked him in a fury.

"How dare you!" she cried, pummeling him with her fists.

Her flying curls blinded him, and had he not quickly braced himself against the table, they both would have fallen in a painful sprawl. Desperate to be rid of her, he swung her toward the bunk and would have dropped her there, but she now clung to his shirt as though he were intent upon hurling her off a cliff.

"Good God, woman!" he shouted. "I only meant to give you the bunk."

Sarah froze, then released a hand to sweep her curls aside. "Liar. But did you actually expect me to sleep through it?"

Chris stared down at her. One of her frantic blows had caught his brow, which had already begun to throb painfully. He had suffered many a black eye, but never from such a ridiculous source. He had thought to be kind and Sarah had reacted like a mad dog.

She was an ill-tempered shrew who looked ready to spit, but instead moistened her lips with a slow lick. He was thoroughly disgusted with her, but she had such an inviting mouth, all glistening pink and poised so close to his. After that undeserved beating, she owed him at least a kiss, and he dipped his head to claim one.

As their lips met, her shocked gasp shuddered clear through him. Her bosom swelled against his chest, while the sweetness of her perfume invaded his senses. Her taste was indescribably sweet and, craving more, he sank down on the side of the bunk with her still cradled in his arms.

She was neither fighting nor responding as she once had, but he took her curious surrender as a victory. He deepened his kiss and did not break away until he was thoroughly satisfied. Her cheeks were now flushed, her breathing shallow, and her gaze held more fright than loathing. It was not the enticing invitation he would have preferred, but at least she was no longer striking him.

"Obviously you'll never sleep through a second with me," he chided, "but I've no time to waste on your foolishness now." He moved her aside and left the bunk while he still could. "You mustn't forget your breakfast. The tea might be cold, but you'll eat the oranges and biscuits right away."

He ripped off his shirt to don another, and was shocked to discover her nails had sliced bloody trails across his chest. "It's a good thing you didn't fight alongside your husband, or the British would be winning this war," he muttered.

"We are winning!" Sarah responded adamantly, but she shrank away from him into the far corner of the bunk.

"Believe whatever you please, it won't make it true." He stuffed the tail of a clean shirt into his pants, pulled on his coat, retied his hair, and grabbed his hat on his way out the door.

Sarah waited until her heartbeat had returned to normal to attempt to stand. She then made her way back to the table with a shaky stride. She poured herself a cup of tea to wash the terror from her throat, but she could not bear to eat. She had sworn not to risk provoking the captain, but he had startled her so badly she had reacted without thinking.

She traced her lips with trembling fingertips. The captain's initial kisses had held a mere hint of the passion he had unleashed just now, and she fought not to imagine where it might swiftly have led. His shirt lay where he had tossed it over the back of his chair, and she was grateful he had not shucked off all of his clothes and ravished her.

Michael had been a slow, tender lover, but Christopher MacLeod possessed a savage strength that terrified her. Worse still was the depth of her response, which thank goodness he had not realized. She slid her hands over her swollen abdomen. At least her babe had not witnessed that shameful scene, but she was nonetheless filled with remorse.

She meant to be a respectable widow, even on board a pirate ship, but she had little faith in her own resolve when the captain could so easily overwhelm her resistance. Her lack of restraint where he was concerned was a worse threat to her virtue than his bold advances, but she would keep that scandalous secret well hidden. Once the babe was born, the captain would undoubtedly use the child to force her to do his bidding. He would have two prisoners then. She looked out the windows, desperately eager for a ray of sunshine, but the ship remained cloaked in gray.

Chris was approaching the idle helmsman when he overheard a gunner snort, "No skirts!"

Annoyed, he signaled to the mate. "Are all the men complaining about having a woman on board?"

Rob had made a concerted effort to suppress the discontent and was badly embarrassed at having failed. "It's the lack of wind and dense fog. When the weather clears, they'll give her no further thought."

"That was not my question, Mr. Corliss."

The curt correction stung and, expecting even worse, Rob squared his shoulders. "This is only her third day on board, so it can't possibly be everyone."

Chris laced his hands behind his back. "The *Island Belle* has as fine a crew as we could hire, but I've never fooled myself into believing they're all honorable men. I could whip a few now, or wait and send the troublemakers off as the crew on our next prize. Which would you recommend, Mr. Corliss?"

"The men know enough to be quiet and listen for

sounds from the British vessels. You whip a man, and his screams might reveal our location to the Royal Navy."

Chris nodded thoughtfully. "That's an astute observation, but a mutiny will make an even greater racket. How do we guard against that catastrophe?"

The captain often asked Rob's opinion on matters he felt poorly equipped to handle. Rob understood he was being groomed for his own command, but as usual, he struggled not to sound like a fool.

"No matter what the problem, Jacob Shorter is the first to complain. Let's toss him in the brig for a day or two. None of the men like being confined, and it's sure to silence the others."

"Assemble the men," Chris ordered calmly. When it was done, he riveted his crew with an icy stare. "You're all aching for a fight, and so am I; but I'll not allow a single word to be spoken against Mrs. Hadley. I swear, I could have sailed with a hundred old women and found more courage than you men display.

" 'No skirts,' " he mimicked. "I'd put the whole lot of you in corsets if it would instill some backbone. Mr. Corliss, escort Jacob Shorter to the brig, and the next time there's even a whisper of discontent, I'll halve the crew's rations until the noise from your rumbling stomachs drowns out your complaints.

"No skirts, indeed!" Chris concluded. "Mrs. Hadley is a better man than most of you. Now get back to work and be quick about it, or you'll not taste a drop of rum for a week. If there's a British ship within range when the fog clears, I want the gunners ready to fire and dismast her."

The men welcomed that prospect with a low whispered

cheer, but just as Chris had on the *Beatrice,* he waited, daring anyone eager for a fight to come forward. As expected, Jacob Shorter complained of being unfairly accused, but when no one came to his defense, he shuffled off to the brig without incident.

Chris was disappointed the coward had not caused at least a minor scuffle and provided him with an excuse for his black eye, which was sure to be a hideous purple by morning.

Sarah was seated on the bunk reading *Evelina* when Chris returned for the noon meal. She looked up, her gaze purposely as blank as the fog.

"I believe you were told to sew," he remarked absently but took the precaution of leaning back against the door while he awaited her reply.

Sarah marked her place and closed the novel with deliberate care. "You've still not returned the muslin, so I'd simply be waving a needle and thread through thin air, which would be most unproductive."

Chris silently cursed his own folly in again completely forgetting the blasted fabric. He removed his hat with exaggerated care and set it upon his desk. He would simply have to ask Charley to produce more—and launder it, he reminded himself. But that Sarah had such a quick wit irritated him anew.

"I'll see it's replaced, but there's something else we must discuss: I've decided not to share my cabin with you any longer."

Sarah cocked her head slightly. "Am I to be confined to your brig?"

"That's a tempting prospect, but it's occupied at present by a man whose company you'd not enjoy nearly as much as mine."

"Which is not at all," Sarah responded.

"Granted, but I mean to share my meals with you and sleep elsewhere, which is what I'd originally intended. Unless, of course, you'd rather I continued to spend the nights with you."

"I'd not describe it as such."

"Perhaps not, and I'd rather not risk further injury."

Sarah laughed in spite of herself. "You are far too strong a man to fear a mere woman might cause you even the slightest harm."

Chris had been serious, but clearly she regarded his comment as preposterous. Two could play that game. He laid a hand on his chest. "You'd not be the first woman to break a man's heart, and I've heard it's quite painful."

"I shouldn't fret if I were you, for you've no heart to break."

Perhaps it was the intriguing tilt of her chin, or the grace of her pose, or the memory of her luscious kiss, but she was more lovely each time he saw her. He looked down and away in a halfhearted attempt to appear annoyed with her, when in fact, he was displeased only with himself.

"We've been using the cabin once reserved for the ship's surgeon for storage; it's where I'd originally meant to stay, and it will suit me for the time being. I'll have Charley come by more frequently to make certain there's nothing you require, and as I said, I'll continue to take my meals here."

"I would prefer to dine alone."

"Yes, so would I, but a captain always dines with his passengers, and I'm a stickler for tradition."

Charley rapped at the door to announce their meal, and Chris stepped aside to admit him. "I see our cook has floated some of his excellent dumplings atop the chicken stew, but I wish he'd sent us a few more."

"I'll fetch more dumplings," Charley offered quickly, and he slid their plates and cutlery onto the table and bolted from the cabin.

"He's quite smitten with you," Chris confided softly. "But then, he meets even fewer women than I do."

Sarah ignored his remarks and took her place at the table. The oranges and biscuits from breakfast remained where they had been placed, and she ignored them too. She lifted her fork to spear a bit of carrot and slid it around in the gravy but guided none to her mouth.

"Would you like me to feed you?" Chris asked. "I could use a bit of practice before your babe arrives."

"You'll not touch my child," Sarah warned, "let alone feed him."

"Well, certainly not at first, when you'll provide all the nourishment he'll require."

Sarah was well aware that women possessed breasts to suckle their young, but she had given no thought to nursing her babe. Now all she could imagine was how eagerly the captain would welcome the sight of her bare nipples. That he might also relish the taste of her milk was doubly disturbing, and she squirmed in her chair.

Enjoying his meal, Chris failed to notice his companion's distress. "I'm not certain how long a mother nurses her infant, but later, when he begins taking solid foods, you might welcome a bit of assistance."

"Not from you I won't." She mashed a dumpling flat, but the painful knot in her stomach still made swallowing impossible. "By that time, the war should be over, and I'll make my way to London."

"Are your late husband's parents awaiting your arrival?" Chris leaned back as Charley entered to place a heaping bowl of dumplings on the table. He said to the boy, "Thank you. Please tell Cook his dumplings are nearly as light as those served at our family home in Virginia."

Charley nodded, tripped over his own feet, and slammed the door on his way out.

"You see," Chris remarked. "The boy sees nothing but you. Now, tell me about your late husband's relatives."

"I'll not describe them simply to entertain you," Sarah snapped.

"You'd rather keep me entertained by other means?"

She could not abide his sly smirk and turned away, but the compact cabin offered no hope of escape. "Regardless of how long it takes me, I intend to reach London."

"I've always admired determination in a woman. I'm sure you'll see London eventually, but I wouldn't be too surprised if your husband's relatives failed to welcome you."

"What a cruel thing to say."

"That wasn't my intention," Chris promised. "I was merely suggesting that the family of an officer killed in the Colonies might not welcome a Colonial maid. Then again, they might be eager to raise Michael's son."

"Don't you dare refer to my husband in such familiar terms."

"What was his rank—major, colonel? Would you prefer that?"

"I would prefer that you not mention him at all, which I realize is a great deal to expect from a pirate." Sarah bit her lip, but it was difficult to exercise restraint when the captain insulted her with every breath.

Chris blotted his mouth on his napkin. "That was a delicious meal, but you must excuse me. Perhaps you would like to list your quaint rules for our conversations while I'm gone, and we can pick up where we've left off this evening."

"Would you abide by any rules I offered?"

"No, but it will keep you occupied until the muslin can be found."

He left with the cast-off shirt in his hand, but the cabin was so thoroughly his that Sarah still felt his near-suffocating presence. She ate three dumplings while attempting to find a better means to govern her temper, which he constantly provoked, and had to reluctantly admit that they were so light they almost slid down her throat.

"Eat," she commanded softly, but when she concentrated on her food, it turned to dust in her mouth.

She was uncertain just when an infant was fed more than his mother's milk but thought it had to be as soon as he had teeth. The way the captain had spoken, he planned to keep her and her child with him for years. How would either of them survive? she wondered.

Then she began to worry that his unwelcome prediction about her in-laws might indeed be true. If they tied her to Michael's death, perhaps even blamed her for it, where could she go? She watched the gravy congeal on her plate and fought to believe a pleasant future would not remain forever beyond her grasp.

Even after it was cleaned, a musty odor remained in the surgeon's cabin. Chris had used the same hammock the previous two nights, but he was now so uncomfortable he doubted he would ever fall asleep. Supper with Mrs. Hadley had been another strained encounter that had left them both feeling abused. All in all, it was a miserable evening.

He had always been so careful in the running of his ship and took only the risks for which success was a near certainty. Until he had found Sarah Hadley and taken leave of his senses. When they took their next prize, he would send Rob Corliss off as captain; surely the Widow Hadley would be safe in Rob's capable care.

He plotted each step of that move from stowing her trunk in her new cabin to watching her black-cloaked figure at the rail fade in the distance as she sailed away. When she would never plead to remain with him, he simply could not understand why the prospect of being rid of her proved surprisingly painful.

Bringing Sarah Hadley on board the *Island Belle* had been a brash mistake, but one he could correct easily enough. All he required was another prize; just one more, and then he would set a course for Martinique. Sarah Hadley would then be reduced to a single reference in his ship's log. But try as he might, he could not shake the uncomfortable sensation that sending her away would only compound the anguishing dilemma he had foolishly caused himself.

He doubted she could sleep any better than he, and thinking a bit of exercise might help them both, he rolled out of the hammock, dressed, and went to his cabin. He knocked lightly so as not to wake her should she be asleep, but she answered immediately.

He opened the door and peered inside. "I thought you might enjoy a stroll on deck."

"At this hour?"

"We can scarcely tell night from day in this fog, so why not?"

Eager to leave the cabin regardless of the hour, Sarah rose, draped her cloak around her shoulders, and slid her feet into her slippers. It would be too dark to befriend his crew, but if she behaved herself this time, Chris might make the mistake of believing that she always would.

Chris allowed her to lead the way but tucked her arm in his as soon as they reached the deck. The men on watch had to rely on their ears rather than their eyes, and not wishing to distract them, he lowered his voice. "The fog has dampened everyone's mood."

"Fog is the very least of my worries."

Chris patted her hand. "Please don't fret. I'll continue to treat you well."

Sarah bit her lip rather than reveal how she regarded his dire threats and unwanted kisses. Men moved out of their way, but the night was so dark, they were little more than shadows. They had nearly completed their first turn around the deck when she sighted a faint beacon of hope.

"Am I merely imagining things, or is that a star?" she inquired.

"Where?" Chris asked, searching the sky.

"To your left, near what ought to be the horizon."

Chris located the soft ray of light, instantly recognized it for the danger it posed, and tightened his hand around her arm. "We'll have to end our stroll. Come, I'll take you back to my cabin."

"But why? If we can see stars, doesn't it mean the fog is lifting?"

It was an innocent mistake, but what she had seen was

a light on board another ship, most probably one belonging to the Royal Navy. But whatever the vessel, it was much too close. "Yes, the fog is sure to lift by morning," he assured her, "which will make it a far better time to take our exercise."

He guided her toward the companionway, but a man standing watch intercepted them first. "There's a light off the port bow, Captain, and the gunners are anxious to fire."

Alarmed, Sarah pulled away, but Chris held her fast. "Await my orders," he replied, and he slid his arm around his captive's shoulders to propel her down the companionway to his cabin, where he hastily drew the velvet curtains over the windows and then doused the oil lamps.

"Don't try and send a signal," he warned. "They'd only fire, and you'd be killed along with the rest of us."

He passed by her on his way to the door, but she reached out to catch his sleeve. "If the fog is lifting, there must be wind."

In the darkened cabin, her voice had a soft, seductive echo, and although he longed to stay, he could not. "Go to sleep. We'll discuss wind currents in the morning."

"Wait," she insisted. "Even if there's sufficient wind to get away, if the *Island Belle* is attacked, I'll be trapped here below."

"I'll leave the door unlocked, and in the unlikely event we actually come under attack, I'll see to your safety myself."

"And if you're slain?"

"Perish the thought," Chris responded. Had she not sounded so desperate, he would have laughed. "If I fall, then Rob Corliss will come for you. Please don't fret; other than being splashed with seawater, the *Island Belle* has yet to sustain any damage from the Royal Navy."

"Your arrogance is scant protection."

"I'd call it confidence; but then, we've yet to agree on anything other than how pretty you are. Now promise me you'll remain here, out of harm's way."

Sarah clamped her mouth shut and wished she had done so earlier when she had foolishly mistaken a dim light for a star. When he waited for a reply, she grudgingly responded. "I'll not leave unless the ship is sinking."

The woman continually pushed him, and he considered her fortunate indeed that the *Beatrice* had not been captured by another privateer, who might not have displayed his exemplary patience. "I'll take you at your word," he offered as he went out the door and, in a race up the companionway, he returned to the deck.

He scanned the night for another glimmer of light. He could feel the wind building, and it would soon clear away the fog, but he would no longer be satisfied with a silent escape. No, he meant to make good on his promise to his crew. Even if they couldn't sink a brig, they could inflict enough damage to make certain they were no longer pursued.

"Sleep," Sarah nearly screamed. "How can the scoundrel expect me to sleep?" Unable to rest quietly, she gripped the back of her chair with a force that made her hands ache.

The crazed captain issued as many ridiculous commands as her father, and she was just as unlikely to obey. She felt like some doomed goddess in a tragic myth. Her father had heartily disapproved of Greek myths as pagan literature, so quite naturally she had loved the tangled tales of heroism and betrayal. The gods were always out-smarting each other with disastrous results, while the goddesses' intrigues were often key to their adventures.

"I should have packed a book of myths," she murmured. "Or better still, I should write one about an arrogant sea-faring rogue and an enchanted mermaid who sprouts legs and runs away the instant his ship reaches port."

Of course, when the *Island Belle* returned to Martinique, she would be surrounded by people who spoke only French and supported the Colonials' inglorious cause. If she leapt over the side now, clad in her night-gown, she might actually be able to swim and reach a British ship. It was too terrifying a prospect to accept as her only hope.

The ship lurched as the wind filled her sails, but Sarah still could not relax. Perhaps if she had not been so stupid as to call Chris's attention to the light, the Royal Navy could have overtaken them unnoticed. Why, she might already have been rescued. It appeared every stroke of good luck for the captain meant an equally horrid dose of bad luck for her.

In the next instant, the booming roar of cannon fire nearly knocked her to her knees. This time it was the *Island Belle*'s own cannon that caused the deafening roar, and her ears rang with the reverberating echo. She braced herself, and tried to recall how many guns she had seen up on deck, but she had not really paid close attention.

She counted silently to herself, but there was no return fire, only the eerie creaks of the ship's timbers. It was like traveling within a giant clock, but one that might at any second explode in a shower of debris rather than chime the hour. Alone in the dark, hysteria crowded the breath from her chest, allowing the escape of only a single muffled sob.

The ship's angle shifted as the *Island Belle* gathered speed and, unable to remain standing or move to the bunk, Sarah slid down the side of the chair and sat clinging to its legs. Someone would undoubtedly be able to create a memorable tale from this wretched ordeal, but she now gave up all hope that it would be her.

She gritted her teeth. "All I have to do is stay alive," she swore. But she dared not think past the coming dawn.

When Chris came through the door carrying a lantern, he was horrified to find Sarah huddled on the floor. He quickly set the lantern on the table and bent down by her side. "Did you fall? Are you injured?"

Sarah's mouth was too dry to curse him as viciously as she would have liked, but even in the dim light her expression was murderous. "No," she explained. "I merely hoped to spare myself a fall should the British finally improve their aim."

Chris helped her to her feet and guided her toward the bunk before relighting the cabin's lamps. "How clever of you. I didn't expect you to sleep through that din, but I'd not meant to frighten you into taking refuge beneath the table."

"You might have gotten us all killed."

"No, once you sounded the alarm, only the British were in peril. Our gunners aimed to shatter their mainmast, but they should have been better able to contain a fire." He spread the curtains to reveal an orange glow in the distance. "You might want to get back under the table, because once the flames reach their powder magazine, we'll surely feel the blast."

Sarah could not bear to look. "You'll not pull any men from the water, will you?"

"This is war, Mrs. Hadley. The British will abandon ship in their long boats, and their sister ship will rescue the survivors."

Not reassured, Sarah felt sick. "I thought I'd seen a star."

"Well, regardless of your error, it was a keen observation, and I thank you for it."

She clenched her fists in her lap. "I'd never willingly help you."

"Yes, I know, but the result is the same—and while I'm tempted to lie in wait for the second brig, I've decided to set a course for Martinique."

"Do you expect me to rejoice in that?"

"No, I didn't dare hope that you would. I'll not disturb your rest any further. I trust you'll be comfortable here alone."

Sarah glared at him. Her only consolation was that he did not intend to remain with her and gloat. It was not something she cared to dwell upon when the reprieve might be short-lived.

Chris paused in the doorway. "I shouldn't have treated you as I would have a sleeping child yesterday. That was an unfortunate mistake."

Amazed, Sarah wondered if he actually expected her to make a similar generous gesture. She refused to consider it. "Your mistakes are too numerous to count, Captain, but I will note that you've apologized for one."

Before Chris could respond, a distant explosion rocked the ship, and despite his reassurance, she felt certain there must have been an appalling loss of life. Feeling at least partly responsible, she ducked her head and let her tears fall into her lap.

Chris took a step toward her, then thought better of it and left. He had not expected to sink a brig, but he would be damned if he would apologize for it. As he strode out on deck, his crew were cheering wildly and, equally proud, he felt a flash of regret that he had chosen to serve as a privateer rather than captain a warship in the United States Navy.

Chapter Six

Chris brought not only the freshly laundered muslin but also a jar of honey to sweeten Sarah's tea and a pot of marmalade for the biscuits. When she joined him at the table without glancing his way, he peeled and sectioned an orange for her and one for himself before attempting conversation.

"This is your fourth day with us, and I'll freely admit your stay has not been nearly as pleasant as I'd hoped."

Sarah's head snapped up. "I can barely tolerate your loathsome presence."

Although Chris was well aware that she possessed a volatile nature, he was still stung by the bitterness of her rebuke. He chose a biscuit and took his time spreading it with marmalade. The cook had found the jelly among the stores brought on board from the *Beatrice,* but he wisely refrained from mentioning its source.

"You continually respond to my hospitality with insults, but I'm blessed with a generous nature and am willing to overlook it."

Sarah refused to dignify that absurd comment with a

response. Her posture remained stiff, and her hands were clasped tightly in her lap.

Chris concentrated upon what he meant to say, and made another attempt to engage her. "Please listen carefully, because it is not my intention to mislead you. While I've endeavored to make you feel welcome here on board the *Island Belle*, the effort has been a miserable failure. I see no reason for either of us to suffer a moment longer than necessary. Should we take another prize, which unfortunately I cannot guarantee, I'll put you on board with Mr. Corliss. Would that prospect serve to appease your virulent anger?"

Sarah blamed herself for that mistaken sighting of a star that had tragically resulted in the destruction of a British warship. That she'd learned a member of the crew had almost simultaneously reported a light failed to diminish her burden of guilt, and she'd had a long, sleepless night as a result. Cursed with a vivid imagination, each time she had closed her eyes she had seen masses of drowning sailors, some hideously burned. Exhausted by those gruesome images and the captain's perpetual torment, she was unable to summon even a particle of hope.

"This is a trick of some kind, isn't it?" she asked.

"No, indeed, but even if it were, would you expect me to admit to it?"

Sarah raised both hands to cover a wide yawn before shaking her head. "No, I expect absolutely nothing good from you, sir."

Chris finished the biscuit and wiped his hands on his napkin. He then sat back in his chair. "Sarah, look at me."

While she would have ignored a harshly worded command, his softly voiced request proved irresistible. She glanced toward him, and was startled to find a bruise shadowed his left eye. It scarcely marred his handsome appearance, but she was amazed someone had dared raise a hand against him.

"You mentioned the man in your brig. Was he sent there for giving you the black eye?"

The injury was not as obvious as he had feared, but he was glad she had noticed. "No, I sent the fellow to the brig for insulting you, and you're the only one on board who's dared to strike me."

Too tired to recall the previous day with much clarity, Sarah responded with a distracted nod. "You deserved it, and if the men are insulting me, you are entirely to blame for that misfortune as well."

"That's a matter of opinion. Now, do you understand what I said about placing you on board a prize ship?"

"Yes. It is merely a tantalizing prospect, not a certainty."

"Precisely."

She was again dressed in the dark blue gown that nearly matched her eyes, but despite the flattering color, he found her usual radiance considerably dimmed. There were pale lavender shadows beneath her eyes, as though she had gone days without sleep.

"Are you merely tired, or are you feeling unwell?" he asked.

Doubting the sincerity of his concern, she closed her eyes and sighed softly. "I'm sick clear through of this dreadful war and the senseless killing. I may not have a peaceful night's sleep until it's over."

He had graciously given her the best bunk on the ship, provided delicious meals, considerately spared her his unwanted company, and still she was unhappy. He doubted either of them would truly rest until she was gone. He forced the indulgent smile he would have shown a naughty child.

"It's clear you're in need of a nap today." He rose and took her hand. "Come, curl up on the bunk. Breakfast will still be waiting when you awake, and I can recommend the marmalade as particularly good."

The warmth of his hand was as appealing as his words, and Sarah let herself be led to the adjacent bed. She kicked off her slippers and lay down, but then she had a truly horrid thought and sat back up.

"Wait. You offered to place me on board a ship with Mr. Corliss, but where would we be bound?"

Chris had expected her to note that significant omission earlier and, moving her skirts aside, sat down on the edge of the bunk. "Not for Charleston, I assure you, unless we've retaken the port. Your destination would depend on when and where we encounter our next prize. I'm sorry not to have better news. I'm not deliberately being vague."

It still sounded like a trick to her, but she lay back down, and he began to rub her back in slow, soothing circles. No one had ever shown her such tender concern, and after a first startled shiver, she had to reluctantly admit it felt rather pleasant. If only it weren't a pirate's touch.

She supposed she must have given him the black eye at the same time she had scratched his chest, but rather than being vindictive, he was gently kneading her shoulders as though she were a beloved pet. She had not expected him to be so considerate. Tears welled up in her eyes and trickled slowly down her cheeks.

Believing his effort to comfort her another abysmal failure, Chris pulled his handkerchief from his pocket and pressed it into her palm. "I am sorry," he offered, and he left to provide the solitude she obviously preferred.

Sarah heard the door close behind him and was swept

with an intense wave of sorrow that nearly rivaled the pain of losing Michael. It made no sense to her, and certainly such an emotional display was unhealthy for her child. She fought to dry her tears but fell asleep on a damp pillow.

Chris scanned the horizon with the spyglass, but since encountering the *Beatrice,* they had not sighted another merchantman. The brisk wind sped them toward home, but he was unable to appreciate what awaited him there.

"I'd hoped for another prize, Mr. Corliss."

"Aye, Captain, we all did. Although, after last night . . ."

Chris snapped the spyglass shut. "Yes, sinking a vessel of the Royal Navy does give one a taste for blood, doesn't it?"

"Aye, sir, that it does."

Chris smiled at the earnest young man and nodded. "Rein in those thoughts for a moment. I intend to put you in command of our next prize, and you'll take Mrs. Hadley along with you."

"Good God!" Rob exclaimed. "Is she to serve as mate?"

Chris laughed in spite of himself. "No, certainly not, although she would make a fine one. I mean for her to be a passenger, on what will surely be a more peaceful voyage than she is currently experiencing."

"May I refuse the honor of her company, sir?"

Chris did not know quite how to respond to such a sensible request. "I've given her my word, and because she finds my company particularly objectionable, I'll not go back on it."

His expression troubled, Rob turned to survey the surrounding sea. "We have to take another prize ship first though, don't we?"

"Yes, I made that point with her," Chris explained.

But he could not send her off with a prize crew made up of the malcontents who had complained of her presence on board the *Island Belle.* That meant he would have to be extremely cautious about whom he chose. But, unlike making a prisoner of the beautiful Sarah Hadley, at least he had foreseen the problem while there was still time enough to prevent it.

Sarah had never been subject to bouts of melancholy and, fearing her current sorrow was unhealthy, she struggled to enjoy the sunlight as Chris escorted her along the deck. She had forgotten her earlier attempts to charm his crew, and now gazed dejectedly at the sky and sea.

Chris had not joined her for the mid-day meal and, hoping she might be sufficiently bored with her own company to tolerate his, he had waited until late afternoon to bring her up on deck. She had such a light step she nearly floated by his side, but she had yet to speak a single word.

"It is a lovely day," he finally offered.

"Superb." She stood with him at the rail and raised a hand to shade her eyes.

Chris searched his mind for a subject that might possibly interest her, but only one came to mind. "Trade routes follow advantageous winds and swift ocean currents," he began. "The northern routes are used by ships like the *Beatrice,* for trade with Britain. We're sailing south now toward the West Indies, but we may encounter a merchant ship out of Jamaica loaded with sugar or molasses."

"I fear I will still be sent to Martinique regardless of the vessel."

"You're forgetting that there are British isles in the

West Indies. Taking you to one would not pose as great a risk for us as sailing into Charleston."

Sarah did not allow herself even a flutter of hope. "I'll welcome that day after I've again set foot on British soil."

Even when Sarah was desperately sad, he could not look at her without feeling the same irresistible desire that had muddled his thinking on board the *Beatrice*. She was easily the most fascinating young woman he had ever met, while she regarded him as beneath contempt. He fought to focus on the clouds, or the sea streaming beneath them, but his gaze was always drawn back to her.

"Perhaps we should go below," he offered. "I've no wish to tire you."

With the muslin now awaiting her pitiful attempts to fashion tiny clothes, Sarah was in no hurry to return to the cabin. "Why don't you see to your duties, Captain? I promise not to make any mischief standing here."

It was not mischief that concerned him. Her downcast expression made him fear she might leap over the side the minute his back was turned. She had the most mercurial temperament he had ever encountered—but then, her circumstances were clearly trying. Unfortunately, she had made his equally difficult. Still, he was worried about her safety.

"I've no pressing duties," he confided. "I love the sea and am content to stay with you."

Rob Corliss watched the pair as they remained motionless at the rail. The captain had angled his stance to protect Mrs. Hadley from being badly buffeted by the wind. Her cloak's hood covered her curls and shaded her face, but he did not need to see her clearly to recall how lovely she was.

Captain MacLeod was a gentleman accustomed to entertaining fine ladies, but Rob was a shopkeeper's son. He had chosen the freedom of the sea when he had turned seventeen, and he had never thought he might one day have to entertain fine ladies at his captain's table.

"I'll choke on my supper and die right there," he worried aloud. He walked away, praying with every step that they would not sight so much as a piece of driftwood before arriving home in Port Royal, Martinique.

The cook prepared ham that evening with yams and spiced apples, and while it was far from Chris's favorite meal, he welcomed the change. He could not draw a deep breath, however, until Sarah took a bite. He waited, hoping she would not quickly spit it out as booty from the *Beatrice*. Thankfully, she swallowed a second taste of ham and then a forkful of yam.

"I'm pleased to see you're eating at last," he said. "You'd be a beauty no matter what you weighed, but with a babe to consider, you must eat."

"My father frequently condemned beauty as the devil's gift," Sarah countered softly. "In fact, whenever anyone remarked on my appearance, it caused him excruciating embarrassment."

Other than describing her husband as kind, she had not disclosed anything about her family, so Chris was doubly astonished by her candid confession. He was also so angry that he had to take a swallow of wine to contain himself. Even then, he was only partly successful.

"You're blessed with an angelic beauty. How could anyone think otherwise?"

She had not meant to beg for compliments, and appalled to have him offer such a sweet one, her fork clattered to her plate. "Thank you, but I shouldn't have mentioned my father's opinions."

"Yes, I know, your life is no concern of mine—you needn't repeat that complaint. But please don't apologize. I've had many a battle with my own father, although I don't believe he ever mentioned the devil."

Sarah was relieved he had changed the subject to his own father. She picked up her fork and speared a bit of spiced apple. "You described your father as being very charming."

He was amused that she remembered. "He has many splendid traits. I have apparently inherited only his fine appearance, however."

Now *he* was hoping for compliments, and she pointedly ignored him. The apple was delicious, and she took another bite before glancing toward him. While she ought not to have confided in him, he had not immediately twisted her remark into an insult, as he so often did. That failure was perplexing in itself.

She supposed all pirates must have families living somewhere, and apparently his resided in Virginia. She did not wish to contemplate anything more than escaping him, but she was too tired to display her usual restraint. She yawned before she could catch herself.

"Yes, I'm tired too," he remarked. "I wish I'd not left you alone here last night. Shall I stay with you tonight?"

There, he had done it again, she fumed. Apparently she had been too congenial a companion, and had thoughtlessly inspired him to press for an advantage. "If I have misled you in any way, sir," she hissed through clenched teeth, "it was completely unintentional."

"I'll take that as a no, then," he replied. "This is my cabin, though, so despite my attempt to be polite, the choice is in fact mine."

"And what would your fine French mother think of your behavior?"

Her eyes were ablaze now, nearly shooting sparks, and he longed to channel her passion in a far more intimate direction. Clearly she did not think much of the French, so she must be truly desperate to avoid him. While not unexpected, it was another blow to his pride.

"Forgive me if I've frightened you," he cajoled. "My mother delights in romantic intrigues, and she would offer me encouragement."

" 'Romantic intrigues?' " Sarah repeated incredulously. "The term certainly doesn't suit our situation. How can you even imagine that I'd welcome your attentions?"

"Yes, I realize the timing is poor. You've been too recently widowed to appreciate my interest. But fortunately that won't always be the case."

Dumbfounded, Sarah sat back in her chair. "Had I been widowed for five years or even ten, I'd not welcome so much as a brief afternoon call from you, Captain."

He smiled and continued eating. "No gentleman worthy of the name gives up so easily, my love."

"I am most definitely not your 'love.' Nor will I ever be," she added for emphasis.

"As you remarked earlier, the war will be over one day. I come from one of Virginia's most respected families, and I can provide every advantage for you and your son. Although I do hope you have a daughter with your golden curls. Let's agree on a name for her, shall we? You said you had a great many from which to choose."

"Dear God in heaven," she cried. "I would sooner beg on the street with a babe in arms than marry you."

"No, you wouldn't. Just imagine the poor little tyke in

filthy clothes and too weak from hunger to utter more than a feeble cry. You'll swiftly change your mind."

"I'll imagine no such thing. This whole conversation is ridiculous. I'm going to London at my first opportunity." She would obviously need her strength to combat this deranged scoundrel, and she picked up her fork and began to eat with a renewed sense of purpose.

Chris bit his lip rather than laugh out loud, but he preferred prompting her anger to dealing with her tears. When she had finally blotted her mouth and set her fork across her plate, he sat back in his chair and smiled.

"What progress have you made with your baby's clothes?" he asked.

In truth, she had not even unfolded the muslin. It was now soft and smelled sweet, but she just did not know where to begin. "I'm having a bit of a problem making a pattern," she offered, which was certainly the truth. "The christening gown was made for a newborn and may not be of the appropriate size for my son."

"Or daughter," he reminded her. "Well, yes, I understand how that might pose a dilemma. Why don't you just begin by fashioning a garment slightly larger than the christening gown, and then the next could be slightly larger than that, and so on."

Sarah thought it sensible advice, if only she knew how to sew. "That's an excellent suggestion. Thank you, but it's really too late to sew tonight."

"Yes, it is. Prepare for bed if you like. I'll not disturb you, although later I'll hang my hammock in here again. I really think you were much happier with my company."

"I was happier before you sank a British warship!" she argued. "And I really wish you'd not reminded me of it."

"Does that mean when Congress awards me a medal, you'd rather I did not give it to you as a token of my affection?"

"Most assuredly. I'd toss it in the sea."

"Pity. Perhaps your little girl will like it." He sprang from the table before she could throw a plate at him, and laughed as he slipped out the door.

Sarah barely stifled a scream. The man flattered her one moment and delighted in infuriating her the next. It was the type of behavior one could expect from someone so unbalanced as he, but it was perplexing all the same. She would simply have to remain on guard whenever he was pleasant, because he never failed to swiftly turn sarcastic, or simply cruel.

At least he had not forced his affections upon her, but when he was so often an attentive companion, she wondered if he might be incapable of pursuing her with more than words. She knew some men suffered in that regard because she had overheard her father and mother discussing such an individual. The man had apparently taken out his frustrations on his poor wife, who had promptly left him. He had then come to her father to plead for help in forcing her return. Sarah had been quite intrigued by the matter at the time, but now she could not recall whether or not her father had successfully influenced the man's wife to honor her wedding vows. She doubted it, for what rational woman would accept such ill treatment from her spouse?

In truth, her mother had left so much about marriage unsaid, Sarah had not really understood the extent of the man's problems until she had wed Michael, who thank goodness had been eager to satisfy her curiosity about men. She could still recall his startled expression when she inquired if he would mind discarding his nightshirt on their wedding night. He had feared a man's body might frighten her, then been thrilled by her wandering touch. He had been the perfect husband for a curious virgin, who had expected making love to be pleasurable for them both.

While it had been a bit awkward at first, they had each learned how to fulfill the other's desires. Tragically, they had been parted all too soon, and were robbed of the many happy years they should have shared. Now all she had was the onerous Captain MacLeod to contend with. Perhaps her temper had convinced him to keep his distance, but whatever the cause of his restraint, her advanced pregnancy or his probable impotence, she was grateful for it. But to accept a marriage proposal from Christopher MacLeod was too horrid a thought to even contemplate, and his wealth would never buy her heart.

It was after midnight when Chris hung his hammock in his cabin. He had done his best not to disturb Sarah, but from her constantly shifting position in the bunk, her unease was clear. Knowing better than to provide her with a choice, he dropped from the hammock and sat down on the side of the bunk.

"I can't allow you to keep me awake all night," he whispered. "I realize it must be difficult to find a comfortable pose, but rubbing your back worked yesterday, so let's give it another try. Then maybe we'll both be able to sleep."

Had his touch not felt so good sliding across her shoulders, Sarah would have protested, but she was too tired to argue now. His soothing touch drew the tension from her muscles with a magical ease. She wondered absently if perhaps he enjoyed touching women because it was all he could do. Poor thing, not that he deserved her sympathy. No, indeed. She yawned, snuggled down into the pillow and, now wonderfully relaxed, finally fell asleep.

When she awoke several hours later, she lay nestled in Chris's arms. He was so snugly curled around her in the narrow bunk that all question of his virility was quite firmly answered. Yet rather than take advantage of her, his deep, even breathing proved he had fallen asleep.

She was positive she had not invited him to share the bunk, which he obviously must have regarded as a mere oversight. He was bare-chested and smelled as always of bayberry soap. It was an enticing scent and thoroughly masculine. For the moment, she allowed herself to be held, but she knew she ought to move to a chair long before he awoke. She really meant to, but the ship's slow, rocking motion lulled her back to sleep before she found sufficient resolve to act.

When Chris stirred and felt Sarah's luscious warmth along his whole body, he was even more surprised than she. He recalled stretching out behind her, but he had not meant to fall asleep. Now his thoughts swiftly ran to how easy it would be to slide her nightgown up her slender thigh past her hip, loosen his trousers, and enter her with a single deep thrust. If he were truly the despicable pirate she accused him of being, he would already have done it.

But he lay still in the dimly lit cabin, with the most beautiful woman he had ever seen asleep in his arms, and did nothing. He simply enjoyed the graceful curve of her back and the subtle scent of her perfume.

He ached to press into her heat and wondered how deep he could delve before she came awake spitting and cursing. Not far, he imagined, perhaps no more than a tantalizing dip, and the thought whet his desire. He was going to have Sarah Hadley, and she would scream his name in ecstasy before he was through. But this just wasn't the night.

He raised up carefully so as not to wake her, and crawled off the end of the bunk, but wanting her so badly that he could not return to the easy sway of his hammock. Instead, he hurried to the surgeon's cabin to find relief with brisk, hard strokes. He closed his eyes to imagine her there in the musty silence and with a stunning clarity felt her wild curls brush his chest in a taunting caress. It was as real a sensation as any he had ever felt and, sagging against the door, he came in violent spurts.

By the time his breathing had slowed to normal, he had begun to wonder just how much of the devil there might truly be in the entrancing Widow Hadley.

Chapter Seven

Charley brought Sarah a boiled egg and a slice of ham for breakfast. "The captain sends his regards, ma'am," he stammered. "If he's able, he'll join you for the mid-day meal."

"Thank you, Charley." Sarah was enormously relieved to be spared Chris's company, but at the same time, she wondered if he might not be too ashamed to face her.

After all, he had claimed only to want to help her sleep and then boldly joined her in the bunk. That he had left while she slept had to prove something. Unfortunately, she was uncertain as to what. But if he were unwilling to admit they had shared the narrow bed, she was only too glad to pretend she was unaware of it as well.

With little to occupy her time, she ate the egg in tiny bites, and the ham even more slowly. She then finished her meal with a biscuit spread with marmalade, which was every bit as delicious as Chris had recommended. It was more than she had eaten in days, or so it seemed.

She stood to stretch her arms above her head, then paced the tidy cabin while she sought another excuse to put off working on her infant's clothes. She had brought along several sets of undergarments, so she did not really need to launder anything today. Without that chore, she could no longer delay, and she unfolded the fabric on the bunk. Next she shook out the christening gown and lay it atop the muslin. It was a beautiful little garment adorned with tiny tucks and exquisite lace. Her mother had made it for her and all the other babies she had expected to have but had not borne.

Sarah had a small pair of scissors, more suitable for mending than for cutting out something new, but it was difficult to concentrate on the task at hand when her mind kept puzzling over Christopher MacLeod's behavior. She could not shake the uncomfortable sensation that she had missed something important, perhaps vital, where he was concerned. She had often heard it said that a man should be judged by the quality of his deeds rather than the eloquence of his words. Because the captain's comments were so often provocative, she paused to consider the manner in which he behaved.

After a moment's reflection, she took her journal from her trunk and using the pen and ink in the captain's desk, began three separate columns. She labeled one CRIMINAL ACTIONS, the second merely SUSPICIOUS ACTIONS and, unwilling to give him more credit than he deserved, the last column was simply WORDS.

He had captured the *Beatrice,* and regardless of how often he proclaimed the righteousness of his cause or referred to her as his guest, she was most definitely a prisoner on board the *Island Belle.* Those actions belonged squarely in the criminal category. But once she had been installed in his cabin, she had not been abused. Fair treatment went into the second column.

The captain's volatile nature and fiery taunts were

something more than words alone, so she listed them across both the second and third columns. That he had threatened to have her tried as a spy was so awful she pondered adding it to the Criminal list, but it really did not seem to fit there. She listed it under Words, and then underlined it.

The man displayed polished manners, which was actually something good. She made a note of it in tiny print at the bottom of the page then added that he was always well groomed and neatly dressed. That was essential when two people were forced to spend so much time together in close quarters.

She still regarded him as a pirate, of course, but if she discounted last night, he behaved in a gentlemanly fashion more often than not. That others might actually regard him as such appalled her.

She paused, wanting to believe she had finished the exercise, but her conscience refused to allow her to overlook Chris's seductive kisses. At the very least, his affection had to be considered suspicious, and she so noted. She then closed her journal with an audible snap and quickly replaced the pen and ink where she had found them.

Disheartened, she returned to the bunk no more able to think clearly than when she had begun categorizing Chris's actions. The man was far too complex for neat lists to hold any meaning, and he was much too handsome. If that weren't distraction enough, his deep voice held such a pleasing resonance that she always found herself anticipating his next word, even when the subject was his extremely unfortunate choice of politics.

An Oxford graduate, her father had been born in Exeter in Devon, England. A Loyalist through and through, prior to the war he had dismissed all complaints against the Crown as the trivial whining of ungrateful subjects. He had missed no opportunity to condemn the passion for liberty espoused by Samuel Adams, Patrick Henry, and Thomas Jefferson. He blamed their misguided followers for maliciously magnifying the discontent he fervently denounced from the pulpit.

Once the fighting began, South Carolina was the site of numerous battles between Loyalists and Patriots, but her father had never wavered in his convictions. When the British had taken Charleston in May of 1780, he had declared it a great day for the city, and their family had celebrated with other prominent Loyalists.

She and her mother had been born in Charleston, and might have been expected to show more sympathy for the Patriot cause. But her mother had never voiced a single original thought, and Sarah had been far too enamored of the dashing British officers who dined at their home to care anything about disputes with the king.

With Michael's death, her world had unraveled faster than a pair of poorly knit mittens. Now faced with too much time on her hands, the fact that she had never agreed with her father on anything made her wonder if perhaps she ought not to have questioned his staunch support of the Crown. Now it was too late, for she would never be disloyal to Michael's memory by siding with the Patriots.

On that question her decision was so easily made, but it still left her dissatisfied with respect to Christopher MacLeod. Even if he claimed his cause was noble, it would not mean he was wholly good. After all, she had been on board the *Island Belle* less than a week, and he had already begun crawling into her bed. That fact alone ought to prove what sort of a man he was, and yet some-how, she sensed there was still a great deal more left to discover.

When Chris sighted the merchantman riding low in the water, he was elated by the prospect of ridding himself of Sarah Hadley. She was a captivating creature, but the searing strength of last night's climax was proof enough that he had become far too attached to her. Not that he didn't crave more of such blissful agony, but her condition precluded it. Of course, her hearty dislike of him provided an even greater obstacle to romance.

After the war for independence was won, he could find her in Charleston, when a man could rightfully pursue his passion for a beautiful woman. With time, who was to say that her heart might not soften toward him? Unless, of course, she actually succeeded in reaching London.

Considering her fierce determination, he came to the sudden and jarring conclusion that she most probably would. Sending her away now might be the wisest choice, but what if she vanished abroad, never to be found? It was definitely a risk, but how great? he worried. There was no easy answer to that troubling question, and he could not ignore the warning knot tightening in his gut.

He still debated whether or not to bring Sarah up on deck, but then, not wanting cannon fire to frighten her unnecessarily, he went below. He knocked politely at his own door, and was surprised when she bid him enter in a pleasant tone.

"Good day," he began. "I hate to interrupt your sewing, but there's a ship on the horizon I want you to see."

Sarah was grateful for any excuse to lay her scissors

aside; she was also intrigued. "Is it the prize ship you've been seeking?"

"It might be," he replied. He watched her don her cloak and tie her pretty bow with a quick twist. "The ship appears to be heavily laden, but as always, we'll stalk her for awhile."

Sarah was first up the companionway, then turned to face him. "Do you ever allow a ship to continue on its way unchallenged?"

"Occasionally," he replied.

She was looking up at him, apparently merely curious rather than about to accuse him of piracy most foul. The breeze feathered the golden curls framing her cheeks, and her eyes shone with an exotic sapphire glow. The radiance he had missed again lit her expression, and although quite unwilling, he was charmed anew.

He took her arm, led her to the rail, and offered the spyglass. "It's a British merchantman ripe for the taking, but you know I much prefer stealth to haste."

The ship was flying the Union Jack, but that was the only proud touch on an otherwise undistinguished vessel. The hull was a weathered gray and the sails were a mottled mix of tan and pale yellow. As for what Sarah could see of the crew, they were standing in idle clumps along the rail in apparent stoic acceptance of an inevitable surrender.

She was badly disappointed it wasn't a more handsome or at least more seaworthy vessel, and handed Chris back the spyglass. "You may have disparaged the *Beatrice,* but I'd not have bought passage on this scow."

The instant the words left her mouth she regretted them. *What had she done!* This was her chance to escape a captain who gave not only heated kisses but blood-chilling threats! She would be a fool to trust him to ever do otherwise.

"The ship looks sound enough to me," Chris argued. After all, he had offered to send her along on his next prize, and he would not allow her to accuse him of going back on his word. At the same time, he was enormously relieved that she had not dashed back to his cabin to pack her trunk. He waved the mate over.

"Mr. Corliss, what's your opinion?"

Rob was loath to accept the responsibility for Mrs. Hadley, and most especially not on board a ship that appeared within days of sinking. "I don't care for the looks of her, Captain. She's likely carrying barrels of molasses that will bring a good price, but this ought to be her final voyage."

Stalling for time, Chris continued to study the ship. He felt sick at the prospect of letting Sarah go, and yet the strength of her appeal posed a greater risk than his own heartbreak. Clearly his crew did not want a woman on board, and while he had quelled their discontent for the moment, it might still erupt in violence. Lives could be lost, to say nothing of the possible damage to the *Island Belle*.

While it would be difficult, clearly the argument for sending Sarah away was the stronger. When she was so eager to go, what did it matter that she thought so little of this particular vessel? he asked himself. He trusted Rob Corliss to look after her, but the decision was still agonizing; he simply couldn't bring himself to make it, at least not yet.

He cleared his throat in a courageous attempt to sound convincing. "That may be a fine ship deliberately made to appear otherwise to discourage privateers. I say we take her and then decide if she's seaworthy."

"As you wish," Rob replied without enthusiasm.

His spirits falling, Chris continued to survey the ship as they closed in. While a merchantman could be expected to carry several small cannon for defense, the *Island Belle* had seldom been fired upon. Still, he remained on guard for the possibility and was quickly rewarded.

A less observant captain might have been fooled, but he saw the eight starboard gunports disguised by the peeling paint and instantly recognized the canvas heaped at the rail must cover as many cannon. That their gunners had yet to move their weapons into position indicated not that they were resigned to their fate but that they were remarkably disciplined. They were no motley bunch of merchant seamen but Royal Navy.

He grabbed hold of Sarah to keep her on her feet and shouted, "That's no battered merchantman, it's a warship. Mr. Corliss, have our gunners prepare to fire the long gun as we come about."

Sarah grabbed for the rail as Chris's order was promptly followed by another to the helmsman. The last time the *Island Belle* had fired their cannon, many fine men of the Royal Navy had surely been lost, and she did not want to witness this slaughter firsthand. Then the slanted angle of the deck threw her against Chris, and she lost all hope of an escape below.

It wasn't until the crew of the merchantman threw open their gunports and rolled out their cannon that she understood all their lives were at risk. The *Island Belle*'s helmsman had changed their course toward the open sea, but she feared Chris's warning had not come in time to save them. She dared not look, and when Chris clasped his hands over her ears, she buried her face in his coat.

The *Island Belle*'s gunners rotated the long gun on its swivel and fired before the merchantman got off a single shot. Standing on deck the noise was deafening, but Chris's waistcoat muffled Sarah's scream. She choked on smoke and might have collapsed at his feet had he not tightened his protective embrace.

The gunners fired a second round, but it wasn't until Sarah heard the men's shouts above the ringing in her ears that she dared peek over Chris's arm. By then, the merchantman was enveloped in billowing clouds of smoke and flame. The ship's mainmast had been shattered, dropping canvas and rigging into the fires on deck. There was a gaping hole in the starboard rail, through which one of their cannon had rolled right off into the sea. While their gunners were scrambling about, they had yet to fire. Several men were floating facedown in the sea.

Sarah longed to pull her hood down over her face and never look out again, but thankfully Chris swung her up into his arms and carried her down to his cabin. He sat her on the side of the bunk and hurriedly backed away.

"You must excuse me," he offered.

At least, that was what she thought he said before he ran back through the door; the painful ringing in her ears had blurred his words. But the meaning really wasn't important. He was a privateer, after all, a man bent on seizing or destroying every British ship he encountered. From what she had witnessed, he had just snatched victory from the jaws of certain defeat and again fulfilled his dreadful mission.

Completely overwhelmed, she curled up on the bunk, still wrapped in her soot-covered cloak. Her babe kicked and jabbed with his tiny elbows and knees, making it nearly impossible to get comfortable. She clung to thoughts of her child, but she longed for him to find a far better world than the violent one that had claimed his father.

* * *

Keenly alert for the next danger, Chris remained on deck until noon. He then went below to the surgeon's cabin to wash away the soot and grime clinging to his skin. As he pulled on a clean shirt, he noticed a medical book their last surgeon had left behind. They had sustained no injuries that day, but with Sarah huddled so close, he had had a vivid reminder of her condition.

He took the book from the shelf, scanned the table of contents, and was relieved to find a chapter devoted to childbirth. He meant to peruse it quickly, but the diagrams so unnerved him that he sat down on the bunk for a more thorough review. It would be far easier to read in his own cabin, but he would not risk alarming Sarah with his lack of knowledge.

At home in Virginia, he had seen all manner of creatures born, from livestock to household pets, but despite his confident boast to Sarah, he had no experience whatsoever with a human mother and child. Now from what he read, a great many calamities could befall a pregnant woman. Her health might be too frail to withstand a prolonged labor, or her hips could be too narrow for an easy delivery. Even with a woman in robust health, an infant in the wrong position could block birth.

All the more frightening, even after her child was safely born, a woman still might bleed to death. The book's author, while claiming to be an authority, offered little advice to alleviate most problems, and freely admitted they frequently resulted in the death of the mother. Should such a tragedy occur during labor, there were concise directions for slitting open a woman's abdomen to deliver her child.

While thoroughly sickened, Chris was convinced the

physician who had authored the tome must know even less about childbirth than he. He returned the book to its shelf and drew in a ragged breath to dispel the lingering bloody visions—but he wished his store of medical knowledge contained more than herbal remedies for fevers and minor aches.

Fearful Sarah might already be in labor, he went straight to his cabin. When he found her asleep, he sat down at his table to rest. He had kept up with the ship's log, and in addition to course headings and weather, he had described their recent adventures in precise detail. There was but a single reference to Sarah having come aboard when they had captured the *Beatrice.* For the time being, her presence was all he cared to disclose.

He poured himself a cup of cold tea from the breakfast teapot and washed down a biscuit, but there was still a slight tremor in his hands. They had escaped being fired upon by a very slim margin. Had he turned toward Sarah while he continued to mull over his options for her, they might have all been killed in the first volley.

He glanced toward her and sighed softly. His men would have cursed her as they died, but he would have held her tight, his final thought one of regret for the time he had wasted. What a fool he had been to even imagine he could send her away; and how incredibly stupid to believe he could deliver a child as though it were no more difficult than birthing a goat.

Sarah felt his unsettling presence before opening her eyes. When she did, he was frowning so deeply, she feared something must have gone amiss. "What's happened now?" she whispered.

Startled, Chris refused to admit his true concern and instead grasped for a believable topic. "What? Oh, nothing to compare with earlier. I've merely been wondering if the two brigs we encountered weren't setting a trap for that heavily armed merchantman. The sea is immense, and to sight them all within days of each other is too great a coincidence."

Sarah sat up and, surprised to have napped in her cloak, she quickly removed it and tossed it over her trunk. "Yes, but I suppose if the Royal Navy sent three ships to stop you, it's some sort of perverted compliment. But you really ought to plot strategy with Mr. Corliss, Captain, not me."

"I wasn't plotting, merely thinking out loud. I'm sorry if I disturbed you."

"No, you needn't apologize. I can barely hear you speak. I hope the cannon fire hasn't permanently damaged my hearing."

"No, it's temporary for the most part, although it's plain from the way the gunners shout at each other that their hearing is no longer keen. I'm sorry there wasn't time to bring you here, and when next we sight a ship, I'll be far more careful."

"I doubt you're ever careless. Are you hungry? Do you suppose the cook prepared anything for us?"

Pleased by her sudden mention of food, he was happy to investigate. "I'll see what I can find, but it may be no more than bread and cheese."

"Have I ever complained of your fare, sir?"

"No, I believe that may be the one item you've overlooked."

Sarah laughed before she recalled how frequently he turned her words against her. This time he had been teasing, though. He presented a confounding array of contradictions, but his sense of humor came as no surprise.

"I believe I've complained of only one thing," she insisted, "and that's that I've no wish to be here."

Chris nodded. "True. But the wind is again strong, and we'll make good time to Martinique. Perhaps you'll find the island more to your liking."

Because he was being pleasant, she chose to be vague rather than insulting. "We shall have to wait and see."

Chris was now so worried about delivering her child that he could not wait to reach the West Indies. At least her appearance was reassuring. Her curls shone, her skin was smooth and clear, and when she smiled as she had just now, she looked to be in excellent health.

Today she had donned a new gown that shimmered between blue and gray. A wide border of lace trimmed the square neckline and sleeves, and seated, she appeared only very attractive rather than quite pregnant. She was definitely slender, though, and he was worried that she might be more delicate than she would admit.

"You appear to be in remarkably good spirits considering our morning," he began. "I trust you are feeling well?"

"I never napped at home," she admitted thoughtfully, "and I'm too often tired now, but I'm well. What about you?"

Chris hated to end what had been a remarkably warm exchange, but he rose and went to the door. "I'm also well, thank you. Now, if you'll excuse me, I'll see if our cook has remembered to prepare our meal."

"Surely he'd not have forgotten."

"No, but he's as distracted as the rest of us." Chris left, intent upon seeing she had plenty of nourishing food, but he really did not feel up to eating.

* * *

While Sarah had fully intended to cut out a small smock that afternoon, the sky began to darken and, easily discouraged when she had no talent for sewing anyway, she laid the muslin aside. Chris no longer left his cabin door locked and, restless, she wondered what he would say if she went up on deck.

He had promised that Charley would stop by the cabin often to see to her needs, but she had not seen the earnest lad since he had cleared away their bowls and the porcelain tureen that had contained an absolutely delicious potato soup. With no way to summon him, she paced the cabin and wished she had been given permission to move about the ship on her own. When Charley at last appeared, she already had her cloak in her hand.

"Would you escort me up on deck for a moment please?" she asked as she crossed to the door. "I'm so tired of being cooped up in here, and I promise not to stay longer than a few minutes."

Certain the captain meant for her to remain in his cabin, Charley extended his arm across the doorway. "The air smells like rain," he warned. "You're better off staying here."

"But if it rains, I'll have no opportunity to go up on deck later," Sarah argued persuasively. "Please, Charley, we can stay right by the companionway and no one will even notice we're there."

It was the way she spoke his name that crumbled Charley's resistance. "Well, I suppose we could go for a few minutes."

Delighted, Sarah kissed his cheek and watched his blush brighten. She swung her cloak over her shoulders and followed him up the stairs. Once on deck, she glanced up to find dark clouds almost brushing the tips of the masts. It was not raining yet, but a fine mist quickly dampened her curls and eyelashes.

Still, she was delighted to have escaped the confines of the cabin. "How do you stand living at sea, Charley? Don't you ever long to run through a meadow?"

"Like a horse, ma'am? I've never even thought of it."

"Pity; it's wonderful fun." Not that Sarah had spent much time in meadows herself, but the idea of it held an enormous appeal. She searched the deck for Chris and found him with Mr. Corliss near the helmsman. Then, mortified by how quickly she had sought him out, she would have fled to his cabin; but before she could take the first step, he glanced over his shoulder and saw her. When their eyes met, his scowl made his displeasure clear.

Sarah grasped Charley's arm. "You needn't worry," she assured him. "I'll take full responsibility for being here."

Chris found it difficult to believe his eyes, but the Widow Hadley had boldly come up on deck as though she were the proud owner of the *Island Belle*. He blamed himself for being such a congenial companion at noon that she had taken such a liberty, but he could not allow her to wander the ship with Charley by her side. He nodded to dismiss the boy, and with a guilty grimace, the cook's helper dashed away.

"It was entirely my idea to come up on deck," Sarah announced as Chris reached her. "I'm just so awfully tired of being left in your cabin, and I'm not in anyone's way here."

Several of Chris's men had already begun moving toward her before he had seen her. Other than to scream for help, Charley would not have been able to defend her. While it would mean frightening her yet again, he could devise no other means to keep her safe.

He took her elbow and guided her to the rail. "You mustn't take advantage of Charley, and if you do it again, I'll whip him for disobeying me."

"Oh, no, you couldn't do that!" Sarah begged. "Oh, I realize you can do whatever you wish on board your own ship, but surely you'd not abuse a mere boy. You're a better man than that."

Chris's mouth nearly fell agape, he was so amazed that she thought he possessed such an admirable character. He believed he did, of course, but it certainly didn't suit his purpose now. Fortunately, huge raindrops began to splatter the deck, and Sarah did not argue about seeking shelter. He waited until they had entered his cabin and then shook the moisture from her cloak and laid it over a chair to dry.

"Mrs. Hadley . . ." he began.

While her hearing had returned as predicted, it did not follow that she wished to listen. She sat down on the bunk and raised her hand to interrupt. "Captain, please. You must first give me your promise that Charley will come to no harm before requiring anything more of me."

"Is that a fact?" Chris wanted to laugh, but she was so completely oblivious to the danger his crew posed that it stuck him as unforgivably rude. "Do you recall the man I sent to the brig for insulting you?"

"Yes, and I remember saying it was your fault, too."

"Let's not repeat that tiresome argument. While I don't agree with your assessment of my crew as cutthroats, you ought not to tease them by parading around the deck on your own. I'd not make this reference in a drawing room in Virginia, but you've been married, so you must understand the danger any man might pose for a woman. You could easily be injured, or worse.

129

"Charley, God bless him, would fight to defend you, but he lacks the strength to succeed. You're safe here in my cabin, but not on deck. Is that point finally clear?"

His tone was actually quite reasonable, but Sarah's dismissive glance slid down to his boots. She might be safe there, but she was still in a prison cell and, depressed by that fact, she glanced to her hands.

Chris had hoped to inspire her to exercise more caution but now feared he had merely crushed her spirits. "Sarah," he called softly. "As long as I'm captain of the *Island Belle,* I'll protect you from harm. But if you're sneaking about, I might not have the opportunity."

She nodded, but he had prompted a question she simply had to ask. "Were you merely protecting me last night when you joined me in the bunk? Oh, forgive me—it's your bed, isn't it? But even if I'm so enormous I take up too much room, you slept with me last night. Don't bother to deny it."

Chris was astonished by how deftly she had shifted the blame to him. He had mistakenly believed that she had slept through the interlude, but he was relieved to learn that she hadn't. "It was very wrong of me to make a joke of your size. That day, I was far angrier with myself than you, and I was needlessly cruel. I'll not seek another prize, so you've no hope of leaving me before we dock in Martinique. Why don't we try and make the best of it?"

"As you did last night?"

"If you like. I'll be happy to share the bunk."

"Well, I'd be most unhappy. If you want your cabin back, then I'll move into the surgeon's."

"No, it's too small for you. You'll stay here and so will I. Now, I want your promise that you'll tell me the instant your labor begins. I'll do all in my power to make you comfortable, but I'll need to know it's time."

"It's too soon for any such concern."

"You've no idea how badly I hope you're right. The coming storm will make for rough sailing. Do I have your word you'll stay here snug and dry?"

Sarah studied his expression for a long moment. He appeared genuinely concerned, but she knew better than to trust him. "What would my word mean to you?"

"Everything," Chris admitted freely and, fearing he had revealed too much, smiled to distract her.

He had a very handsome smile, but Sarah had heard the slight catch in his voice and wasn't fooled. His crew might be an ill-mannered lot, but he was the one who posed the real danger.

Chapter Eight

The *Island Belle* dove and pitched through storm-tossed seas and each shuddering thump heightened Sarah's fears more cruelly than a threat of medieval torture. The wind blew with a ferocious howl. Sheets of rain pelted the windows above her. Each flash of lightning was near blinding, quickly followed by bone-rattling jolts of thunder.

Raised on the coast, she was well aware that most summers hurricanes came swirling out of the warm Caribbean Sea to devastate Florida's coast. Trees were uprooted, buildings blown away, and the coastal settlements were flooded by high tides. The lives of many good citizens were lost. The fiercest hurricanes sent their torrential rains clear into South Carolina. Following the storms, tangled debris littered Charleston's streets, but other than a leaky roof, their home had never suffered much damage. Plus, they had always had solid ground beneath their feet.

The *Island Belle* might be beautiful and swift, but tonight her timbers creaked and moaned like a dying beast, and the ocean was awfully deep. Terrified the ship would break apart, she clung to the side of the bunk and wondered how well it would float.

When Chris returned to his cabin for dry clothes, she dared not leave the bed and merely propped herself on an elbow. "Are we seeing the worst of this storm, or is this merely the outward edge?"

Wet and cold, he was in no mood for conjecture. He turned toward her as he peeled away his waistcoat and shirt, then thought better of going any further with her observing him so closely. Instead, he gathered up warm clothing to carry to the surgeon's cabin to dress.

"The barometer began falling at mid-day, so we knew a storm was brewing even before the dark clouds appeared. As to how long it will last or how much worse it might get, it's impossible to say. While it might be difficult, you must try and rest."

Dissatisfied with his cool dismissal, Sarah paid no attention whatsoever. "If we're sailing into a hurricane, shouldn't we change course to avoid it?"

"Madame, really, you must trust me to set the wisest course."

"I have little choice," she challenged. "But we'll all be equally dead if you're not as magnificent a captain as you assume. Do you usually remain on deck during storms?"

"Yes, often I do, and I'll not have our arrival in Martinique delayed by a little inclement weather. Now, for the last time, go to sleep."

"I doubt that I shall be able to, but I wish you every success. Please take care not to fall overboard, as I've no wish to face your crew with no more than Charley to defend me."

"Have you forgotten that Mr. Corliss will see to your comfort should I be lost?"

"No, but without you, he'd have problems enough of his own."

While that was certainly true, Chris thought better of continuing their discussion when she was unlikely to ever fall silent. "I'll return as often as I'm able to see to your comfort; now, good night."

He had gone through the door before she could exclaim that she had never been less comfortable, and his unflappable confidence failed to allay her fears. The storm was not the only thing frightening her, either. She kept reliving the sinking of the brig, and their narrow escape from the merchantman. In her flowing cloak, the captain of the British vessel must have seen her on deck. Apparently he cared little for the welfare of women and children, because in another instant he would surely have fired all of his cannon into the *Island Belle*.

While Chris might have again outwitted the British, their escape had led them straight into this dreadful storm. What if his extraordinary good luck had run out? It was impossible to sleep with that terrifying prospect magnifying her fears.

She fidgeted nervously, and her back had begun to ache so that even her usual pose on her side brought no relief. She thought perhaps if she stood for a moment she would feel better when she lay back down. She had to time her step to that of the roiling sea, but once on her feet, she retained her balance easily enough. She felt better too—until she reached out for the back of a chair.

As if mirroring her gesture, the ship suddenly pitched forward into a deep trough. Sarah made a frantic grab for the chair, missed, and landed so hard on her hands and knees that pain shot clear to her shoulders and hips. Sobbing, she remained where she had fallen to allow the worst of the pain to subside, but now with the ship rocking wildly, she lacked the courage to stand.

Chris had found her huddled on the floor once before, so he would not be surprised, but now the ache in her back rivaled the throbbing pain in her hands and knees. She had donned her lace-trimmed sleeping jacket over her nightgown for warmth, but it did not extend as far as her knees, so only a single layer of linen had cushioned her fall.

To feel so utterly ridiculous heightened her anguish, and the next bolt of lightning lit a trickle of tears on her cheeks. She had barely covered her ears when thunder came rolling out of the sky. She had never worried about her hearing until that day, but between the cannon fire and thunder, she thought she might soon be deaf.

Unless, of course, the *Island Belle* sank and they all drowned.

She turned to crawl back toward the bunk on her bruised hands and knees, and if that were not misery enough, she had begun to feel seasick. She imagined the whole crew was ill in these rough seas but hoped she would feel better if she could just reach the bunk. She waited for the bow to tilt upward, pushing the stern down, and used the ship's own momentum to propel herself back into the bed. There she curled up on her side, and feared Chris must be doing even worse on deck.

After he had discounted her concerns so quickly, any worry for him was misplaced. But she had thought of his safety, and the guilt of that concern stung worse than her poor hands.

Chris had fully intended to dock the *Island Belle* safely in Port Royal before the first hurricane of the season tore through the Atlantic. Obviously he had miscalculated the date, because they were sailing right through it. He scarcely needed Sarah's suggestion to change course, but the storm was so wide and its path so erratic, they had been unable to escape.

Now they could only fight to keep the ship afloat. With waves crashing over the bow, the crew continually manned the pumps and even so were barely able to stay ahead of the sea pouring in. They were taking turns at the wheel as well, for no man could steer the ship through such rough seas for the whole watch.

They were strong men, and used to hard work, but even with frequent breaks to rest, there was a limit to their endurance. That none of them would prove equal to a hurricane was a fearsome prospect. If that weren't awful enough, Chris kept thinking of Sarah huddled alone in his cabin and wished he could hold her and make the seas calm.

His crew was too busy fighting the storm to complain aloud of the woman on board, but had the men had the breath, they surely would have. Unwilling to ever blame Sarah himself, Chris relieved the man at the wheel and fought the storm bravely for all their lives.

When he finally went below, Chris was so exhausted, he could barely shove open the door. He had promised to look after Sarah, but he prayed she would not request so much as a crust of bread. When lightning lit the cabin, he could not mistake her tears.

"I hate to trouble you . . ." she whispered.

Chris lacked the energy to pull off his wet coat and, stumbling across the cabin, slid to the floor beside the bunk and leaned back against it. "Just let me catch my breath," he begged.

Sarah tried to be quiet but, caught by a wave of pain,

she cried out. "I know it's much too soon, but I don't think the baby will wait."

"What?" Horrified, Chris turned to face her and, grabbing the side of the bunk, he hauled himself to his knees. "Are you sure?"

She caught his hands and peeled off his sodden gloves. "You feel like ice." She rubbed his fingers between her hands to warm them, then laid his half-frozen palm on her abdomen to feel the next contraction for himself. "There, now do you think I'm lying?"

"No, I'd never accuse you of it, but we should be better prepared. We'll need towels and blankets and . . ."

"Chris, you swore you knew how to do this. Can you even stay awake?"

He laced his fingers in hers. God help him, he had nearly drifted off. He fought to recall everything he had read about childbirth, but exhaustion had muddled his thoughts. "First babies take their time," he explained. "I'll just change my clothes, gather what we need, and stay with you. Please don't worry."

"You make such impossible demands," she complained through clenched teeth. "This hurts!"

"Yes, I know it does, but it will be over the instant your beautiful baby is born."

"Which may not matter." She sighed fearfully.

"Stop that! The *Island Belle* is the finest ship afloat. We built her in our own shipyard, and it will take more than a little rain to sink her."

"A little rain?" Had she been able to draw a deep breath, she would have laughed in his face. "Go on, take care of yourself or you'll be of no use to me."

For once he did not argue, but shoved himself to his feet. He braced against the bunk and next to the table to shrug out of his wet clothes down to his skin, without a thought to sparing her the sight. Then he had to face the challenge of pulling on dry clothes while he shivered and tried not to let his teeth chatter. He simply could not wear wet boots, and so remained barefoot.

"I have plenty of towels here," he assured her. "Did your mother provide any instruction on what to expect?"

He wished that he had paid more attention growing up when his own mother had come home after delivering a baby. His father had taken him away from the house when his brother had been born, so he had missed that event entirely.

Sarah could not recall her mother providing a single bit of useful information. "My mother refused to admit that men and women exchanged more than polite conversation. If she recalled the details of my birth, she never shared them." She had to pause to allow a contraction to pass. "I'm sorry, I expected to be in a four-poster bed in a fine house in London with a midwife who would know exactly what to do."

"London is filled with fools," Chris mumbled to himself. He now wished that he had not discovered the medical book, so he would still be blissfully unaware of the dangers she faced. *They faced,* he corrected himself.

A ribbon he had yet to use in his hair would serve to tie the cord, which he could cut with his razor. He thought that would be all right, but it might alarm her. "Do you have scissors?" he asked.

"Yes, in my trunk with the muslin. Will you need them?"

"Yes." Chris tried to explain how babies were attached to their mothers, but his explanation sounded confused even to him. "I'll do a good job, and he'll have a handsome navel, you'll see."

"I hadn't thought to worry about it."

"Good, don't." Chris thought he had assembled the necessary supplies, and was grateful the seas were too rough to light the lamps. He did not want her to be embarrassed by how much he would surely see, but neither did he wish to make some awful mistake in the dark. He welcomed each bright burst of lightning while she cringed against the pillow.

He sat down on the end of the bunk. "Your bag of water will break first, so I want you to put these towels underneath you so the bed isn't soaked."

She silently cursed her own ignorance, but her kindly family physician's only concern had been that she might miscarry after Michael was killed. She followed Chris's directions but did not really understand what would happen.

"Are you just making this up?" she asked.

"Oh, Sarah, you don't know anything, do you? I'll explain as best I can." He could not swear that he was even coherent, but her expression reflected more interest than fear, so apparently she was able to follow his rambling description of the birth process.

She swallowed hard. The storm had created utter chaos all around them, and yet he projected a soothing calm. Even if it were a vile trick, she wanted very badly to believe him.

"I keep telling myself babies are born every day," she murmured. "So I should be able to give birth too."

"Yes, that's the spirit. Just rest between the contractions; then you won't be too tired to push when it's time."

"You ought to be resting too," she countered. "Come on, stretch out here beside me."

He was sorely tempted but shook his head. "I'd fall asleep."

"Is there anything you can do for me now?"

"Unfortunately no, but I can at least hold your hand."

"Come on, lie down. I promise to wake you."

He thought her screams would do that, and he could not bear to think of her being in pain. "Giving birth shouldn't hurt so much. It isn't right, not when women give men so much pleasure."

"I agree," she gasped, and gritted her teeth as the next contraction tightened around her. Not only were the pains getting more intense, there were shorter intervals between them. That her only help was a brigand who knew more about childbirth than any man should was scant comfort.

Chris had leaned back to rest his head against the window, but he now reached forward to take her hand. "You were fine when I last went up on deck. Did the pains begin the minute I left?" He was now very sorry that he had not returned often simply to reassure her, but he had lacked the opportunity—truly he had.

She needed a moment to draw a breath. She was not going to admit she had fallen, but she had only left the bunk in a foolhardy attempt to ease her aching back. Had she been in labor even then? she wondered.

"What does it matter when the pains began? I'm more concerned about when they'll end. How long can this agony last?"

"A day, or longer, I've read," Chris answered.

Already worn out by fear and pain, she began to cry in earnest. "A whole day? Oh, no, I'll not survive nearly that long."

He cursed his stupidity for frightening her and tightened his hold on her hand. If she became hysterical, she would be unable to assist in the birth, and that possibility terrified him. Desperate for a means to calm her, he had a sudden inspiration. While it would be cruel to use such a diabolical threat, if it succeeded, no harm would be done.

"Sarah, you must survive or I'll raise Michael's son as my own. He'll never even suspect that I'm not his true father."

Her eyes widened as she absorbed his calmly voiced vow, and then she snarled, "You bastard!"

"No, my parents are quite happily wed, but I'll do it, Sarah, I swear I will. He'll be my son. Is that what you want?"

Before she could scream another outraged reply, Rob pounded a fist on the door and, unwilling to have the mate enter should he not respond, Chris got to his feet. His hip struck a chair as he lurched across the cabin, but he shoved away to reach the door without further mishap.

He opened it only a crack. "What is it, Mr. Corliss?"

Rob looked beyond to find Sarah lying in the bunk amid the tangled sheets, then down at Chris's bare feet. For the captain to lose himself in her during such desperate times was so completely inappropriate he could barely control his rage.

"Pardon the intrusion, Captain, but the pumps can't stay ahead of the rising water, and our situation is truly grave."

His mate's tone was more caustic than informative, but Chris had no time to waste on a reprimand. "Do you actually expect me to order the men to abandon ship in this storm?"

"No, sir, that would be suicide, but—"

"Shorten each man's turn at the pumps and form a bucket brigade to bail out whatever you can."

"Aye, Captain, I'll do that, but you need to be there to inspire the men."

"You'll have to inspire them, Rob. Mrs. Hadley's child has chosen tonight to be born and I'll not leave her."

Drenched, Rob's hair lay plastered to his brow, and his hat was askew. There wasn't an inch of him that wasn't wet, but with their problems so acute, he had yet to even notice that discomfort. He stared at Chris a long moment, then shook his head in dismay.

"You're choosing that woman over the *Belle*?" he asked incredulously.

Chris understood how his crew would think so. He had faced anguishing choices in his life, but now he had no doubt what was right. He could no more leave Sarah to give birth on her own than he could have sprouted wings and flown through the storm. Still, it hurt to have Rob and the others condemn him for shirking his duty to them and the ship.

"Have you safely delivered a child?" he asked pointedly. "If so, you may stay with Mrs. Hadley and I'll see to the pumps."

Rob took a step back. "Either way, the babe will drown. Why bother?"

Chris reached out to grasp Rob's lapels and yanked him close. "No one is going to drown," he swore in a menacing whisper. "Now go back and convince the crew of it."

He released the mate with a rude shove, shut the door in his face, and turned back toward Sarah. The ship's shuddering timbers were making so much noise, to say nothing of the howling wind and booming thunder, that he hoped she had not overheard the man's words. He managed to avoid being slammed into the table and chairs as he returned to her side, but he had no hope of a welcome.

Sarah pulled her knees up closer to her chin. "I hate you."

She had snarled like a wounded animal, but Chris was elated to find she still had so much fight left. "I knew you'd break my heart, but this really isn't the night to discuss our romance, is it?"

She would have silenced him with a truly imaginative curse, but the pain was now so severe she was gasping for breath. Then Sarah felt a rush of fluid and feared it was blood. "I'm all wet."

"Yes, that's just the water. It's a sign it won't be much longer." At least, that was what Chris thought he recalled. He wished it were a sunlit morning on a day so calm the sea was mirror smooth. Instead, it was all he could do to stay seated at the end of the bunk with the ship bucking so wildly.

"Turn on your back, and I'll fold your nightgown over your knees. On the next pain, push as hard as you can."

She managed to turn, but as his fingertips brushed her inner thighs, she was gripped by an excruciating contraction. It felt as though her insides where being clawed to shreds, but when it finally passed, her baby still had not been born.

"Don't let the baby die with me," she begged.

"No one is dying here, Mrs. Hadley. You're almost through." Chris had no idea if that was true or not, but he needed hope as much as she.

Sarah bit her lip and tasted blood. Michael had loved her dearly and been thrilled when she had conceived a child so soon. He had sent the news to his parents, but if he had received a reply, he had not read it to her. Maybe their response had never arrived, but now, when she needed her husband's family most, they were no more than names with no good wishes attached.

The next pain caught and held, but she was too weak to scream. Michael's dear face blurred with Chris's in her mind. She felt as though she were falling and only Chris's insistent encouragement kept her tethered to the bunk. She fought to push and thought she heard a newborn's wail, but utterly spent, she feared it was only the wind.

Furiously angry, Rob damned Christopher MacLeod with every filthy curse he knew and then began again at the beginning. He could not tell if the captain sincerely believed they would survive the storm, or if he was convinced they would not and had chosen to spend his last hours with a beautiful woman.

He didn't believe the story about the baby, either. That was just a convenient excuse to justify remaining with Mrs. Hadley, which had to mean Chris thought they were all as good as dead. Well, he wasn't ready to quit. He had just expected the captain's help, was all. If he had to go it alone, so be it.

Rob sloshed through the knee-deep water in the hold and, after clearing his throat, addressed the men manning the pumps. He relayed the captain's orders without providing any excuse for Chris's failure to appear. When the men nodded wearily without asking any questions, he organized the bucket brigade, and secured the last men with ropes to make certain they were not tossed overboard by the storm as they emptied the buckets.

The whole effort struck him as not merely exhausting but very possibly futile. And yet he rotated the men through the pumps and lent a hand himself with the buckets as though he had every confidence in their success. To his utter amazement, the water level in the hold gradually subsided to the point that the pumps alone could handle the sea water flowing in.

He congratulated the crew and sent as many as he could off to sleep, but he could not rest. Instead, he toured the ship time and again, searching for leaks that might present a new peril. The *Island Belle* had been built with a copper-plated hull to defeat the shipworms that feasted on wooden hulls. The captain also kept every seam in the deck well caulked, and even in these heavy seas she was sound.

After being so disrespectful to Christopher MacLeod, Rob feared his job was not. They had sent the best of the hands off with the prizes they had taken, and any man who might have replaced him as mate was no longer on board. That did not mean he would not be replaced as soon as they docked in Port Royal, however. In fact, Rob thought he would be a fool not to expect it.

He wasn't certain when he actually began to believe his own shouted orders, but as dawn neared, it appeared as though they had escaped the worst of the storm and might even see clear skies. He had to admit begrudgingly that Chris had been right, he and the men had saved the ship. It would be a shame if he could no longer sail with her.

"It was them buckets what done it, sir," Charley assured him. "Saved us all. Cook has some bread and cheese for you."

"Thank you. See all the men are fed." He was ravenously hungry himself and bit off a hunk of bread. It had been the worst night of his life, and he had not once stopped to wonder how the captain had fared with Mrs. Hadley.

* * *

When Sarah awoke, a light rain was all that remained of the fierce storm, and the cabin was filled with a soft light. The seas were calm and the boat rocked gently on the waves. Chris lay sprawled across the bunk with his cheek against her thigh, and the tiny baby in her arms slept just as soundly.

She recalled the faint cry and being too exhausted to remain awake, but here was her child snugly wrapped in a small blanket, clearly at peace in her arms. She combed the infant's smooth cap of dark hair, and counted the sweet little fingers. Not wanting to wake the sleeping child, she eased the blanket apart and was surprised by the silk ribbon Chris had used to tie off the cord.

He had also covered the baby's bottom with a handkerchief. She thought he must surely have announced whether the child was a boy or girl, but she simply had not heard. Now too curious to wait, she shifted her pose slightly. Chris moaned softly in response but failed to wake. She carefully untied the ends of the handkerchief and discovered she had borne a son. Despite coming early, he had plump arms and legs and appeared to be a fine little fellow.

She was an only child, and this was the first baby she had ever held. It should have been an ecstatic moment, but that her infant son had no father nor home was so incredibly sad she began to weep softly. He was perfect in all respects, but so completely dependent upon her, when she had not even been able to fashion any tiny clothes, that she felt overwhelmed.

Then he yawned, showing pink toothless gums, and opened his eyes to look up at her. She had expected him to have his father's green eyes, but his were blue, although not as dark as hers. In fact, his eyes were very nearly the same shade as . . .

Startled, she glanced over at Chris and found him observing her all too closely. "People will swear he has your eyes," she told him accusingly. "But he'll never be your son."

Chris sat up slowly. He had understood her exhaustion and had not tried to wake her before cleaning away all evidence of the birth. He had bathed her and changed her nightgown, then tossed the afterbirth and bloody sheets over the ship's side so she would not see them. He had not expected all that blood, and did not understand why any woman dared to have more than a single child.

"Please forgive me for that comment last night," he offered sincerely. "I'd hoped it would keep you alive. Obviously it did."

She would have called him a liar yet again, but her son began to cry. He waved tightly clenched fists and kicked as though miserably unhappy with the world. Sarah looked first at him and then to Chris. "We can settle that argument later. What do I do now?"

Her question astonished him. "Well, you're his mother; you must know."

"I'd not have asked you if I did!"

Chris shook his head and shoved himself to his feet. He glanced out the windows at the new day and was amazed by how good it appeared. "I have a medical book you can consult for how best to proceed. I'll fetch it before I go up on deck, but for now, just rest your son against your shoulder, pat his back, and bounce him a little."

For once, Sarah did as told and, after a slight hiccup, her son fell silent. She continued to pat his back and watched Chris as he searched through his lockers for clean clothes. Beard shadowed his cheeks and his hair had come loose from its tie. While far from his usual neat appearance, his presence was so comforting, his lack of grooming mattered not at all.

That did not mean she would excuse his vile threat. No, indeed, but she had a vague memory of the lullaby he must have sung while he bathed her baby. Unable to hide her tears, she looked away and kissed her dear infant's cheek. She wanted to hate Christopher MacLeod and, after all, she and her son were his hostages, but could any man who sang such sweet lullabies be truly evil?

Chapter Nine

Chris had feared the worst, but when he stepped out on deck, he was disappointed not to have even come close to imagining the extent of the damage. The storm had not merely tangled the rigging, it had snapped the yards on the mainmast and half of those on the foremast, leaving the once tightly furled sails to tear in the wind. He kicked a frayed rope out of his way and continued along the deck to Rob Corliss's side.

"Good morning, Mr. Corliss."

"It is now afternoon, Captain. Although after such a storm, losing track of time is understandable. How is Mrs. Hadley today?"

Chris sent him a warning glance. "She was safely delivered of a fine son, but she could not traverse this deck were she able. I want every bit of this rubble cleared away before nightfall."

It was a near impossible request, and Rob nodded as though merely considering it. "Aye, sir, but the men are exhausted and—"

"And?" Chris repeated. "We could not fight off an assault mounted from a long boat with debris piled this high. Has it slipped your notice that the Royal Navy still wants us?"

"No, sir, it certainly hasn't."

"I'm relieved my confidence in you is not misplaced."

As Chris turned away, Rob called to him. "Captain, did Mrs. Hadley really give birth to a son?"

"Yes. Did you think I'd simply made up the story to amuse you?"

Too late, Rob realized how much he had revealed. "No, sir, I merely meant—"

"I know what you meant." Chris turned away without voicing his disgust. He then went to the helmsman to re-set their course, but until their repairs were complete, they might just as well hold up their handkerchiefs to catch the wind and hope it blew them to Martinique.

"Michael?" Sarah caressed her babe's cheek, but he was again fast asleep. She laid him lengthwise on her legs and bent her knees to observe him closely. He was definitely a beautiful baby, all pink, with such cute chubby cheeks. The next time he awoke he might be hungry, and she thumbed through the medical book resting at her side for advice.

It was a very thick book, with well-worn pages. She found the drawings of the skeleton most intriguing, and followed one to identify all the bones in her hand. Then little Michael made a soft sucking noise, and she hastened to locate the chapter on infants. Unfortunately, it was rather brief. The only advice on newborns was to immediately employ a wet nurse should the mother not produce sufficient milk.

Her nightgown closed with a ribbon at the neckline, but

as she debated loosening the bow, she found not the gown in which she had gone to bed last night but another. She understood why Chris would have changed her nightgown and sleeping jacket, but she was still badly embarrassed that he had. Of course, after he had helped birth her son, she had had little left to hide, but she was no less embarrassed.

Her skin now held his familiar bayberry scent, and while she must surely have needed a bath, she wished he had not been the one to attend her. She feared he could have done more than rub a cloth along her skin, but also fondled and caressed, or even dared to kiss her.

When Charley rapped at the door, she was nearly too flustered to invite him to enter. He was carrying bowls and the soup tureen, but he glanced between the table and the bunk, unable to decide what to do.

"Can you come to the table, Mrs. Hadley, or should I bring the soup to you?"

Sarah had no appetite at all but thought for the baby's sake she ought to eat something. "Let's see, Charley. If I lay Michael here beside me, I ought to be able to eat. Although I certainly wouldn't want to spill hot soup on him."

Charley set the tureen and bowls on the table and approached her hesitantly. "May I see the baby, ma'am?"

"Yes, of course, come close. Isn't he precious?"

Charley took a couple of steps but stopped at a respectful distance. He then leaned forward and craned his neck to see better. "He sure is small."

"Do you think so? I've no experience with babies, so I thought all infants were this size."

"Well, yes, of course, sure they are. I didn't mean to say he was puny."

Chris came through the open doorway in time to hear their last exchange. "Cook's looking for you, Charley. I'll see to Mrs. Hadley myself."

"Aye, Captain, I'm on me way."

Chris closed the door after him. "I don't want the men near the baby."

Sarah instantly took offense at his imperious tone. "I'm not hosting a christening party for the whole crew. Charley was curious, and I didn't see any harm in introducing him to Michael."

Chris ladled the thick pea soup into a bowl. "During the storm, the men worked well past the point of exhaustion. Some may fall ill. We need to protect the baby from any possible harm." That he was desperately worried she might develop a fever as some new mothers did was better left unsaid.

"Yes, I agree," Sarah murmured, but she hated being confined to the cabin for any reason, even if she currently lacked the strength to leave the bunk. "I'm not really hungry, so please finish the soup."

"It's delicious, I'm sure, but you have to eat or you'll not be able to nurse Michael, and we've no cow on board. Had I known we'd need milk, I'd have found room for a goat, but your arrival was completely unexpected."

He had delivered his comments in an off-hand fashion but Sarah was mortified nonetheless. She had been shocked the first time he mentioned nursing her baby, for men simply did not discuss such intimate subjects in polite society. Not that he belonged in refined company, but his remarks were far too personal.

"I appreciate all that you did for me—for us—last night, but I really must insist that—"

Chris carried the bowl to the bunk, sat down beside her,

scooped up a spoonful, and raised it to her lips. "You're in no position to insist upon anything right now, Sarah; just eat."

She opened her mouth but, while the pea soup was good, she still wasn't hungry. He was sitting very close so there was no danger he would spill on the sleeping baby. His black eye had faded to a pale green that would have escaped anyone else's notice, but she appreciated each delicate nuance in coloring.

"Here, give me the spoon," she insisted. "I'm not an invalid."

Chris turned the handle of the spoon toward her. "Have you tried nursing Michael yet?"

Blushing deeply, she set the spoon back in the bowl. "I want to believe that you mean well, but you're embarrassing me very badly."

She was gazing down at her son rather than looking directly at him as she usually did, but Chris assumed her eyes held their usual defiant gleam. "Fine, we'll discuss the weather rather than anything of vital importance. Would you rather leave Michael on the bunk and come to the table to eat?"

"Yes, I'd like to try." She waited for him to rise, and then tenderly lay her little boy by her side. When he did not wake, she pushed the covers away. Her nightgown had rolled up her legs and, before she could adjust the hem, Chris saw her knees.

"You're badly bruised, and I know I didn't cause it. When did you fall?"

"I wasn't hurt," she insisted, but now she felt rather dizzy and slid her legs back under the covers rather than attempt to stand. "Maybe I should wait until tonight to eat at the table."

"As you wish." Chris suspected she had fallen during the storm, and he blamed himself for not being with her. Not that she would have cared; she had made her continuing disdain for his company plain. Still, he had to try. He retook his place by her side and again offered her the spoon.

"Did you find anything of interest in the medical book?"

"Yes, I rather liked the study of the skeleton. I had no idea a body had so many bones."

She was the most perplexing creature. She was obviously very bright, but Chris wondered if perhaps her family had not employed the best of tutors. Or maybe they had considered many worthwhile subjects unsuitable for a young lady to study. Whatever the cause, he considered it a shame that she lacked a wider store of knowledge. He certainly wished she spoke French.

"I meant about babies," he prompted softly.

"Oh, yes, of course," she insisted too quickly. "No, there's very little about babies, but perhaps the doctor who wrote it had yet to have children."

"Yes, that's undoubtedly the cause of his oversight. I'm trying to be helpful, Sarah. I'm not just prying."

She nodded absently and took another sip of soup. Chris held the bowl in a light grasp, but with a single glance toward his hands, she again felt his fingertips slide up her thighs. He had had an excellent reason for such an intimate touch, a very kind one, in fact, but the shocking memory proved nearly impossible to suppress.

"It would be a mistake," she cautioned hesitantly, "to assume that because an extraordinary event called for an unusual degree of familiarity, that it would be welcomed later."

Chris chuckled at her polite protest. "Yes, I understand. I won't expect to undress you every night, although should you require assistance, don't hesitate to call on me."

Sarah replaced the spoon in the near empty bowl. "I'd not wait up if I were you."

"Of course not, but it may be difficult for either of us to get much sleep with a new baby crying to be fed. See if he won't nurse when he wakes. As I recall from when my brother was small, babies nurse every few hours. I just can't remember when they begin to eat soft foods like pudding."

He carried her bowl to the table, sat down, and filled his own. "I've always loved pea soup," he murmured.

"I shall make a note of it."

She was being her usual flippant self, but he hid his smile rather than accuse her of being insincere. Then he had a devilish impulse he simply could not repress. He said: "Your breasts, while as exquisite as the rest of you, aren't the first pair I've seen; and I'll certainly not object should you nurse Michael in my presence."

"Were you still sitting here, you'd have a second black eye for that crass remark," she shot back at him. "I have absolutely no interest in your affairs, which are undoubtedly many and brief, and I would prefer to be accorded a respectful privacy when I feed my son."

The soup was especially delicious, and Chris refilled his bowl. "Privacy is in short supply on board a ship," he advised sympathetically. "But I will continue to do my utmost to guard yours."

Sarah turned away from him to gaze down at her son, but she knew Chris too well to expect more than an occasional burst of gentlemanly behavior. She would simply have to endure his insufferable company for the time being, but she would escape him at her first opportunity.

"How long will it be before we reach Martinique?" she asked.

"It's difficult to say. We sustained some damage during the storm, which will take time to repair. You can tell by the way we're rocking on the water that we're not under sail."

Alarmed, Sarah turned back toward him. "Do you mean we're just floating adrift?"

"We are floating, my love, and, for the present, be grateful for that blessing."

Rather than repeat how little she appreciated his endearments, Sarah waited until he had finished eating and gone to the door. "Captain," she then called. "You're not the only one who's had the opportunity to appreciate a beautifully proportioned body. However, I'll refrain from drawing comparisons if you will."

She had drawn out the word *proportioned* in a husky whisper so there was no mistaking her meaning. While he was positive he compared quite favorably to most men, it had not even occurred to him that her late husband might have been equally well endowed.

"Believe me, Mrs. Hadley, I'll strive not to disappoint you."

Sarah nodded, but she doubted that was even possible where he was concerned.

When Chris returned to his cabin a short while later, both Sarah and the baby were crying pitifully. He crossed to the bunk in two long strides and sat down on the edge. "Here, give me the little tyke and tell me what's wrong."

Sarah was relieved to have any help, even his, and handed him her son. She then wiped away her tears with her fingertips but neglected to retie the bow at her neckline. "I thought babies were born knowing how to nurse, but he knows no more than I do."

Chris had to bite the inside of his mouth to keep from laughing, but he did not wish to make light of what was clearly a desperate situation for her. He cradled the baby in his arms and, instantly soothed, Michael yawned and stared up at him rather than continue to howl.

"Look," he exclaimed. "He's smacking his lips, so just as you expected, he's ready to do his part."

"That may very well be, but I'm a failure at mine. What if I can't produce any milk?"

"Sarah, I wish there were some kindly woman on board who had raised a dozen children. Lacking that, perhaps you just need a little practice. Please try again." He returned the baby to her.

"Shall I turn my back?" he asked.

"Please." Sarah opened her nightgown to expose her left breast, but when she raised her infant to her nipple, he gave only a hesitant nip and again began to cry.

Chris glanced over his shoulder. "If I'm to be of any help, I must be allowed to look."

Sarah was almost too distraught to care. Almost, but not quite. "First you must promise not to make any lascivious remarks."

He was glad she could not see his face, and he was deeply grateful she had not sought to curb his thoughts, which were definitely running in a lascivious direction. "I swear. May I please turn around?"

Had there actually been a goat on board to provide an alternative, she would have refused, but alas, she was her baby's only hope for survival. "If you must."

Chris focused his attention on the baby. Sarah was holding him so awkwardly in her arms, he thought perhaps that was the problem. "Michael needs to be held so that he can breathe while he's nursing. Let's adjust the angle. May I touch you for a moment?"

All Sarah could manage was a small nod.

"Here, draw the babe close and let's just raise your breast a bit so he can take more of the nipple in his mouth. There, he seems to like that better, doesn't he?"

When Chris looked up, he found Sarah studying him rather than the baby. He tried to read the expression in her eyes, and prayed it was more wonder than loathing. Unable to decide, he switched his gaze to the baby, who was suckling quite happily now.

Sorry he had had such immediate success, Chris reluctantly drew back and got to his feet. "You two appear to be doing fine now, so I'll leave to provide the privacy you require. Michael will sleep when he's finished, and you should too."

He was out the door before he could catch his breath, but he had expected to maintain an admirable detachment and clearly lacked sufficient restraint. Sarah was still pale from her ordeal, and her curls were in tangled disarray. But even with a darling infant at her creamy smooth breast, he saw only an extremely desirable woman rather than a tense new mother.

He planned to visit her frequently throughout the day and share the cabin at night, but he was ashamed of the strength of his desire when she felt none for him. Sadly, he would be forced to use the surgeon's cabin often to tame the aching need he dared not ask her to satisfy. At least, not yet.

* * *

As predicted, Michael fell asleep after only a few minutes at Sarah's breast. She could also have used a nap but was far too anxious to rest. That she had not even known how to hold her baby properly reinforced her dread that she somehow lacked an innate talent for motherhood.

Then there was Christopher MacLeod, who had worn such a tender expression while helping her to nurse. She had fully expected an obnoxious leer, but he had been smiling at Michael as though he loved the child too. In that unguarded moment, his expression had been one of genuine delight. She would have been touched, had she not feared that he truly did wish to raise her babe as his own.

Once spoken, threats, like insults, were impossible to forget, regardless of how sincere the apology. She was firmly convinced he had meant it. He could have been away from his home in Virginia for years. If he returned with a son and some heartbreaking story of how the dear little boy's mother had been lost, everyone would believe him.

She could have cried but dared not risk waking Michael when she had such little skill in tending him. She would simply have to bide her time and see how they fared on Martinique, but for now, she was too tired to overcome an oppressive sense of dread.

On his next visit, Chris ripped the muslin into squares. "I don't suppose there is any hope that you know how to fold a diaper?" he teased, and her befuddled frown provided an all too clear answer. "I'm sorry. It doesn't matter; I do."

"You appear to have learned a great deal from having had a younger brother. Are you two close?"

"I'm eight years the elder, and I fear my parents believed I set a very poor example."

"Yes, that's easy to understand." Michael was asleep in her lap, and she envied him his innocent contentment. "What's your brother's name?"

"Stephan. He wanted to sail with me, but I refused to consider it. Our parents ought to have at least one son survive the war."

Sarah was taken aback by his remark. "You expected to die?"

"Yes, and long before this. I consider myself daring rather than reckless, but fate can play nasty tricks."

"So can the Royal Navy," she reminded him.

"Yes, but *they* are so very easy to elude. I believe we were talking about our families. Other than the fact that your father is suspicious of beauty—"

"Scornful is a better word."

"Well, you would certainly know, but I find it difficult to believe that your mother wasn't at least pretty."

He sat down by her feet and after his having done it so often now, she did not think to object. "She is such a shy creature, her beauty is often overlooked."

"Then you are nothing like her." Chris reached out to stroke Michael's wispy hair.

"No, I don't take after either of my parents. My father is an Anglican priest and a very proper gentleman. He knows precisely how things are to be done. He's rather like you in that respect."

Chris chuckled at the unexpected comparison. "You must have found that unbearable."

Sarah feared she had confided too much, which was never wise, and especially not with him. "I mustn't keep you when you need to supervise the repairs. Shouldn't they be completed with all possible haste before the Royal Navy overtakes us?"

Her abrupt change of subject disappointed Chris. He wanted to know everything about her, and she had provided a mere glimpse. "The Royal Navy was most probably blown even farther off course than we were. They'll not find us."

"Wouldn't they know your home port is Martinique? It seems to me they'd attempt to intercept you on your way there."

Chris stood and ran a hand through his hair, which suddenly felt as though he had pulled it much too tight. He loosened the bow at his nape and retied it but still had no quick answer to allay her fears.

"I swear, I don't know how we managed to remain afloat before you, Mrs. Hadley, but you needn't fret. Should the British appear, which is less than unlikely, I'll put you and Michael in a long boat and row you to their ship myself."

"And then attack them with us on board?" Sarah responded accusingly.

"Oh, Sarah, there's simply no pleasing you, is there?"

"It would please me to survive!" Startled awake, Michael began to cry, and she scooped him from her lap and hugged the babe close.

Chris leaned down. "Would you like me to take him?"

"No. We'll be fine, but I do wish you'd see to the repairs."

"Aye, my love, I'll race right up on deck to check on them and keep watch for any sign of the Royal Navy." He turned toward the door, but she called him back.

"Wait. If you do sight them, will you consider surrender?"

Had he a serviceable sail larger than a tablecloth, he

would escape them again, but that day his prospects were rather dim. "I would scuttle the ship before I'd surrender. That's why Stephan isn't on board. Now, tend the baby, and this time sleep when he does."

Sarah let him go. That he would prefer to die rather than surrender did not surprise her, but it certainly wasn't the choice she would make, nor what she would choose for her son.

Simon Beasom took a place beside Jacob Shorter and Sean McBean in the stern to aid in mending the sails. He threaded his needle, pulled the canvas across his lap, and began to work on a tear. "Heard tell the bitch whelped a pup."

"Aye, that she did. I overheard the captain say so." Jacob had been released from the brig to fight the storm, but he was no happier than when he had been confined. He preferred mending sails to untangling rigging, but he felt he was owed a good lot of rum and a peaceful rest, which were a long time in coming.

"Ship's become a floating nursery," he muttered under his breath. "I don't recall ever looking for work as a nanny."

"A nanny?" Sean McBean's laughter was closer to a donkey's bray, but once begun, he had a hard time containing it.

"Hush up, you fool," Jacob scolded. "You want the captain mad at us all?"

"No, that I don't," Sean blurted, but he still had to swallow a giggle.

"The way I see it," Simon whispered, "I've earned enough on this voyage to retire. I'm gonna build me a nice house in St. Pierre and get me a plump little wife— one who'll know how to keep a man happy."

"Think she'd want to keep the rest of us happy too?" Sean asked, and once again dissolved into hoarse giggles.

"You stay away from me wife!" Simon shouted.

"Hell, Simon, you don't even got one yet!" Jacob reminded him, but he couldn't help but laugh too.

Chris would have told them to save the jokes for later, but after the men had worked so hard in the storm, he was inclined to be forgiving. He kept searching the horizon, however, unwilling to relax his usual vigilance. He was more concerned than he would admit to Sarah that the British did indeed know where they were bound. He just wished she had not realized it so quickly.

She was so wonderfully bright and fiercely independent, he did not understand how she could have been a Loyalist. There was far more to her story than she had revealed, but she was apparently determined to parcel it out in tiny bits. That annoyed him to no end. He himself had no secrets and was desperately eager to learn hers.

"Most of the hens drowned in the storm," Chris reported apologetically. "So we'll be eating chicken for the next couple of days, and then we'll have to make do with ham."

"You left the hen's cages on deck?"

"No, I did not leave their cages on deck; the cook did. I was busy elsewhere, as you might recall."

Sarah recoiled slightly. "I did not mean to accuse you of murdering the poultry. I've also thanked you effusively for staying with me, which it is now plain you will never let me forget."

Chris stood at the table cutting her meal into bite-sized

pieces. "It's been too long a day to argue after sunset. Don't leave the bed; I'll bring your plate to you."

Sarah could barely keep her eyes open, so she was relieved he had more appetite for chicken than controversy. "Thank you. I'll get up tomorrow, I promise."

"No, take as long as you like. There's no rush."

"Perhaps not, but I need to get up and about." Michael was sleeping by her side, so she could balance her plate on her lap. "Do you think Michael ought to have a cradle?"

Chris carried her plate to the bunk and handed her a fork and napkin. "I'll make him one as soon as we reach my home on Martinique."

"Can you fashion one yourself?" She scooped up a bite of chicken and thought she detected a hint of curry. She would have to meet the cook one day soon to thank him for his meals.

Chris brought his plate to the bunk and sat down to eat with her. "Of course. I built the *Island Belle*. A cradle would scarcely be a challenge."

"If making a cradle would delay my arrival on a British isle, I'll wait and have one made there." She dared not look up at him, but neither did she take another bite she would be unable to swallow.

He sorted through possible replies, none of them plausible, and finally went with the truth. "It's too late now to send you away. You and Michael will stay with me."

Confused, Sarah frowned pensively. "Do you mean it's too late in the war?"

Again, he wished he could evade her question without burdening his conscience. "No, I mean it's simply too late for me to give you up." But Sarah clearly hated being his prisoner. Heartsick and furious to lack another choice, she threw her pewter plate to the floor, where it clattered in a slow spin and splattered chicken stew over his neatly polished boots.

Startled by the noise, Michael awoke and began to scream. "Now look what you've done," Sarah moaned, close to tears herself.

"I may be responsible for a great many things but not waking the baby," Chris argued. "Can't you understand why I'd be reluctant to part with your charming company?" He carried their plates to the table, then used his napkin to clean the mess from the floor and his boots. "You need to begin acting more like a responsible parent and less like a spoiled brat, Mrs. Hadley. But we're both tired. See to your son, and if his diaper is wet, just toss it in the bucket beside the bunk. I'll wash them all tomorrow."

"You're going to wash diapers?" Sarah could not believe her ears. She thought he would be much more likely to hand the chore to Charley.

"Yes, I'll do it until you're able. My men have enough work without looking after you and a baby."

She held Michael pressed to her shoulder and patted his back in a frantic rhythm, but he continued to howl. "You needn't try so hard to make me to feel indebted to you."

"You're far too bright to believe gratitude is all I want." He leaned over, took a handful of her tousled curls, and kissed her hard on the mouth.

When he straightened, he couldn't tell if she was outraged or merely astonished. Whichever, her lashes nearly swept her brows, and her parted lips simply in-

vited even more lavish affection. Seizing his last bit of
restraint, he left before she found the breath to curse
him, but he was already plotting how to win her heart on
Martinique.

Chapter Ten

For the next three days, Chris forced himself to remain on deck for the majority of the daylight hours. Not only did he keep watch for the enemy, he made certain each repair was done so expertly that once under sail, the *Island Belle* would not merely regain her former speed but exceed it.

The moment the last sail was unfurled, the crew broke into hoots and wild cheers, but Chris responded with no more than a slight smile. There had been no sign of the Royal Navy, nor any other vessel that far south, but he remained uneasy all the same.

He provided a double ration of rum for the crew but took not a sip of his own private stock of spirits. Eager to reach the comfort of home, where he could spoil Sarah shamefully, he continually circled the newly caulked deck. When Rob approached, he greeted him with a barely perceptible nod.

"Captain," Rob began awkwardly, "I wonder if I might pay Mrs. Hadley a visit. I don't want her to assume that you're the only one on board who is concerned for her welfare."

"How thoughtful of you," Chris replied without a trace of a smile. "However, I'm the only one who needs to be concerned."

"Be that as it may, sir, I would like to speak with her and offer my congratulations on the birth of her son."

Despite Chris's fears, none of the men had fallen ill, but he still believed it wise to take the precaution of keeping Michael isolated from the crew. "The baby was born at least a month early and, while he appears sturdy, Mrs. Hadley would be devastated should he fall ill. I will relay your good wishes, however, as she will surely appreciate them."

"Perhaps you should allow Mrs. Hadley to decide whether or not she cares to have visitors. She might be very tired of her own company."

"And mine as well?" Chris asked, insulted.

"Certainly not, but I don't want her to believe that I am so lacking in manners that I have not even inquired about her health. After all, Charley sees the baby several times each day, and I promise not to tire Mrs. Hadley or her son."

Rob had once been an exemplary mate, but Chris could identify the precise hour when he had grown argumentative and distant. Good mates were difficult to find, but an extraordinary woman like Sarah Hadley was a priceless treasure.

"You may be assured that I'll convey your request, Mr. Corliss."

"Thank you. I would appreciate the opportunity to extend my best wishes before we reach Martinique."

"If it can be arranged," Chris emphasized, but he sincerely doubted it.

When he mentioned Rob's curiosity later, it was in an off-hand manner intended to garner a prompt refusal.

"Like Charley, Mr. Corliss is infatuated with you. It would be very unwise to encourage him."

"I believe you're missing the point, Captain. Charley is the only one who has seen Michael. Perhaps the other men do not believe he actually exists."

"Well, of course he exists." Chris turned his back on her to pace the cabin. He now found it nearly impossible to sit for the length of a meal, let alone to chat with her. He flexed his hands in time with his steps rather than ball them into fists.

"Yes, we know that, but it might be wise to allow Mr. Corliss to see Michael with his own eyes. You could remain with us to limit the visit to a few minutes. It would be nice to speak with someone new."

"Have I already begun to bore you?"

He had tossed the question over his shoulder, but Sarah sensed her answer mattered a great deal. "No woman will ever grow bored with you, Captain, but you have a ship to sail, and as yet, Michael is unable to hold up his end of a conversation."

Chris halted facing her. "Then you do want to see Mr. Corliss?"

"Yes, I do. I appreciate your warning, and I promise to assiduously avoid encouraging his affections."

Chris clamped his mouth shut rather than admit that she had done nothing to encourage his either, and still he had been charmed. He had never been a jealous sort. No, indeed, but then, he had never thought enough of any other woman to care whether or not she preferred another man.

"You've not even begun to dress the boy," he pointed out. "Did you complete any of the little clothes you were making?"

Sarah had completely forgotten them. She had been so worried about her lack of skill as a seamstress, and her son had been fine with nothing more than a blanket and diaper.

"No, as a matter of fact, I lacked the time before he was born; then we used the muslin for diapers. Now I dare not sew for fear of poking him with my needle."

"That's undoubtedly wise." Chris rocked back on his heels. "Do you plan to receive Mr. Corliss in your nightgown?"

It was so much easier to nurse Michael while wearing one, Sarah had not once bothered to dress since his birth. Each morning, a freshly laundered gown lay at the foot of her bed, and she was only too happy to wear it. Michael lay sleeping in her lap, and she took care not to disturb him as she tugged nervously on her lace-trimmed cuffs.

"I'll wear my sleeping jacket over it. Surely he'll understand if I'm not more fully clothed. After all, Michael is less than a week old. He's sleeping so peacefully, would you care to invite Mr. Corliss to visit us now?"

"No, I'd not like it at all, but I gave you the choice and unfortunately shall have to abide by it."

His annoyance was so plain in his tone and frown, Sarah could not let it pass. "I appreciate just how difficult this is for you. Thank you for considering my feelings."

Chris nodded stiffly. To say their relationship had grown increasingly strained was an understatement. At least he had made his intentions clear, but as long as she had no wish to fulfill them, he had no choice but to wait until she did. Unfortunately, he was very nearly out of patience.

* * *

Rob Corliss doffed his hat and took only a single step past the door before offering a greeting in a reverential tone. "I'm pleased to see you looking so well, Mrs. Hadley. To give birth during such a violent storm must have been a terrifying ordeal."

"Is that your idea of witty conversation?" Chris chided sarcastically. "I expected better."

"Captain, please," Sarah begged. "I appreciate your expression of concern, Mr. Corliss. I'd love for you to see my son. Would you care to come closer?"

"Yes, I would." Rob shuffled forward but, like Charley, chose to remain at a respectful distance. "He's a handsome lad, but I'd not expected him to be quite so small."

Rob was the second person to remark on Michael's size, and Sarah feared their assessment must be correct. "Well, he may be small now, but his father was nearly the captain's height, so I imagine he'll be tall when he's grown."

"Oh, yes, I expect so, ma'am. I wonder if I might visit you again tomorrow."

"If you can spare the time," Sarah responded graciously. "Are the repairs complete?"

Rob shrugged unhappily. "Most are, but some will have to wait until we dock. Not that the *Island Belle* isn't seaworthy, you understand, but belowdeck she has been in far better condition."

"Thank you, Mr. Corliss, that's quite enough." Chris came forward to take the mate's arm and turn him toward the door.

Sarah waited until Rob could be heard climbing the companionway steps before she spoke, and even then she whispered. "That wasn't too awful, was it?" she asked Chris.

171

"Perhaps not for you, madame. Now you must excuse me as well."

She nodded, but then laughed to herself when he had gone. She was his prisoner, and yet Chris behaved as though he feared being jilted for the mate. How preposterous! Not that Mr. Corliss wasn't attractive, because he was, but she had swiftly recognized how foolish it was to expect assistance from the crew.

Michael stirred in his sleep and stretched his little arms. She envied the way he napped throughout the day, while she still found it difficult to sleep for even an hour.

The next day, Rob watched Chris take the helm. Thinking it might be the only opportunity he would have to speak candidly with Sarah, he rushed to the captain's cabin. When she bade him enter, he hastened to her side.

"You're looking well today, ma'am, as is your son. Please forgive me for hurrying through this, but I'm unlikely to be the mate of the *Island Belle* once we reach Martinique, and I'd never forgive myself if I missed whatever chance I might have to be of service."

He was so obviously troubled that Sarah was immediately intrigued. "Thank you, but what service did you wish to perform, Mr. Corliss?"

"I know you're from Charleston. Once we reach Martinique, I believe passage could be arranged for you, perhaps on a Dutch ship bound for the British island of Jamaica, and from there to South Carolina. I can only imagine how badly you must want to return home with your son."

Horrified by the offer, Sarah barely swallowed a hysterical shriek before it escaped her lips. Home? Her father's house was the last place she would ever wish to go. Even if the rest of South Carolina had beckoned invitingly, she could not bear the thought of another voyage through pirate-infested waters.

She had once intended to escape Christopher MacLeod the moment her feet touched dry land, but now she could more fully appreciate the risk such a dangerous course would pose for Michael. She would simply have to learn to be more circumspect in both her words and her actions while her son was so small.

She inhaled deeply to still her racing heart and waited a moment longer before responding. "I'm touched by your concern for our well-being, but it is entirely misplaced. I have absolutely no wish to ever return to Charleston, nor to immediately embark on another ocean voyage once this one is complete. Thank you for paying us another call, but Michael is beginning to squirm, so he must be hungry."

Mortified to have misread her situation so completely, Rob backed right out of the cabin and ran up the steps. He then went straight to Chris, who had relinquished the helm and now stood in the bow.

"I owe you an apology, Captain. Mrs. Hadley came aboard under the worst of circumstances, and my attitude as to your involvement with her has been uncharitable, to say the least. It is plain to me now that she is content to remain with you once we reach Martinique."

Amazed by the mate's revelation, Chris cocked his head slightly. "How did you come by this remarkable insight, Mr. Corliss?"

Too late, Rob realized his mistake, which forced him to stretch the truth shamelessly. "I stopped by your cabin just now to inquire if I might be of some service, and in the course of a brief conversation, Mrs. Hadley intimated as much. I believe she's quite taken with you."

Chris simply stared at Rob, who was so badly embarrassed, his freckles had disappeared beneath a deep blush. "She actually said so?" he asked.

"Well, no. She is a lady and by nature discreet, but it was clear to me nonetheless."

It was easily the most bizarre bit of news Chris had ever received. He looked up at the sails as though he were comparing the ones they had just fashioned from their store of canvas with those they had been able to mend. "I would appreciate it if you would keep Mrs. Hadley's remarks in the strictest confidence, Mr. Corliss. She is a very sensitive young woman, and she must not be hurt by careless gossip."

"Oh, no, sir. I would never violate her confidence. I had completely misunderstood her feelings, but I will cease to give her welfare any further thought. I know you have her best interests at heart."

"Indeed I do," Chris agreed, but if Sarah had any tender feelings for him, she was maddeningly disinclined to show them when they were together. Still, Rob was a perceptive young man, and if he believed she had come to care for him, then surely she had.

That night, Chris lay in his hammock, his hands behind his head, his left leg dangling over the side. He had not felt this relaxed in weeks; but now that Sarah might soon come to love him, even if the level of her affection remained unequal to his own, he had every hope of a promising future.

He could accept her reticence to offer him any encouragement, and yet he could not help but believe they had been destined to meet. When Sarah sat up to nurse Michael, he heard the faint rustle of the bedclothes.

"Do you believe in destiny?" he asked softly. The lamps were turned low, but he was careful to ensure her privacy by not glancing her way.

"No," she responded thoughtfully. "With the exception of my marriage and dear little Michael, I've not led the happiest of lives. I would hate to think sadness and tragedy were all fate had in store for me."

"No life is without some sorrow," he offered, "but I'm saddened to learn you've not been happy. You already know how gladly I'd welcome the opportunity to provide for a blissful future."

Sarah shifted Michael slightly, but he was often an awkward bundle in her arms. "I'm sorry if we woke you. It's very late and I'd rather concentrate on my son than speculate on the future, if you don't mind."

"Good night, then," Chris responded, but he would much rather have talked until dawn.

"Chris?"

He loved the way she said his name. "I thought you wanted me to be quiet, Mrs. Hadley."

"Yes, I do, but first tell me if you think Michael is too small."

"He was born early, and that accounts for his size. He nurses well, doesn't he?"

Sarah was sorry she had asked his opinion now that he had strayed into what appeared to be his favorite topic. "Yes, I believe so." Her breasts were now heavy with milk, and being able to feed her son was no longer a concern. "Good night again."

"Good night. Wake me if you need me to hold Michael or change his diapers. I'm rather good at it."

"I'm sure you're good at everything you attempt, Captain."

"I work at it," Chris confided with a low chuckle, but he was disappointed when the whole night passed without her again calling his name.

The lagoon was more beautiful than Sarah could have imagined. The aqua waters of the Caribbean Sea lapped against sparkling white sand, while palm trees and verdant vegetation ringed the deserted beach. She doubted paradise could be any more inviting, but she was too badly frightened to leave the *Island Belle.*

"I thought we'd be disembarking at a sturdy wooden dock," she exclaimed. "I won't climb down a rope ladder with Michael, even if there is a man in the long boat to catch us."

Standing behind her, Chris rested his hands lightly on her shoulders. "Your trunk has already been taken ashore. Were we to leave the ship when it docks in port, we'd then have a long carriage ride over treacherous mountain trails to reach my home. Here, you can see my roof just above the trees. Please trust me, Sarah. I'll have you ashore in less than ten minutes."

Sarah clutched Michael even more tightly. The baby looked up at her, his bright blue eyes aglow. He was a remarkably good-natured baby who spent most of each day sound asleep.

"I realize we've been on the water for weeks," Sarah argued. "But this is different."

It was the first time she had been on deck since Michael's birth. It was too warm for her cloak, and she was dressed in her navy blue gown, which now hung loosely from her shoulders. Her curls were flying in the breeze, but with Michael to tend, there had been no op-portunity to style her hair. She could feel every last member of the crew staring at her, many undoubtedly chuckling at her reticence to leave, but she was near tears.

Chris pressed closer, molding his body to hers. "Let's ask Rob to hold Michael for a moment, and I'll help you down into the boat. Then I'll come back up for Michael and bring him to you. Please don't worry so. No one will fall into the water and drown."

"I can swim," Sarah protested softly. "My husband taught me."

"Was this before or after you were wed?"

"After, of course. It would have been most improper earlier."

"Yes, indeed." Chris leaned down to whisper, "Michael would be very uncomfortable on a long carriage ride. He might cry the whole way, and then so would you."

His deep voice inspired confidence, and Sarah almost believed him, but her feet remained firmly attached to the deck. "I'm sorry to be so frightened."

"It's understandable," Chris coaxed as he moved around to face her. "You take your responsibilities as Michael's mother very seriously. I'm just as serious about my duties as captain of this ship. Now, hand Michael to me."

Before Sarah could object, he had plucked her son from her arms and passed him to a startled Rob Corliss, who clutched the babe tightly. She wanted to trust both men, but the distance to the shore looked impossibly far. "Wait, isn't there another way . . . ?"

Chris swept her up into his arms and lifted her over the side, where she made a quick grab for the rope ladder. He then swung down beside her, wrapped one arm around her waist, and with a firm grasp on the ladder with the other, carefully guided her down into the waiting boat. Simon Beasom held the oars balanced across his lap. He flashed a gap-toothed grin and nodded a welcome.

Chris saw Sarah safely seated in the stern and then, as promised, climbed the ladder to fetch Michael. In a moment he'd laid him in her arms. "There, you see how easy that was?" He sat down on the bench opposite her and urged Simon to row with all possible haste.

Sarah felt sick. While she had been afraid to climb into the long boat, she was equally terrified of being stranded at Chris's home. Until he tired of her, of course, and then she would surely be promptly sent away. That she had no safe haven awaiting her and her son compounded her heartache. She was so tired of travel that London might as well have been on the moon, but she was obligated to take Michael there one day. Fortunately, the war was an excellent excuse to put off the voyage, but she could at least send her in-laws news of their grandson's birth.

She risked a quick peek toward the shore and discovered a remarkably tall woman running down the path toward the shore. She was clad in a wild mix of patterned and plain green cotton, with a long white apron and a knotted orange kerchief about her head. Her skin was the shade of weak tea. As she reached the sand, she clapped her hands and broke into a lively jig.

Sarah stared at Chris, her gaze narrowed in shocked disbelief. "Is she one of your slaves?"

"I take it you are opposed to the practice?"

Her posture stiffened. "Vehemently. I'll not set foot in your house if it's staffed by slaves."

Chris leaned forward to pat her knee. "I've never

owned a slave and I never will. Ramona is my housekeeper. She claims Spanish and French blood, but she has always appeared more Indian to me. This is her home as well as mine. Smile please, so she'll believe you're pleased to be here."

"But I'm not!"

"Then pretend to be, for Michael's sake as well as your own. You've disparaged fate, so I'll blame circumstance for making us companions. Let's make the best of it."

"It was not circumstance but you, sir, who captured the *Beatrice*!"

"Then let's regard it as providence," Chris insisted.

Sarah shot him a truly malevolent stare, which served to silence him until they reached shallow water and the boat's rounded bottom grazed the sand. "You see, we made it here safely. Now, I'll step into the water and then carry you and Michael up to the beach."

Ramona was still dancing happily, and Sarah feared the housekeeper would assume she was Chris's wife. But when the woman began to call to them excitedly in French, she doubted she would ever learn the truth.

"You must tell me what she said," Sarah urged in a frantic whisper, "and I expect an accurate translation. If she says I'm so thin I resemble a rope with a frayed end for hair, please say so."

"My God, Sarah. You're such a beautiful woman. Why would anyone describe you in such derogatory terms?"

"When have people needed an excuse to be cruel?"

"I hope that's not how you would describe me." He forced a smile as they approached Ramona, but he was beginning to wonder if Rob Corliss had not completely mistaken Sarah's feelings for him.

Ramona hurried across the damp sand to meet them. She took a quick look at Sarah and then cooed happily at Michael. She smiled coyly at Chris and began an animated conversation filled with graceful gestures and sly winks.

Chris placed Sarah on her feet, then turned to send Simon and the long boat back to the ship. He nodded to acknowledge Ramona's welcome, but swiftly realized he should have prepared a tactful introduction for Sarah, rather than allow the housekeeper's imagination free rein.

He slid his arm around Sarah's shoulders, and when Ramona paused for breath he interrupted with the story of how he had rescued the lovely widow at sea. While certain elements of the tale were true, like Michael's birth, when Ramona's expression filled with harsh skepticism, he feared nothing he had said had been believed.

"She mistook you for my wife and was elated to think I'd not only married but produced such a beautiful child," he told Sarah.

"I refuse to pose as your wife," she vowed through clenched teeth.

"Nor do I expect you to. It may take me a day or two, but everyone will soon learn you are merely, well, my . . ."

" 'Hostage' is an appropriate word—or 'captive,' if you prefer."

"I prefer 'guest,' " he insisted, but even after he had expanded his explanation with a description of their differing political views, Ramona clearly remained unconvinced. She rested her hands on her hips and shook her head sadly before issuing a terse parting comment and walking back up the path.

"She appeared to be very badly disappointed. What did she say?" Sarah asked.

Chris dropped his arm to encircle her waist as they made their way across the sand. "It really wouldn't translate well."

"Do your best, and it would be a grave disservice to offer only flattering commentary rather than the truth. If I'm to be surrounded by servants who despise me, I deserve to be warned."

Chris had already cursed his own folly in not being better prepared for Ramona, but at least he could request a moment to fabricate a translation of her remarks. Then he realized Sarah would be twice as difficult to fool as the housekeeper.

"Ramona has been with me for years and sometimes feels entitled to offer opinions she knows I would not tolerate from anyone else."

"Was it so awful you can't even say it? Maybe I should return to the ship." Sarah glanced over her shoulder and was disheartened to find the *Island Belle* had already sailed out to sea.

Chris took a deep breath and rushed through the housekeeper's parting insult. "Ramona said a gentleman should buy a house for his mistress and bastards, rather than bring them home."

Sarah halted in midstride. "And you let her walk away? Is that how I'm to be treated here? You'll allow anyone to assume what they will and won't contradict them? I'd be better off staying here on the beach. If you'll just fetch me a blanket, I'll suspend it between those two palms and call it a tent."

"No, I will not have you living on the beach. You may

be assured that once you and Michael are comfortably settled in your room, I'll reprimand Ramona in such blistering terms her eyebrows are likely to burst into flame."

His fierce expression was proof he would follow through on his promise, but Sarah still felt abused. "No one has ever called me a whore."

"Not a whore, a mistress. There's a difference."

"Only in the number of men, not in the activity, surely."

Chris could not dispute her succinct definition, especially when he thought she would make such a magnificent mistress. "Look up ahead. Now you can see my house. I'm sure you'll be far more comfortable there than you were on board the *Island Belle*."

They had reached a rise on the path, and while Michael had fallen asleep, Sarah stopped to stare. The house was built of wood and stone found on the island. It was huge, with a spacious veranda surrounding the first floor, and wide louvers on the windows to entice a cooling breeze. An abundance of deep pink and purple orchids grew up from vine-covered trellises to drip over the railing of the second-floor balcony.

"You built this house too, didn't you?" she asked.

"Yes. It kept me occupied for a while. Do you like it?"

Sarah did not want to like anything of his, but it was impossible to dislike something so hauntingly beautiful. "It could be an enchanted mansion from a fairy tale."

Delighted she had been distracted from his opinionated servant, Chris grew inspired. "Shall we write one about a lonely princess and the handsome prince who rescues her?"

Sarah rocked her sleeping son in her arms. "What about a lonely princess who is besieged by a hideous troll? That might be far more amusing. For the moment, however, I'd appreciate a bath. Do you by any chance own a magnificent copper tub?"

"I most certainly do, and I'll see that it's immediately filled with perfumed water."

"Plain warm water will do," Sarah cautioned.

As they neared the veranda, three women burst through the front door. Two were younger than Sarah, with tendrils of auburn hair escaping their lacy white caps. Their gowns were gray cotton, and hastily tied aprons drooped over their narrow hips. They had lovely smiles, but nearly as many freckles as Rob Corliss.

The third was a plump woman in her fifties who was also dressed in gray and white, although far more neatly than the girls. Her hands were dusted with flour that spotted the air as she bobbed a shaky curtsy. All three squealed with delight and greeted Chris excitedly in French.

He braced himself and presented the trio to Sarah. "Mariette and Michelle are sisters who assist Ramona in caring for the house. Madame LeFleur is our quite excellent cook." He then switched to French to describe Sarah as a charming widow he had rescued at sea.

All three servants appeared confused, but only Madame LeFleur offered a flurry of questions in a surprisingly high-pitched voice.

Having learned his lesson, Chris was not even tempted to translate her words accurately. "Madame LeFleur has offered several tempting options for supper."

"The truth," Sarah chided. "She was asking about me."

"Well, yes, she did wonder why there was no hoop under your skirt and asked if perhaps hoops were no longer considered fashionable." That was at least an approximation of one of her queries.

"I thought a hoop would be a poor choice for the close confines of a ship and expected to purchase a new wardrobe in London after Michael's birth. I'm sorry not to be more knowledgeable about current fashions."

Sarah had been smiling, but Madame LeFleur merely looked perplexed and waited for Chris's translation. "She thanks you and expressed some surprise that you do not speak French."

"Please explain that not everyone you 'rescue' at sea is cursed with a French ancestry."

Chris could not help but laugh, but neither would he convey her haughty opinion of the French. "I hope you'll not mind if I take certain liberties in the translation of your remarks. After all, you will have to rely on my servants during your stay here, and I do not want them to deliberately neglect you or Michael. That would make us both very unhappy indeed."

"You may censor my words however you please, but at least you'll understand my true meaning."

"Yes, and that's of primary importance, isn't it?"

Sarah nodded to agree, but as she entered his home, she found it merely a well-appointed prison.

Chapter Eleven

Sarah almost floated in the brightly polished copper tub. It sat on a wooden platform in a bathhouse located down a fine pebble path behind the main house. Chris had brought her there himself, and now sat outside while Michael slept in his arms. She had already washed and rinsed her hair, but the now tepid water was still so soothing she was reluctant to climb out.

Her parents had owned a tub made of tin that took forever to fill with buckets of hot water and even longer to bail out with that same bucket. Her mother had always bathed first, and then Sarah had stepped into the same soapy water. They had employed only a single servant, a woman who both cooked and cleaned, so filling and draining the tub had been left to Sarah.

Here, Chris had simply asked that the tub be filled, and it had been readied for her. She yawned and wiggled her toes. The fragrance of the cinnamon-scented soap permeated the air, creating a mood as exotic as the beautiful island. For a brief moment, she felt perfectly at peace; then, believing she had already imposed upon Chris's patience, she stood and shook slightly to send the last droplets of water cascading down her body.

She really was too thin now, except for her breasts, which were more than gently rounded. Whenever Michael fell asleep while nursing, milk would leak from her nipples in a most embarrassing fashion. She had brought clean undergarments out to the bathhouse, but she hated to wear anything other than a linen nightgown that could be easily laundered. Even after she had patted herself dry and turned the spigot to drain the tub into the garden, she remained reluctant to don several layers of clothing.

"Chris?"

He rose to stand just outside the door so he could whisper and still be heard. "Yes? Do you need more towels?"

"No. I was just wondering if I really had to dress for supper."

"Of course not. Please feel free to dine with me in the nude. It would certainly be a novel experience, and now that you've suggested it, I see no reason to refuse."

Sarah wrapped her damp hair in a towel. "I'm sure you would enjoy that, but I wondered if I could simply wear a nightgown and dine in my room."

"You may dine wherever you please, but I plan to be there with you."

Sarah slipped her chemise over her head and shook out her petticoats. "We are no longer on board ship, Captain, and I shall not be insulted if you wish to dine alone."

"I would be a very poor host if I abandoned my guests on their first night in my home."

Sarah peeked out the doorway and found him hovering near. "When you have insisted to anyone who will listen that I am not your mistress, why do you insist upon behaving as though I were?"

It was such an intelligent question, he relied upon a smile rather than offer an absurd reply. "Let's discuss the subject later. I'll not have sufficient time to construct Michael's cradle this afternoon, so why don't we carry him in a basket and have supper on the beach? The nights here are warm and very pleasant."

"You want to picnic on the beach?"

"Yes, why not? You were ready to string up a tent and reside on the sand."

"True. If I may picnic in a nightgown, then I'll go."

"Wear whatever you wish, Sarah. I'll see only you."

Sarah immediately ducked back inside the bathhouse and sat down on the wooden bench. While Christopher MacLeod always got his way, apparently he planned to court her with romantic moonlit suppers and effusive flattery. She would have to put a stop to such foolishness immediately, but because she would prefer not to do so in front of his curious servants, a picnic on the beach would be the perfect setting.

Near sunset, Chris arrived at Sarah's door carrying a basket woven from palm fronds lined with a pale blue woolen blanket for Michael and a wicker picnic basket containing their supper. He had a dark blue blanket for the picnic folded over his arm.

"Other than those who work for me, there's no one living near us, so we'll have the lagoon to ourselves."

He was obviously delighted by their isolation, while Sarah merely felt alone. Not wishing to be maudlin when they had such an important matter to discuss, she focused instead on the palm basket.

"What a charming basket. Perhaps Michael won't need a cradle after all."

"No, he must have a proper cradle. I've already selected some cherry wood I'd left here. Once the cradle is finished, I'll build you a rocking chair. Babies ought to be rocked to sleep, and most especially a boy who was born at sea."

Sarah snuggled Michael down into the basket and carried him balanced on her right hip. "You have clearly given the matter more thought than I have, Captain."

"I enjoy making furniture. I'd have made everything in this house had I had the time."

"I wish you had taken the time rather than turn pirate," she replied with her usual aplomb.

Chris took her hand as they climbed the rise overlooking the lagoon. "You have called me a scoundrel so often, I'm beginning to believe it. You mustn't complain should I behave as one."

"When have you not?" Pulling free of his grasp, Sarah raised her nightgown slightly rather than risk tripping over the hem.

The sea glowed in the twilight with a thousand twinkling lights, and while she had no wish to dwell on romance, the setting was truly ideal. She paused to remove her slippers and walked barefoot across the sand. The fine grains reflected the last of the sun's rays and met each of her steps with a warm caress.

Chris spread out the blanket, took Michael's basket from her, and placed it on the side farthest from the water. "I had no idea babies spent so much time asleep. I'd feared you'd soon tire of bouncing him in your arms all day."

"Does he sleep too much?" Sarah inquired anxiously.

"No, I don't believe so. He's growing bigger every day, so clearly he's thriving."

"Yes, he's grown, but is he still too small?"

"Sarah, he's a fine boy. Now, please be seated and have

one of these delicious pastries Ramona baked this afternoon. They're filled with olives and cheese rather than fruit, and always delicious."

Still unconvinced of her son's health, she sat down and, while not really hungry, took a bite. "Yes, these are good. I meant to thank your cook personally for his many delicious meals but completely forgot to ask you to introduce him before we left the ship. I do hope he wasn't offended."

"Raymond Fox is not easily insulted," Chris assured her, "but I'll introduce him at my first opportunity. He's so thin, it appears he does little more than sample the food he prepares."

Sarah could not recall ever seeing a man of that description, but perhaps she had been too preoccupied to distinguish one man from another while they prepared to leave the ship. She wondered if ascending the rope ladder would prove to be as frightening as the descent had been. But she could not inquire without appearing eager to sail with him again, which she most definitely was not.

"How will you summon your ship—or will Mr. Corliss simply return when the repairs are complete?"

Chris gazed out at the waves slowly rolling against the shore. "Rob will send word when the repairs are complete, and then I'll make my plans. Should I wish to contact him, my house borders a sugar plantation. I'd dispatch one of the workers."

"Wouldn't the owner of the plantation object?"

He shook his head. "I own the plantation, Sarah, and I pay excellent wages, by the way. The workers and their families live on the other side of the fields, so I doubt you'll ever see them."

She was already convinced the island was populated with all manner of interesting individuals she was unlikely to meet. That he was her only companion was simply part of the problem, however. Thinking she ought not to delay what must be said, she laid her half-eaten pastry aside.

"I understand why you've brought me here tonight, but I really must—"

"Wait. You'd be more comfortable if I sat behind you and you leaned against me." He moved, and with his left knee bent and the right extended, he turned to prop himself on his right arm and pulled her back against his chest with his left. "There, isn't that far more comfortable?"

She had only to turn her head slightly for their eyes to meet. It would have been a wonderfully comfortable pose had she been with someone of her own choosing.

"Captain," she scolded softly, "should anyone see us sitting this close, they would quite naturally assume I am much more than your house guest."

"They'd be correct too, wouldn't they?" He wound his fingers in her cinnamon-scented curls. While he had liked her floral perfume, the tangy spice was a far better match for her vibrant spirit.

"It's such a lovely night, and I want to know so much more about you," he coaxed persuasively. "Let's talk rather than argue."

"Well, yes, I'd hoped we'd be able to have a rational discussion."

"Good, then we agree for once. From what little you've told me, your mother must have been a very timid soul. While your father was undoubtedly respected as a priest, was he an overbearing parent?"

She had barely mentioned her father, but it was clear Chris understood him perfectly. An obedient daughter would have defended both her parents, but she was too appreciative of his insights to protest. She was also amazed by how masterfully he had manipulated the conversation away from the topic she had wished to introduce.

"Yes, that's precisely the word to describe him," she concurred wholeheartedly. "He regarded even the most innocuous question as a rude attack on his authority, and he quoted Scripture to settle every argument in his own favor."

"That explains everything." Chris sighed wearily. He adjusted his position slightly to slice a pear grown in his garden, and handed her a piece. "Your father must have been at his wits' end coping with an extraordinarily beautiful daughter who was also blessed with a keen intellect. I'll bet you insisted upon logical explanations for his undoubtedly absurd demands. It's no wonder you were such an unhappy child."

Her gown had a gently rounded neckline, and he brushed light kisses across her bare shoulder. "Michael Hadley must have been a dashing sort to win your heart, but I'm surprised you hadn't already run off with the first man to ride by on a fine horse."

After he had been so wonderfully sympathetic, Sarah regarded that insulting observation as doubly cruel. She shoved his right arm to knock him off balance, but before she could scramble to her feet, he caught her waist and pulled her back down on top of him. She braced her palms against his chest and shoved hard, which only made him tighten his hold.

"The picnic's over. Now let me go," she spat out angrily.

Instead, Chris rolled over with her still cradled in his arms. He propped himself on his elbows to spare her his weight, and then kissed her gently.

"I own a very fine horse," he whispered against her lips, and his second kiss was insistent, the third demanding. When she still failed to respond, he drew back slightly. "Oh, Sarah, I know you have feelings for me—you needn't pretend otherwise."

"How preposterous! You've obviously confused me with all your women with the magnificent breasts."

"Sarah—" He was so amused by her insult he had to laugh.

With a sudden brutal clarity, she understood him all too well. "This is simply a game to you, isn't it? But I'll never regard love as a sport."

"Does this feel like a game?" Chris whispered, then traced the gentle curve of her lips with the tip of his tongue. "You are the most maddening creature I've ever met, perhaps ever borne, and yet I love you. How can you think otherwise?"

Sarah swallowed hard. She was furious with him, but his words and expression were so tender she felt herself being drawn in, lured to what she had always feared might be an inevitable surrender. But just as quickly, she imagined him gloating as he left their bed.

"No," she argued, more with herself than him. "If you loved me, you'd not believe that I'd leap on the back of any obliging man's horse."

"No, not just any horse. It would have to be a very fine mount, although I might have carried you away on the back of a mule."

"You are the most arrogant—"

Chris interrupted her with another slow, sweet kiss. "I

do love you, Sarah, and I'll never take advantage of your feelings for me."

That he could not even grasp how little she liked him infuriated her anew. With sudden inspiration, she issued a biting question of her own. "Were I your widow, how long would you expect me to mourn for you?"

Never having had a wife, much less having worried about leaving the dear woman a widow, the question caught him completely off guard. He was well aware that the war might cost him his life, however, and that Sarah would surely dread being widowed twice. To give her question the respect it deserved, he raised up and moved to lie down beside her. He took her hand and brought her fingertips to his lips. A bright canopy of stars covered them now, but looking up, he saw only the sadness in her eyes.

He needed a moment to consider his answer, but it was easy to choose what would be best for her. "I'd hope that you'd love me forever, but I'd not want you to spend the rest of your life alone. I'd hope another man would touch your heart and be a loving father to Michael. If you met him a day after I died, or years later, it wouldn't matter. I'd always want you to be loved."

Sarah's tears blurred the stars overhead, and she hurriedly wiped them away on her sleeve. She did not understand how he could have summoned such a profoundly comforting answer. That he had included Michael in his hopes for love overwhelmed her completely.

He turned toward her to rest on his side, but kept hold of her hand. "Sarah?"

"Hmm?"

"Did you ever ask Michael that same question?"

She sighed and turned toward him. "Michael was the

exuberant sort, and so very charming. He loved a good joke and had a wonderful laugh, but while we talked of going to England after the war, neither of us ever considered that he might become a casualty. It seems very foolish of us now, doesn't it?"

"No. It just sounds as though you were very much in love."

Sarah had always found Christopher MacLeod devilishly attractive, and she was grateful to him for his calm presence at Michael's birth and his continued devotion to her son. But it wasn't his handsome appearance, nor mere gratitude that made her lean over to kiss him now. It was a very light kiss flavored with a pear's subtle sweetness, and when he lay back to pull her into his arms, she rested her head against his shoulder rather than insist they return to the house.

They lay under the stars in that relaxed embrace until Michael awoke. Chris then sat behind her again to provide a comfortable backrest while she nursed him. Neither of them said anything more, but in a single night, everything between them had changed.

Chris had placed Sarah and Michael in the bedroom adjoining his, and not simply to be near should she need help with Michael, as he had sworn to her and Ramona. He was happy to tend the baby, of course, but his real goal was to be close to her.

It had been past midnight when they had returned to the house, and she had bade him good night at the bottom of the stairs. Rather than follow, he had gone to his study and sat in the dark until he was certain she had had time to fall asleep. Tomorrow he would send a man to Port

Royal for the latest news, but tonight the war was as distant as his home in Virginia.

Now he stood in the doorway connecting their rooms, his ankles crossed in a relaxed pose, his arms folded over his chest. He enjoyed watching Sarah sleep and, surprisingly, it was enough. When he could no longer remain awake, he stretched out on his own bed and wished they were still in his cabin on the *Island Belle*, where she slept only a few feet away.

Mariette and Michelle brought a breakfast of fresh pastries and sliced mango with a pot of tea to Sarah's room shortly after she awoke. The sisters placed the tray on the table beneath the window overlooking the garden, and then, giggling to themselves, darted from the room.

Still yawning, Sarah carried Michael to the table. There she sat down to nurse him while she nibbled a raisin-filled pastry which, while similar in shape, was sweeter than a scone. A white orchid in a small silver vase sat on the tray, and she moved it to the table to enjoy for the day.

The room was lovely in the morning; the dark paneling shone with frequent polishing, and with the windows and louvered shutters open, sunlight brightened the deep rose walls. The furniture was far finer than anything they had had in her home, and the rose and green carpet presented a magical swirling garden in itself.

It was a delightfully feminine room, and while she had not cared to investigate yesterday, she felt certain Chris would occupy the master bedroom next door. He had decorated this room for his wife, and although it was lovely, she felt as out of place there as she had in his cabin.

At least here she could wander the garden or stroll down to the sea, and she wished the opportunity to spend a pleasant hour were enough to ease her troubled mind, but sadly it wasn't. Then she heard Chris calling her name and stood to look down into the garden.

He waved to her from below, where he sat astride the most magnificent white stallion she had ever seen. She laughed as she shifted Michael in her arms. "I expected to see you on the back of a mule, sir."

He appeared shocked. "Is this not a mule, then?"

"No, it is a very fine horse. Where are you bound?"

"Anywhere you'd care to go. Do you have a preference for either the cane fields or the lagoon?"

The sun lent his hair the iridescent glow of a raven's wing, and his expression was so inviting, she hated to refuse. "While either would be diverting, I'll not take Michael on a horse when there's a danger we could be thrown."

"Michael can sleep in his basket on the veranda and Mariette and Michelle will watch him. We'll return in five minutes if you're too worried to stay away any longer."

Afraid to rely on the sisters to care for him even that briefly, Sarah frowned pensively. Then, remembering that the girls spoke only French, she gave a truthful reply. "I'd not trust that silly pair to watch bread rise."

"I'll ask Ramona to tend him, then," Chris replied.

Sarah shook her head. "She doesn't like me, so she would be even worse."

"You're forgetting that everyone believes Michael is my son, and they'd never allow him to come to any harm."

"You didn't disabuse them of the idea?" She thought it utterly ridiculous to discuss such a personal matter through an open window, and yet when no one else spoke English, there seemed no possible harm.

"I tried my best, but they don't believe me. I'll ask all three to watch Michael and promise to bring you back before he even notices that you've been gone."

It wasn't until Sarah glanced down at her son that she realized she was nursing him in plain view of the whole world. Horribly embarrassed, she backed away from the window.

"Sarah! It's too beautiful a day to stay inside. Come riding with me."

She hoped that from where he sat astride the horse, the baby in her arms had covered her more discreetly than she had first feared, but in the future, she would simply have to be more careful. As for riding a horse, surely it was no more outrageous than lying on the sand until the stars began to fade.

She first made certain she was modestly covered, then again rose and went to the window. "I neglected to pack a riding habit."

"You don't need one; anything will do."

Chris meant it too, but when Sarah appeared on the veranda in a black cotton gown a Puritan would have considered severe, he wished he had encouraged her to wear a nightgown. She had twisted her hair into a bun atop her head, and while she was no less beautiful, she looked more like a recent widow than he cared to see.

She carried Michael in the basket, and he dismounted to summon Ramona, who promptly appeared on the veranda. The housekeeper immediately put the basket containing the sleeping child on a low table and pulled up a chair to watch him even more attentively than his mother.

Eager to get away, Chris took Sarah's hand and led her down the steps to his stallion. "This is Winter, and while it's warm here the year round and we never see snow, the name is still a fine one for a white horse."

Now standing beside Winter, whose flowing mane and tail were neatly brushed, she saw not merely a beautiful animal but one of an impressive size. "Do you own three others to represent spring, summer, and fall?"

"Alas, I do not. Please don't be afraid; the man who tends the stable gives him plenty of exercise even when I'm away, and neither of us is likely to be thrown." He swung himself up into the saddle and then leaned down to offer her his hand.

"Just take hold and I'll pull you right up in front of me."

Sarah glanced back toward the veranda, where Mariette and Michelle had jointed Ramona. All three were seated near Michael's basket and were cooing to him softly. "Do you promise to bring me back in a few minutes?"

"You have my word on it." Before her reluctance became a stubborn refusal, he reached out to grab her hand and lifted her onto Winter's back. Encircled by his arms, she rested her back against his broad chest.

"There, I hope you're comfortable. We can just ride through the garden if you'd rather not stray too far from home."

Sarah had ridden in carriages but never on the back of a horse. Quite naturally apprehensive, she wound her fingers in Winter's mane and focused her attention between his ears rather than look down to judge the distance to the ground.

"Are the cane fields close enough to visit?"

Chris urged Winter forward with a tap of his heels.

"Yes, and when we return, I'll work on the cradle. I'm sorry I didn't have one on hand."

"You needn't apologize; it's not the type of thing a bachelor would think to include in his furnishings."

"Perhaps not."

Chris waited until they were away from the house, and then he could no longer keep still. "I hope that is not your favorite gown, because quite frankly, it is the ugliest garment I've ever seen."

Sarah turned to look at him, found his mouth much too close, and instantly turned back around. "I've always considered it hideous myself, which is why I don't care a bit if it's ruined when we ride."

"I'm enormously relieved to hear it."

"It was still very rude of you to criticize my clothing. A widow is expected to wear mourning attire for at least a year, and no one cares if it's unattractive."

"Please accept my apologies if I've offended you yet again, but I do care what you wear, Sarah. I'd love to buy you beautiful new gowns, and lacy lingerie, and—"

Last night she had discovered an appealing depth in him, but despite an appalling weakness for his affection, her feelings for him were still fragile at best. That he wished to shower her with expensive gifts was too much.

"I think you had better take me home now, Captain."

"Not unless you promise to burn that dress."

"I shall wear it every day if you do not take me back this instant."

"That's the edge of the cane field just ahead. It grows even taller than corn, perhaps twenty feet high."

"How fascinating. I had no idea you possessed an interest in agriculture."

Chris placed a kiss behind her ear, then plucked the combs from her hair to send her curls tumbling down her back. "You're the only thing that fascinates me."

His deep voice washed through her like the most intimate caress. Relaxing against him, she dipped her head. "Chris, what are we doing?" she whispered.

That she would even refer to them as *we* thrilled him. "We are touring the plantation, because it's the only excuse I could find to hold you." He tightened his arm around her waist. "Do I sound like all of your besotted suitors?"

"There was only Michael; I had no others." She was perched upon his lap with her feet resting atop his left boot, which suddenly struck her as far too intimate a pose. But then, he was always too close. "Now will you please take me home?"

Chris was too puzzled to honor their agreement just yet. He could not understand why she had not been the belle of Charleston, where dozens of young men should have been lined up for a chance to kiss her. Unless, of course, her father had insisted that she refuse all party invitations. Certain that must have been exactly what had happened, he disliked the man all the more.

"Am I only the second man you've kissed?"

"Yes, but then, respectable young ladies are not allowed to take as many lovers as you undoubtedly have, sir."

"I've not kept a tally, but it's not nearly as many as you apparently think."

Sarah raised her hands to cover her ears. "Don't you dare tell me a word about any other woman. I refuse to listen. Now, if you do not wish me to risk breaking my neck leaping down from this horse, you'll take me back home."

Chris reluctantly turned Winter toward the house, but he did not believe their first ride had gone all that badly. Tomorrow he would take her a little farther, and a little farther the day after that. When she dropped her hands, he nuzzled her ear.

"You see, I'm taking you back just as I promised."

"If that was a fair sample of how well you keep your promises, I shall take Winter out by myself tomorrow."

Chris pulled her close in an enthusiastic hug. "You'd do it, too, wouldn't you? I swear, while I was struck by your beauty, it's your spirit I love. You should have been born a queen of some splendid but isolated country where I would be the only captain to ever arrive at your shores."

He had just given her an intriguing idea for a book, and while she had abandoned her original idea based on her own experience, she rather liked the thought of creating a fantasy world.

"You would have become my prisoner then," she suggested with an impish smile. "I might have tossed you into my dungeon and forgotten you."

He again tightened his grasp on her waist. "Never. You would have made me a duke, so that we could wed."

Sarah turned to look up at him. "Would you have been a devoted husband, or would you have quickly become bored with my kingdom and sailed away?"

She had been teasing, but when a shadow crossed his gaze, she knew exactly what he had been thinking. "Oh, Chris, I know we won't stay here forever. You needn't pretend that we will."

He had not realized he was so transparent, but with a woman as perceptive as she, he doubted he would ever be able to keep any secrets. Fortunately, he did not wish to. "Let's just enjoy every day," he suggested. But he looked forward to the nights with a longing he dared not name.

Chapter Twelve

Chris left Sarah by the steps to the veranda and walked Winter around to the stable. Henri, who cared for his horses with a remarkable devotion, was a grandfather of twelve. He also bred his own mares to Winter and sold the foals. Chris was aware of what was happening, but when he was so seldom in residence, he saw no point in firing Henri when his replacement would undoubtedly do exactly the same thing and not take nearly such good care of the horses.

He spent the rest of the day in his workshop fashioning the cradle. It was a simple but elegant design that showed off the beauty of the wood grain. He secured the pieces with pegs and carefully sanded the rockers to achieve a perfect balance. Very proud of his efforts, he carried the cradle to Sarah's room and knocked lightly at the door.

Sarah was still clad in the black dress, but her hair had remained loose and floated over her shoulders. "You've already finished!" she exclaimed. "Oh, Chris, it's absolutely beautiful. I didn't expect you to complete it so quickly."

Her ecstatic smile warmed him clear through. While

the cradle had not been a challenge, he was pleased to have delighted her. "I made it of sufficient size to last Michael a while. A firm pillow will make a fine mattress."

He carried it into her room and placed it beside the bed, which might have been the four-poster Sarah had expected to find in London. Michael, who was lying in the middle of the high bed wide awake, watched him with a curiosity Chris was certain he had inherited from his mother.

"May I hold him a moment?" he asked.

"Please do." Sarah had not realized men might be charmed by babies who were not their own. That Chris might very well be the only father Michael would ever know created a painful lump in her throat. She crossed to the open window and focused on the garden rather than the sorrow that was never more than a single breath away.

"It's nearly sundown," she commented absently.

"Yes, it is. I'm sorry if you felt neglected. What have you done all day?"

"I took Michael through the garden and down to the lagoon, but he slept most of the time. And no, I did not feel neglected."

She had also recorded her thoughts in her journal, for having missed that opportunity with her late husband, she wished to confide every detail from her son's birth to that very hour. She intended to keep those thoughts private as well.

Chris carried Michael to her side. "We can dress for dinner and dine here tonight, or I'll catch us some fish and roast them on the beach. Which would you prefer?"

Sarah took Michael from his arms. "I believe fresh air to be beneficial for a baby, or at least it ought to be, so it might be best if we dined on the beach."

"I'll need a moment to rinse the sawdust from my hair and catch the fish, and then I'll come for you."

"We'll wait right here."

Chris barely brushed his lips across hers before leaving, but on the off chance that the fish weren't biting, he stopped to request Madame LeFleur prepare them another picnic supper.

"You ought to hire a scullery maid," she scolded crossly. "I can prepare the meals when there are only a few of us here to eat, but if you plan to fill the house with your women, I will need more help in the kitchen."

Chris stared at her coldly, but she did not even flinch. "I've no intention of filling this house with anyone other than our children once Mrs. Hadley and I are wed, provided that she'll have me. For the time being, have Mariette and Michelle assist you, but I expect you to do your best under the horrible burden of our presence. If that's simply impossible, it's a new cook I'll need to hire, not a scullery maid."

He left her sputtering incoherently but obviously convinced any further criticism of his guest would result in her prompt dismissal.

Taking advantage of their informal setting, Sarah licked her fingers before reaching for her napkin. "I don't believe I've ever tasted a dorado, but it's a truly delicious fish—or perhaps it's merely the way you've prepared it."

Chris was delighted to see her display more of an appetite. "I can't take credit for the taste when all I did was toss it on the grill. Are you sure you wouldn't like some wine? It is French, of course, which you may be unable to swallow, but I wanted to at least offer more than tepid tea."

He was seated in front of her tonight, and she enjoyed

being able to read his expression. Michael slept in his basket, and she was rather sleepy herself. She had worn a nightgown over her chemise, and brushed a few crumbs from her lap.

"Thank you, but I'd rather not have wine no matter what its source. Perhaps you'll have time tomorrow to take me through the garden. There were so many exquisite flowers I couldn't name."

"I may not be able to name them myself, but I'll certainly try. Ramona tends the garden, but until you learn to speak French—"

"Did you not understand the first time I refused that I will never study the language?"

"Someday you may change your mind." He pulled apart a roll and tossed a bite into his mouth. "Would you object if I spoke to Michael in French?"

"Go right ahead. He understands neither English nor French at this point."

"True, but I mean later, when he begins to talk."

"You're being presumptuous again, Captain, and I'd rather not plan past tomorrow."

He leaned forward slightly. "What about tonight? Shouldn't we have made plans for more than a picnic supper?"

His sly smile indicated that he already had. "I'm sure it's too soon for what you obviously have in mind. So please think of another entertainment."

Chris was uncertain whether she was referring to her husband's death or her son's birth, but he had not allowed himself to even dream they would make love that night. It certainly wouldn't be a moment too soon for him, but whatever her reason, he respected her reticence. Still, it did not mean they couldn't exchange some affection.

He was in his shirtsleeves, and lay back on the blanket to prop his head on his hands and be even more comfortable. "I'm not usually a man of unlimited patience, but I'll make an exception where you're concerned. I'd like nothing better than to make love to you all night long, but I'll wait for you to come to me."

Sarah had not known such a thing was even possible. "All night? Are you simply bragging again, or do you routinely spend that much time?"

"I've no set routine, Sarah, and no, I've not devoted that many hours to anyone else. But I'd need at least that much time with you."

"Should I be flattered?"

"Definitely."

"No, I believe it would be more prudent to wait and see just how well you keep your promise."

Her voice held a delicious husky edge, as it so often did when she chose to be provocative. His hopes soaring, he offered a suggestive hint of his own. "There are many ways to make love, Sarah. We should try them all."

She raised her brows slightly, for as usual she thought he was at least stretching the truth, if not boldly ignoring it. "How is it we so easily stray into such improper conversations?"

"Improper? Good Lord, I had no idea. Do you suppose someone will report us to the king?"

"Of course not. Why should he concern himself with anything we do?"

"Careful, Mrs. Hadley, that's the Patriots' argument." He sat up to again face her squarely.

"There's always a warning note in your voice when you call me Mrs. Hadley, but I do believe the Patriots' complaints are somewhat more complex."

"Yes, indeed, but . . ." He took a deep breath, intending to impart an eloquent defense of the cause, but then, sensing how poorly she would respond, he let it go. "Tonight is too perfect to waste on politics. Tell me what you think of Martinique. Could you be content living here?"

Finished eating, Sarah twisted her napkin between her hands, and then still took her time before responding. "Contentment is fleeting, so even if I loved the island, everything could change in a heartbeat. But you're the one who's fought for independence for the Colonies. Why would you prefer living here to Virginia?"

"I don't. This is merely a temporary refuge."

He could have been describing her marriage, how she had fled to a place of safety instead of great happiness, wonderful though Michael had been, and the sadness of that thought brought a sudden chill. "I'm afraid it's getting too cold for Michael to remain here. I need to take him back to the house."

Chris stood with her, but in his view, the night was as pleasant as the previous evening when they had tarried at the lagoon far later. He blamed himself for reminding her of the war, which seemed to be the eventual topic no matter where their conversation began.

"You carry the baby and I'll clean up here and bring everything else," he offered with more good humor than he had known he possessed. Before he had tossed the remains of their picnic into the basket, she had already crossed the sand.

"Damn it all!" he swore under his breath. Frustrated his best effort to provide another wonderfully romantic evening had come to naught, he kicked sand into the still glowing coals at the bottom of the fire pit and left the grill in place to cool. He shoved the cork into what truly was an excellent bottle of wine, and followed her up to the house fearing it would be a very long evening indeed.

But there was a black horse tied in front of the house, and a man he recognized awaiting him on the veranda. The gray-haired fellow was barrel-chested but with legs so short he rocked from side to side as he hurried down the steps to greet him.

"Captain, sir, I came just as soon as I heard you were home." He turned his tricorn hat in his hands and glanced over his shoulder. As an added precaution, he peeked behind Chris before he continued. "I've business of a most private sort, and I would not dream of inviting myself into your home, but—"

Chris gestured toward the steps. "Mr. MacBurney, isn't it?"

"Yes, sir, it is, and it's good of you to remember me." He followed Chris into the house and, once they had reached the study, took the offered chair and sat forward. "Now, I supply all manner of privateers what comes to Martinique, but you have never cheated me, which I can't say for many of the others."

Chris had left the blanket and basket on the veranda, but he still held the wine. "Would you prefer brandy, Mr. MacBurney, or wine?"

"Neither, thank you, for I must ride straight home on our curving roads." He laughed briefly at his own joke, then hurried on. "Have you by chance met the Marquis de Lafayette?"

"Unfortunately, I've not had the honor, but the last I heard, he was fighting in Virginia." Chris sat down behind his desk and, while tempted to uncork the bottle and pour the contents straight down his throat, he placed it unopened near the tray holding the decanter of brandy.

"Yes, sir, Lafayette and his men are there still, but we'll soon be having even more of the French with us, which is a wondrous blessing. That's why I'm here tonight. The French Admiral DeGrasse has been in our waters with a fleet of warships since the last of April. I heard tell he's bound for the Colonies, so before he buys every last crumb and sip in both St. Pierre and Port Royal, I thought you'd want to resupply the *Island Belle*."

While most welcome, Chris found MacBurney's news difficult to accept. "Just how many warships is DeGrasse commanding?"

"Twenty ships of the line, sir, plus transport vessels. So you see, there is no time to waste in purchasing your supplies."

Chris nodded thoughtfully. If the French were prepared to engage British Admiral Thomas Graves's fleet with such a large force, then he intended to be with them. He was thrilled by the prospect, but the woman he adored was upstairs, and he hated to consider her reaction. For the moment, the less she knew the better.

"Thank you for coming here tonight, Mr. MacBurney. I appreciate hearing your news."

He quickly wrote brief instructions for Rob Corliss, signed the heavy vellum with his usual flourish, and blotted the ink. After folding the note, he stood and handed it to the enterprising merchant. "Please give Mr. Corliss my authorization. He'll provide the list of what's needed and arrange for payment."

MacBurney slipped it into his coat pocket. "Thank you, Captain. Should you wish another service, I'll be pleased to do my best for you."

"Yes, there is one thing. Send word when Admiral De-

Grasse's departure for the Colonies is imminent. Come straightaway, and I'll reward you for your trouble."

"That I will, sir; you may count on it."

Chris walked him to the front door and waited until MacBurney had ridden away to cross the veranda and take a seat on the steps. Despite what he had insisted to Sarah, and even with an alliance with France, the war had not been going well for the Patriots. Washington was a masterful general, but even he could not supply his troops from thin air. Nor could he keep soldiers who were weary to the bone from simply going home. If the French were now sending warships and fresh troops, it was not merely a blessing, as MacBurney believed, but a miracle that would save them all.

He wanted very badly to believe Admiral DeGrasse's fleet was not mere rumor, but he would wait until he actually sighted the masts of the impressive French warships before he made his final plans. Until then, he could only dream.

Sarah had nursed Michael, but unlike all other nights, rather than promptly falling asleep, he had begun to cry. She had found the perfect pillow with a soft linen slip for his cradle and was eager to use it, but she could not even put him down while he was so unhappy. When Chris rapped lightly at their connecting door, she hurried to open it.

"He won't stop crying, and I'm so afraid he's fallen ill."

Chris touched the baby's forehead. "He's not feverish. Sometimes babies suffer from colic, which I believe is simply a fancy name for a stomachache. I'll hold him for a while." He took Michael from her arms, laid him against his shoulder, patted his back, and walked him slowly up and down the room. While the baby did not quiet immediately, gradually his cries softened, and after giving a wide yarn, he closed his eyes and fell asleep.

"There, that's all he needed," Chris whispered. "Shall I put him in the cradle?"

"Wait just a minute please," Sarah begged. "I don't want him to wake and be frightened."

"No, of course not," he agreed. "Why don't you brush your hair and get ready for bed? I'll just take him into my room." He turned and walked back through the door. Sarah followed.

"This is so easy for you," she complained in an anxious whisper. "But I worry constantly that I'm doing everything wrong."

"You're a very loving mother and you're doing fine. You need more sleep, though. With Michael nursing every few hours, I don't know how you manage to stay awake all day."

Sarah had given up all hope of banning that topic and simply shrugged. "I have no choice now, do I?"

Chris turned and walked back toward her. "If you'll agree, I'll be happy to employ a wet nurse. There must be a recent mother among my workers' wives who could nurse Michael as well as her own child."

"No, absolutely not." She shook her head so vigorously her flying curls resembled Medusa's snakes. "I won't even consider it. Michael is my son, and I'll be the one to care for him."

"It was merely a suggestion," Chris replied. "I don't want caring for Michael to be too difficult for you. If you become exhausted, you'll be the one to fall ill."

Chris was now rubbing the baby's back, and as always

Sarah envied how relaxed he was with her son. "I just didn't realize—" she began hesitantly.

Her anguish was too painful to observe, and Chris slipped his free hand around her shoulders. "No one realizes how much care a baby requires until they have one, and perhaps new mothers need even more attention. Now, let's put little Michael to bed."

He took her hand to lead her back into her room and gently laid Michael in the new cradle. He knelt and gave the cradle a nudge. "It's balanced to rock gently, see?"

Sarah knelt beside him. "It's perfect. Is there anything you can't do exceedingly well?" she whispered.

Chris frowned slightly, as though searching his mind for an example, then broke into a wide grin. "No, actually, nothing worth doing." He stood and drew her up beside him. "Come with me. We'll be close enough to hear the baby if he stirs."

Before she had time to think better of it, he led her through the doorway back into his room and pulled her into his arms. He ran his hands over her shoulders and down her back to press her close.

"You need someone to care for you, my love. You've spent too many years all alone."

Touched that he understood her so well, she relaxed against him, then slid her arms around his waist. He felt rock solid but so warm and alive. He was all muscle and sinew, and yet his cheek was smooth against her own.

He turned slowly as he caressed her arm, the curve of her ear, her neck. He traced her hairline at her temple, then slid his fingers through her curls. She could have leaned against him all night, but then he tilted her chin.

There was nothing tentative in his kiss. She wavered, skirting the narrow bridge between passion and tears.

213

And yet, if everything were as fleeting as she now believed, it would be foolish not to wring every drop of bliss from each moment they shared. He was certainly willing, and she slid her hand between them to caress the whole, hard length of him.

Instantly, he locked his hand around her wrist. "You mustn't do that." He sighed regretfully.

"Why not? You want to make love to me all night, and yet I'm not allowed to touch you? That's very unfair."

He eased her hand to his hip. "Do you recall touching me here?"

"I most certainly do. It prompted you to accuse me of being a spy, but I still believe you rather enjoyed my touch."

"Oh, yes, I did—*do*—but I don't want to hurt you."

He had moved her hand, but she now grazed her hip-bone across his pelvis. He moaned way back in his throat, but she refused to stop. "If there are so many ways to make love, why not show me one that won't cause me any harm?"

He knew what he wanted to do, but he feared he would shock her so badly she might never come near him again. "There's no rush," he assured her, and after loosening his cuffs, he tugged his shirt off over his head.

She leaned close to lick a leathery nipple.

"Sarah!" he hissed, for the shout he almost gave might have wakened Michael.

"What? Am I not allowed to touch you there either?" She regarded him with a wide, innocent gaze, while her smile was tinged with mischief. She slid her fingertips through the wiry curls fanned across his chest. "What about this?"

He laughed and gave up all hope of controlling her. Instead, he took a step back, sat down on the bench at the foot of his four-poster bed, and yanked off his boots and socks. "There's a wildness in you that a man would be a fool to try to tame."

She stepped between his outstretched legs, rested her hands on his shoulders, and slid her thumbs along his neck. "Is that a complaint or a compliment?"

"A bit of both." He caught her hands as he stood, led her around to the side of the bed and, sitting down again, pulled her up beside him. He leaned across her to force her back against the pillows. "Comfortable?"

"Almost." She reached up to untie the ribbon at his nape and like ebony silk, his hair spilled through her fingers. She had been so afraid her weakness for him would betray her, but there was no danger now that he had become so dear. "Kiss me," she begged, before pulling him down into her arms.

He covered her mouth in a luscious kiss that he deepened so easily, it might have gone on for hours had there been no need to breathe. He placed his next kiss in the hollow of her throat, the next along her exposed shoulder. She moaned in a soft purr and pressed against him to caress his whole body with her own.

"I just want to kiss you tonight," he whispered against her ear. He kissed her eyelids, her lashes, her cheeks, her chin. Then he drew her fingertips into his mouth to suck gently one at a time.

Sarah was beginning to see how he could indeed consume an entire night making love, but she could not lie still. She caught one of his hands and drew his thumb into her mouth. He closed his eyes, and when he opened them, desire was so bright in his gaze, he appeared feverish.

She had neglected to retie the ribbon at her neckline,

and she opened her nightgown in a blatant invitation and touched her left breast. "Kiss me here."

Her breasts truly were exquisite, with pale areolas and sweetly puckered pink nipples. It did not even occur to him to refuse. He was no babe who needed to suckle, but a man who knew precisely how to kiss and lick the fullness of her breasts as well as the sensitive buds.

She arched her back into his whisper-soft kisses and slid her fingers through his flowing hair to hold him closer still. The windows were wide open to fill the room with the perfume of a thousand flowers, while birds whose song she didn't recognize chirped happily in the distance.

"This truly is paradise," she whispered, and while she ached for more of him, Michael was not yet a month old, and she wanted to cry Chris's name in passion, not pain. She did not want him to have that memory of their first time together, either; but when he leaned back to pull her nightgown off over her head, she was filled with such a languid warmth, she had to rely upon him to do no more than kiss her.

"You have the most beautiful skin," he breathed out against her navel. "It's as smooth as cream, and you taste like our cinnamon soap. Would you mind if I kissed your toes?"

Amused, she shifted her hips to twist down into the bed. "I'm afraid you'll tickle me, and if I burst into raucous laughter, it will wake Michael."

Chris moved down and kissed the inside of her ankle. "What about here; does this tickle?"

"No, that's rather pleasant, but you ought not neglect my knee."

"No, certainly not." He then kissed her calf. He

doubted her proper British officer husband would have introduced her to the type of affection he had begun to believe she might welcome. He changed positions again to spread tender kisses up the inside of her thighs.

"I'm just going to kiss you tonight, love, that's all."

"Hmm." When he gave such wonderful fluttering kisses, she had no wish to object. When he reached the top of her thighs and combed the soft triangle of curls, she was lost in his knowing caress. Then she felt the hot flick of his tongue, and it was too late to demand he stop—or to even want him to.

He slid her knees over his shoulders to angle her hips toward his mouth. He was afraid to slide his fingers up into her, but he hoped slow, wet kisses would be enough. He listened to her initial startled gasp turn to deep moans and kept coaxing her toward a climax so stunning he felt it shudder clear to her pretty pink toes.

When he relaxed his hold on her, she lay sprawled on his bed in a satisfied heap. He had intended for it to be enough, but with her, it wasn't. He quickly loosened his breeches to free himself and then aligned his cock with her cleft. He slid ever so slowly, his motion controlled, to again caress her most sensitive flesh. She opened her eyes, her glance dazed, but then she reached up to draw him down into a kiss so hungry it lapped at his very soul.

He wanted her too badly to torture himself for long and, rather than break his word, he came against the hollow of her stomach. A long while passed before he could bear to loosen his embrace and roll to the side. Chagrined not to have been able to show more restraint, he grabbed his shirt from the floor and wiped her clean, then again lay down beside her and drew her into his arms.

She thought he had a most unusual definition of what

constituted a kiss, but when they fit together so comfortably, she was inclined to be as liberal as he.

Chris heard Michael's first whimper, and he got up to change the infant's diaper. He carried him in to Sarah, who was sleeping so peacefully he hated to wake her. "Sarah, my love, can you sit up?"

She feared he had melted her bones, but after covering a wide yawn, she propped herself against the pillows. Chris had pulled on a pair of drawers, and she was back in her nightgown, which came as a complete surprise.

She reached out to take her son. "Please talk to me so that I'll stay awake. Most birds don't sing at night. What kind are those?"

Chris sat down beside her, stretched out his legs, and leaned back against the headboard. "They're actually tiny frogs, but those new to Martinique always mistake them for birds."

"Frogs? How curious." Sarah closed her eyes and listened carefully, but they still sounded like birds to her. "I didn't have a chance to ask, but who was the man waiting to speak with you? I saw him pacing the veranda and, not wanting to again be mistaken for your mistress, I circled the house and entered through the garden."

Chris had hoped MacBurney had arrived after she had gone upstairs, but he was very sorry she had rushed to hide. Her honor was important to him, even if she now shared his bed. Her politics, however, were another matter entirely.

"His name's MacBurney, and I've done business with him in the past. He saw the *Island Belle* in port and came to sell me provisions."

"He traveled over supposedly treacherous mountain roads at night simply to do business?"

"Yes. As you might suspect, as a French colony, Martinique is a haven for privateers. MacBurney is an ambitious fellow who hoped to beat out his competition to resupply the *Island Belle*."

Sarah cuddled Michael a little closer. She smelled like Chris, and while the lush garden scented the bedroom, a far more primitive odor also hung in the air.

"We just arrived here," she pointed out warily. "Are you already making plans to leave?"

Chris scrubbed his hands over his face while he searched for the right words. "I'm a privateer, and while I've no wish to encounter another fierce tropical storm in the next few months, you can't have expected me to remain here indefinitely."

That a merchant would pay a late-night call at a captain's isolated home to sell flour and beans made as much sense to her as singing frogs. Chris was up to something, and because he had reminded her that he was a privateer, as if she could have forgotten, it could not possibly be anything good.

"What I expect from you, Captain, is the truth," she announced calmly. Now wide awake, she tightened her grasp on her son, moved off the opposite side of the bed, and returned to her own room.

Chris could have followed, but to swear that he had already told her the truth would have only compounded the lie.

Chapter Thirteen

"This waxy red flower is an anthurium," Chris explained. "It doesn't look real, does it?"

"No, it's wonderfully strange," Sarah agreed.

Michael slept in his basket on a nearby bench while they toured the garden. After her bath, Sarah had dressed in her navy blue gown and taken the time to style her hair far more attractively than she had yesterday. Chris was doing his best to provide an informative tour of his garden, but she was far too distracted to appreciate the unusual variety of flowers growing there.

Rather than feign further interest, she gave up the pretense. "I'm really not in the mood to discuss flowers. I know I'm the enemy, Chris. You needn't confide in me, but I don't want to wake up some morning and discover you've gone back to sea and left Michael and me alone here."

"I'd never do that," he denied emphatically, shocked that she could even think such a thing. "I'd not strand you anywhere, and most especially not here, where you can't even converse with the servants."

He lowered his voice and leaned close. "I know I

pleased you last night, so why do you have such a low opinion of me this morning?"

"Did you say these unusual white blossoms are called passion flowers?"

"Yes. There are other vines with the purple variety. Some people consider them prettier. Now if you just answered my question with a flower metaphor, I didn't understand. Try again."

"I've never been adept at crafting clever metaphors. I merely meant that passion is one thing, and looking out for my own best interests and those of my son is quite another. Forgive me if I merely confused you. You're a superb lover, but even in this paradise, the world is bound to intrude. When it does, if it hasn't already, at least do me the courtesy of allowing me to make my own plans."

Had she added another word, Chris would have begun ripping flowering vines out of the ground by the roots. "Do you actually believe I'd casually toss you aside the way some men treat their mistresses? That's simply insulting. Would you care to marry me today? I'm sure it can be arranged."

Dumbfounded by his clumsy proposal, if it could even be described as such, Sarah felt more like slapping him than dissolving into joyful tears. "I don't believe either of us is in the proper frame of mind to discuss marriage, at least not this morning."

"I don't care whether we are or not. I'm serious. Let's get married today."

Before she could make herself even more clear, Ramona stepped out into the garden and announced Rob Corliss's arrival. Sarah comprehended only the name, but after yesterday's late-night visitor, she was not surprised.

"Perhaps he also wishes to discuss provisions," she

suggested. "Please don't keep him waiting on my account, and wish him a good day for me."

"Stay right here; I won't be long."

Sarah sat down on the bench to watch her son sleep, but she feared that in an effort to settle things with Chris, she had only made everything worse. That had not been her intention, nor had she wanted to goad him into a marriage proposal. He had brought up the subject himself while they were on board his ship; but she had taken it as a boast, as though it were a challenge for him, rather than out of any deep regard for her.

Now he spoke of love, and it flavored his kisses, but everything between them had been so rushed—which was entirely his fault. Her parents thought she was on her way to England to be with her late husband's family; she absolutely refused to consider how they would react should she reappear wed to a privateer. She would never include such an outrageous pairing in a book because their romance would never be believed.

Perhaps that was her problem, she mused. Other than an adorable child she could cuddle in her arms, nothing seemed real—not a swaggering seafaring bandit nor this wondrous paradise. It was all a mere dream, from which she would surely wake all too soon.

Rob paced the study and spoke excitedly. "DeGrasse's *Ville de Paris* is the largest warship afloat. She carries more than a hundred guns. Can you imagine what it must be like to sail on a ship of that size?"

"Exhilarating, to be sure," Chris commented dryly.

Rob turned on his heel. "What do you plan to do, stand atop Mt. Pelée and watch the French fleet sail past?"

"No, we'll sail with them. While DeGrasse will most likely order us to stay out of his way, I don't want to miss what is sure to be the largest naval battle of the war."

"I'd hoped you'd say that. I'll have the *Island Belle* ready with plenty of munitions. What will you tell Mrs. Hadley? Do you plan to leave her here?"

"No, I'll have to take her home."

"To Charleston? The British hold little more of South Carolina than the city now. If we landed down the coast, she could be sent overland by coach."

"No, I mean to take her home to Virginia." He could see no other way to keep track of Sarah when winning her hand appeared to be well nigh impossible. "I realize it will be difficult."

"Impossible is more like it, sir. I'd leave her here."

"You would, would you?" Chris was too upset with Sarah to laugh at how little Rob understood. "Go on back to port. I've spoken with MacBurney, and he'll contact you about supplies. We won't need to speak again until DeGrasse appears."

"As you wish, but I wonder if I might bid Mrs. Hadley a good day before I leave?"

"You can only try," Chris offered truthfully. "Let's see if she's still in the garden."

Even knowing Sarah to be unpredictable, Chris was astonished to find her on her hands and knees beneath the trellis supporting the passion flower vines. "Rob hoped to say good morning, my dear," he called in warning. "Have you lost something?"

"What? Oh, no, I was merely searching for the tiny frogs you mentioned." Embarrassed to have been caught in such an unguarded moment, Sarah stood so quickly, she snagged her hair on the trellis. Chris stepped forward to help free her, but fearing her hairstyle was simply ruined, she removed the combs and shook out her curls.

"Good morning, Mr. Corliss, how are you today?" she asked, hoping to have recovered at least a modicum of decorum.

Simply entranced by the lovely, if slightly disheveled, young woman, the mate held his hat pressed to his chest. "I am well, Mrs. Hadley. You appear to be enjoying Martinique."

"It would be difficult not to be happy here," she responded sweetly. Despite being flustered, she was pleased with her reply, which while cordial, veiled her true feelings. "I hope you did not have to endure too arduous a carriage ride to visit us."

"Why, no, I rigged a sail on one of our long boats and sailed here."

"We wish you an equally swift journey on your return," Chris interjected pointedly. He stood with his hands behind his back and rocked back on his heels.

"Well, yes, thank you." He stepped closer to the bench to gaze down at the sleeping child. "I must say, Mrs. Hadley, your little boy appears to have grown in the two days since I last saw him. He's sure to be a handsome lad."

"Thank you, Mr. Corliss, good-bye." Sarah tried not to laugh as Chris took the attentive mate's arm and escorted him right out of the garden. Perhaps they still had business to discuss on the way to the lagoon, but it was more likely that Chris simply wanted him gone.

She sat down on the bench and covered a yawn. She had felt so well-rested when she had awakened that morning, but now the day was growing warm and making her sleepy. She had almost nodded off when Chris returned and sat down beside her.

He took her hand in a fond clasp. "I'm sorry we were interrupted. Now, while I doubt that we could find an Anglican priest here on Martinique, there has to be a magistrate who could marry us. We're closer to St. Pierre than Port Royal; what do you say to our making our way there this afternoon?"

"On a twisting mountain road with Michael crying the whole way?" she asked. "No, I'd rather not."

She appeared merely peeved with him, so he persisted. "Are you objecting to the journey, or to taking me as your husband?"

Sarah released an exasperated sigh. "I may marry you someday, Chris, just not today."

He glanced away but found no solace in the colorful garden. "With such a vague answer, it's difficult to hold much hope."

"Please, let's not quarrel. I didn't refuse you, I merely asked for more time." She still wore Michael's ring and slipped her hand from Chris's to twist it on her finger. "You needn't worry that I'll leave you for Rob Corliss or any other man. That has to be enough for the moment."

"Unfortunately, it isn't," Chris swore darkly. "Now you must excuse me. Rather than take you for another ride on Winter, I want to work on your rocking chair. I doubt I'll see you before tonight. Let's plan to dine here for a change."

Clearly, he could barely contain his anger, and it showed in the taut line of his jaw. Sarah fought to control her own temper. "Dinner here would be lovely. Would you please inform Madame LeFleur so that she'll have sufficient time to prepare more than a picnic?"

"Of course. I'd not overlook such an obvious detail."

Sarah had done her best to protect his feelings, but he

was sulking as though her every word were an intentional affront. She would definitely welcome some time away from him.

As she watched Chris walk toward the house, the pride in his bearing was unmistakable. There was so much more to him than stubborn pride, but clearly he was seldom crossed, and she did it all too often. Perhaps by the evening he would accept that she would not be rushed into marriage—but that he had not kissed her good-bye still hurt.

In the worst of moods, Chris lumbered about his workshop kicking scraps of wood out of his way. He had crafted several chairs and could easily add rockers for Sarah. He had mahogany left from the house's interior paneling; it was beautiful wood and would make a fine chair.

He had always enjoyed working with wood, whether it was building a ship or a footstool. He liked the feel of it in his hands and how easily it could be shaped. But as he began to assemble the pieces for Sarah's chair, he could not get the proportions right. The legs were either too short or too long, and the seat and back refused to fit together properly.

He had to stop to sharpen the blade on his plane, then nicked his thumb in the process. He used his handkerchief to stem the flow of blood, but he had never had such a difficult time building anything. Giving up for the moment, he lay his tools on his workbench and walked down to the lagoon, where he planned to just sleep in the shade.

To his utter dismay, he found Sarah there swimming in her chemise. She was near the shore and waved to him as she made her way slowly through the surf. Even without the sea water dripping from her hair, her chemise was soaked and transparent. There was no mistaking the roundness of her breasts, nor her tightly puckered nipples. She had long slender legs, but all he saw was the tantalizing V where they met her body.

She resembled a mythical goddess born in the sea, and yet there was nothing remote in her expression. She simply looked carefree, as though she swam in the lagoon every day. He quickly looked around for Michael's basket, and found it beneath a palm tree where he must have walked right past the child when he left the path. But that took only a moment, and then he could not stop staring at Sarah until she was so close that the water dripping down her legs splashed on his boots.

"Have you already finished my chair?" she asked.

For a moment he could not even recall what a chair was; then he realized how foolish he must look and cleared his throat. "Not yet. I thought perhaps I should have taken a few measurements to make certain it fits you perfectly."

"All right, but I shall have to bathe and dress again first."

"No, come with me to my workshop just as you are."

Sarah saw the real invitation in his gaze but refused to lose herself with him as she had last night amid scattered hammers, saws, and nails. That was simply too much to expect. She dared not be so blunt, however, with a man as sensitive as he.

"I'm afraid your workshop might be too dusty for Michael, so please, let's just wait."

Chris caught her arm before she could continue on her way. "I frequently remind myself that while you may be wise beyond your years, you're still awfully young. Perhaps it did not occur to you that if Rob Corliss could sail into this lagoon, so could any other man. You ought not to swim all alone."

Sarah turned to face the lagoon and raised her hand to shade her eyes while she assessed the view. "We can see for miles. Is there a boat on the horizon?"

"No, not at this moment there isn't," he observed, clearly annoyed that there weren't half a dozen.

"There wasn't one earlier either, or I'd not have entered the water. Nor did I leave Michael for long. The sea is very pleasant. Would you like me to keep watch while you swim?"

"No one is likely to attack me!" he exclaimed, and she jumped back so quickly, he knew that he had frightened her. "I'm sorry, I didn't mean to yell, but—"

"Yes, I understand, you're used to standing on the deck of the *Island Belle* and shouting orders, but it doesn't work with me."

She walked around him and over the warm sand to fetch Michael's basket. Then she gazed back at him. "Until tonight then, Captain."

He wanted to believe the promise in her voice, but even more, he longed to believe that she would soon come to care for him.

Sarah came downstairs for dinner wearing the beautiful black satin gown she had worn the day Chris had captured the *Beatrice,* but now it was laced tightly to show off her narrow waist. Her curls were again coiled atop her head, while a few enticing tendrils tickled her nape. She had seriously debated the wisdom of looking her best with a man who adored her even soaking wet, but then Chris came forward to take Michael's basket from her arms and she swiftly decided the effort had been well worth her time.

Chris was dressed for the evening in a fine suit that was as rich a black as his hair. His shirt was a snowy white and his waistcoat pearl gray. The lace at his throat and cuffs made his deep tan all the more appealing. There was a clear warning in his gaze, however, that he was approaching the limit of his patience where she was concerned.

She smiled as though they had never exchanged a cross word. "Michael should sleep all through dinner, but I didn't want to leave him in my room all alone."

"No, he's always welcome." Chris took the infant's basket and carried him into the dining room.

The mahogany table would have easily accommodated eighteen, but fortunately Sarah's place had been set at his right rather than at the far end. The tablecloth was a lovely ivory damask, and a silver candelabra with six glowing candles lit their places, which were set with ornate sterling silver. A crystal vase held a magnificent spray of white orchids.

Sarah waited to comment until Chris had placed Michael on the chair to her right. "You are always handsome, Captain, but tonight you can only be described as dashing."

He wanted to pay her an equally extravagant compliment, but her elegant black gown was too vivid a reminder of her wish to remain a widow rather than become his wife. He held her chair and, once she was seated, leaned down to kiss her cheek.

"Thank you, but I should have been the one to pay the first compliment. I hope I've not insulted you yet again."

"Not at all. Everything is so beautiful tonight. Have you hosted many wonderful parties here?"

"No, this is the first. Did you entertain in Charleston?"

"No. Michael and I lived in his room above an inn, but we were invited to many lovely parties and elegant balls. I never understood why a war called for such lavish parties, but Charleston is home to many respected Loyalist families, and they were eager to entertain British officers."

Mariette appeared with crab cake appetizers, and Chris thoughtfully waited until Sarah had taken several bites before he continued their conversation. "Did you consider their need to entertain at such a difficult time unseemly?"

"Unseemly is a good word, along with irrelevant and inappropriate." She sat back as Michelle cleared away their plates and returned with a clear consommé. "I hope that doesn't sound too harsh, but I wanted the gatherings to be more than simply an excuse for music and dancing."

He appeared merely thoughtful, but he was eating very little of his dinner. She had been served a refreshing mint tea, but he had taken only a few sips of wine from his silver goblet. "I'm sorry," Sarah apologized quickly. "I didn't mean to belittle your efforts tonight."

"You haven't, and I'm the one who asked about Charleston, remember? I've not been to a formal party in years, and I've not missed them either. It wasn't that the young ladies in Virginia weren't charming, but like you, I felt it was a very poor use of my time."

"Yes, that was precisely my complaint. Everyone else had such fun, but I often felt as though I were standing outside on the terrace, looking in."

Michelle removed their soup bowls, and while they heard a plate clatter to the floor and break in the pantry, she soon reappeared with an avocado and pear salad sprinkled with pecans.

"Have you ever tasted an avocado?" Chris asked. "They're really quite good."

Sarah agreed. "Yes, everything is delicious." Confident she would enjoy the pear, she began with a bite of it before sampling the avocado. "Oh, yes, this is good. Do they grow on vines like squash?"

"No, they grow on a tree that can become so tall, you simply have to wait for the avocados to fall to the ground. The plummeting fruit can actually pose quite a hazard."

She preferred his lazy smile to the strained expression he had worn when she had joined him that evening. "You're teasing me, Captain, but because I am your only guest, I'll not make an issue of it."

"How very kind. I meant to say this earlier, but your gown is stunning with your fair coloring. Have you always worn black?"

"Before I became a widow, you mean? Well, yes. It's a very proper color, restrained, but I did have some prettier, more colorful clothes. I didn't pack them for London, though."

"Because you regarded them as unseemly?" he asked.

"Now we're back where we began. No, wait a minute, that's not quite true. No evening with you is ever dull."

It was Mariette who served the tuna crusted with sesame seeds, and Chris was relieved Madame LeFleur had taken the preparation of a formal dinner so seriously. He would have hated to fire her, but neither would he allow anyone to be disrespectful toward Sarah.

"I may never be dull," he remarked once they had both tasted their tuna, "but I know you haven't always enjoyed my company. I intend to do better from now on."

Sarah reached over to touch his arm. "Please don't

strive to be something other than what you are. It would cheat us both."

He nodded and sat back in his chair. She was the most serious young woman he had ever met, and after having been raised by such a stern father, he could understand why she would welcome a lighthearted suitor. Still, he imagined her husband had looked forward to the very parties she found so tedious, which meant in the long run they were not truly a good match.

Both Mariette and Michelle served the savory roast duck nestled in a bed of parsley-laced rice. "I hope you're fond of duck," he said to Sarah between bites.

"Why, yes, I am, but I'm afraid I've eaten too much and either won't be able to sleep tonight or will be plagued with hideous nightmares."

"I'd not worry about tonight if I were you," he offered with a sly grin.

Sarah knew that suggestive smile too well to mistake his meaning, but she waited to respond to his tantalizing advice until she had swallowed the last bite of an exquisite caramel custard dessert.

"Captain, I hope you won't fear that, though I'm not ready to marry, I'm not inclined to share you bed."

Her comment was so unexpected, and yet so welcome, he nearly choked on his wine. When he at last regained his composure, he hoped he had not misunderstood what she had said. "If after chasing frogs and swimming in the lagoon you'd care to spend more time with me, I'd be delighted."

"There's only one point I wish to make clear," she warned.

Fearing the worst, he held his breath and nodded. "Whatever you like, Mrs. Hadley."

"A mistress is paid for her favors, but I'm not interested in a business proposition. I'll accept nothing from you other than pure emotion. Will you agree to my terms?"

He took a moment to appear to be considering her proposal, which in truth was far more advantageous to him than to her. Finally, he shrugged. "Yes, but I've already given you a cradle, and I don't want it returned. As for the rocking chair, I worked a little longer on it without taking your measurements, but it's meant to make both you and Michael more comfortable. It's not a proper gift for a man to give his mistress, even if you were mine, which you've no desire to be, is that right?"

"Yes, you've understood perfectly. The cradle and chair are merely furnishings for a mother and child. Now I have a question."

"I'm almost afraid to hear it," he replied truthfully.

"You needn't be." She leaned close. "Is it possible for me to kiss you, and I'm using the word very broadly here, the way you kissed me last night?"

Her expression was one of polite interest, as if she were merely curious, and he was very grateful she had not asked that question when he had just taken a sip of wine. "It's a very good thing you're my only guest tonight, my love, because if you'd asked me that in the midst of even the most fascinating assortment of guests, we would have had to excuse ourselves and leave the table."

"Then I may take that as a yes?"

"Yes, indeed. Now, why don't we pretend to be enjoying a stroll through the garden for at least a few minutes."

She turned to pluck Michael from his basket. "I'm afraid you'll have to tour the garden by yourself tonight. We tarried so long over dinner that Michael is awake, and he'll soon be hungry again."

Chris would have liked to have told her to spend as long as she needed with her son, but at that moment he was positive he needed her more.

Sarah removed the black gown and accompanying lingerie, then slipped into her nightgown. She truly was anxious to be with Chris, but unwilling to neglect her son for even a minute, she took extra time to tickle his tiny feet and play with him before he began to nurse. She looked forward to having a rocking chair but now could only walk with him a bit as Chris had done until he was sound asleep. She lay the babe in his cradle and rocked him awhile to make certain his dreams would be sweet.

She brushed out her hair and then knocked softly on the connecting door between her room and Chris's. He opened it almost immediately, and quickly drew her inside. She said, "I'm sorry to keep you waiting, but—"

He muffled her apology with a welcoming kiss that would have been bruising had he not checked his desire. "You are worth the wait," he whispered between tender kisses, loosening the neckline of her nightgown to send it pooling at her feet.

She laughed and reached for the drawstring on his drawers, but he laced his fingers in hers before she had succeeded in loosening the tie. "I believe you're even more handsome without your fine suit, but you're not allowed to be so modest if I'm expected to cavort in the nude."

"I'd hoped to do more than cavort, but we ought to at least dim the lamps."

"You can't be embarrassed. I simply won't allow it."

"I've no reason to hide," he assured her, "but not all women enjoy gazing at men's bodies."

"You have too splendid a physique to garner such silly complaints, Captain, and I know how men look when they're aroused. You'll not frighten me. Although, I do expect you to tell me exactly how to please you."

He closed his eyes and moaned softly. "This has to be a dream."

"When you made love to me, the delicious heat spread all the way to my toes. Will it feel as good for you?"

"Enough, woman," he cautioned, but he could not keep from making a predatory growl as he lifted her into his arms, swung her in a full circle, and then carried her to the bed. He had the spread pulled all the way back so they could lie on freshly ironed sheets. He set her down on the side and then stepped back to peel off his drawers.

"You're such a handsome man, Chris—tall, muscular, yet lean through the hips." When he came back to the side of the bed, she reached out to trace the dark curls that grew in a thin line down his belly, then framed his cock with a thick fringe.

She had brought along the medical book he had shown her. It contained such interesting diagrams of the male body, but when he kissed her as though he had not been in port in years, she knew it was not in anticipation of an anatomy lesson. She needed both hands to encircle his cock, and gently rotated her fingers in opposite directions. He was rock hard, and a pearl of moisture glistened at the tip. She rubbed it away with her thumb.

Her adoring massage sent a bolt of pure sensation clear through him, and he caught her shoulders. "I'm going to have to lie down."

"Well, of course, I want you to be comfortable." She waited until he had stretched out beside her and then leaned over to lick a nipple. He gasped, as he had the night before, and she laved its mate before trailing her fingertips up his inner arm.

"I love touching you, but am I being too bold? I've never flirted behind a fan. In fact, I doubt I could even find one in my trunk."

From her first venomous stare, he had known she would be a magnificent lover. Now her gaze was as soft as her lips, and he was so hungry for her loving touch, he could barely lie still. He pulled her down into his arms and gave silent thanks for her limp wisp of a mother, who had been too timid to fill her head with the nonsense most virgins believed.

"I love everything about you," he swore, and took care not to add that she was a pirate's dream. "Any man you'd shock with your affection isn't worthy of you."

She pressed her lips to the pulse pounding at the base of his throat. That she excited him so easily was an enormous thrill. She spread kisses across his collarbone. "Do you mind if I begin here?"

"You may begin wherever you please, just as long as you begin."

He was laughing way back in his throat, and she dipped her head to brush her long curls over his chest. "I rather thought the end was important too."

"Oh, yes, it is." He ran his fingers through her hair and thought it as pretty as spun gold.

He closed his eyes, but Sarah didn't mind at all if that was how he wished to savor her every kiss and lick, while she enjoyed watching him. She moved lower to straddle his leg, and this time grasped his cock more firmly. When she licked the tip, he arched his back and came clear off the bed, but if he felt any pain, it was the most exquisite kind.

She ran the tip of her tongue up the shaft, tracing the veins, then sucked the smooth, plum-sized head deep into her mouth. He was moaning now, all laughter forgotten as she swirled her tongue around the corona. She freed a hand to rake her nails up his inner thigh and then tenderly thumbed his scrotum.

Chris had known several women who prided themselves on their artful loving, but none had ever touched him with such joyful abandon, nor given him such intense pleasure. Before he lost all control, he caught her hair, then drew her up into his arms and rolled her beneath him.

He slid through her cleft, timing each of his thrusts to his own heartbeat, but when she bucked beneath him, he came against the smoothness of her stomach. Utterly spent, he still could not sleep, for he had no idea how to convince his volatile beloved to marry him before they left Martinique.

He would hide the reason for their departure as long as he possibly could, but both their lives would be so much easier if she would agree to become his wife. "Will you marry me tomorrow?" he whispered against her ear.

Sarah pulled the ribbon from Chris's nape and sighed into his glossy hair. "I don't know. I rather like the way you're striving to convince me."

He moved to her side. "Are you simply toying with my affections?"

He was scowling as though it were a serious concern, and she turned her back on him and fluffed her pillow. "I can't marry a man who doubts my sincerity. You might as well have called me a liar. Why don't you go sleep in my room; I don't feel like moving from your bed."

"I don't either," Chris responded, and he pulled her

back against his chest, where he held her until she had to go to Michael. But it was her heart he longed to snare, and she guarded it even more closely than she did her darling son.

Chapter Fourteen

Chris guided Winter toward the shade beneath a coral tree where the ground was scattered with red blossoms, which might just as well have been drops of blood. "We seem to be at an impasse," he remarked solemnly.

They had again left Michael on the veranda with three rapt attendants, and up until then, Sarah had been enjoying their second ride. "Are you referring to the path, or to our perpetual lack of accord?"

He nearly snorted. "We've not been acquainted long enough to describe anything between us as 'perpetual.'"

"You see, that's precisely what I mean. Last night's dinner was superb. Could we agree upon that at least?"

In truth, he had been so involved in their conversation, he could not even recall what had been on the menu. "Yes, the meal was awfully good, as was the company."

"Thank you." Sarah relaxed against him, and his chest provided a solid wall of comfort. "I know I pleased you later too."

"Oh, yes, you were sublime—until I dared speak of marriage."

She absolutely refused to repeat that bitter argument

today. "You'd grow bored with me in a week if I answered, 'Aye, Captain,' each time you ordered me about."

"Is that what you believe I'm doing? Is it so difficult to believe that I have only your best interests at heart?"

When she fell silent, he brushed her curls aside and nuzzled her neck. In truth, she was still a captive, and as much a prisoner as a guest in his home. He just did not want her to consider herself as such and become even more rebellious.

"Most women are such vapid creatures," he confided. "Which isn't their fault. They're raised to please their parents, then their suitors, their husbands, and even their children. I could have had my pick of beautiful young women in Virginia, but when we couldn't even complete a country dance without my wishing the music would end, I wasn't tempted to pursue any.

"Then I found you—or perhaps you were the one to find me—and if we spent the next fifty years together, I cannot imagine a single moment when I'd be bored. Agree with me all you please. You needn't say, 'Aye, Captain,' either. It won't make you any less dear."

Sarah laid her hands over his. They were such handsome and capable hands, definitely a gentleman's. "Thank you, but I suspect there are some important things you've neglected to tell me. But then, I'm not a 'vapid creature' who would be so thrilled by the prospect of marrying you that I'd cease to think."

Now it was Chris who remained silent too long. He intended to take her home to Virginia, which carried a grave risk to them all, but there was absolutely no point in fighting about it for the next month.

"I'm really not the devious sort," he argued as persuasively as he could, considering it was a barefaced lie.

240

His softly voiced comment gave Sarah a moment's pause. While she would never admit to being devious, she did keep her own counsel. She believed he did the same. "I could ask you again what we're doing, but now I'm afraid to look too closely."

When his motives would not bear close scrutiny, he shared her trepidation, but at least her tone was reasonable. He also thought a wise man would swiftly change the subject before the ground beneath him dissolved into quicksand.

"I love coral trees," he told her. "I've taken the seeds home to Virginia and planted some there."

She turned to smile at him. "Is that a metaphor?"

"Possibly. Love often grows from small seeds of affection."

Her feelings for him were far deeper than passing affection, but she had buried the last man she loved and did not want to doom Chris as well. "Some people lack sufficient patience to grow more than weeds."

"I believe we could combine our thoughts and write a truly awful love poem. Let's fight the impulse and ride back to the lagoon to swim."

Sarah brightened instantly. "Oh, yes, let's do."

The joy that lit her expression brought Chris a welcome sense of relief. That she craved the freedom other young women never even thought to pursue was definitely an odd trait to seek in a bride. But when she gave affection with the same unabashed delight, he would not utter a single word of complaint.

When the following days passed without Chris making any further reference to marriage, Sarah assumed they had reached a tacit accord. The lack of animosity brightened their days, and enriched their nights, and she loved the hours past midnight when, accompanied by a frog chorus, they conversed in hushed voices as she nursed her son.

She had few happy memories to share, but Chris told many amusing stories about his childhood. He had grown up in his father's shipyard, and had ventured out in his own little boat as soon as he was old enough to hold a paddle. His younger brother, Stephan, preferred horses to boats, and had spent his childhood exploring their land astride a succession of spotted ponies. While Chris could appreciate the beauty of a mount as fine as Winter, he had never understood why Stephan had shown no interest in the sea until the war began. They had never been particularly close, and now saw each other so seldom, they might have been distantly related rather than brothers.

"My life would have been much simpler had I had an elder brother," Sarah mused aloud. "My father would have concentrated all his energies on him, and I would have been grateful to be ignored."

"You would still be as lovely, but perhaps you'd have been closer to your mother and—"

"That's highly unlikely," she scoffed. Yet she could not help but wonder if a happier young woman would have wed the first man bold enough to propose. It was a disconcerting insight, and she worried that her initial haste to marry might be influencing her decided reluctance to accept Chris's proposal now.

She was still pondering the question the next day when they strolled down to the lagoon. They spread their blanket on the sand where Michael's basket would be shaded by the palms. When they sat down, Chris handed her a small wood carving.

"I'll carve something else for Michael, but this little mule is for you."

Sarah turned it in her hands. It was perhaps four inches tall and fashioned with such marvelous detail that it looked as though it might gallop right off her palm. "You are shameless, Chris, but thank you. This is a perfect keepsake. You made me such a beautiful rocking chair, but I had no idea you liked to carve too. What are you going to carve next?"

"I've not decided. I could build a little barn and make horses, cows, goats, and pigs, or perhaps an ark filled with wild animals like elephants, giraffes, and lions. It will be years until Michael can really play with them, so I could do both. What do you suppose he'd like best?"

"An elephant would fit nicely in a little boy's hand, but I'm sure he'd love whatever you made for him. I love this mule, but if you'd simply ridden by on one, I might not even have noticed you."

"That's impossible," he swore, and drew her into a playful hug.

As they laughed together, she marveled at the lively fun they shared. It was another glorious summer day, and they had planned to swim but, as usual, they would not rush through the afternoon. When he made her so happy, it suddenly struck her as foolish not to marry him.

Her mouth went dry, and she skimmed her tongue over her teeth. "Chris," she began hesitantly, gathering her courage to propose to him if she had to; but he was now gazing out toward the sea with an expression of such undisguised joy, she turned toward the shore.

One afternoon they had seen dolphins leaping into the air, but today a ship had come into view. It was not a sluggish merchantman, nor a sleek schooner like the *Island Belle,* but a French man-of-war in full sail. She had to admit it was a magnificent sight, but while Chris was obviously thrilled, she saw only the ship's destructive threat and felt sick clear through. After overcoming anguishing doubts, she had finally reached a decision that would affect all their lives, and it had seemed the right choice just a few seconds ago. Now it felt so horribly wrong, she was glad she had not caught Chris's attention.

"You seem overjoyed," she commented sadly, "but I don't have to guess where that warship's bound. You must excuse me, I've lost interest in the seaside."

She rose, tossed the little mule into Michael's basket, and carried him away. She knew Chris was too entranced to follow, which made the glimpse into his bloodthirsty soul all the worse. He had cleverly lured her into separating the charming man he was from the violence of his privateer calling. She was appalled to have forgotten for even a minute that her life had not been truly her own since he had claimed her as a diverting bit of booty from the *Beatrice.*

Chris did not follow Sarah because he couldn't—at least, not until he had found a way to describe his plans that wouldn't make her even more furious. Since the night MacBurney arrived, he had paced his workshop and practiced one explanation after another, but none had sounded sufficiently convincing to share with her. There was simply no way to soften the obvious fact that while he had fought the British as a privateer, he now intended to take a far more active role in the war. She could not possibly wish him to succeed, either. That was what hurt most, that she did not think enough of him to at least accept, if not encourage, his commitment to the Patriot cause.

He had not killed her husband, but she had just regarded him with a gaze of such pure loathing, she might just as well have called him a murderer. That he had no way to counter the unspoken insult only served to intensify his dread of their next meeting.

He stood, shook out the blanket, and folded it over his arm. If French warships were circling Martinique, then he could count on Rob to appear soon. This time he would go with his mate and find a way to meet with De-Grasse. He doubted that Sarah would take one of his horses and ride off in the few hours he was away, but he would make a point of asking Henri to guard the stable just in case.

"And this is the woman you want for a wife?" he asked himself in a perfect imitation of his father's easy sarcasm. "Oh, hell, yes, she is most definitely the one."

He was simply going to have to find a way to convince her that what they shared had nothing whatsoever to do with warring countries and everything to do with their hearts. He hoped it would be enough for a while at least, but when he reached the house she was not in her room, nor was she in the garden.

Alarmed by her absence, he found Ramona in the kitchen helping Madame LeFleur prepare dinner. The housekeeper was slicing string beans, while Mariette and Michelle were rolling out pastry for a berry pie and had flour up to their elbows.

"Have any of you seen Mrs. Hadley in the last few minutes?" he asked.

"No, sir," they said in unison.

Ramona looked at him askance. "We have not been looking for her either. If she walks through the kitchen looking for you, shall I send her to your study?"

"Please do." He left knowing there were only so many places Sarah could be, but when a more thorough search of the house failed to reveal a trace of her, he went back outside into the garden. He was about to begin looking under the shrubbery when he heard Michael's high-pitched cry.

It was coming from the bathhouse, where he found the infant's basket inside on the bench, and Sarah seated in the empty tub, fully clothed. Her hands were clasped tightly over her mouth to muffle her sobs, and she was crying as though her heart were broken.

Poor little Michael's face was contorted in a mask of enraged indignation, for he had always been cuddled the moment he had uttered the faintest whimper. Unwilling to allow him to suffer, Chris scooped him up from the basket and placed him in Sarah's lap. He then climbed into the tub behind her and wrapped her in a confining embrace.

"I'm sorry the world is such a terrifying place, but please tend to Michael, and then I'll cry with you if you like."

Chris's comforting words only made Sarah feel worse, but she was not too distraught to care for her son. Tears streamed down her cheeks as she loosened her bodice and brought him to her breast. It took a moment to quiet him, but then he began to nurse in thirsty gulps.

Chris stroked her hair. "Clearly I've disappointed you very badly, but please don't turn away from me."

She sat stiffly, trapped in his arms, for mere disappointment did not begin to describe the severity of her pain. They had been happy, for a while at least, but it had been an all-too-brief respite from the chaos her life had become. While Chris's deep voice was soothing, there had always been a dangerous gleam in his eye, and surely a lust for blood in his heart. How could she have overlooked his true nature for even a moment? she agonized. Now utterly lost, when Michael at last fell asleep, she let herself be led back to the house. As empty as a ghost, she floated up the stairs to her room.

Chris was frantic himself, but at least he was calm enough to change Michael's diaper and place him in his cradle before helping Sarah out of her blue-gray gown. He fumbled with the ties on her petticoats but left her in her chemise. He had believed she would surely feel better after a nap, but her expression was still filled with such abject despair, he could not bear to tuck her into bed and leave.

She had demanded the right to make her own plans, while he had longed to forge such a strong bond between them that she would never leave. Now he feared his silence about their French allies had done irreparable harm, and he could think of only one way to bring her back to him.

He stripped off his clothes and joined her in bed. He savored the smoothness of her skin as he held her close and brushed her lips with tender kisses. "Surely there has been enough time since Michael's birth," he whispered. "Let me make love to you."

She lay relaxed in his arms without a ripple of desire, but she understood his passionate sense of urgency. Drained of all feeling save an enduring loneliness, she caressed his cheek and let him believe whatever he wished. She tasted the sweetness of his kiss, shivered at his adoring caress, yet his affection flowed over her as lightly as spring rain.

He entered her with slow, shallow thrusts, stretching her with such deliberate care that when he at last lay buried deep within her, she had not experienced a twinge of pain. Instead, there was only his delicious heat, and the devotion etched in his face as he rocked above her.

She had wept too hard to feel anything other than the strength of his release, but when he rolled to her side and gathered her into his arms, she closed her eyes and, exhausted, welcomed a numbing sleep.

Chris paced his study with a long, angry stride. "No, you don't understand, Mr. Corliss. I can't wait for DeGrasse to assemble his entire fleet. We're sailing for Virginia now. If the crew is scattered about the island, find as many as you can and, the minute all the supplies are loaded, sail into the lagoon."

"But I thought that—"

"Yes, I know what I led you to expect, but we can rendezvous later with DeGrasse."

Rob had been eager to sail with the French fleet and didn't know what to think of this sudden change in plan. "If there's no need for extra men to form prize crews, then I should be able to summon enough to sail. The only question is whether or not the men will want to remain with the *Island Belle* without the lure of prize shares to split."

"You're right; some are bound to refuse," Chris agreed darkly. "Tell them the war will soon be over, and there will be no more privateers, so if they'd rather not make their homes here on Martinique, they'll come with us. If that doesn't work, then to hell with them. I'd not miss Jacob Shorter, so you needn't look too hard for him. We can sail home with a couple dozen hands if we have to."

"Yes, the Dutch have always made do with smaller crews, and their ships are no easier to handle than the *Belle*. I just wish that you would come to Port Royal with me."

"I had intended to," Chris assured him. "But I could do little there that you can't handle. Let's just see how swiftly we can be ready to sail for home."

Rob failed to share Chris's newfound sense of urgency, but it did inspire him to speak with unusual candor. "We've both come of age during the war, and I might not be able to manage a voyage myself without an enemy to chase."

"Quite frankly, I doubt I'll have the same passion for sailing either, but the war has cost everyone at home too much, and they'll all be glad when it's over."

He again walked Rob down to the lagoon and kept watch until his mate's boat rounded the point. He then hurried back to the house to be nearby when Sarah woke. For all he knew, she had been overcome by grief for her late husband and had hidden rather than burden him with her sorrow. It was a plausible explanation for her hysterical tears, and he could not bear the thought that she might have been dreaming of a dead man while they had made love. There could be no worse betrayal than that.

Chris entered her room quietly, but she was already awake, again clad in the blue-gray gown and rocking Michael in the new chair. The slight puffiness of her eyes was the only indication that this day had not been as pleasant as any other.

"Please forgive me," she greeted him. "I won't allow it to happen again."

Her icy calm was almost more frightening than her tears had been. "You needn't apologize. I expect you to cry when you're unhappy, and I fear I was the cause of your sorrow today." He reached for the chair at the desk and brought it up to sit close to her.

"Admiral DeGrasse is commanding a French fleet that has been sailing through the West Indies since the end of April. That was one of his ships that we saw today. The rumor in Port Royal is that they're preparing to depart for America. I've not met the admiral, nor am I privy to his plans, but I believe we may be near the end of the war, and I'd like to go home rather than remain here on Martinique."

That was at least the truth, but if she was surprised by his revelations, it failed to show in her maddeningly blank expression.

"We should be able to sail for Virginia in a few days. Rather than minimize the risk involved, I'll admit it will be dangerous, but I'll take you to my parents' home, where I know you and Michael will be safe and comfortable.

"You may regard it as a temporary stay if you like," he stressed. "Or, if you'll agree to marry me, we'll build our own home there."

Sarah lifted Michael to her shoulder and rubbed the babe's back. "If you'll recall, I asked you for nothing."

"No, you asked for emotion, for love, and that's why I need to keep you with me."

"Am I the only one on Martinique who had not heard of Admiral DeGrasse?"

Chris shrugged. "I have no way of knowing, but I wish now that I'd mentioned him earlier. Instead, I avoided the subject of the war, which I'd still rather do with you."

"Yes, I understand. We don't trust each other, and now you must fear that I'm unstable. Perhaps even—"

"Stop it. I think anyone who's suffered through what you have in the last few months is entitled to cry as often as they please."

"No, there simply aren't enough tears," she responded, her voice strangely hollow. "You must promise me something."

Chris sat back with his hands clasped loosely between his thighs. "Not until I hear what it is."

"I suppose that's fair. Once we reach Virginia, if I choose to end my 'temporary stay,' promise that you'll let me go."

"No, not without a chance to change your mind I won't. Besides, you'll like Virginia, and my family will welcome you."

"You might fool me, but don't try to fool yourself, Chris. They'll not welcome a British officer's widow and her child. They'll believe you're daft, and it will be horribly uncomfortable for us all."

He leaned forward again and placed his hand on her knee. "It has been nearly a decade since I required my parents' approval for anything. I certainly don't need them to tell me whom to love."

A sad smile played across her lips. "You don't love me, Chris. I'm merely a challenge, a small part of the adventure you crave. If you can't find a battle at sea, then you'll bring one into your own home."

Her reasoning continually astounded him, but this time she was completely wrong. "I may have gone to sea for the thrill, but it's worn off by now. While I definitely admire your spirit, when have I ever provoked you simply to enjoy a fight?"

"You do it so often I've lost count, but the mule you carved is a good example."

He nodded. "All right, I said some things on board the *Island Belle* that in retrospect don't appear wise. It won't happen again."

Sarah believed that it would, but she preferred to wait and catch him at it rather than argue. "Thank you. By the way, I do appreciate your advising me to behave as an adult and consider my son's welfare. In the future, I'll endeavor to do better in that regard than I did today."

"The fault was entirely mine," he emphasized, so grateful she had not mentioned her late husband that he would have accepted the blame for almost anything. "If you're feeling up to it, let's take Michael out to the garden and enjoy the sunset."

Sarah went with him, but it seemed as though years had passed since the last time they had strolled the mossy paths.

The next time Chris mentioned Virginia, he spread out a worn map on the dining room table. He pointed out the James River and where it widened into Hampton Roads, which opened out into the Chesapeake Bay. "My home borders the river here, near Williamsburg. I'll not make my final plans until we get closer to home and I learn where the British are encamped."

The map was so intricately drawn that every little marshy inlet was included in the coastal detail. "What if the whole area is swarming with British troops?" she asked.

"Then we'll dock somewhere it's safe, and I'll take you in a carriage overland. There are places to ferry across the James River if we must approach from the south."

Michael was asleep in his cradle upstairs, so it was just the two of them sharing the soft circle of candlelight. "And if we're stopped?"

"Mrs. Hadley, if you had given half so much thought to your voyage to England, you'd never have boarded the *Beatrice*."

"You're right, I didn't consider the risks as I should have. But have you no plan other than to avoid the British?"

"No, I enjoy creating elaborate plans, and if we must reach home by carriage, I'll dress in old clothes and serve as your driver. You'll be thoroughly convincing in the part of a recent widow journeying home."

She raised her glance to his and was appalled by his smug grin. "You'd trust me not to betray you?"

"Yes, I would."

She shook her head sadly. "Then you're a fool, Captain."

That she would actually claim she'd betray him at the first opportunity did not surprise him. He rolled up the map and tapped it against the table. "I intend to sail up the river at night, so you needn't practice any pretty speeches to use with British sentries."

Sarah could no more betray him than she could her own darling son, but she thought it best he believed otherwise. Despite his certainty, she doubted his family could possibly be pleased to meet her. She came from a respected South Carolina family, it was true, but the MacLeods would want Chris wed to a young woman they knew—preferably a lovely virgin from a family as wealthy as their own, rather than a Loyalist widow with an infant son.

Of course, she could appear content until Chris left and then side with his parents and promptly leave. They would probably offer her a sizable sum of money to disappear, which, for her son's sake, she would have to seriously consider accepting. What did it matter how little they thought of her? she wondered. She simply could not bear to remain with them and be among the first to hear the awful news of Chris's death.

He slid into his chair at the head of the table. "I know what you're thinking. You're planning to leave Virginia the minute my back is turned. I'll warn you just this once not to bother, because I'll find you no matter where you've gone."

"If your home is such a marvelous place, why would I ever want to leave?" she asked sweetly.

He had a ready answer. "To prove something to me, or to yourself, or simply because you can."

"If you'd hoped to provoke an argument, you've failed. I'll not fight about what I may or may not do once we arrive at your home, if we are in fact able to reach it. The whole exercise would be absurd."

Chris leaned over to kiss her and then lowered his voice to a husky whisper. "I don't want to fight with you. I want to take you upstairs where nothing matters but how good you taste."

"That's an inviting thought, but you're wrong. Everything, even the smallest detail, matters. As an example, the way your lace cuffs fall over the backs of your hands, or how your spine curves into your hips."

That she observed him so closely was surprising, but then, he doubted she missed much. He laced his fingers in hers to draw her to her feet, and led her from the dining room to the stairs.

"Yes, I see what you mean," he said. "I'm quite fond of

how the lace on the hem of your chemise brushes your ankles. Or the feel of your curls across my—"

He leaned close to whisper a request, and she raised her brows as though she might only consider it. Then, startled by the sound of rain splattering the roof, she reached for the banister. "I didn't expect another storm so soon."

"It's only a little rain," he assured her. "Not every summer storm is as violent as a hurricane."

"One hurricane was quite enough, thank you." She was even more certain that loving him had proven to be far more destructive.

Chapter Fifteen

The *Island Belle* had sailed into the lagoon, and Sarah sat on her trunk on the sand holding Michael while she and Chris waited for a long boat to reach shore and ferry them out to the ship. Michael's cradle, with his basket tucked inside, and her rocking chair were resting on the sand beside them.

"I understand why I ought not to remain here," she told him, "but I don't relish the prospect of again being on the water, nor confined to your cabin."

Chris stood behind her, gently massaging the tension from her shoulders. "I know. Here we've been free to come and go as we pleased, to say nothing of the joy of sharing a full-sized bed. But this voyage won't be long, and my home will offer many enjoyable diversions."

She sighed softly. "Not without you it won't."

He moved to her side to study her expression, but she appeared merely introspective rather than desperately sad. He sincerely hoped the war would soon end, but he would not make a promise that might prove empty. As captain of the *Island Belle*, he had always decided where they would sail and which ships to capture, and other than to avoid severe weather, he had felt no pressing need to return to port. But then, Sarah had not been waiting for him.

Before he left her in Virginia, she would undoubtedly demand at least an estimate of when he expected to return. He would devise a sensible reply at his first opportunity, and hope she would accepted it. However, she was not the type to embrace uncertainty with any enthusiasm, and he no longer could either.

"Here come Madame LeFleur, Ramona, and the sisters," he whispered. "I've given them all ample bonuses, but they still wanted to bid us good-bye."

"Should I do anything more than say *merci?*"

"My God, are you actually going to speak French?"

She gave him a withering glance, but rose and turned toward the servants advancing across the sand. Ramona had been thrilled by their arrival, until Chris had explained he had neither a wife nor a son. As for Madame LeFleur, she had kept to her kitchen, so Sarah had seldom seen her, but if possible, she had been even less friendly than Ramona. The sisters had been sweet, but she and Michael were merely curiosities to them.

"Please tell everyone how much I appreciate all they have done to make my stay here a comfortable one. I'm especially grateful for the time they spent looking after Michael, and the little clothes Mariette and Michelle made for him this last week. I'm sorry I've no presents to give them in return."

She smiled as Chris translated her appreciation and added effusive thanks of his own, but when Mariette and Michelle giggled into their hands, Ramona looked ready to spit, and Madame LeFleur rolled her eyes, Sarah was too upset to be still.

"Are they making fun of me?" she asked apprehensively.

"No, not at all. I simply said that when we returned, you'd be my wife."

"Have I mentioned that you tend to be presumptuous?"

"Yes, on several occasions. Now here's the boat; we'll go first today, and then I'll send men back to fetch your trunk and the furniture."

Sarah turned to scan the beach. Her eyes filled with tears as she recalled the picnic suppers under the stars. Chris had such high hopes for Virginia, but Martinique possessed not merely a remarkable beauty but also a serenity she feared they might never recapture.

Chris slid his arm around her shoulders. "I'll bring you back here every year if you like. Now, I'm sure you'll find going up the rope ladder far easier than coming down."

He helped her climb into the boat, and she held Michael tightly as they were rowed out to the *Island Belle*. The perils posed by a swaying rope ladder were no longer her major concern.

That night Raymond Fox served their dinner himself. "The captain said you were eager to meet me, ma'am, and I am truly sorry I neglected to introduce myself before this."

The cook was as slim as a reed, and Sarah would now recognize him anywhere. "I'm very happy to meet you," she assured him. "I was relieved to learn you were among those returning with us."

"Yes, ma'am. I've got a wife and two children who are long overdue for a visit. As for the men with a greater thirst for gold than freedom, we'll be just fine without them, won't we, Captain?"

"We certainly will." Chris closed the door behind the cook before joining Sarah at the table. "That's more than

I've heard Raymond say in two years. How is the chicken stew?"

"As delicious as always, but the shredded coconut is something new."

Chris began to laugh and had a difficult time containing himself. "Actually, he's used it before, but he'd run out by the time you came on board. It will be in a custard tomorrow."

"I shall look forward to it, then."

Chris reached over to give her hand a fond squeeze. "You never made that list of rules for our meals, but when we get home, I want you to keep track of everything you'd like to do when I come back. I'll make a list too. For one thing, I'd like to meet your parents."

Sarah blotted her mouth on her napkin. "All right, that can probably be arranged, but you mustn't expect it to be a joyous occasion."

"Perhaps if I make a generous donation to your father's church, he'll be more inclined to welcome me."

"A bribe, you mean? No, I shouldn't think so."

When she rested her fork across her plate, he was sorry a mention of her parents had spoiled her appetite. That he could take no credit for giving them a fine grandson was a shame, but he thought the boy might distract them sufficiently for a privateer to slip into the family almost unnoticed.

They had placed Michael's cradle at the end of the bunk, but the rocking chair had been stowed in the hold. They were going to be even more crowded than before, but he would do all that he could to make the voyage pass quickly. He glanced toward the bunk, which had never seemed so narrow, and thought the next time he built a ship, he would give the captain's cabin a much larger bed.

* * *

There were islands scattered along the Atlantic coast of the peninsula Virginia shared with Maryland and Delaware. Many were frequented by privateers, and with Sarah asleep in his bunk, Chris went ashore on one before dawn. He laid the map of Virginia on a scarred tabletop in a deserted inn and asked the shrewd innkeeper for news of the war.

"You know I keep my eyes and ears open," Samuel Peabody murmured with a conspiratorial wink. "Couldn't stay in business if I didn't. Cornwallis was raiding deep into Virginia in June, but now he's pulled back to York-town and digging in there. Looks to me like if a man had to, he could come up through North Carolina, or down from Maryland and walk right through the heart of Virginia. Or a daring man might sail right up the James River some dark night."

Chris rolled up the map and slipped it back in his pocket. Samuel Peabody had an unparalleled talent for ferreting out the news, and he tarried to learn all that he could from the wily innkeeper before returning to the *Island Belle*. Peabody was the third person he had questioned since nearing the Virginia coast, and each had told the same story.

General Washington and the French General Rochambeau were preparing to attack New York with their combined armies, but the arrival of Admiral DeGrasse's fleet might inspire a swift change in plan. At least Chris thought it would, which meant he had no time to lose in taking Sarah home.

Chris was certain his crew must have noted the difference in Sarah's manner toward him whenever they were on deck. Of course, the men believed they had been lovers since the capture of the *Beatrice,* which had been impossible to convincingly refute. Now, their love affair could not be denied.

Despite the narrowness of his bunk, they had made love every night. Sometimes their passion for each other had been so slow and sweet they had explored it until nearly dawn; other times they had quickly exhausted themselves in a heated rush.

That night, Chris had savored Sarah's taste and with an intimate caress brought her to climax again and again before seeking his own release deep within her. Now she lay nestled in his arms, sleepily waiting until Michael's hunger forced her to move.

Chris sighed deeply, for he hated to leave her. "I have to go up on deck," he whispered. "After you nurse Michael, dress and pack your trunk. I'm taking you two home tonight."

Panicked, Sarah pushed against his chest to sit up. "This very night? Couldn't you have told me earlier? I ought to have known why you were being so loving."

He shoved himself into a sitting position to face her. "I'm always loving, and so are you, but I didn't want you to fret any longer than you had to."

"How thoughtful of you." She wanted to scream at him for being so unfair, but it would only wake Michael and spoil what little time they had to share. "I can't walk into your parents' home reeking of you. You'll have to fetch me some hot water to bathe. Oh, how I wish we had your beautiful big tub."

Chris left the bunk and began to dress. "I don't want to ever wash off your scent, but I'll bring you some hot water right away. You'll have to stay here below; if Michael cries, there will too great a risk someone along the river-bank will hear him. I'll come for you after we've tied up at my family's dock, but it will be very late."

"I'll be ready, but even under the cover of darkness, will it be safe to go up the river?"

"Lord Cornwallis is massing his troops at Yorktown. That's where the York River meets the Chesapeake Bay." Chris paused as he hurriedly pulled on his shirt. "There must be a fifteen-mile stretch of land between the York and James rivers where we're bound, and with Washington and Rochambeau near New York, Cornwallis won't have troops posted on the James. Or at least I don't believe he will. We'll soon see. I imagine you've met Cornwallis, haven't you?"

"Yes. I even danced with him a time or two at balls in Charleston. Did you hope I'd introduce you?"

"No, I was simply curious. Does he dance well?"

"Frankly, I can't recall. Could we discuss something else, please?"

She looked so bewildered, he chose to review his plan in greater detail. "I was born on the James River. I know every dip and bend. The *Island Belle* was launched on the river, and she's as at home there as I. As soon as we reach our dock, I'll send Charley running up to the house to wake everyone. I'll introduce you, but I won't be able to stay more than a few minutes. I don't want you to feel abandoned, but we have to be out at sea before the first hint of dawn lightens the sky."

Sarah pulled her nightgown on over her head and sank into her chair at his table. He sat down on the bunk to pull on his boots. She feared she was going to be sick, and swallowed hard. "I doubt I'll be able to draw a deep breath until we're safely inside your parents' house."

"Now I'm sorry I told you so early, but I've always found doing the unexpected to be exhilarating."

"Yes, you would." She rested her head on her crossed arms, but the table was still uncomfortably hard.

He rose and placed a kiss atop her curls. "How many times have we talked about this?"

"More than I can count, and I appreciate your taking me into your confidence, but I can't help but fear we'll all end up dead."

"Sarah, no one is likely to die tonight. Why don't you go back to bed? I'll come to check on you in a while."

She raised her hand in a feeble wave. "Just give me a moment to make the cabin stop spinning, and then I'll move."

This time Chris brushed her hair aside to kiss her cheek. He hadn't meant to frighten her so badly, and now it was too late to rethink his plans.

Chris had avoided telling Sarah that the real danger might very well come at Hampton Roads, where the James River flowed into the Chesapeake Bay. The darkness of the night as well as the *Island Belle*'s speed gave them the advantage, however. Even if a sentry caught a glimpse of sail, the ship would have entered the river and disappeared before the soldier could confirm the sighting and order cannon fire. He thought it far more likely they might have to fight their way back out to sea, but Sarah and Michael would be safe, and they were his primary concern.

The entire crew was as alert as he as they sailed closer to land, but their extraordinary good luck held, and they reached the MacLeods' private dock without raising a single cry of alarm. As Charley sprinted up the riverbank,

Chris brought Sarah and Michael up on deck. Her trunk, the cradle, again containing the handy basket, and the rocking chair were already there.

"You see, we've made it safely," he whispered. "Let's hurry on up to the house."

Sarah held her breath the whole way, for even on friendly soil she expected a shouted challenge or, worse, gunfire. The dew on the lawn dampened her slippers, and she might have tripped and fallen had Chris not maintained such a firm grip on her arm.

As they neared the three-story brick house, the glow from a lantern passed through two rooms on the second floor, then disappeared briefly as the man carrying it ran down the stairs. He burst through the front door, nearly colliding with Charley, who had remained on the porch, and ran to greet Chris.

"My God, what are you doing here?" he whispered hoarsely.

"Sarah, this is my brother Stephan. You'll find the rest of my family possesses far better manners."

Sarah could not really get a good look at Stephan until they reached the front door, which was now filled with a couple who had to be Chris's parents. His father was every bit as tall and handsome a man, with only a few streaks of gray in his dark hair. Even clad in a wrinkled nightshirt, he appeared muscular and fit.

His mother was holding an ornate silver candlestick and wearing a nightgown that was more lace than linen. While her blond hair had a faint silver cast, she was quite lovely. As for Stephan, he looked enough like Chris to have been his twin, but at a second glance his youth became more apparent.

They were a very handsome family, but all three were

staring at her and Chris with such astonished gazes, she wondered if perhaps he had not been home in years. "Good morning," she greeted them rather shyly. "I'm so sorry to have disturbed your rest."

Now fully awake, Catherine MacLeod handed the candlestick to her husband and flung herself into her son's arms with an enthusiasm Sarah's parents had never shown her. She wished Chris had introduced her first, but he spoke as soon as his mother stepped back to wipe away her tears.

"Charley, run help them bring up the trunk and furniture," he directed. Then he gestured toward the door. "I can stay only a minute, but please welcome Mrs. Hadley and her son. She'll soon be my wife, and I'd like you to treat her as such."

"Mrs. Hadley?" his mother repeated, clearly perplexed. "Please do come in. I shouldn't want you or your baby to catch a chill on our doorstep."

Sarah had worn her cloak over her black satin gown, and swept over the threshold with the grace of the night. "Please call me Sarah, and this is Michael. I promise we won't be a bit of trouble."

Stephan was simply gaping at her; he had hastily yanked on a shirt and breeches, and loose, his hair fell over his shoulders. "I didn't think you'd ever marry, Chris, not when—"

"That's enough," Chris ordered sharply. He withdrew a letter from his coat pocket and handed it to his father. "This is my will. Should I not return, I'm leaving everything to Sarah and Michael. She is the bride of my heart even if we're not yet legally wed. I'm so sorry I can't stay any longer, Mother."

He kissed his mother, then leaned down to kiss

Michael's cheek before again hugging Sarah. "You wait for me, you hear? I'll be back as soon as I can." He turned to his father. "Father, I—"

Brendan MacLeod handed the candlestick back to his wife, took Chris's arm, and turned him toward the door. "We'll talk on the way to the dock." He closed the front door behind them and then lost his tenuous grasp on his temper.

" 'Bride of my heart?' What nonsense! She's obviously your mistress. We've heard no word of you in months, and you blatantly bring your mistress into your mother's home? I thought we'd taught you to show more respect."

Chris slammed to a halt and forced a more respectful tone than his father had just used. "I've no time to argue, and I'll not insult you by lying. Sarah and I are lovers, but it's no business agreement in which I've paid for her favors. I beg you to treat her as my wife. Give her my room, and as I've directed, my share of the family's wealth should I be unable to return."

He rushed through what he knew of Admiral De-Grasse's expected arrival with a French fleet. "The *Island Belle* may be able to do no more than ferry the injured, but I want to be there when he engages the British fleet. Now, unless you'd like to sail with me, bid me good-bye here."

"Do not presume to give me orders," Brendan shot right back at him. "I'm the captain here in our home, not you."

Stung, Chris remained silent as three of his men carried the trunk and rocking chair by.

Charley trailed with the cradle, and all four were clearly straining to hear what was being said. Not sorry to disappoint them, Chris kept his mouth shut.

"Wait!" Stephan called as he came running down the

grassy slope. He was carrying only his boots and a coat. "I'm coming with you."

"Stephan, go back to the house," his father exclaimed.

"No. I'm old enough to sail with Chris," Stephan argued.

Chris hoped the sound of the churning river would drown out their angry voices, but he had no time to fight with either member of his family. "It doesn't matter what you want, Stephan, I won't take you along. You're needed here."

Stephan swore under his breath. "You'll take me or I'll seduce Mrs. Hadley."

That ridiculous threat made it plain how desperate Stephen was to fight, but Chris laughed, which infuriated his younger brother all the more. "You're a handsome lad, but you're no match for Sarah, so don't even try. Believe me, she'd eviscerate you with a single glance. I've already tarried too long, so please, Father, I beg you to take good care of Sarah and Michael for me."

Brendan waited until Chris had reached the dock to call a begrudging, "Good luck, son!" He then cuffed Stephan hard on the shoulder. "If I catch you anywhere near Mrs. Hadley, you'll have to answer to me rather than Chris."

Chris boarded the *Island Belle*, quickly followed by his four men, who had returned from the house. While he waved to his father and brother, he doubted they saw him before his ship again disappeared into the night.

Catherine MacLeod tightened her grip on the candlestick and gestured toward the stairs. "Let me show you to Chris's room."

"Thank you." Sarah raised her skirt to follow.

Catherine paused on the landing, regarded Sarah with

267

an enchanting smile. "Do you by any chance speak French?"

"I'm sorry, I don't speak the language."

Although clearly disappointed, Catherine shrugged as though it were a small failing. "I did not think you looked like a French girl, but one can always hope." She continued up the stairs, and when they reached the second floor, she led the way down the wide hall and into Chris's bedroom. "We have kept the room clean in anticipation of Chris's return. You should be very comfortable here." She set her candlestick on the dresser and then lit the candles on the desk and beside the bed from it.

The room was painted a pale green, and the dark furnishings were quite handsome and masculine, but Sarah was immediately drawn to a bookcase filled with small models of ships. She shifted Michael in her arms to pick up one from the top shelf.

"When did Chris make these?"

"He was perhaps ten years old when he began whittling little boats. As he got older, they became more complex, and he added masts and sails. I believe he might have been an artist had he not gone to sea."

Chris's father and brother carried her trunk up the stairs and into the room, where they dropped it just inside the door. Stephan then went back down to the foyer for the cradle and rocking chair.

"I don't believe we've ever had a guest arrive with their own furniture, have we, my dear?" Brendan asked his wife.

"I'm so sorry," Sarah rushed to apologize before Catherine could reply. "I know my arrival has created an awkward situation for your family, and I'll do my very best not to make it worse."

Stephan carried the rocking chair through the door and then left to fetch the cradle. Brendan glanced down at his bare feet, and appeared startled to discover he was wearing no more than a nightshirt. "We should have this discussion in the morning. Come, Catherine, let's give Mrs. Hadley time to settle in."

Stephan paused to catch his breath before entering the room and placing the cradle beside the bed. "There, now what did I miss?"

"Nothing, dear," his mother assured him. "There will be plenty of time for all of us to become better acquainted tomorrow." She reached for her son's hand to hurry him along, and Brendan closed the door on their way out.

Michael had slept through their arrival, but Sarah doubted she would be able to sleep before it was again time to wake. She simply shrugged off her cloak and sat down in the rocking chair.

Chris's bedroom was huge, much larger than her parents' parlor, and while she had not been able to fully appreciate the size of the house during their hurried approach from the river, it appeared to be at least as large, if not larger, than Chris's house on Martinique.

That was a good thing, for it meant she would be able to stay out of everyone's way. But it was also an impressive reminder of the MacLeods' wealth, which they would quite naturally fight to protect.

Chris had not once mentioned a will before that night, and she had been astonished when he handed one to his father. Rather than an inheritance, she wanted Chris to return very much alive, and she was terrified now that he would not. He had referred to her as the wife of his heart, which was such an endearing thought. She was ashamed not to have said how much she had come to care for him. She could only hope it was not too late.

When Catherine knocked at Sarah's door to invite her to join them for breakfast, Sarah had just donned her navy blue gown. Catherine's own dress was an icy lavender that complemented her fair complexion beautifully. Sarah eyed the billowing skirt and wished she still owned something as pretty, but she offered no excuse for her own modestly tailored gown, which lacked a hoop.

"Michael's awake this morning," she told Catherine as she plucked the boy off the bed.

Catherine came close to see the little baby, but when he looked up at her with eyes as blue as her own, she gasped. "With those eyes, he has to be Christopher's son. Why didn't he tell us so last night?"

"It isn't true. Michael is named for his father, my late husband." Catherine did not appear convinced, so Sarah added another vital bit of information. "He was a British officer serving with Lord Cornwallis, but he was killed in March."

Greatly alarmed by that revelation, Catherine's glance remained suspicious, and she studied the infant a moment longer. She then gestured toward the door. "Let's not keep everyone waiting, for I do believe we will have a most interesting morning."

As Sarah left the room, she nearly ran into Stephan, who had been leaning against the wall just outside her door, obviously eavesdropping. "Good morning," she greeted him warmly, but she did not appreciate his lurking about. He might closely resemble Chris, but she sensed that was the only similarity between them.

"Mrs. Hadley," he responded with a polite nod.

The dining room was painted a bright buttercup yellow. The early morning sun filled the room with a shimmering light, but Sarah was far too apprehensive to appreciate the pretty setting. Brendan came forward to seat her to his right, but his smile did not reach his eyes as she thanked him.

"Her son is such a handsome lad, isn't he, dear?" Catherine asked.

"Why, yes, of course he is," Brendan answered absently, but then he too noticed Michael's distinctive blue eyes. "Well, Mrs. Hadley, is it merely a remarkable coincidence that your son's eyes are as vivid a blue as my son's?"

Brendan's eyes were a smoky gray that held not a spark of good humor. After Chris's fond description, Sarah had expected his father to be quite charming, but she had yet to see a hint of his supposedly engaging manner.

She shifted her son to the crook of her arm and repeated what she had told Catherine about Michael Hadley. When she was met with incredulous stares, she described how she and Chris had met under what were surely the worst of circumstances.

"However, Chris has been very good to me," she added, "and I miss him already. You must all be wondering where my loyalties lie, but you have my word that I would never betray Chris or your family."

Brendan propped his head on his hand and closed his eyes for a long moment before speaking. "Let me see if I understand you correctly, Mrs. Hadley. You lost your husband approximately six months ago. Since then you have been taken prisoner at sea, given birth to a son, and also captivated Chris so completely that he can't wait to take you for a wife. I dare not contemplate what you might accomplish in the next few months."

"Brendan, really, that was totally uncalled for," his wife scolded softly. "The poor dear has been beset by misfortune, and yet blessed by love. I for one am touched."

Sarah responded to Catherine's sympathy with a tremulous smile, but she feared she would never win Brendan's approval. As for Stephan, he was leaning forward, listening with a rapt awe. She refused to even look his way.

A young woman in a prim black gown with a snowy white apron brought platters of scrambled eggs and sausages to the table. On her next trip from the kitchen, she carried a plate of warm biscuits. Sarah tried to eat but managed little more than a biscuit smeared with honey. It was plain from the servant's startled glance that gossip of her presence had yet to reach the kitchen. She could only imagine what the help would think once they learned that Chris intended to marry her.

"We are fortunate in that we raise most of our own food," Catherine explained, "but the war has taken a terrible toll nonetheless. Many a night we have only fish from the James River with seasoned rice."

Brendan heaved a weary sigh. "I'd rather not burden our guest with complaints of shortages."

"Please, I've no wish to add to whatever problems you may be experiencing here. Whenever Michael is sleeping, which is often, I'd be happy to help with whatever needs to be done."

"Absolutely not," Stephan nearly shouted. "You're our guest, not another servant."

Brendan raised his hand in a plea for quiet. "Hush, Stephan. Let's finish our breakfast, and then you and I will decide how best to spend the day while your mother and Mrs. Hadley make their own plans."

Despite Chris's repeated assurances, Sarah had not expected to be welcomed into his family. Sadly, she had imagined a more loving circle than she found. She searched her mind for a useful task she could actually perform before she was asked to do one of many she could not.

"Mrs. MacLeod," she began hopefully, "Chris mentioned that you were adept at creating herbal cures. I wonder if I might assist you in your garden, or with whatever you require to prepare efficacious remedies."

Catherine's expression lit with delighted surprise. "How wonderful! I have longed to have an apprentice, but with no daughters, I feared there would never be anyone to teach. But I insist you call me Catherine. If you're finished eating, I'll provide a brief tour of my herb garden before it grows too warm."

"Why, yes, I'd be delighted to see it."

Brendan rose to help her from her chair, and Sarah thanked him before following Catherine from the room.

Brendan sat back down to finish his tea. Chris's adventures had provided an ample supply, while many of their neighbors had gone without the favorite beverage. "You ought to tuck your napkin into your collar if you're going to drool each time you glance at our guest," he said to his son.

Stephan snorted a rude protest. "You have to think she's lovely too."

"Yes, she's an extraordinarily beautiful woman, but I sincerely doubt anything she says is true. Look how eager she was to ingratiate herself with your mother. Be very careful around her."

Stephan nodded as though he would, but his imagination had taken another path entirely.

Chapter Sixteen

Sarah was on her hands and knees weeding Catherine's herb garden when she heard a distant rumble. Mistaking it for thunder, she looked up, but the skies were clear. Puzzled, she rose and brushed the dirt from her hands.

They had all been waiting for news of the battle that was sure to come at Yorktown, but she had quickly learned that Brendan MacLeod forbade any mention of the war during meals. In his view, it was not a fit subject for conversation, which condemned them all to mealtimes where a lack of enthusiasm for trivial subjects inevitably resulted in a strained silence.

Had Chris been the one to insist upon such a silly rule, she would have defied him with every breath, but she dared not debate the issue with his father. Catherine appeared unaffected by her husband's edict, and remained a gracious hostess while apparently unaware that more might be required than flavorful fare and fresh floral arrangements.

The progress of the war consumed Stephan, however, and she sympathized with his frustration at his father's mute disapproval. He had become an unexpected ally who eagerly shared whatever news he gleaned from the men who, unlike his father, gathered at the Raleigh Tavern to discuss the war.

When he came barreling around the corner of the house on his way to the stables, she called to him. "Did you hear something just now?"

"Yes, it's cannon fire." He hurried over and spoke in an animated rush. "The British Admiral Graves's ships must have arrived from New York, but he won't break De-Grasse's blockade and Cornwallis will be trapped. Washington and Rochambeau are moving south, and Lafayette is crossing Virginia. They're bringing twice the troops Cornwallis commands. It's exactly as Chris predicted; this could be the last major battle of the war, and the victory will be ours."

"Let's pray an end to the war is near, but I'd feel better if I knew where Chris was," she replied.

Stephan's expression grew sullen at the mention of his brother. "He should have taken me with him. I'm old enough to fight."

"Has it not occurred to you that, should the British prevail, you might be needed here to defend your home?"

Stephan backed away. "You'd be happy if the British won, wouldn't you?"

Sarah stared at him coldly. Her husband was dead, and while she would never dishonor his memory, she was trying very hard to separate her past allegiance from the one now tugging at her heart. Perhaps that made her a traitor to both sides.

"I'll not be happy until the war ends," she remarked wistfully.

Stephan appeared unimpressed. "Tell Mother I'm off to convince Father to sail down the river while there's still something to see."

As he walked away, his proud posture and long stride reminded her so much of Chris that she had to close her eyes. That was when she again heard the low, rumbling roar of cannon fire. A warship could carry a hundred guns, all larger than those aboard the *Island Belle*, where the firing of the single long gun had been deafening.

She turned toward the house and, swept with an almost unbearable sorrow, fought to hide her tears as she went inside to tend her son.

Chris stifled a yawn and leaned back against the rail. He had slept little during the three days DeGrasse's magnificent warships had so skillfully fought Admiral Thomas Graves's fleet. Rather than continue a lengthy battle the British were sure to lose, Graves had prudently withdrawn his ships to the safety of New York waters. The French blockade was now unopposed, which meant the end of the war was near.

It was a deeply satisfying thought, and Chris could have gone below for a nap, but without Sarah and Michael, his cabin was heartbreakingly empty. He expected to find them whenever he swung open the door, but only his footsteps broke the unwelcome silence. While he and Sarah had been together almost constantly since the hour they met, he had not anticipated missing her this badly.

Lost in sweet memories of her, he failed to take warning at the suspicious rustling of the reeds along the shore, giving one of Cornwallis's marksmen a clear shot. The musket ball tore through Chris's right shoulder with a shattering force. Blood sprayed out in a ghastly shower, and he dove toward the deck to escape a deadly second shot. He landed in an awkward sprawl, and as Rob Corliss ran toward him, his vision had already begun to blur.

"Stay down!" Rob cried. "There must be British troops lying in wait along the bay." He pressed both hands against Chris's shoulder, but blood seeped between his fingers in a gory trail.

"Get me home," Chris whispered, and while his crew clustered around him, all he saw was his beloved Sarah rushing toward him with her bright curls flying.

Rob heard Chris faintly murmur Sarah's name and yelled the course change over his shoulder. Terrified, he prayed night would fall quickly to ease their way home. He had never thought he would become captain of the *Island Belle* by such an awful turn of luck, but hiding his fear of assuming command, he vowed to make Chris proud.

While neither Sarah nor Catherine had expected it, Stephan succeeded in convincing his father to sail to the coast. Brendan built swift schooners, not massive ships of the line, but if the Royal Navy had arrived to engage De-Grasse, he felt justified in having a look at the warships involved.

With her best source of information away, Sarah fell prey to all manner of desperate fears. Then, late one night, she heard a commotion downstairs. There were muffled men's voices, a shouted warning and, as she lay Michael in his cradle to investigate, Catherine knocked lightly and opened the bedroom door.

"Chris was been wounded, and his crew have brought him home to us."

Horrified, Sarah quickly moved Michael's cradle over by the rocking chair to clear the way to the bed. She then stood back so as not to block the way herself. She recognized Rob Corliss and the faces of the seamen who carried Chris through the door, but they all appeared as frightened as she.

Chris was unconscious, but not limp as dead men were, and when the men laid him on the bed, she rushed to adjust the pillow beneath his head. He was in his shirtsleeves. His right shoulder was heavily bandaged, but blood had still seeped through the muslin strips.

"We were to guide transport ships up the Chesapeake Bay and drew fire from Cornwallis's troops on Gloucester Point," Rob hurriedly explained. "Some coward shot Chris in the back. I did my best to stop the bleeding. I only hope we have not arrived too late for you to save him."

Several days' growth of beard heightened Chris's pallor, but he was most definitely alive, and to Sarah, that was all that mattered. "Thank you, Mr. Corliss. We're grateful for the chance to tend him here."

Catherine ushered the men to the door. "Thank you for all you have done for my son. Help yourselves to anything you like from the pantry before you go."

She came back to the bed and felt her son's forehead. "He is cool, which may be a worse sign than a fever. There are quilts in the chest in our room. Please run and fetch several, and bring the lengths of muslin you'll find with them."

Sarah did not waste a second before tearing from the room. She grabbed an armful of colorful quilts along with the plain fabric and raced back down the hall to Chris. Catherine was carefully unwinding the bandage from his shoulder, but Sarah could not bear to look as she removed his boots and folded the quilts over his legs and hips.

"I kept a medical book Chris had on board the *Island Belle*. While I'm sure you must know more than the physician who wrote it, it does have marvelously detailed drawings of the skeleton. Not that you would need them," she hastened to add.

"I have set a bone or two," Catherine murmured under her breath. "But that is not what is needed here. Please dampen a cloth and bring it to me."

Sarah passed by Michael as she hastened to do as was requested. Her child was sleeping quite peacefully, despite the many visitors to the room. At the washstand, she wet a cloth, wrung it out over the bowl, and hurried to hand it to Catherine.

"Thank you. Now, I would like you to carry what's left of this shirt and these bloody bandages to the fireplace and burn them."

Sarah could barely bring herself to touch them with a light pinch of her fingers. There were no glowing coals on the grate, for the September night was warm, but telling herself she was merely burning rags, she lit them with a candle.

Catherine took her time examining her son's wound before looking up at Sarah. "The musket ball went clear through his shoulder. See here, it entered through his shoulder blade and exited just beneath his collarbone. It could not have nicked his lung or he would have drowned in his own blood long before this. He might still have bled to death had Rob not acted so quickly."

Sarah's heart was pounding with fright, and yet a wave of dizziness nearly buckled her knees. She grabbed for the nearest bedpost and with sheer force of will remained focused on Chris's welfare. He had always been so strong; it was difficult to recognize him as the helpless man on his bed.

"I'm sorry not to show more courage," she apologized in a strained whisper.

"You are doing very well, Sarah, but if you faint, I will leave you lying on the floor and step over you." Catherine tore off a yard of muslin, folded it tightly, and then slid it beneath and over Chris's shoulder.

"Come close and hold these fresh bandages in place to make certain he does not begin to bleed again, while I fetch some balm to make a compress. I have everything I need handy and will return in a few minutes."

"I'm happy to stay with him." Sarah sat down on the side of the bed to apply the necessary pressure, but she wished Chris would wake if for only a moment and smile. "Please, we must keep him alive."

"Yes, of course, that is my intention." Catherine raised her skirt and ran from the room with such light steps that her feet barely grazed the floor.

Sarah leaned forward to kiss Chris's brow. His skin still felt too cool, and she wished she had had the presence of mind to lay a real fire when she had burned the bandages.

"I'm sorry to be of such little help, my darling. You did such a wonderful job caring for me, I wish I were better at repaying your kindness. Do you remember how I complained of the way you ordered me about? I would welcome it now simply to hear the sound of your voice."

The grandfather clock downstairs chimed the hour with a deep gong, and she wondered how long ago Chris had been shot and if he had suffered horribly before losing consciousness. It was agony simply to sit beside him, but Chris's own faith in his mother's expertise as a *sage femme* sustained her hopes.

Catherine had taught her that balm was an ancient remedy for wounds. It was believed to ward off infection as well as relieve pain. Eager to learn, Sarah had applied herself to Catherine's lessons, all the while hoping there would be no need to rely upon them anytime soon.

As promised, Catherine made a swift return, and she continued to teach Sarah as she worked. "You've helped to collect the herbs and dry them. Now you will have the opportunity to see how several are used. Should you need to prepare a balm compress yourself, boil the dried leaves, strain the water, and apply it on a clean cloth."

She had prepared two and now removed the plain muslin and applied one compress to his shoulder blade and the other to the wound below his collarbone. She held it in place with the dry bandage. "Tear some of that muslin into strips for me, please."

Sarah ripped into the muslin with a vengeance and soon had a mound of strips ready. "Won't he be in terrible pain when he wakes?" she asked fearfully.

"He will not awaken for a day or two, and I have some laudanum for pain."

"Yes, I understand, we need to take things one at a time." She had been so eager for Chris to return, but not like this. She had not seen her husband's body, but she had been told he had died instantly. Still, there must have been a great deal of blood.

She again felt faint, and had to sit down on the foot of the bed. She did not understand how Catherine could tend her son in such a calm fashion; but then, she had little choice. "Someday you must tell me how you met your husband," she said to distract them both.

"Yes, I will give it some thought to make it an exciting tale, but my life has been quite placid compared to yours."

"I would welcome a more serene life," Sarah assured her, but then she recalled Brendan's comment about what the next few months might bring and hoped he would not blame her for Chris's awful wound. With a sinking feeling, she feared he might.

Catherine gathered up the strips she had not used and rolled them over her fingers to save. "I know it will be difficult, but you must try to sleep whenever you can. You will be of no help to either your son or Chris if you become exhausted. I will brew some chamomile tea for you to sip before you go to bed."

"Thank you, but I'll not be able to sleep."

"You must at least try. Curl up beside Chris. He will feel your warmth, and your presence may well do more for him than all my herbs."

"Thank you for saying so." Sarah felt certain she had an ally in Catherine, but Brendan had never regarded her with a friendly gaze. She hoped her devotion to Chris might sway him, but if he were like many men, once he had formed an opinion, he would stubbornly cling to it no matter how wrong he might be.

Chris moaned in his sleep, and Sarah sat up with a start. She felt his forehead and found it was merely cool rather than a near-deathly chill. She left the bed and rearranged the quilts for his comfort before kneeling beside the cradle. She envied Michael his blissful sleep and, too anxious to again lie down, she began to pace at the foot of the bed.

The bedroom faced the east and, as the new day dawned, bright rays of sunshine slowly spread across the floor. She paused to wrap an arm around a bedpost and watched Chris sleep. It wasn't like him not to be up and about at first light, but today, he lay unnaturally still.

Keeping to his usual schedule, Michael soon woke with a sputtering yawn. Sarah changed his diaper and sat down with him in the rocking chair. Unaware of his mother's distress, he nursed contentedly, until Brendan came flying up the stairs and burst into the room, with Stephan and Catherine close behind. Sarah sat up so abruptly she startled the baby, who began to cry.

"Get them out of here," Brendan ordered his wife. "They ought not to share Chris's room."

Catherine sent Sarah a sympathetic glance and followed her husband to the bed, while Stephan appeared more eager to observe Sarah nurse Michael.

Catherine laid her hand on her husband's back. "My darling, you must not shout at our guests. They are precisely where Chris wished them to be. I shall not ask them to move until he instructs me to do so."

Brendan turned to glare at Sarah. "This is your doing, isn't it? You're trailing tragedy like an ermine cloak. If you truly care for Chris, you'll be gone before he wakes."

In an effort to preserve her modesty, Sarah held the neckline of her nightgown closed with one hand while she cuddled her son in the other. "We are all distraught. If it helps you to blame me for Chris's misfortune, then please do so. I prefer to blame the British soldier who shot him."

"He'd not have been in harm's way if not for you," Brendan swore.

Sarah had spent a lifetime arguing with a master and

she did not even flinch as she responded. "That's where you're mistaken. Once Chris had learned DeGrasse was taking his fleet to America, he could not have stayed on Martinique. I'm surprised he had not talked the admiral into giving him the command of a warship."

Unable to find a suitable insult to counter that insightful comment, Brendan turned his back on her to concentrate on his son. "Tell me the truth, Catherine. Will he recover?"

"Divination is not one of my talents, but I believe he will—although his recovery will be a slow and painful one. Now I would like to change his bandages, and unless you plan to be a real help to me, I would prefer that you and Stephan left us."

Brendan circled the bed to take Chris's left hand. "He feels, well . . . alive."

"He feels very good to me too," Catherine assured him.

Stephan was hanging back as though he were uncertain whether to press close to the bed or walk out the door unseen. Sarah was tempted to gesture for him to come close; if he was eager to see her breasts, she wanted him to take a good look now and never come near her again. It seemed like a fine plan to her, but as Chris would be unlikely to agree, she maintained her modest hold on her neckline.

Chris felt as though a cannon had rolled over his shoulder and left him trapped beneath its wooden truck. Where were the gunners who should have pulled him free? he agonized, but he was too weak to shout for their help. Pain shot down his spine and clear to his fingertips. Nausea he could barely force down filled his throat.

Sarah heard Chris gasp and rushed to the bed. "Chris, are you awake? Can you hear me?"

He fought to open his eyes, but even that pitiful effort was almost too much for him. He barely managed to flutter his eyelids, but it was enough for a glimpse of Sarah. She raised his head and brought a cup to his lips. His mouth was dry, but he recognized one of his mother's remedies. That meant he was home—but that was impossible.

"Chris, stay with me," Sarah urged. "You've been shot, and I know it must hurt terribly. I'm going to call your mother, but I'll come right back. Don't move."

Move? He was being crushed under an enormous weight and she ordered him not to move? He would have laughed had it not hurt so badly just to breathe. Surely he was dying, but he had seen Sarah one last time. He tried to say her name but managed only a hoarse groan. He had never thought he would die in his own bed. After the life he had led, it was a very bad joke.

Catherine swept into the room in a sweetly scented rush. "Are you awake, my darling? Here, I have laudanum to ease your pain. Drink it for me."

Sarah stood on the opposite side of the bed. She had not left Chris, not for an instant, but she was still amazed to have heard his faint gasp. She feared she had worn a path in the deep green rug, pacing between the door and windows. She had fed and rocked Michael, even attempted to read, but mostly she had paced the room like a caged beast waiting for Chris to stir.

Catherine stepped back, holding the now empty cup. "Did he say anything?"

"No, I think he just drew a deeper breath. He looked up

at me, but it was no more than a blink. It is a good sign, though, isn't it?"

"Yes, it is a very good sign. The next time he wakes, he may be able to say a few words, but you must not force him to speak."

"No, I understand. He must save whatever energy he has to get well."

"Yes, that is it precisely. I am concerned about you too. This would be a good time to take Michael out to the garden. Chris will not wake again for hours, and I will sit here with him until you return."

Sarah did not want to go, but neither did she wish Chris to wake and find she had lost her mind trapped in his sickroom. "Yes, thank you. A little sun would be good for both of us."

She carried Michael through the flower garden to the bench beneath a coral tree. It barely exceeded her height now, but she remembered how beautiful the mature trees had been on Martinique. Propped against her shoulder, Michael appeared to enjoy being outside as much as she.

The MacLeods employed capable servants, and the girls had asked to tend her son. Catherine doted on him too. If she had to rely on others to look after Michael while she stayed with Chris, then she would have to do so. Strengthened by that decision, Sarah swiftly made another not to sit through any more meals with Brendan managing every word. He might want her out of Chris's room, but they had shared one too long to be separated now.

She tried to focus on the beauty of the roses and the fragrance of jasmine and honeysuckle in the air, but it was nearly impossible to sit calmly. All she could think of was Chris, and how badly he would need her loving attention, and how forcefully he would reject it.

"Mrs. Hadley."

She had not heard Brendan approach until the man was within a few feet of her, but he always spoke her name with the same hint of reproof Chris had once used. Catherine called her Sarah, her voice softly accented by her native French, but Brendan always addressed her in a clipped, formal tone. She was not pleased he had found her, and held her breath as he joined her on the bench.

"It will undoubtedly be several weeks before Chris is well enough to leave his bed," he began. "You'll grow bored with him long before that, and I'll not risk your eventual departure hurting him even more than he already is. I want you to leave now, before he is fully aware of your presence. I'll arrange an escort for you and your son to your home in Charleston. If you'll stop to consider what is best for Chris, I'm certain you'll see the wisdom in my plan."

Even before their arrival, Sarah had anticipated his offer, and she was ashamed to have ever considered accepting it. It still hurt to have Brendan think so little of her, however. "I will say this only one time, so please listen carefully, Mr. MacLeod. I will never leave Chris. You may rest assured that I'll not reveal the details of this unfortunate conversation to anyone. Let's forget it ever occurred. Please excuse me."

As she began to rise, Brendan caught her arm. "Mrs. Hadley, I'd planned to send you home with a generous gift to ensure your welfare."

Sarah pulled away from him. "Now you're compounding the insult. There is not enough money in the world to influence me to change my mind. I swear I knew you'd offer me money even before Chris and I left Martinique, but I had no idea just how badly it would disgust me."

She left him standing by the bench, scowling fiercely, but she no longer cared what he thought of her; Chris's health and happiness were what mattered most.

"Laudanum will dull the worst of his pain," Catherine confided in a hushed whisper. "Then I prefer an infusion of white willow bark. Some refer to it as a tea, but an infusion is allowed to steep longer and is therefore stronger and more efficacious."

"Yes, I understand," Sarah replied. "I should write everything down, so you'll not have to repeat it endlessly."

"Nonsense. You're very bright and learn quickly."

They were standing at the foot of Chris's bed. He had awakened again briefly yesterday afternoon, but they both hoped to see him fully conscious that day. Sarah had lain beside him during the night but slept only fitfully between the times she had been up to nurse Michael. She was already near exhaustion, and the real work of caring for Chris had not even begun.

"Would you mind if I took Michael into our room for a bit?" Catherine asked. "I would like to make more little smocks for him and will need to take a few measurements."

"That would be so nice of you. I'm afraid my needlework isn't what it ought to be."

Catherine graciously shook her head. "When you have such remarkable gifts, Sarah, that small failing is easily excused."

Having endured a lifetime of criticism, Sarah was touched. "You're very kind to say so."

When Catherine left carrying Michael, Sarah again stretched out beside Chris. She had bathed him so his skin was again scented with bayberry soap rather than gunpowder. Cuddled against his left side, she laced her fingers in his and willed him to awaken, but she fell asleep before he opened his eyes.

Chris felt Sarah, and caught the subtle scent of the cinnamon soap she had brought from Martinique. He was too weak to do more than squeeze her hand, but that action filled him with a peaceful sense of comfort. Then his shoulder began to throb even more painfully, and he wondered why she had not done something to ease the ache.

"Sarah?" he hissed.

She came awake instantly. "Yes, I'm here."

"Am I still alive?"

She sat up and brushed his hair off his forehead. "Yes, you're very much alive, and you're going to stay that way. I'll give you more laudanum for the pain."

"Wait. I can stand it—for the moment, at least."

"But you shouldn't have to."

Chris wiggled his toes. That meant he still had legs and could walk, but he did not feel up to it that day. In fact, just smiling at Sarah was exhausting. He tried to recall how he had been hurt, then did not want to.

"I'm sorry," he whispered, and his eyes fluttered closed.

"Chris?" Sarah could not imagine why he had wished to apologize, but she regretted not being better prepared to talk with him before he again fell asleep. She ought to have planned what she wished to say, and now the opportunity was lost.

The next time Chris awakened, it was with a scream of pain. "Yes, I know this hurts," his mother responded soothingly, "but your bandages must be changed. Your wounds are healing nicely due to the balm compresses, but they must be replaced."

Chris snarled as though he might bite her, but he restrained the impulse until she had completed her work. His brother was standing at the foot of the bed with his father. They both looked worried and tired.

"Where's Sarah?" he asked.

She was on his left, and leaned in close. "I'm right here. I'll not go away."

"That's good." He reached for her hand and brought it to his lips. "Make it stop hurting."

Sarah looked over at his mother, who reached for the bottle of laudanum and poured the last drops into a glass. "We're doing our best," she promised. She helped him raise his head, and he swallowed the tincture of opium in a grateful gulp.

Catherine waited a moment to be certain he was asleep. "That's the last of the laudanum, but he should be over the worst of the pain. We'll rely on white willow bark the next time he wakes."

"At least it appears that he *will* wake," Brendan whispered.

Sarah doubted he had slept much either, for the lines in his face were deeply etched. As for Stephan, the young man's clothes were rumpled, as though he had fallen asleep in them, and his hair was tied so loosely several lank strands had escaped the bow.

Catherine alone appeared confident, but then, she had kept busy working with her herbs. Clearly she was the heart of the MacLeod family, which would have been equally troubled regardless of which of them had been injured or fallen ill.

What Sarah did not see, however, was any part for herself in the tightly knit group. She might stand by Chris's side, but outside of their inner circle. She could not bear to think how poor little Michael would be pushed even farther away. She and Chris would love him, and the three of them would form their own family circle. Still, she could not help but wish Brendan MacLeod had been delighted to meet her rather than appalled.

Sarah leaned forward to hold the spoon to Chris's lips. "I thought this was awfully good," she exclaimed, "and I recall you saying pea soup was your favorite."

"Don't coddle me like Michael," he ordered gruffly. "I don't need to be coaxed to eat."

"And I do not appreciate being yelled at for being kind." She moved off the bed and set the bowl back on the tray. She shoved it close to his left side and handed him the spoon. "Here. Feed yourself. I've got much better things to do."

She walked out the door before he had time to offer an apology, but she refused to cry in front of him. Michael was asleep in Catherine's room, but she could not face Mrs. MacLeod either. Instead, she slumped down in the hallway and buried her face in her hands.

At first, Chris had been too weak to utter more than a hoarse word of thanks for her attentive care. After a week in bed, he was so frustrated not to be well that he was simply mean. She could understand his distress at being unable to perform tasks that he had never even paused to consider, like standing up without falling or using two hands to shave. She had been patient as well as sympathetic, but she was through, at least for that afternoon.

"Sarah?" Stephan knelt down in front of her. "What's wrong? Did you slip and fall?"

"No, I simply enjoy sitting here in the hallway." She wiped her eyes, but it was too late to hide her tears.

Stephan sat down next to her and slung his arm around

her shoulders. "I know, we've all been crying, but we don't want Chris to see."

Sarah had not expected him to understand, but perhaps they were more alike than she supposed. "Thank you. I'll get up in another minute."

Brendan reached the top of the stairs and stopped to stare. "I don't even know which of you to condemn," he uttered crossly, and marched down the hallway with a long, angry stride. "You ought to know that woman's poison, Stephan. As for you, Mrs. Hadley—"

"If we want to sit here and cry, we'll damn well do it!" Stephan shouted. "You needn't twist it into something obscene."

"My God, has something happened to Chris?" Brendan roared.

Catherine opened the bedroom door. "Why are you making so much noise out there, Brendan? The baby's trying to sleep."

"I'm not the one causing all the trouble!" he insisted. "I'm going back to the shipyard. Come with me, Stephan."

The young man unfolded upward, letting Sarah's hand slowly slide through his until only their fingertips touched before he stepped away. "You'll not find a better man anywhere," he called over his shoulder.

"Yes, I know," Sarah replied.

His mother took a step closer. "Was he referring to Chris or himself?"

Sarah now felt utterly ridiculous sitting there in a wrinkled heap. "Chris—and I believe I need a very long nap." She rose with a clumsy stretch and covered a wide yawn. "Could you please point me toward a spare bed?"

"Yes, my dear, come with me, and I will see you are not disturbed."

Sarah smiled sleepily and shook out her skirt. "All my gowns are a fright, aren't they? It's no wonder Chris is tired of looking at me."

Catherine opened the door into a guest bedroom decorated in opulent shades of gold. "Your gowns are modest as befits a widow. I will summon my dressmaker if you like. I am sorry not to have thought of it sooner."

"Thank you, but no. My wardrobe isn't really the problem."

"No, the problem is that we are all worn out. You will feel much better after a nice rest and a warm bath."

Sarah nodded and went straight to the bed. She kicked off her slippers, and as her head touched the pillow, she thought how nice it was to have someone pamper her for a change. In such a beautiful room, it was almost like being royalty.

Her next thought was of a playful conversation of a princess who took a sea captain prisoner. She had thought it a charming idea at the time, but now they were living out a ghastly parody, not an amusing fairy tale. Unless, of course, she made the enchanting version real.

Chapter Seventeen

Chris meant to swing his legs over the left side of the bed and use his left arm to hang onto the bedpost and stand. It had made sense when he had begun shifting his weight across the bed, but now he was stranded in the middle, too tired and sore to move another inch.

He rested his head against the headboard and closed his eyes. He had not been so helpless since he was Michael's age. Where were Sarah and Michael? Hours had passed since she had flounced out of his room—*their* room.

Where was his mother, with her magic potions that blurred the pain? Where was his father, or brother, or the servants? Had he been abandoned by the entire household? he fumed.

He was hungry, but it was still difficult to eat more than a mouthful of food without becoming nauseated. He could use a drink of his father's finest whiskey, which would never stay down. Maybe he could just swish it around his mouth and spit it out. But first, someone would have to bring him the bottle.

* * *

Sarah entered his room at sundown carrying a dinner tray with asparagus spears wrapped in thin slices of ham and smothered in cheese sauce, sweet potatoes, and bright green peas. Slices of freshly baked bread and newly churned butter rested on a smaller plate. There was also a cup of hot tea. She removed the tray with the bowl of congealed pea soup, which Chris had somehow managed to shove to the end of the bed, and placed his dinner on his left side.

Stephan had been there a moment earlier to help Chris relieve himself, but Sarah had confided the details of her plan, and he had not tarried. Until that afternoon, she had been happy to feed Chris whatever he could eat, but from now on, he was on his own.

She had donned her black satin gown and let her curls tumble over her shoulders in casual disarray. She sat down in the rocking chair and assumed a regal pose. "We once talked about a princess of a tiny kingdom who captured a dashing sea captain and kept him prisoner in her dungeon." She wore an inviting smile. "Do you remember that day?"

"In exquisite detail," he said. "Aren't you going to help me eat?" He reached for the damask napkin and flopped it across his lap.

"No. You're my captive now, Captain, and this room is my dungeon. There's no need of chains, but if you wish to eat, you'll have to feed yourself."

"I don't feel up to playing any silly games," he countered crossly.

"But this isn't really a game. It occurred to me this afternoon that we've switched places. But I do believe you make an even more disagreeable captive than I did."

"You were never my captive," he swore, his frown darkly menacing.

"Then your memories are far different than mine. You threatened me with being hanged as a spy. Do you imagine I regarded that horror as playful teasing?"

"I've already apologized for the stupid things I said on board the *Belle*."

Sarah folded her hands in her lap and rocked slowly. "No, I believe you characterized them as merely unwise."

He refused to quibble. "Stupid or unwise, what's the difference?"

"Apparently none to you. You really ought to eat your dinner before it gets cold." She got up and went to his desk to take out a sheet of expensive vellum stationery her father was sure to appreciate. She sat down, opened a bottle of ink, and took out a pen.

"I've neglected to contact my parents, but I'll write to them while you eat."

Chris was tempted to throw the fork at her like a dagger but restrained himself. "What will you tell them?"

She turned toward him and rested her arm on the back of her chair. "What a bizarre question. I shall tell them the truth."

"No, you can't." He shifted to sit up straighter, and shuddered at the resulting jolt of pain.

"And why not, Captain? Do you fear they would not regard you in a favorable light?"

He nodded. "That's one way of putting it."

"So, you're advising me to lie to my parents? I thought you'd hoped to meet them soon."

"Well, yes, of course I do—provided I am ever able to leave this blasted bed."

"You were fortunate your wound was so high on your

shoulder. Had it been a few inches lower, you would not have come home at all."

"Yes, I know, my remarkable streak of good luck hasn't run out." He regarded his dinner with a desultory glance, plucked an asparagus spear from the plate, swiped it through the cheese sauce, and took a bite. It was warm but tasteless. "You know I've never liked ham."

"What a shame. Virginia is noted for its flavorful hams, and I do believe that is a very tasty example. Perhaps if you combined it with a bit of sweet potato it would taste better to you."

"I don't require advice on how to eat."

"Then I will continue with my letter." She had written no more than the date, and now added a greeting.

"Wait a minute. We still need to decide how we met."

Sarah again turned in her chair. "What is there to decide? You're a privateer who boarded the *Beatrice,* and I was taken prisoner. How's that?"

"Why don't you explain how fortunate you were to be intercepted by a charming privateer shortly after you'd begun your misguided voyage?" He reached for another asparagus spear and chomped it in two.

Sarah laughed. "I rather like that. Can you repeat it?"

He did. He also flexed the fingers on his right hand and wondered if he would ever be able to grasp a pen without feeling a searing pain. "Then you could say I not only delivered your son but took you to my beautiful home on Martinique, where if you would only admit it, you fell in love with me."

"Now who is playing silly games?"

"You'd not be here if you didn't love me," he murmured grudgingly, and instantly wished he could take it back.

"After being rescued from a misguided voyage and assisted through childbirth, I'm quite naturally grateful for the opportunity to repay your kindness," she snapped.

"No, you love me desperately." He fumbled with the fork, but managed to raise some sweet potato to his mouth. "How did you expect me to eat these peas?"

"Roll them through the cheese sauce or mash them into the sweet potatoes, and they'll cling to your fork. You're a very clever man, Captain. I'm surprised you have to ask."

Chris swore under his breath. "And you're too damn clever by a half."

"Yes, that's why I'm the princess and you're in my dungeon."

"I refuse to play that game!"

"Then you will have to eat your ham, get strong, and walk out of this room. Now you must excuse me; I need to complete this letter. I've left it unwritten for far too long."

Furious with her, Chris hacked off a bite of ham and guided it to his mouth. He chewed and swallowed without tasting it; then he had had enough and dropped the fork to the tray.

"I wish you'd bring me something stronger than herb teas."

"A glass of milk, perhaps?"

"No, spirits of any kind."

Sarah signed regretfully. "That's quite impossible. In your present weakened state, you could too easily become tipsy, fall out of bed, and reopen your wound. You haven't got that much blood left, and think how that would look in the *Virginia Gazette*: 'Heroic privateer succumbs to injuries after fall from bed'." She shook her head. "No, I simply can't allow you to come to such an ignominious end."

Chris would have argued, had he not feared a fall might

very well be the end of him. He tilted his head against the headboard. "Read me your letter," he commanded.

"Very well. 'Dear Father and Mother, You will quite naturally be shocked to learn that I am living in Williamsburg, Virginia, rather than London. You have a fine grandson, whom I've named Michael Christopher, for his father and the remarkable man who delivered him. I will write to you again soon. With love, your daughter, Sarah.'"

"You're naming him for me? When did you decide to do that?"

"Just now, but it's a fine idea, isn't it?"

He thought it far better than fine. "Come here, Sarah."

His voice was now honey-smooth, and she was tempted, but remained at the desk to blot and fold her letter. "I am the princess, remember? You don't order me about."

"That was a request, not an order," Chris insisted.

"I'm sorry to disappoint you, but I need to care for Michael now. I'll see you again in the morning."

"What do you mean, in the morning? Aren't you going to sleep here with me?"

She stood and slid her chair into place at the deck. "No, a princess never sleeps with her captives. It simply isn't done."

"Damn it all, Sarah. This is real, not a game. I need you here with me."

"Yes, I know, but I don't need to be with you. Stephan will come back to see to whatever you need, and your mother will bring you something to help you sleep. Your father will probably sit with you a while too, so you'll not be lonely. Good night."

She had gone out the door before he could fling his plate across the room, but when his grip wavered, he doubted he could hurl it off the bed. He dropped it to the tray. "Damn the woman," he moaned.

He could barely twitch, let alone get out of bed, and she had walked out on him. Well, if she wanted to play at fairy tales, he would soon show her who was king. Just as soon as he could get out of bed.

Catherine tied the sprigs of sage with ribbons and hung them up to dry in the room off the kitchen, which she referred to as her herb pantry. "I prefer to use sage to preserve meat rather than to treat wounds. It has a wonderful aroma, doesn't it?"

Sarah brought a leaf to her nose and agreed. "This whole room smells divine. I'm just having difficulty keeping everything straight. The rosemary smells especially good. Did you say it could also be used as a preservative?"

"Yes, indeed. It has many uses. Some like to hang it in sickrooms, but I believe it would only have made Chris ill. It is also believed to make for an especially potent love charm."

"Really?" Sarah doubted she would have any need of one, but getting away from Chris for several hours each day had served to improve her mood—while unfortunately, his had grown increasingly surly.

"I'm ashamed to be so woefully ignorant when it comes to herbs, but my mother kept only a vegetable garden."

"Please do not apologize. I would receive no praise for my skills if everyone were equally adept," Catherine teased.

Sarah laughed with her, but she knew she was going to have to make a careful listing of the ingredients Catherine recommended because she lacked an innate talent for healing herself. She had not made any new entries in her diary of late, so she could put the journal to a new use.

"Just for curiosity's sake," she inquired, "how does one make a love charm of rosemary?"

Catherine considered the request for a long moment. "You must promise never to use this on anyone other than Christopher. Should you ever need to do even that, which I doubt."

Sarah could not imagine loving anyone else either. "You have my word on it."

"Good. First, you must wait until the rosemary is blooming. Then all you need do is tap him with a branch bearing a blossom."

"Just tap him, as though I were making a point?" Sarah laughed again. "Surely the magic is in the person doing the tapping, rather than the rosemary."

"Perhaps, but you cannot expect me to admit having worked such a charm on Brendan," she responded coyly. "And I do wish you would excuse his current belligerence. He used to be as charming a man as his sons, but he is quite passionate about our winning independence, and it has come at a terrible price."

"Yes, for both sides," Sarah added.

"Oh, forgive me, I did not mean to—"

"Yes, I know. It's easy for everyone here to forget I'm a widow. Thank you again for your lessons; I'll endeavor to remember them all."

Chris cursed angrily, "Stephan, you have to help me get out of this blasted bed!"

Stephan rather liked being the stronger brother for a change, and he shook his head. "Mother insists that when you're actually well enough to leave your bed, you'll be able to do it on your own."

"Mother is dead wrong. If you won't help me, then go and ask Father to come in here." He tried to plump up his pillow, but he was so clumsy with his left hand, he might as well not have tried.

Stephan slanted his hip across the foot of the bed. "Father's spending all his time at the shipyard. You could have died, and it might have killed him too. Don't say that I'd still be here, because I'm sick of just being here, taking up space."

"Then do something for a change—help me escape this wretched bed."

Stephan responded with a careless shrug. "Why are you so anxious to get up? Even if I helped you stand, you'd not be able to walk on your own. Then I'd have to peel what's left of you off the floor and roll you right back into bed."

"I'm not that weak," Chris muttered, but he feared Stephan was right and exhausting himself to stand would only provide the additional problem of how to cope once he had. "I want to see my wife," he added in an exasperated plea.

"Unless I've missed a day and not noticed, she's still Mrs. Hadley."

That she preferred being a dead man's wife wasn't lost on Chris, but he was determined to prevail sooner rather than later. "Don't make me crawl down the hall looking for her."

"All right." Stephan reluctantly gave in and pushed to his feet. "I'll go and find her. I think she's actually beginning to like me."

"Is that supposed to make me feel better? Go on, get out of here, and don't come back without Sarah! No, wait; tell her I miss seeing her and Michael. Will you do that? Ask her to bring Michael to see me."

Stephan paused at the door. "I don't recall your ever asking me for anything. It's about time."

When his brother left, Chris found the wait as humiliating as begging for the favor. Stephan was almost grown, and if their father had not absolutely forbidden it, he would be fighting with Lafayette's forces, as other boys his age were. Chris had been a firebrand at Stephan's age and gotten away with it. It was no wonder his brother felt abused by the way their father continually exerted his authority over him. Perhaps all parents were more protective of their second son, but he had a newfound appreciation for Stephan's plight.

He had been home more than a week and he had not once thought to ask what had happened at Yorktown. At least he had witnessed DeGrasse easily outmaneuvering Graves, and it had been as spectacular a battle as he had expected. He could recall little after that, though.

He would have to ask Stephan for news of the war, and thank him sincerely when he provided it. He had never been an exemplary elder brother, which he had blamed on the eight-year difference between their ages. He could at least try to do better now that they were older.

Where was Sarah? he wondered. He raked his fingers through his hair and hoped he did not look too unkempt. Perhaps he was too thin for her to still consider him attractive. He could easily remedy that complaint once he regained his appetite.

He hated staying in bed, but he had not imagined how

confined Sarah must have felt, locked all alone in his cabin. Maybe that was all she wished to teach him: how horrible it had been. If so, she had succeeded without much effort.

Sarah knocked lightly at his door before looking in. "Is this a good time for a visit?" she asked.

Chris bit the inside of his cheek rather than shout at her. "Yes, please come in. I've missed seeing Michael, and he appears to have grown."

Sarah carried her son to the bed and sat down on the foot. "Not a single person here has remarked on his diminutive size, so perhaps he is catching up."

Just looking at them filled Chris's chest with a painful surge of emotion. He loved them dearly, but he thought they ought to know that. Then he recalled how quickly he had left them to follow Admiral DeGrasse. The price had not been worth it if he had lost Sarah's love. He refused to ask such a dangerous question while in this pitiful state, for she would surely claim to love him whether or not she truly did.

"Chris, are you all right?" Sarah shifted Michael in her arms to come close and rest her palm against his forehead. "Thank God you're not feverish, but you're frightening me. What's the matter?"

"You said it yourself; I make a very poor captive." He caught her hand and placed a kiss in her palm. "I'll get better, Sarah. I won't stay like this forever."

"Of course you won't. I'll fetch us some tea, and your cook has made the most delectable berry tarts. I bet you'd love them."

His stomach lurched. "Only if you'll stay here with me to enjoy them."

"I'll be happy to remain with you."

When she left, Chris could not wait for her to return, but the sweetness of her manner bothered him. He could not bear to be treated like an invalid rather than her lover, but what if every time she brought her son to her breast, she thought of her late husband? he agonized. What if every hour they spent apart, she was lost in memories of Michael Hadley? What if she always had been?

"Your shoulder looks better each time I change the bandage," Catherine exclaimed. "You'll have scars, but I have added aloe to sooth your skin."

"At least I'm no longer screaming," Chris mumbled under his breath.

"I am also grateful for your silence," Catherine agreed. "But you are not eating enough."

"Nothing tastes right. Even the cook's berry tarts might as well have been sawdust," he replied.

"Oh, Chris, they were delicious. Could you not eat even one?"

"I ate one—at least I chewed and swallowed it. It didn't have any flavor."

"Everything will taste better soon." She tied the ends of the new bandage and stepped away from the bed. "You should be fine until morning."

"Not unless Sarah comes in to sleep with me. You know how to make love potions, don't you?"

Her son looked so serious, Catherine fought not to laugh. "I know a few, but when Sarah is so devoted to you, why would you need one?"

"Never mind, even if it worked, I'd be too weak to take advantage of it." Ashamed to admit that sorry fact, he looked down at his hands rather than at the dear woman who had raised him.

Catherine bent down to kiss his brow. "You are talking about making love, which isn't the same thing as loving someone with your whole heart. It's a shame you don't trust Sarah's affection for you to last through the few weeks of your recovery." She shook her head. "You need not worry that I will reveal your fears to her, either, when it would surely break her heart. It is not only your body but your spirit, as well, which was wounded. Please give yourself more time to heal."

"Do I have any choice?" He sounded obnoxiously cynical even to his own ears.

"Let us hope not." Catherine regretted that he needed more than medicinal herbs could supply, but she willingly put her faith in the strength of Sarah's affection, even if he could not.

Brendan had always loved to watch Catherine brush her hair before they went to bed. His wife swayed in front of her mirror and used long, fluid strokes from her scalp to the ends of the gentle waves. It was a beautiful dance she did only for him, and a seductive ritual.

He stepped up behind her, slid his arms around her waist, and pulled her back against his chest. "I swear you're more beautiful every day."

"Thank you, and you are a very handsome man."

"I was once." He hugged her and stepped back. She resembled an angel in her lacy nightgown, but his thoughts strayed in the opposite direction. "I don't know what to do about that woman."

Catherine set her brush aside to take his hands. "You need not do anything about Sarah. Chris's survival is assured due in large part to the love those two share. He is a grown man, and he adores her. As I adore you. Why don't we share some of our own affection tonight?"

Brendan shook his head, dazed. "Have I ever won an argument with you?"

She snuggled close to kiss him. "We have never had an argument. Unless you wish to count that unfortunate incident in Acadia."

"No, that is best forgotten." He was lost the instant his lips touched hers, and all without a whiff of rosemary.

Sarah was also brushing out her hair, but her strokes were more frantic than relaxed. She had wanted Chris to channel his frustration into getting well instead of simply stewing in pity. Removing herself, temporarily at least, appeared to have done it. From what Stephan reported, Chris was nearly clawing his way out of bed. Surely that meant he had earned a nice reward.

She waited until Michael was fed and tucked into his cradle, and the rest of the house was still, before she went to Chris's bedroom. He turned toward her as she slipped through the door.

"You can't sleep?" She climbed up on his bed and knelt beside him.

"All I do is rest. By nightfall, I'm too tired to sleep. Come here and kiss me."

She ran her fingertips up his left arm and licked her lips. "*Where* would you like me to kiss you?" she asked in a sultry whisper.

Chris moaned. "Is this your idea of torture, princess?"

"No." She leaned close to spread tender kisses across his mouth. "This requires no thought at all."

Chris knew what he wanted and, unlike food, he could

actually taste this. She had the sweetest mouth, and she knew precisely how to tease him with a gentle swirl of her tongue. He could almost feel her silken curls spilling over his hips, but what he could not feel was his usual swift arousal whenever she was near.

She thumbed his nipple, and he grabbed her wrist to push her away. "You've kissed me good night," he stated coldly. "Go on back to wherever it is you'd planned to sleep."

She rested her hand on his knee. "I'd planned to sleep here with you, for awhile at least."

"No, go on back to Michael. He needs you more."

She hesitated, for while she had wanted him to look after himself, she had acted out of love, not pity, and yet he sounded as though he was ashamed to need anything from her. She would not argue, nor would she take what he would not willingly give. Instead, she left him as silently as she had come and closed the door quietly.

Rob Corliss could not stop grinning. "I can't believe how good you look. The night we carried you in here, I swear we felt like pallbearers."

"I'm sure I was a sorry sight, and it's not something I'd ever care to repeat." Chris worked his right hand into a fist, though every time it hurt. "Where's the *Island Belle*?"

"Your family's dock. British troops won't bother us today. DeGrasse ran off the British fleet, and Cornwallis will soon be surrounded. I'm tempted to fight with our boys, but it will be almost too easy to push Cornwallis's forces right into the Chesapeake Bay."

Ashamed that he had once been equally cocky, Chris stared at him. "Fight with whomever you please, but don't for a minute think it will be easy. Come here and help me get out of bed. I need to walk around a bit."

Rob immediately stepped close. "Swing your legs off the side, and then I'll grab your left arm."

Swing your legs off the side..Rob made it sound so easy, but it was all he could do to turn his body to the right. "Just give my knee a push," he suggested, as though it were a small favor. He was wearing linen drawers and his chest was swathed in bandages, so he did not feel exposed.

"There, you're all set." Rob bent to catch Chris's left arm, and slung it over his own shoulder. When he straightened up, Chris came right off the bed. "You've lost weight."

Chris saw shooting stars and his vision blurred alarmingly, and his stomach lurched, but he was standing up for the first time since he was wounded. Sweat beaded on his forehead and upper lip, and his legs felt as if they were made of straw. Afraid Rob couldn't hold him much longer, he eased himself back down.

"Thanks, but that's enough. Don't you dare tell the crew I'm weak as a kitten, either. Just say I'll see them all soon."

"I'll do that. But believe me, they'll be real glad to hear you're getting well."

Sarah heard Rob's voice and peeked in the room. "Good morning, Mr. Corliss. It's so nice to see you under better circumstances."

Elated to see her, he took a quick step toward Sarah, then caught himself and widened his stance. "That's what I told the captain. I knew he'd be most likely to get well here with you."

Sarah saw where Chris was seated and fought not to

appear troubled by it. "You've become very bold, calling here by the light of day. Is it safe?"

"I believe so, but I don't wish to tire the captain so I'll be on my way. We're taking care to keep the *Island Belle* well out of range of anyone else who might wish us harm, but I'll send word, or come back myself, so you'll always know we're close."

"Thank you," Chris said. Relieved, his shoulders slumped when Rob had gone out the door.

"Just what is it you think you're doing?" Sarah asked. She circled the bed to confront him, resting her hands on her hips. "It looks as though you talked Rob into helping you out of bed, and it didn't go well, did it?"

"No," he confessed between short gasps. "Just give me a minute to catch my breath and I'll be fine."

She reached for him, and he batted her hand away. "You needn't fuss over me."

She had simply wanted to touch him, to please herself, not humble him. She went to the rocking chair. "All right, I'll simply sit here and watch you struggle. Then I believe I'll post a sign on the door so your next visitor will know better than to help you leave your bed."

"Now who's making threats? Besides, you wouldn't do it."

"Oh, but I will." She rose to go to his desk and took out a sheet of stationery. Inspired, she sat down, picked up the pen she had used previously, and opened the ink. "It may take more than a single sheet to list all the activities you should avoid."

"Not if I just avoid you."

She smiled at him. "You know I'm right. You're the daring sort who is used to commanding everyone around him. When you say 'Come here' and 'Do this or that,' people quite naturally respond. Today it was Rob, tomorrow it might well be one of the servants. Unfortunately, becoming overtired won't aid in your recovery."

"And your meddling will?" He snorted.

"Yes, of course it will. Perhaps I can summarize all the prohibitions in a single sentence: 'Please disregard all of Chris's requests.'"

He hoped she was merely teasing him, but he felt too sick to his stomach to continue the argument. "Just come here and help me get back into bed."

He sounded too wretched for her to insist he say please. She left her notice unwritten and came to the bed. "I know how torturous this is for you, but it's been equally difficult for all of us."

"You don't even know the meaning of the word," he complained.

She eased his legs back onto the bed, with a caress so tender it brought tears to his eyes. For the first time he was faced with the awful possibility that he would not be well in a few weeks or even months, but perhaps would need a year or more to regain his strength. He doubted he could survive a whole year without making love to her.

"Thank you," he mumbled. "You may go now. I want to sleep."

"I hope you have beautiful dreams."

"I just hope I wake up," he countered bitterly. He could not decide which was worse: to suffer the humiliation of admitting he was too weak to make love or to continue to force her to keep her distance and barely exist without her.

He had always been strong, but with a hole torn through his shoulder, he could barely move his arm. If he got no better, how was he even to dress himself, let alone command a ship? he agonized. It would be ludicrous to always circle the deck in a clockwise direction to be able to grab for the rail with his good left hand whenever the ship lurched with the waves.

If there was much wind, should he stumble and fall, he would then slide across the steeply angled deck like an unsecured barrel. The crew would not dare laugh in his face, but they were sure to break into boisterous howls once he had gone below. He could not captain the *Island Belle* by sending up commands from the safety of his cabin either. No, unless he could again be among the most fit on board, he could not captain any ship.

In time, he supposed he could train himself to write and draw with his left hand. But their shipyard would be a dangerous place for a man who had to guard his right arm and would be easily knocked off-balance. He could buy land and grow some useful commodity, but damn, he knew no more about farming than Sarah did.

He had the wealth to buy her whatever she desired, but what he really longed to give her was the vigorous young man he had once been. Sick with despair, he sighed deeply. He was simply going to have to get well; and he would, if the effort itself did not kill him.

Chapter Eighteen

Catherine's dressmaker, Madame LeBlanc, spread fabric samples across the bed. She was a petite woman who loved nothing better than designing beautiful clothes. Her hair and eyes were a rich, rusty brown, and she was dressed in a flattering yellow satin gown with a green bodice. A matching hat perched atop her elegant coiffure.

"With your fair hair and dark eyes, Mrs. Hadley, vibrant colors would show off your beauty to the best advantage. What do you think of this lush burgundy shade?"

Sarah caressed the glossy satin, but her melancholy expression failed to lift. "It's glorious, but while I'm not without resources, this may be too expensive for me."

"Please do not concern yourself with the cost," Catherine emphasized. "This is my treat."

"Thank you," Sarah replied, "but I doubt I'll be attending any grand parties in the coming months. What I truly need is a more practical wardrobe, simple gowns made of your more serviceable fabrics. I've not worn a hoop in months and prefer to go without one."

Catherine hid her disappointment behind a sympathetic smile as Sarah sorted through cottons and muslins in muted blues and grays. "Choose whatever you think is best, dear, but I want you to have at least three new gowns."

Sarah skipped a fingertip across the intricate floral design on a bolt of lace and pulled a pink satin ribbon across her palm. She and her mother had always had fashionable wardrobes. If they had not owned as many gowns as some of her father's wealthy parishioners, it had not mattered to either of them. It had been Michael who had purchased all the pretty gowns she had left behind.

"I have other gowns, or at least I did, but I left them at my parents' home," she recalled.

"They should have received your letter by now," Catherine said. "They may send them to you here."

"They probably just gave them away. Could you finish taking my measurements, Madame LeBlanc? My baby should wake soon, and I don't want to keep you waiting while I see to him."

"But of course," the dressmaker agreed, and she quickly completed the task and made the appropriate notations in her order book.

Catherine waited until Sarah had left for her own room before she spoke candidly to the modiste. "Sarah will soon be my daughter-in-law, and after you complete her selections, I want you to create something spectacular for her from the burgundy satin."

Madame LeBlanc nodded. "I understand completely. She is preoccupied with the care of her son, but she will surely need prettier clothes."

"Yes, she most certainly will, and I want you to make everything for her—silk lingerie as well as lovely new nightgowns."

"As always, it will be my pleasure. Now, what would *you* like to order today?"

Catherine was tempted but shook her head. "Nothing today, but we will talk again when Sarah's garments are finished. Perhaps I'll need something new then."

"As you wish, Mrs. MacLeod. You are my favorite customer, and I love making beautiful gowns for you."

Catherine assumed Madame LeBlanc flattered all her clients equally, but she tactfully hid her suspicions behind a bright smile. When Madame LeBlanc departed with Sarah's order, she went straight to Chris's room.

Sarah had moved the cradle out first, then had her trunk transferred to the gold room, and finally the rocking chair. While it was merely a matter of clothing and furniture, in Catherine's view, they provided tangible evidence— proof, she supposed, that something was amiss between the lovely young woman and her stubborn son.

Chris was sitting up in bed with a copy of Choderlos de Laclos's *Les Liaisons Dangereuses* open on his lap. "That is not a novel I would recommend for you," Catherine warned. "Justice does prevail, but the lovely heroine—"

"Wait!" Chris begged. "Don't give away the ending. While I've read the first page a dozen times, I might someday find the necessary concentration to finish the book."

Catherine came around the bed to make certain he had a fresh cup of tea on the nightstand. "You ought to be reading to Sarah. Have you not even thought of entertaining her?"

He shook his head. "There's so damn little I can do, I'm just not good company."

"You may not be able to chase her around the room,

but you could certainly read to her, play cards, or simply engage in conversation. She has just ordered new gowns from Madame LeBlanc, and she asked for plain, practical garments. Why do you suppose she requested those rather than something as pretty as she?"

"Her father was very strict. I doubt she is used to wearing clothing as beautiful as yours. I wish I'd known Madame LeBlanc was coming. I would have encouraged Sarah to order whatever she wished."

"That would have been very sweet of you, and appreciated, I am sure. Are you speaking to Sarah at all?"

"Yes, of course I am. She was here only this morning with Michael." He refused to admit how relieved he had been when she had not tarried. It hurt to look at her and remember how easily he had once carried her in his arms. Now he would have difficulty holding even Michael.

Catherine sat down on the side of the bed. "I fear you have not made her feel welcome here, when you ought to have been planning your future together. You cannot be a privateer after the war. Do you wish to enter the merchant trade?"

"All I've ever wanted to do is sail, but if I have only one good arm, I might lack the necessary balance to cross the deck without falling. In a storm, I'd swiftly lose my footing and be tossed overboard." He sighed sadly. "But I've no desire to leave Sarah and Michael for months at a time, either."

"Have you told her so?" Catherine reached out to take her son's hand in a fond clasp.

"What promises can I make?" He almost shrugged, but stifled the impulse before causing himself an unnecessary torment.

"You're a wealthy man in your own right. You will have

a comfortable home here with your family until you build your own. It seems to me that you could promise Sarah a great deal. But before I forget, I neglected to mention that she told me you were the one to deliver Michael."

He wished he could forget that night. "I've never been so frightened, but she was in too much pain to notice. You're not to tell her, either."

"Of course not," Catherine assured him. "We were discussing herbal remedies, and she remarked on how grateful she was that I had taught you so much about childbirth. Because we had never discussed the subject, I simply replied that you were a remarkable man in every respect."

"Thank you, but we were lucky Michael came into the world so easily. I could not have stood it had I lost Sarah, and it would have broken her heart had her baby not survived."

"She believes that you were supremely confident. Why not show her some of your characteristic confidence now? Talk about your future. It is sure to be bright."

Chris feared his mother was being overly optimistic. What difference did it make if he had considerable wealth when he was unable to lift a child? "Once I'm well, and I'm holding to that hope, there will be time enough for Sarah and me to plan our future."

Catherine rose gracefully and leaned close to kiss his cheek. "You cannot love Sarah only when it is convenient. You must simply try harder, my darling, to think first of her welfare rather than simply your own."

"That's all I've been doing," he swore. But if he remained an invalid, he could not bear to think Sarah might feel obligated to marry him out of some misguided sense of duty. Then he had a truly horrible thought:

"Could Sarah have ordered what you describe as practical gowns because she has no intention of becoming my wife? Could she be preparing to leave us?"

His anguished expression tore at his mother's heart. "I have no idea what she might be planning other than to be useful. It is almost as though . . ."

"As though what?" he asked.

"As though she feels she has to earn a place here. Your father has not been unkind, but he certainly has not shown her the warmth he usually displays toward guests. As for Stephan, he is entranced by her, which I doubt she enjoys. I do believe she is sincerely interested in learning my craft, but perhaps she also feels she must. Oh, Christopher, we ought to have had the wedding just as soon as you were able to speak your vows."

"That would have been pathetic. I have to be able to stand. It doesn't matter how wealthy I might be, or what I can provide, if I collapse each time I leave my bed. I'll not make Sarah a captive to my tragedy."

Catherine sighed unhappily. "You're so like your father, and that is not always a compliment. You could at least have given Sarah a ring and spoken of how eager you are to marry her. I fear you have chased her away to save your pride. Fortunately, she is far too sensible a young woman to go far."

Chris thought Sarah might also be too sensible to stay, but he kept the sour thought to himself as his mother left the room. He had to regretfully admit that without her chiding, he might never have considered how Sarah felt about living in his home. He had thought only of his mother's hospitality and the physical comforts his family could provide.

He had not once reflected upon how different the usually gracious MacLeod household must be from her parents' spartan rectory. He would have to build her a fine residence as beautiful as she was, but he would not even begin to plan until he was certain he would not have to be carried over the threshold on a stretcher.

Had he been shot in the leg, he could have at least carved the little animals he had intended to make for Michael. Unable to hold a knife securely, he could not even make toys. All he could do was think about getting well, toward which goal he had not accomplished a damn thing as of yet.

Determined to regain his strength, he inched his way to the other side of the bed, where he could more easily grab the bedpost. When Stephan came into his room, Chris swore him to secrecy.

"Mother isn't to know I'm getting up to walk. Father won't think to ask. As for Sarah, don't tell her either."

"All right, if I must I'll help you stand, but just for a minute at a time." He leaned over to grab Chris around the waist and pulled him upright. "I'll bet I outweigh you now."

Chris gritted his teeth. His legs were only marginally stronger than on his last attempt, but he was on his feet. He counted to ten, then sagged back down on the bed. "Thank you. I can't do this alone. You'll have to keep quiet about it."

"I will, but clearly you're stronger every day. It may be difficult to have patience, but—"

"No, it's impossible. Go get me something to eat— meat, cheese, bread, anything that tastes good, along with some ale." He slid his legs back under the sheet, but even that small effort was a chore.

Stephan remained beside the bed. "First, you must promise you'll take me along the next time you sail on the *Belle*."

"How do you expect me to walk up the gangplank when I can't even stand on my own?" Chris shook his head and slumped back against the headboard.

"I know it won't be today, but it will happen soon."

"Not soon enough. Just bring me something to eat and then find Sarah. I have to see her."

It was now Stephan who became adamant. "I'm not taking a single step until you give me your word that I'll sail with you."

Chris gripped the sheet tightly in his left hand. "I may not sail any farther than the length of the Chesapeake Bay, but you may go with me. There, are you satisfied?"

"For the moment, but I fear you lack sincerity. If you no longer wish to captain the *Island Belle,* may I have her?"

"I didn't just strut on board the day she was christened and assume command," Chris stressed. "I had learned how to sail long before her keel was laid. You'll have to earn your captain's papers too. If that's what you really want."

"The MacLeods build ships—it's the family business—so I ought to be able to sail."

"I can't argue with you. Talk it over with Father. He'll help you make your plans."

"Yes, but he'll insist it be after the war."

Chris's voice was surprisingly tender. "That's good advice. In the meantime, race your horses. Enjoy what you have, because it could all be lost in an instant."

Stephan cocked his head slightly. "You'll be fine soon. You haven't really lost anything."

"No, but Michael Hadley did. Now please, fetch me something to eat before I faint from hunger."

"All right, but you promised." Stephan exited the room

so quickly he nearly collided with Sarah, who was passing by in the hall.

She stepped aside and looked in on Chris. She was wearing her blue-gray gown, and her curls were caught in a blue ribbon at her nape. "What have you promised your brother?" she asked.

"Nothing of any consequence." He patted the bed at his side. "Come sit here beside me."

She sat down and picked up his book. "I should have thought to bring you something to read. I'm sorry, I—"

"Please don't apologize. I didn't feel up to reading until today, but my heart isn't in it."

"Where is your heart?" she inquired softly.

"I suppose it's still rattling around my chest. I've never been sick a day in my life, and while that's no excuse for my ill temper, I'm sorry I haven't been better company. I'll have to be more amusing or you'll never release me from this detestable dungeon of yours."

"That's right, but I might accept a bribe."

He welcomed her smile, but he dared not encourage anything more, despite how badly he longed for it. "If there's anything you want or need, we can probably find it in Williamsburg or have it made. All you need do is ask. I don't want you to be unhappy."

He was all she needed, but for the time being, he had to concentrate on himself, regardless of how little she appreciated being set aside. "I'm not unhappy," she assured him, though it was untrue.

When she leaned forward to kiss his cheek, he pulled away. It was a subtle flinch rather than an obvious aversion to her touch but equally devastating. It made the wait even more difficult than when he had been away.

Hiding the hurt, she rose quickly and shook out her skirt.

"Michael will wake soon and I want to be there. Do you need anything before I go?"

"No, thank you, Stephan's seeing to it." He let her leave, but her sad, sweet smile pierced him clear through.

When Stephan came back with his food, he would ask his brother's help to stand another time. Just as soon as he could stand on his own, he would begin walking. It did not matter if all he could do was take a few shaky steps around his bed, he would force himself to walk farther with every attempt.

"I am going to get well," he swore, and then he would become Sarah's favorite husband.

Later that afternoon, Brendan MacLeod found his son clinging to the bedpost. He rushed to Chris's side and eased him back down on the bed. "What were you thinking?" he cried. "You ought not to get out of bed alone!"

Chris had counted to twenty before his father interrupted him, and he flashed a cocky grin. It occurred to him that in addition to what he could manage on his own, if both his father and brother helped him to practice standing, he might get well in half the time.

"I can hold on tight with my left arm and should I tire, I'm smart enough to fall backward onto the bed rather than on my face."

Brendan stood with his hands fisted on his hips. "I've never been impressed by how smart you think you are. There's too great a risk you'll reopen your wound. I won't allow it."

Chris nodded as though he would actually obey.

"Could you come by more often to help me, then? A tankard of ale would be welcome too."

"I'll be glad to help you because you obviously need supervision. As for the ale, we'll have to be careful your mother doesn't catch us."

"I'll still drink her teas. She'll never suspect that I'm drinking anything stronger. You're here now. Come on, help me stand again."

"You need to give yourself more time to heal."

"Yes, I know, but I'm fresh out of patience. I want to get married, and I imagine Sarah is tired of waiting for me to be a proper groom."

Brendan gave in reluctantly. "Tell me when you're tired," he cautioned. He took a firm hold on his son's waist to lift him off the bed. Chris grabbed hold of the bedpost, and Brendan released him to take a hesitant backward step.

"Sarah is a recent widow," he advised with what he hoped Chris would mistake for mere fatherly concern. "You ought to give her more time to grieve before you press her for marriage."

Chris was counting in his head, and did not reply until he reached twenty-five and was ready to sit down. "She'll never forget Michael Hadley, and I don't expect her to. But believe me, it's high time we were wed."

"I fear I might just as well be addressing the bedpost, but if you insist upon a wedding, you must give your mother and Sarah time to plan. You know how much women love giving parties and handling all the details involved."

"No, I've never really paid much attention. But obviously I need to be more aware of their feelings."

"That's always wise." Brendan began to pace beside the bed with his hands folded behind his back. He appeared preoccupied as he continued. "My intention when I came in here was to let you know that both American and French artillery have opened fire on Cornwallis's fortifications at Yorktown. It's only a matter of days before the British will be forced to surrender."

"That is good news. But we can't expect Sarah to celebrate the victory with us."

"Which is precisely my point. She's still too attached to her first husband to take on a second."

"I'll allow Sarah to decide for herself," Chris promised. But he was counting on his most potent powers of persuasion to convince her to finally accept his proposal.

By the time Chris was strong enough to walk from his bed to his bedroom door and back, it was near the end of October. As predicted, Cornwallis had surrendered. Chris's father and Stephan had gone to watch the nearly eight thousand British troops lay down their arms in a grassy meadow south of Yorktown, but they had described the solemn scene to him in private rather than risk hurting Sarah with their jubilant hoots and laughter.

Chris was positive she had heard about it, though, as his mother would surely have disclosed the British defeat in a sensitive manner. He knew he should have been the one to tell her, but whenever she was near, he encouraged her to talk about how she had spent the day, or they played with Michael, which was much more fun. One stormy afternoon, he had even swallowed his pride long enough to disclose his uncertainty about what work he might be able to do. But anything was preferable to a discussion of the progress of the war. It simply did not exist within the confines of his room.

Tonight he had remained awake. He wondered if Michael still woke to nurse near midnight. He thought it would be best if Sarah were tending her son when he went to her room. That way he could simply count it as a milestone and wish her a good night. Of course, if they were both asleep, he would still know he had been there.

But if Michael was sound asleep and Sarah was wide awake, he did not know what he would do. He could move his right arm if he kept it close to his chest, and flex his hand without cringing in pain. But a lingering ache still throbbed in his shoulder, and he was far from agile. He was also so desperate to be with Sarah again he could not stand waiting another long, lonely night.

He heard the deep echo as the clock chimed twelve and waited a while longer before pushing off the bed. He paused at his door and ran his hand over his chin. He could at least shave himself now, but he hoped he had done a good job. Not that Sarah would complain. She would congratulate him for arriving at her room, but he needed more in the way of warmth than a polite welcome.

He opened his door and stepped out in the hall for the first time in the nearly two months he had been home but kept his hand on the wall to guide his way. All his life he had taken his robust good health for granted, and now it had taken far too long to get even a portion of his former strength back.

When he reached Sarah's door, he drew in a deep breath, and at the last minute remembered he ought to knock lightly rather than just burst in. He did, and she opened the door almost immediately. The delight in her expression overwhelmed him, and he had to lean back against the doorjamb to brace himself rather than grab her in a clumsy hug and risk causing them both a disastrous fall.

"I was just out for a stroll and thought I'd stop by," he whispered.

"My goodness, Captain, you appear to have escaped my dungeon. That's certainly cause for celebration. Won't you come in?" She took care to close the door quietly behind him.

A candle burned on the dresser, and another on the nightstand. He would have preferred to snuff them both, but they needed to be able to make sure Michael was sleeping peacefully. "Will the baby wake soon?" he asked.

"No, he's just gone back to sleep." She glanced toward a comfortable chair near the window before looking toward the bed. "Where would you like to sit?"

Chris reached for the edge of the dresser to steady himself. "Would you mind if I lay down for a while?"

"Oh, Chris, why didn't you say so sooner?" She took his left arm to guide him to the bed.

Chris sat down on the side where she slept and slid his legs under the covers. He had spent so much time longing to get there; now he wished he had given more thought to what he could actually do.

"Come lie down here beside me," he coaxed. "I've really missed having you near me at night."

Sarah circled the bed to climb up on the other side to be on his left. "I've missed you too."

He was wearing a pair of linen drawers, and his shoulder had only a light bandage. She snuggled close and rested her arm across his chest. "Do you mind if I touch you?"

"I will die if you don't. Oh, I shouldn't have said that, should I?"

"It's all right, you'll not plunge me into deep mourning."

"Good, but I appreciate just how lucky I am to be alive when so many fine men have perished. I want Michael to know his father was an admirable man, not simply my enemy."

"I had no idea you ever thought of my husband."

"I think of him constantly. It's only a quirk of fate that Michael Hadley is dead and I'm alive. I don't mean to depress you, it's just—"

Sarah raised her fingertips to his lips. "Hush. You needn't apologize. Michael was a fine man and I'm proud to have borne him a son, but there's something more you should know."

She wondered where to begin, and then found the perfect place. "You were right about me, Chris. I was so eager to escape a home where I never really belonged, I'd have run off with you had you simply walked by."

Chris laughed in spite of his best efforts. "Oh, Sarah, I wish I'd never made that thoughtless remark."

"No, it was very perceptive. You have keen insights, even if I refused to admit it when we first met. Please don't interrupt me again."

"I'm sorry, please continue."

"My parents frequently entertained British officers. They were charming young men who always spoke to me as though I were their own dear sister, until I was old enough to be more. I adored them all, and when I turned eighteen, I married the first one to propose.

"I was truly heartbroken when I lost Michael, but the affection I felt for him, while genuine, doesn't begin to compare with the love I feel for you. You truly are the husband of my heart."

He could only hug her with his one good arm, but she moved up to find his mouth, and he was lost in her hungry kisses. He was also fully aroused as he feared he might never be again. When he had to gasp for breath, he whispered, "Lock the door."

"I already did." She had also laid her wedding ring on the dresser. She slid her hand between them to rub his erection. "If you'll lie still, I could move across your hips and—"

"Don't say it, just do it," he nearly sobbed.

"I will, but not just yet." First she wanted to kiss him until they were both dizzy with desire.

But when he peeled her nightgown over her head with one hand, she understood how eager he was to sink into her heat. She helped him discard his drawers, then warmed his cock between her palms, but he was already steaming hot.

"Sarah," he whispered in an urgent plea.

"Yes, my love." Still stroking, she straddled him and lowered herself slowly to take only the smooth, rounded tip of his cock before raising up on her knees to slip free. On her next dip, she slid a bit lower to take more of him, but just as quickly rose up again.

Chris opened his mouth to beg her to stop the exquisite torture, but this time, she took him deeper and for a few seconds longer, before again straightening up. She was so beautiful with her curls trailing over her breasts, and she wore such an inviting smile. He loved watching her and slid his thumb through her cleft, coasting on her own slippery wetness to fan her desire until she lowered herself to take him deep again.

She rocked forward to stroke his nipples, and he bucked under her. He could feel his climax approach, coiling around him, tightening with each slow, rolling motion of her hips until he came within her in an explosive rush. He called her name, but she smothered his grateful moan with both hands as she leaned forward to grind against him and find her own release.

When she fell asleep still sprawled across him, her head lay on his left shoulder where she would cause him no pain, but he could not have found the breath to complain even if she had.

"Chris, are you in there?" Catherine knocked frantically at Sarah's door.

"It's your mother." Sarah sat up and pushed her tangled curls from her eyes. She dimly recalled waking to nurse Michael during the night, and later at dawn. Both times she and Chris had made love again, and he had not returned to his own bed. Sunlight filled the room, and she knew they must have slept very late.

"Yes, I'm fine," he called to her, and pulled Sarah back down with his left arm.

"That is good to hear, but there is a Reverend Godwin and his wife here to see you and Sarah."

"Oh, my God," Chris howled. "They're here now?"

"They are in the parlor," Catherine replied.

"Please tell my parents that we'll be with them in a few minutes," Sarah called and, as horrified as Chris, nearly shot up in bed this time. At least her father had not marched right up the stairs to find her himself.

Chris listened for his mother's footsteps retreating down the hall before pulling Sarah back down on his chest. "They can wait."

She loved the familiar rakish gleam in his eye, but this was no time to take advantage of it. "The longer my father has to wait to meet you, the more infuriated he will become, and he could not possibly be happy at present."

Chris reluctantly acknowledged her concern. "A valid point."

"Just get back to your room and get dressed. It won't matter what he says, or what insulting names he calls any of us. I'm staying with you."

Chris would never reveal how worried he had been that she might leave him, or that he would have to send her away. He struggled to pull on his drawers over his erection, but that he was so hard was a renewed source of pride rather than embarrassment.

"Your parents will be thrilled with their grandson. Dress him in the christening gown and we'll have your father baptize him."

"What a wonderful idea. Hurry and put on some clothes, so we'll not greet my parents looking like Adam and Eve."

"Undoubtedly a wise choice." But Chris could not stop laughing at what a stunning family portrait that would make.

Catherine and Brendan MacLeod had done their very best to put their guests at ease, but William Godwin refused to be seated and paced their parlor with a measured stride. He was dressed in black and clutched his tricorn hat, which he tapped against his thigh. A tall, thin man, his ginger-colored hair was tied back with a narrow bow. His piercing blue gaze darted around the parlor as though he were seeking some damning relic to denounce.

Mary Claire Godwin sat beside Catherine on the

striped satin settee. Her gown, while of fashionable design, was dove gray. She wore a matching bonnet, and her gloved hands were tightly clasped in her lap. Blond curls brushed her forehead, and her pale blue eyes were firmly focused on the tips of her slippers.

Brendan stood beside the fireplace, attempting to look far more confident than he felt. He was certainly concerned by the Godwins' sudden appearance, but the reverend's abrasive manner gave him an unexpected burst of sympathy for what Sarah must have endured as a daughter. Not that he had shown her anything in the way of affection, and growing increasingly ashamed of how coolly he had treated her, he straightened up.

"Please excuse me a moment," he begged. "I want to make certain my son doesn't need my help to come down the stairs. I don't want you to be kept waiting unnecessarily."

He bolted before Catherine could suggest strongly that he remain, but he walked past Chris's room to Sarah's and rapped gently at her door. "It's Brendan, may I please speak with you?"

Sarah was fully dressed and had just brushed her hair into an attractive crown of curls, but she was not eager to greet him. He was frowning, which he did so often that she had begun to wonder if he possessed any other expressions. Afraid he would embarrass them both with another financial offer to entice her to leave his home for her father's, she had already begun to shake her head before he spoke.

"Forgive me for intruding like this," Brendan began hesitantly. "But I want to set things straight between us. Without French allies, we would have surely lost the war, and when you arrived, I was haunted by that dire possibil-

331

ity. I was astonished when Chris asked that I look after you, and when I learned that you were the Loyalist widow of a British officer, I immediately began regarding you as an enemy."

Amazed by his candor, Sarah watched him struggle for words as he inched toward an apology. Grateful, whatever had prompted it, she sought to ease his way. "I understood how you felt."

"No, what you don't understand is my confusion at your devotion to my son. You gave him such tender care, and he was too stubborn to admit how much he needed your attentions. It would not have surprised me had you left him when he grew surly, but you stayed, as though this were truly your home, despite how rudely I had treated you."

Sarah nodded rather than admit how deeply she had appreciated Catherine's friendship, while he had barely acknowledged her presence with a twitch.

"That I offered you money was unforgivable. What I am attempting to say, and rather poorly I fear, is that you prove your love for Chris in your every gesture. I had not believed he could ever find a woman as loving as his mother, and I am enormously glad that he has. I wish I had trusted his judgment and welcomed you into the family on the night you arrived. I hope that you'll accept this sincerely felt welcome now."

When he offered a hopeful smile, Sarah finally saw the man Catherine adored. "Thank you, I'm honored to join the MacLeods, and let's agree to never again speak of your desire to send me away. I've told no one of it, and I never will."

"Thank you. You have my word it will remain our secret," Brendan hurriedly agreed. "Now, I fear I have left my darling wife alone with your parents too long. Will you excuse me?"

Sarah leaned close to kiss his cheek. "Yes, of course, thank you again for seeing how deeply I love your son."

"If unfortunately late," Brendan apologized before hurrying down the hall.

Catherine greeted her husband with a grateful smile, but she was elated by the sound of footsteps on the stairs. "At last, here are my sons."

She presented them to the Godwins, and waited for them to provide what could not possibly be a gracious response. She was overjoyed that Chris was able to leave his bed but wished he had not been sleeping in Sarah's when Sarah's parents arrived.

Chris was dressed in his usual navy blue. With Stephan's help to bathe and dress, he was confident his appearance could not be faulted. His shirt was spotless, his navy blue pants and waistcoat neatly pressed. His boots shone with a high polish. He had had to drape his coat over his shoulders, but it was the best he could do. And yet, all he saw in the Reverend Godwin's eyes was pure loathing.

"Good morning, sir. I had hoped to take Sarah to visit you soon. Please forgive me for not offering my hand, but I'm still recovering from a recent wound."

He turned to Mrs. Godwin, who was peering up at him with a frightened gaze. He thought it likely that she had also married for the wrong reasons, and it saddened him. "It is a pleasure to meet you, Mrs. Godwin. I do believe Sarah resembles you, and you are both exceptionally pretty."

"We've not come to suffer through meaningless flattery. Where is our daughter?" the reverend asked accusingly.

"I'm right here, Father." Sarah had come down the stairs so quietly, her approach had gone unnoticed until she came up beside Chris and Stephan. She smiled as though she were actually pleased to see her parents so unexpectedly. She had donned one of her new gowns, which was a heavenly blue with deep lace cuffs.

"This is Michael. There has been no opportunity to have him baptized, and I would be so grateful if you would do it today. Here, Mother, would you like to hold him?"

Mary Claire's eyes filled with tears as she gathered her grandson into her arms. "What an adorable baby," she cooed softly, and he looked up at her, entranced by a new face.

The Reverend Godwin did not even glance Michael's way. "Fetch your belongings, Sarah. You are leaving with us. Your son will be baptized in our church in Charleston, although I must say I am surprised you even remember such a sacrament exists."

Sarah gripped Chris's hand more tightly. "I've not forgotten anything you taught me, but my home is with Chris now, and I'm not leaving. I promise to bring Michael to visit you, but my place is here."

The Anglican priest regarded Brendan and Catherine with a hostile sneer. "You've condoned their living in sin? I had heard that you possessed questionable politics, sir, but it appears the same can be said for your morals."

"Father, please, this is totally unnecessary."

Brendan swiftly agreed. "I'll not allow you to insult my family or your child, who is one of us, within my hearing. Chris has left his sickbed to meet you, but his intention has always been to marry your daughter."

Chris was elated by his father's righteous announcement. The man had once harbored so many unwarranted doubts about his son's choice of wife, but clearly he had embraced the match now. It meant the world to Chris. He was leaning on Stephan for support rather than Sarah. He could not deny that he and Sarah had already enjoyed the benefits of marriage without a legal bond, but that was easily remedied.

"We would all be thrilled if you could perform a marriage ceremony for us today, as well as the christening." Chris squeezed Sarah's hand and felt an encouraging press of her fingertips.

"Have I shamed you into it?" the reverend asked. He appeared to be appalled by his success, rather than pleased. "Sarah, if you insist upon marrying this, this . . ."

"Why not refer to me as Christopher MacLeod?" Chris offered with another warm smile.

"This *person,*" Sarah's father continued, "I will indeed perform the ceremony forthwith, but only to provide salvation for your souls."

Chris was tickling her palm now, and Sarah suppressed a giggle. "That is so generous of you, Father. Where should we stand?"

Catherine wished there was time for Sarah to change into the beautiful burgundy gown she had had made for her, but the young woman could wear it to the wedding supper that night. It was not the elaborate wedding scene she would have planned, but with the war, such stark simplicity was appropriate. She quickly offered a suggestion.

"You should stand in front of the fireplace, Reverend Godwin, and Sarah and Chris opposite you. Stephan, stay right beside your brother to assist him to a chair should one be needed."

"Yes, Mother." Stephan straightened proudly.

"I want you for my best man," Chris insisted. "You've

been a great help to me, and I intend to be a better brother from now on."

Stephan shrugged off the praise. "And I promise to treat your beautiful wife as a beloved sister." But he winked at her, which belied his vow.

"I hate to interrupt your heartfelt exchanges, but if you could just move into place," Reverend Godwin urged shortly.

When everyone had, Reverend Godwin removed his Book of Common Prayer from his coat pocket and turned to the marriage ceremony. His wife was still seated, cuddling their grandson, while Catherine and Brendan were standing behind the settee holding hands. Their servants were tiptoeing into the hall to peek into the parlor, and the priest nodded to acknowledge their presence.

"Oh, wait," Catherine cried, and she quickly removed a diamond-encircled amethyst ring from her right hand and gave it to Chris. "This will have to do for now."

"Thank you." Chris was beginning to feel a bit dizzy, but he intended to remain on his feet long enough to be legally wed. "You may begin, Reverend Godwin," he urged, but he had to lean a bit harder on his brother. Sarah felt Chris tremble and stepped closer to his side.

The last time she had been married, it had been in her father's church, surrounded by Michael Hadley's fellow officers and her parents' friends. She had blushed appropriately, and cast admiring glances toward her soon-to-be husband, but she had had no real appreciation of her vows.

This morning, each word was spoken from her heart and rang true. When Chris slid the amethyst ring on her finger, tears brightened her gaze, and they were joyful tears. She reached up to kiss him the moment her father pronounced them man and wife.

"If we have a daughter," she whispered, "I'm going to name her Beatrice."

Chris wished he could pluck her off her feet and spin her around, but he had to content himself with a deep kiss that sent her father into a coughing fit.

"What do you mean 'if'?" he replied. "It ought to be 'when.'"

"Do you see what I mean? You argue simply for the sport of it."

"I do not," Chris insisted, and he pulled her close to smother her laughter against his chest. They still had a son to christen, and he had new in-laws to somehow impress, but for the moment, he held paradise in his arms.

NOTE TO READERS

While *Midnight Blue* is a work of fiction, French Admiral François DeGrasse (1722-1788) was actually the commander of the French naval contingent. While most Americans recognize the name of the Marquis de Lafayette, Admiral DeGrasse, who never set foot on American soil, played a more significant role in the outcome of the Revolutionary War. Lord Cornwallis's defeat at Yorktown forced King George's cabinet to resign. The new cabinet then opened peace negotiations, which led to the end of the war and independence for the United States of America.

Lord Cornwallis (1738-1805) had personally opposed the war with America and, after its end, went on to distinguished service as Governor of India, where he worked tirelessly on behalf of the Indian people. He was also appointed Lord Lieutenant of Ireland, and was highly respected by the Irish.

Sarah Godwin Hadley and Christopher MacLeod may be fictional characters, but it is my hope that their passion for life and each other will live forever in your hearts.

I love to hear from readers. Please send a SASE for a newsletter and bookmarks, or contact me via e-mail at phoebeconn@earthlink.net.

The Pirate Prince
CONNIE MASON

She is a jewel among women, brighter than the moon and stars. Her lips are lush and pink, made for kissing . . . and more erotic purposes. She's a pirate's prize, yet he cannot so much as touch her.

Destined for the harem of a Turkish potentate, Willow wonders whether she should rejoice or despair when her ship is beset by a sinfully handsome pirate. She is a helpless pawn in a power play between two brothers. She certainly had no intention of becoming the sex slave of a sultan; and no matter how much he tempts her, she will teach her captor a thing or two before she gives her heart to . . . *The Pirate Prince*.

The Care & Feeding of Pirates

Jennifer Ashley

Honoria Ardmore is as prim and proper as they come. Her sole moment of indiscretion was when she fell for a roguish pirate. But he died, or at least, that's what she assumed—until the night he showed up eager to pick up where they had left off....

Christopher Raine cheated death, and he believes life owes him his just rewards. So he sets out to reclaim the woman of his dreams. And this insatiable pirate is not one to let trivial details get in his way.

Dorchester Publishing Co., Inc.
P.O. Box 6640
5281-4
Wayne, PA 19087-8640
$6.99 US/$8.99 CAN

Please add $2.50 for shipping and handling for the first book and $.75 for each additional book. NY and PA residents, add appropriate sales tax. No cash, stamps, or CODs. Canadian orders require an extra $2.00 for shipping and handling and must be paid in U.S. dollars. Prices and availability subject to change. **Payment must accompany all orders.**

Name: _____

Address: _____

City: _____ State: _____ Zip: _____

E-mail: _____

I have enclosed $_____ in payment for the checked book(s).

CHECK OUT OUR WEBSITE! *www.dorchesterpub.com*
_____ Please send me a free catalog.

THE PIRATE HUNTER
JENNIFER ASHLEY

Widowed by an officer in the English navy, Diana Worthing is tired of self-important men. Then the legendary James Ardmore has the gall to abduct her, to demand information. A champion to some and a villain to others, the rogue sails the high seas, ruthlessly hunting down pirates. And he claims Diana's father was the key to justice.

When she refuses to tell him what she knows, James retaliates with passionate kisses and seductive caresses. The most potent weapons of all, though, are his honorable intentions, for they make Diana forget reason. They make her long to believe she's finally found a man she can trust, a man worth loving—a true hero who could rescue her marooned heart.

BOOK YOUR PLACE ON OUR WEBSITE AND MAKE THE READING CONNECTION!

We've created a customized website just for our very special readers, where you can get the inside scoop on everything that's going on with Zebra, Pinnacle and Kensington books.

When you come online, you'll have the exciting opportunity to:

- View covers of upcoming books
- Read sample chapters
- Learn about our future publishing schedule (listed by publication month *and author*)
- Find out when your favorite authors will be visiting a city near you
- Search for and order backlist books from our online catalog
- Check out author bios and background information
- Send e-mail to your favorite authors
- Meet the Kensington staff online
- Join us in weekly chats with authors, readers and other guests
- Get writing guidelines
- AND MUCH MORE!

Visit our website at
http://www.kensingtonbooks.com